PRAISE FOR
THE TAGGART BROTHERS NOVELS

"[Bingham] reaches deep into your heart with a story that will stay with you long after the last sigh, the last laughter, and the last tear."

—Carolyn Brown, *New York Times* bestselling author

"Bingham knows her readers well and hits all the notes."

—*Publishers Weekly*

"Bingham's latest . . . is a keeper . . . Jace's genuine heart and sexy manner will have readers falling in love from the start. Jace and Bronte's romantic connection is passionate and tender. With a cast of heartwarming secondary characters, this modern western romance is sure to please."

—*RT Book Reviews* (4 1/2 Stars)

"An enjoyable read, sure to suit lovers of contemporary romance set in the West, whetting their whistle for the next books in the series."   —New York Journal of Books

"Wild West Games, ranch country setting, bruised characters with pasts? Count me in. It wasn't long into the story that I decided that I made a good decision. Things get off to a feverish start as far as combustible attraction."

—Delighted Reader

Berkley Sensation Titles by Lisa Bingham

DESPERADO
RENEGADE
MAVERICK

MAVERICK

❖

LISA BINGHAM

BERKLEY SENSATION
New York

BERKLEY SENSATION
Published by Berkley
An imprint of Penguin Random House LLC
375 Hudson Street, New York, New York 10014

Copyright © 2016 by Lisa Bingham

ISBN: 9780425278581

First Edition: November 2016

Printed in the United States of America
1   3   5   7   9   10   8   6   4   2

Cover illustration by Danny O'Leary
Cover design by Lesley Worrell
Book design by Kelly Lipovich

To Christian.
Read the books and learn.
And to Connie . . .
You're welcome.

ACKNOWLEDGMENTS

I'd like to take a moment to acknowledge all those who were instrumental in helping the Taggart Brothers series come to life.

To my mother, all my love in the world. Thank you for always being so incredibly supportive.

I'm grateful to all the gang at Multimedia, Danielle, Abby, and Joanna, as well as the awesome team at Berkley, Kristine, Ryanne, Deborah, and Leis.

My warm appreciation also goes to my sounding boards, Nancy and Danice, and my fellow members of the Utah Chapter of RWA. It's so nice to have people around who "talk my own kind of crazy" or don't mind if I mumble incoherently to myself as I'm trying to figure out a plot twist.

I'd also like to recognize Syd and Helen, who introduced me to the world of SASS and the fantasy of shooting in full Victorian regalia. I'm blessed to have found such great friends, and I truly appreciate the way you refrained from laughing at my "slower than tar" times at Hell on Wheels. Your marriage is the epitome of "happily-ever-after," and your love for your children and grandchildren knows no bounds. You are an example to us all.

And last, but certainly not least, I'd like to thank all of the fans out there who have been so supportive. I have received so many wonderful notes, posts, tweets, and reviews, and I'm touched by your kind words.

To anyone who'd like to connect, I'd love to hear from you. Join me on my website, www.lisabinghamauthor.com, www.Facebook.com/lisabinghamauthor, or on Twitter at @lbinghamauthor.

Lisa Bingham

ONE

———◆———

BODEY Taggart loved to win.

He craved the surge of adrenaline that came with a wager, the fire that settled into his chest at a challenge, the pounding of his heart that accompanied the competition. As a kid, he'd joined every team, run every race, and fought to the bloody end for every point. He'd started with Little League, worked his way through junior varsity and varsity sports. Once in high school, he'd added rodeo to the list with bronco busting and bull riding—and he'd given it his all, returning home at night with bruised ribs, bloody lips, and black eyes. He'd been driven to be the best—to the point where his mother had despaired of his reaching adulthood in one piece. Time and time again, she'd warned him that if he only set his sights on winning, he'd never be satisfied with anything for more than a moment.

"That glittering prize is short-lived," she cautioned. "Don't spend your whole life looking for shiny things, or you're bound to end up with a room full of tarnish."

Bodey still didn't know what the hell he was supposed to make of that statement. Maureen Taggart had died before he'd turned twenty. If she hadn't, he was sure that he would have argued the point. He would insist to his mother that the trophies filling the boxes in the garage didn't motivate him. It wasn't as simple as that. He competed because something deep inside of him, some restless, prickly portion of his nature, demanded that he push himself to the limits, physically and mentally. He craved that oblivion of spirit as much as an alcoholic obsessed over booze.

Granted, things were getting a little out of hand. Where once, he'd been content to use sport and athleticism as his sole means of getting his "fix," lately everything he did had become a contest: cow cutting competitions, quarter horse races, fantasy sports, and poker. Hell, if someone was willing to play along, he'd make a bet on which side of the hill a heifer would leave a cow pie—and he'd do his best to make sure the animal cooperated.

Sad to say, even women had become a game to him. Bodey relished the thrill of the hunt, the excitement of the chase, the tender intricacies of wooing. He reveled in the first headiness of attraction, the anticipation of that first kiss, first caress, first connection. Hell, he loved women plain and simple, and he continued to love them, in his own fashion, after the female in question decided to call it quits. Even then, he considered all of his "exes" his friends. He didn't intend to be a "love 'em and leave 'em" kind of guy. Each time he set his sights on a new conquest, he was sure that *this was the one. This* was the woman who would ease the battling compulsion within him and give him the sense of peace his brothers had found. Maybe then, he could settle down, abandon the never-ending need to prove himself, and consider a long-term commitment without feeling like a noose was wrapping around his neck.

But as he squinted against the blazing hot July sun and packed his long guns into his cart, Bodey realized that this time, *this time,* his need to win might kill him.

Good hell, almighty. He'd made a huge mistake. *Huge.*

In lingering with the practice posse for the regional SASS Hell on Wheels Competition, he'd stayed too long in the hundred plus temperatures of a Wyoming summer. Belatedly, he realized that he should have bowed out thirty minutes ago when he'd begun to feel the familiar throb of a headache blooming behind his left eye. But, no. He'd insisted to himself that he could finish one more stage, one more round of marksmanship. He'd been showing off in front of his buddies and the newest female recruit to their group, and he'd been driven to finish . . .

On top.

Yup. That was the crux of his error. There was a new member to the Single Action Shooting Society—or at least to Bodey's circle of friends—who went by the moniker of Ima Ontop.

As SASS nicknames went, it wasn't terribly subtle.

But it *was* effective.

From the moment she'd appeared on the range, testosterone levels had soared within the predominantly male group. Men who usually spent the practice rounds laughing, joking, and slinging bullshit . . . well, let's say they snapped to attention. What would have been a relaxed afternoon of marksmanship became a life and death struggle for the best score.

And Bodey hadn't been immune. He'd been immediately attracted to the tall, scantily-clad brunette—and, *duh*, who wouldn't be? The woman had come to the practice match wearing nothing but calf-high Victorian boots, striped hose, tight ruffled shorty-shorts, and a leather corset. The getup hovered somewhere between saloon girl and Miss July. A man would need to be dead not to notice her.

But as the heat of the day wormed its way through his head, and the remnant side effects of a recent concussion made each movement an exercise in torture, Bodey's interest waned. Especially when it became clear that she was a talker. For the past twenty minutes, she'd gone on and on and *on* about loading her shells with shot and glitter for a little extra "sparkle" on the range.

What the frickin' hell?

Normally, Bodey would have been more than happy to

pick up on her "let's have some fun while we're in Cheyenne" signals. There wasn't a red-blooded male within a hundred miles who wouldn't have been interested. She was tall and voluptuous with legs up to her armpits and boobs that threatened a costume malfunction at any moment. Even better, she was a "no strings" kind of gal.

But as the dull ache over his eye began creeping toward his nape and he broke out in a clammy sweat, the woman's chatter soon dissolved into a drone akin to adults in the Charlie Brown cartoons.

Wah-wah-wahwah-wah-wah.

Then it got worse.

The white-hot drill bit which had been screwing into his eye socket plunged straight through to his brain. The pain ricocheted through his skull, spreading like wildfire. Sweat popped out on his forehead and upper lip and his stomach lurched ominously, reminding him that he hadn't eaten yet today but he'd drunk lots and lots of water in an effort to stay cool. The liquid sloshed in his stomach, threatening to make a reappearance.

Which meant he was going to have to bow out.

Leave the competition midstream.

Lose.

But, damnit, he had to get out of here. Now.

Grasping the handle of his gun cart, he turned away from the group without explanation, forcing one foot in front of the other as his head began to pound in tandem with the jarring thud of his footfalls. Tugging his hat low, he ignored the curious calls from his friends, knowing that if he tried to talk, the sound would reverberate through his cranium. Then, he'd lose his tenuous control on his stomach and begin yakking up all that water.

Squinting, Bodey tried to gauge the distance to his truck, but the glint of sunshine radiating off the trucks and RVs stationed in the distant parking lot seared through his retinas.

Damnit. If he could get to his trailer, he could pull all the curtains, turn on the AC, crash on the bunk, and pray he'd caught the migraine in time so that it only lasted an hour or two rather than days.

But he'd taken fewer than a dozen steps when he realized that he wasn't going to make it. His knees felt as if they were made of wet spaghetti. And even if he got to his "home on wheels," he'd have to take the time to unload his ammo and weapons from the gun cart and stow them away. Right now, he wasn't sure if he'd be able to go another few feet, let alone traverse several hundred yards to his truck.

Shit, shit, shit.

He quickly scanned his surroundings, his gaze settling on the tent city which had sprouted overnight opposite the length of the range. Vendors from all over the country had set up shop, selling everything from hand-tooled holsters to wigs, artisan knives to Victorian hats. The cool shade beneath their awnings beckoned to him. He could imagine the reaction if he stumbled inside and crawled beneath one of their tables.

But sweet heaven above, he was sorely tempted.

Bodey forced himself to keep moving as more cold, clammy sweat began pooling beneath his shirt and his head felt as if it were being squeezed in a vice. He was close to moaning aloud when a series of befuddled thoughts eased through the pain.

Tents.

Shade.

Syd and Helen.

Bodey altered his trajectory mid-stride. Syd and Helen Henderson—friends from Bodey's hometown of Bliss, Utah—had rolled into camp the night before. Most of the summer, they traveled from one SASS competition to the next, selling Victorian garments that Helen designed and sewed. Bodey hadn't arrived in time to help them erect the spacious canvas tent from which they sold their wares, but he'd heard his brother Elam talking about it. If Bodey could find Helen, he was sure she'd have a stash of headache medicine in that massive carpetbag of hers. If not, he could at least sit in the shade until he felt steadier on his feet.

Scanning the line of tents, Bodey found the right one easily enough. Positioned squarely in front of its entrance was Virgil, a metal sculpture of a bowlegged gunslinger welded together from old farm machinery and mounted to an industrial-sized spring. The piece had been made by Jace, Bodey's older brother. Even now, gusts of hot wind caused it to sway back and forth, inviting customers into the yawning opening.

Normally, Bodey would have steered clear of the canvas structure with its racks of female frippery and chattering customers. Syd usually parked their motor home somewhere to the rear where Helen used a generator to run her sewing machine and make onsite alterations. Unless he was on the range, Syd took refuge there. But Bodey was afraid the additional twenty yards would make his head pound with even more ferocity. So he stepped beneath the awning, braving the racks of calico and silk, ruffles and lace, making a beeline for a folding chair next to the cash register.

He didn't know how long he'd sat there, head bowed, eyes squeezed shut, hands wrapped around the back of his neck, when a voice asked, "May I help you?"

The question speared through him like a bolt of lightning, even though the question had been uttered softly enough. Without even opening his eyes, he rasped, "Is Helen here?"

"No. She and Syd went into town to get some supplies."

Damn.

Bodey dared to open one eye, just a crack.

Again, he was confronted with a WTF moment. Where his companion on the posse had been intent on showing off her assets, this woman had gone to the opposite extreme. She was petite, probably only an inch or two over five feet, with a girlish figure that had been entirely obscured by a gathered chintz skirt, a schoolmarm blouse buttoned up to her chin, and a battered straw hat topped with flowers which had clearly seen better days. Ima Ontop had displayed her wares for all to see, but this woman was openly declaring hers off-limits.

Bodey clenched his jaw tight, his stomach pitching as he

realized he was going to have to make it all the way to his trailer after all.

The woman's eyes narrowed suspiciously. "You're going to be sick, aren't you?"

Before he could answer, she dodged around the counter and grabbed a wastepaper basket, which she thrust into his hands. Bodey considered the invitation to purge his stomach, but the trash can was made of wicker and unlined. Not the most effective of containers.

She seemed to realize the same thing at about the same time. Muttering an unladylike, non-Victorian curse under her breath, she grabbed a shopping bag from the pile next to the register, snatched the basket away, and handed him the sack.

Clutching the plastic, Bodey debated whether or not to use it as his stomach roiled dangerously. But one look at the woman peering down at him changed his mind. He didn't want her seeing him so completely . . . unmanned. Which he would be if he let loose the Technicolor rainbow.

Hell. Why couldn't he have found Syd behind the counter?

The woman's head tipped slightly to the side, and Bodey had the fleeting impression of a bird sizing up the situation, mentally calculating the threat before making a decision to fight or fly.

She must have decided to "fight" because she stepped slightly to the side—out of his field of range should his stomach start its heaving again—and asked, "What's wrong? Flu?"

Bodey shook his head, then wished he hadn't. "Migraine."

She folded her arms under her breasts—revealing that she did have a figure under that awful shirt she wore.

"Do you have something for it?"

"Not . . . on me." He waited a moment before finishing, "It's in my trailer."

He closed his eyes again but not before he saw the way her lips pressed together and her brows furrowed in silent deliberation. Once again, she reminded him of a bird; one of the baby swallows which had hatched in a nest they'd built against his bedroom window. In the past few weeks, they'd been learning to fly. He'd seen that same expression of quick intelligence as they'd judged the distance to the nearest branch against their ability to get there safely.

Abruptly, she said, "Wait here."

Bodey couldn't summon the wherewithal to inform her that he didn't plan on going anywhere, so he grunted, only dimly aware of the rustle of her skirts as she strode from the tent. Seconds later, he heard her approach. Then, to his utter amazement, he felt her remove his hat and place an icy cold pack against his scalp.

Daring to open his eye again, he saw her watching him with something that approximated concern. But somehow, he knew the sentiment had more to do with the danger that he might woof his biscuits on the merchandise rather than anything personal.

"I filled a shopping bag with ice from one of the water stations on the range," she said, referring to the large plastic totes that were regularly stocked with crushed ice and bottled water to encourage the participants to stay hydrated in the scorching summer heat.

"Drink this." She held out a can of Pepsi that was wet with condensation and more bits of melting ice. "Helen keeps a cooler in the back loaded with her secret stockpile. I don't think she'd mind if you had one."

Knowing that the caffeine would help, he gratefully took it, popping the top.

She dug into the voluminous pocket of her skirt and pulled out a pill bottle. "It's over-the-counter stuff from the RV. Do you need something else?"

"This will work." Bodey had a prescription painkiller, but the thought of waiting even a moment longer for relief held no appeal. He grappled with the lid and shook four pills into his palm, then swallowed them with a swig of soda and leaned back, closing his eyes again. "Thanks."

There was a beat of silence. No, not silence, exactly. In the background, Bodey could hear the staccato *bang* of gunfire, followed quickly by the sharp *ping!* of bullets striking metal targets. Laughter and good-natured jeering rode softly on the breeze.

"So you know Syd and Helen?"

He opened his eyes again when the woman spoke, and the caffeine must have hit his system because he didn't feel the need to wince. Even so, he was struck by her intent expression. There was something strikingly . . . odd about her. She had delicate, gamin features and huge blue-black eyes. Rather than donning the Victorian wigs worn by most of the women at the matches, she'd kept hers natural—a tousled pixie cut that accented her wide eyes. But the wind and the heat had caused wispy curls to form around her face. Even so, there was no hiding that the naturally dark strands had been highlighted with a subtle shade of blue. Nevertheless, even though her offbeat hair, slight build, and too-large clothing could have made her look like an orphan, she was obviously a grown-up woman. It was there in the "I've been knocked down by life but I've come back swinging" shadows in her eyes and the way she appeared comfortable in her own skin—if not the costume she'd been forced to wear.

Her brows lifted in silent query, but this time, there was a mocking hint to the dead-pan set of her features. As if she'd heard his thoughts out loud.

Too late, he realized that she'd asked him a question.

Syd and Helen. Did he know them?

"Yeah. Syd and Helen are neighbors of mine in Utah."

"Ah."

He held out his hand, grimaced when he realized it was wet from the ice pack and the soda can, and swiped it down his thigh. Then he held it out again. "Bodey Taggart."

Her eyes narrowed for a moment.

Damnit. What stories had Helen been telling?

But she finally slipped her hand into his. Bodey liked the way that it felt there, small and warm but with a firm grip. "Beth."

She didn't offer her last name, and there was no further explanation of her relationship to Helen—friend, relative, acquaintance—which left Bodey curious. Beth wasn't from Bliss. He would have seen her around. So how did she end up working with Helen?

"That's it? Just plain 'Beth'? No last name? Or are you one of those people who only needs one name, like Cher or Usher?"

It was a weak attempt at humor—mainly because he already felt like an idiot. He'd stumbled into the tent like one of the Walking Dead and nearly up-chucked all over her shoes. He didn't like anyone seeing him that way, not even his brothers. He'd lived too long under a single motto: never let them see you sweat; never let them see you weak.

"I try to keep things simple."

Simple?

Oh, yeah. One name.

For some reason, he'd forgotten that he'd even asked a question. Instead, he'd grown conscious of her soft skin against his own calloused palm. Even as he debated prolonging the contact, she tugged free—not quickly, not self-consciously. No, she did it . . . dismissively. As if she would be more than happy for him to remain a stranger. Then, very subtly, she slid both hands into the pockets of her skirt.

Well, hell. If that wasn't a "keep your distance" move, he didn't know what was.

Nevertheless, even with his head pounding and his stomach tied in knots, Bodey found himself responding to the challenge—though, for the life of him, he didn't understand why her attitude rankled. He was a nice guy—charming as hell, if his sisters-in-law were to be believed. She didn't have to assume he was Jack the Ripper.

Or worse.

Weak.

She'd seen him at his lowest. He didn't want her to think that was all he was.

At the very least, she could smile.

"Thanks for your help." He held her gaze, searching her expression, her eyes, for any hint of emotion. "I'm pretty sure I would have face-planted it if I'd tried to get back to my trailer."

Dipping into his arsenal, he offered her a crooked grin, one that was guaranteed to get even the frostiest woman to lighten up.

But her features remained absolutely still. "Mmm."

Mmm? That's all the response he got?

He sat back in his chair, still holding the makeshift ice bag to his head, and regarded her curiously. He usually didn't go for females like her. No, he gravitated toward women who fell into certain molds: girl-next-door, Rodeo Queen, or Miss Boobs and Legs. He liked females who were tall and stacked and willing to indulge in a little harmless fun. Like Miss Ima Ontop. But this one . . .

There was something brooding and intense about her. And she was tiny. Hell, he could tuck her under his arm with room to spare. But that didn't make her delicate. The way she looked at him warned that she had a will of iron.

He must have been staring because she looked away, offered a slightly annoyed sigh, then asked with a little more conversational warmth, "Do you get them often? The migraines?"

He shook his head, and this time, rather than feeling like his brain was crashing against his skull, the movement merely inspired a dull throb. "I had two concussions within a month of each other. The migraines are a side effect. Hopefully, not a lingering one."

Especially since his brothers had "grounded" him for the summer. No cow cutting, no bronco busting, no sky diving, no ATVs. He was lucky that they hadn't forbidden him to ride horseback altogether—although he wouldn't be surprised if they threatened to restrict him to the corrals back home and his little brother's aging pony if they caught wind of this latest headache.

Bodey couldn't blame them. The first injury had occurred on the ranch when they'd taken a load of cattle up to the summer pastures. A rabbit had darted from beneath a bush, startling his mount. The horse had zigged and Bodey had zagged. Next thing he knew, he'd been flying through the air. When he'd landed, his head had struck a rock and he'd been out like a light. The second concussion had been more serious. On his way home from a competition in Jackson, he'd been T-boned by a drunk driver and had spent two days unconscious in the hospital. When he'd finally been allowed to return home, he'd been plagued by double vision, vertigo, bouts of nausea—and headaches that made the one he had now seem like a cake-walk. But, over time, most of his symptoms had disappeared.

Until today.

He should have known better and worn dark glasses rather than the lighter protective lenses he used for shooting.

A pair of women entered the tent and Beth backed away, murmuring, "Excuse me."

Bodey appreciated the way she kept her voice soft and soothing, unconsciously encouraging the other women to do the same. Soon, their conversation washed over him like lake water, allowing him to close his eyes again and sip his Pepsi. By the time the women disappeared with one of Helen's hand sewn ensembles in a shopping bag, the banging against his temples had eased to a dull ache. When Beth approached him again, he smiled ruefully.

"Feeling better?" she asked.

"Yeah. Thanks to you."

Nothing. She gave him the same inscrutable look Spock would give Captain Kirk if he announced he was beaming down to the inhospitable planet below where it was guaran-teed he would be attacked by life-sucking aliens.

Shit. He'd spent too much time watching television with Barry during his recuperation.

"I'm serious. I doubt I would have made it back to my trailer."

He flashed her another broad grin.

Nothing.

Was he losing his touch? He'd hoped for some kind of reaction. But her eyes grew shadowed with emotions that he couldn't translate and her face remained neutral.

And damned if that didn't egg him on even more.

TWO

———— ◆ ————

"SO you're a friend of Helen's?" Bodey probed, hoping
for a little more information.

"Not exactly."

He stood and was pleased to find that he was steady on
his feet. Rather than lurching, his stomach responded with
a twinge of hunger.

Good sign.

The makeshift ice pack had completely melted by now
and the water was growing tepid, so Bodey grimaced, tossing it and the empty can into the waste paper basket.

"I owe you a Pepsi at least."

"It's Helen you owe."

Again, although she gave no hint of emotion, Bodey
sensed that she knew exactly what he was up to, that he was
bound and determined to make her react. But she remained
outwardly unimpressed. So much so, that he sensed she was
toying with him, like a cat with its paw on a mouse's tail,
taking great delight in watching it squirm.

But Bodey wasn't so easily cowed. "Then tell *Helen* I
owe her a drink."

"If you insist."

He couldn't prevent a soft laugh. "I do." Moving toward her, he watched the way she subtly drew herself up to full height. Even so, she wasn't any bigger than a mite.

As he closed the distance between them, he saw the first chink in her armor when her hands clenched in her pockets and she rocked back on her heels—and once again, he was struck by the innocent high-necked blouse and voluminous skirt. The old granny charm of her outfit was completely at odds with her rocker hairstyle and the dark liner around her eyes. He'd bet money that the costume had been supplied at the last minute.

"Are you shooting on one of the posses?" He gestured to the range.

He saw tiny lines appear at the corners of her eyes and he knew she was amused. "Me? Uh . . . no. I'm helping Helen in the tent."

"Are you staying with them in their motor home?"

She shook her head again, and this time her lips actually twitched. Clearly, she knew he was fishing. "No."

He waited, but she didn't add anything more, so he was finally forced to say something to ease the silence. "I see."

Nothing.

And he didn't really know anything more about her than he had when he'd begun this conversation.

Bodey knew that was his cue to leave but he found himself curiously loathe to do so. He couldn't remember the last time a woman had been so . . . unaffected by his easy charm. Normally, he could coax a self-conscious giggle out of even the most hard-hearted female, whether she was ninety or nine. But Beth . . . she was proving hard to fathom.

"I'd love a chance to properly thank you." Bodey lobbed her a softball flirt, figuring it was worth a try.

"Consider me properly thanked."

Strike one.

Apparently she wasn't willing to play. At least not with him. But he couldn't resist trying again. "Maybe I can follow up that vote of thanks with lunch."

Her head tipped back, a lock of blue hair falling over her brow. Normally, he didn't like that kind of thing. God had given women perfectly good hair. Why would they adopt a hue not found in nature? But with the rest of her tresses so dark, the color was subtle—reminding him of the blue-black tones of the crows that gathered around the silos during harvest time.

"Thanks, but no. I have to stay in the tent while Helen is gone."

Strike two.

"What about later?"

She didn't immediately answer.

"You've gotta eat sometime," he said, purposely dropping his voice. But his attempt at tempting her backfired.

"Maybe. But not necessarily with you."

You're out!

Bodey lifted a hand to his chest as if wounded, but to his surprise, rather than feeling rejected, her comment made him laugh.

"You don't like me much, do you?"

She crossed her arms, eyeing him from tip to toe. "I don't know you well enough to like or dislike you. But . . . as I said. Helen's told me about you."

Ouch. He was going to have to meet up with Helen and find out what horror stories she'd been recounting. For the life of him, he couldn't think of anything so awful that this girl would immediately dismiss him.

"And what has she been saying?"

He anticipated a recital of the large number of women he'd dated, but her response took him by surprise.

"That you're an adrenaline junky. A risk jockey."

Risk jockey?

He laughed, supposing he couldn't argue too much with that label. "And that makes me non-lunch-companion material?"

She regarded him with those dark, dark eyes, and again, he wondered if she could read his thoughts.

"I don't know. But I'm only helping Helen until the shoot is over, so there's not much point in finding out, is there?"

Bam! Not only out for the inning, you're ejected from the game!

But again, rather than being put off by her frankness, he said, "You really don't pull your punches, do you?"

"I didn't think I was throwing any. Merely telling it like I see it."

And damned if he didn't feel a stupid-ass grin threatening to slide all over his face. How the hell could this woman shoot him down in flames and make herself even more intriguing?

He closed what little space remained between them. To her credit, she held her ground.

"Tell you what. If you're not opposed, I'll check back a little later. Maybe if Helen returns and you decide you're hungry—*and* you can bring yourself to endure my company—I'll take you down the row for a brisket sandwich. That shouldn't be too . . . risky . . . for either of us."

She didn't jump for joy, but she didn't refuse the offer. Bodey decided to count that as progress.

"What if I'm a vegetarian?"

"Then I'm sure we can scare up some lettuce and rabbit food somewhere."

Bodey wasn't sure, but he thought her eyes grew softer, the tiny lines in the corner appearing once more, so he decided to press his luck. "After that . . . if you're up for it, I'll take you to the practice lane they've got set up for the scholarship fund. You can't leave Hell on Wheels without shooting at something."

"You're sure of that, are you?"

Again, the thread of mockery, so Bodey pushed things even further, leaning down so that his lips were a mere hairsbreadth away from her ear.

"Oh, yeah, darlin'. I'm sure."

Then, knowing that he'd better get the hell outta Dodge before she could think up a snarky refusal, he snagged the handle to his gun cart and scooped his hat off the counter, settling it over his brow. He touched a finger to the brim.

"Later."

Then, he braved the glaring sunshine.

BETH silently counted to ten before stepping beneath the awning and casually glancing up and down a dirt access road which had somehow become a Wild West main street in the space of twenty-four hours.

Not a person prone to flights of fancy, she had to mentally remind herself that she hadn't somehow been dropped into a nineteenth century boom town. Tents had sprung up overnight all along vendor's row. Tables and mannequins lined the makeshift street, tempting visitors to step inside. A hot breeze stirred up dust-devils that frolicked and dissipated around racks of canvas dusters and clothes trees laden with hats.

Although the competition wouldn't officially start until the next day, that hadn't stopped most of the participants from donning their Victorian finery. Women—wearing gowns supported by bustles and hoops—strolled down the lane, their faces shaded by lacy parasols. The men—who were probably even more slavishly attuned to accuracy—had donned frock coats, ornate Spanish gaucho regalia, military uniforms, or— dear sweet heaven above—breechclouts and leggings.

Clinging to the shade, Beth wondered what made a sane person dress in buckskin or wool—*wool!*—when it had to be over a hundred degrees in the sun.

Unwittingly, her eyes scanned the crowd until she found one particular cowboy making his way to the parking lot on the opposite end of the lane. Bodey Taggart looked as if he'd stepped down from his horse after a cattle drive north. Even from this distance, Beth could see how the historical garb molded itself to the taut musculature of his body. He wore tight woven trousers that clung far too intimately to powerful thighs and perfectly rounded buttocks. His tab collared shirt was made of hanky-soft linen, caught above the elbows with bright red arm garters. Leather tipped suspenders, buttoned at his waist, dissected his spine before flaring out to accentuate the width of his shoulders. His hat was obviously one he didn't wear only at the shoots because it had shaped itself to the curve of his head, the brown felt dusty and darker at the crown. It was the kind of cowboy hat worn by a man who worked and worked hard. But the icing on the cake was a holster rig positioned low on his hips, the grips of his pistols glinting in the sun, slender cords wrapping around his taut thighs.

Gunslinger personified.

Although Beth tried her best to resist the appeal of a red-blooded, hard-bodied male dressed tip-to-toe like a walking, talking, figure from the Old West, she couldn't completely tamp down the way her heart skittered in her chest.

Not your type, she reminded herself firmly.

But she was lying. There wasn't a woman alive who wouldn't respond to the sight of a male dressed head-to-toe in cowboy finery, and Beth was no different. Too many old television shows featuring big families, green ranches, and gun-toting lawmen willing to defend their kin to the death had been drummed into her head as a child for her to react any other way.

Even if she knew it was all a fairy tale.

Stop it!

"We're back!"

Beth jumped, turning to see Helen breezing back into the tent, her arms loaded with sacks. "Sorry we're late. I talked Syd into stopping at the local fabric store because I was short on thread—and look what I found!" Helen's eyes snapped with excitement as she began laying bundles of cloth on the counter.

Having never learned to sew, Beth wasn't sure what the proper response was supposed to be as Helen extolled the virtues of each sample. As far as Beth could tell, her boss had a whole lot of the same thing—material with big flowers, little flowers, stripes and flowers, plaids and flowers.

Beth had learned enough about Helen Henderson to know that the woman had a gift. She'd seen the way Helen could look at a length of calico or silk and picture exactly what she would make. Next thing you knew, there was a new creation hanging from her racks ready to sell. In the few days since Beth had been hired, Helen had designed and created over a half dozen items. They were girly, girly prints worn by the kind of women who had long curly hair extensions, false eyelashes, and big boobs.

Beth had never fallen into that category. Except for a few skirts, there wasn't a stitch of black or the sheen of leather anywhere to be seen on the racks. What Helen needed were some steampunk items with dark, dramatic colors, brass rivets and buckles—which would be more in keeping with the kind of fantasy attire that Beth preferred.

"Did you have many customers drop by while we were gone?" Helen asked breathlessly as she tucked the fabric back into the sacks and stowed them under the counter.

"Quite a few. I sold a couple of dresses and two men brought some trousers in to be hemmed." Beth hesitated before adding, "You know they're buying them from one of the other shops and bringing them to you, right?"

Helen laughed. "Of course I know. The other vendors don't have a machine or the know-how to do it, so they send them my way." Her eyes twinkled as she pushed a strand of hair back into the elaborate switch of ringlets attached to the back of her head. "More often than not, when the gentleman in question comes back to retrieve them, he brings his wife or significant other, and the woman in question walks out with something too."

"You're a sly one."

Helen winked. "How do you think I got Syd into a fabric store," she said, gesturing to her husband as he pushed through the tent flap carrying more sacks of brightly colored cloth.

Beth could only imagine the stir they'd made in town. Helen wore a deep red riding habit trimmed with broad strokes of black soutache braid, and Syd looked like a nineteenth century banker, complete with a dark suit, embroidered vest, cravat, and bowler hat.

"Anyone else stop by?"

Beth hesitated. But since Helen would find out soon

enough that he'd taken refuge in the tent, she nodded and said, "Bodey Taggart was here."

That caused Helen's fussing to cease. She stood so still she could have been a participant in a game of freeze-tag. "Oh?"

The question was completely innocuous, so "I'll pretend I don't care about the answer even though I'm dying to know" casual that Beth rolled her eyes.

"The man had a migraine. He needed a shady spot to sit and some painkiller. I gave him one of your Pepsis and some of your over-the-counter pills from the RV."

Helen immediately "unfroze."

"Poor thing."

Poor thing? Helen's tone implied the man was six years old.

"He's so used to jumping from one venture to the next, I don't think he knows how to relax and enjoy himself. I do believe this is the first summer I've seen him participate in a SASS regional competition since the one . . . what would you say, Syd? Five years ago?"

Syd, who had claimed the seat that Bodey had so recently vacated, stretched out his legs and absently stroked his full beard—taking great care not to jar his waxed mustache. "I'd say more like six."

"He's usually on the cow cutting circuit this time of year."

Cow cutting?

What did that mean?

Since Beth had been hired to help Helen and Syd with the Cheyenne shoot, she often felt as if she'd been dropped down a rabbit hole where playing dress up was normal, and people were governed by an odd set of unwritten rules—and an even more foreign vocabulary.

The job had appeared simple enough when Beth had seen the hand-printed advertisement for full-time help at a nearby convenience store. Eager to land the position before someone else could snap it up, she'd come to interview with Helen at an out-of-the-way spot a few miles from town.

At that time, the place had been nothing more than a

large dirt parking lot and open fields, a few scattered out-buildings, and an incongruous event tent erected in the middle of what appeared to be a large pasture. Dismayed, Beth had been sure the address and the offer of employment were someone's twisted idea of a joke. But Helen must have been watching for her arrival, because she'd waved from the steps of a bus-sized motor home.

Immediately, Beth had been welcomed inside. As Helen had brewed blood orange tea and set out finger sandwiches, she'd explained that her regular helper had been forced to return to Utah for a family emergency, so she needed someone to handle the customers part of the day while she and Syd played "redneck golf."

When Beth had blinked at Helen uncomprehendingly, the older woman had laughed elaborating with, "Sweetie, it's a bunch of crazy folk who like to play dress up and shoot guns. There's really nothing to it."

But when Beth emerged from the motor home—with a job and a list of tasks to help get the Hendersons' merchandise unpacked—a Wild West tent city had already begun to sprout like a patch of mushrooms in the prairie grass.

Working throughout the afternoon and well into the evening, Beth had swiftly realized that to the SASS participants these regional matches were a really, *really* big deal. No money was exchanged, no expensive prizes were awarded. Winners of the multi-day competitions—which included shooting and practice posse rounds—were rarely given anything more than a plaque and bragging rights. And somehow, that was enough for a bunch of grown-ass people to take competitiveness to a "whole 'nother level."

There were contests for the best working costume, best shooting costume, best formal costume, and best couple. They competed to see who had the most unusual gun cart and the fanciest rig. They had at least a dozen categories—male and female—for marksmanship, and a casino night where the proceeds from roulette and card games were donated to charity or scholarship funds. And this year, according to Helen, there would even be a "Dueling Tea" contest.

Huh?

She soon learned that the costumes weren't merely for fun but were a mandatory regulation. Even more confusing, no one used their real names. Instead, each one had a registered SASS alias. Helen and Syd were Queen Helen and Syd Sheleen. And Beth was soon introduced to "Bad Gene Pool," "Slick Willy," and "Calico Cate."

Sometimes Beth felt like Alice, transported to a Wild West Wonderland where reality was turned topsy-turvy. And other times . . .

She envied them all. Envied their ability to dive headfirst into the fantasy, creating a world and a community that drew people together from disparate walks of life.

"How long did Bodey stay?"

Beth blinked, then realized her brain, once again, had veered down a meandering path. But this time, thank heavens, the thoughts had been harmless enough.

"Probably twenty, thirty minutes."

Helen became ultra-casual again.

"Did you talk about anything interesting?"

Beth shot Helen a pithy look. "No. After he nearly lost his lunch, I left him in the corner with his eyes closed while I helped a couple of customers. By the time I got done, he was ready to leave."

Not exactly a true recitation of events but it was the closest version that Beth was going offer. Even so, just to cover her hiney, she added, "He said he'd drop by later to bring you a Pepsi to replace the one from your stash."

Helen offered a dismissing wave. "My cooler—and anything else—is always open for those Taggart boys. They're good people, even if Bodey strays a little too close to the wild side."

As far as Helen was concerned, being "good people" was one of her highest forms of praise.

Now that she had all of her fabric safely tucked away, Helen stood and set her sights on Beth. "You've been tending to the store all morning and it's getting late. Go get yourself something to eat."

Why was everybody so obsessed with food?

But before Beth could object, Helen said, "It's hotter than Hades outside and it will only get hotter. If you try to skip on the meals and water, you'll get heatstroke for sure. Go. I've got sandwich fixings in the fridge or you can get something from one of the vendors. Either way, I don't want to see you back for at least an hour. Two would be better."

Two hours? What was she supposed to do in Little-House-on-the-Prairie-Land until then?

"Go! Once you've got a meal in your stomach, put your feet up in the RV with the cooler turned up to HIGH."

In their brief acquaintance, Beth had already learned that it was useless to argue with Helen once she had a bee in her bonnet, so Beth reluctantly murmured, "Fine."

When Beth would have dodged out the back and headed straight for the RV, Helen shook her head and wagged her finger. "Eat first."

"Yes, ma'am," she said facetiously, then mumbled, "but I'm not heading out there in this getup."

"Why not? You'll blend into the crowd." But Helen's stern tone quickly dissolved into a rich chuckle. "Okay, fine. Take it off, if you want. It really doesn't suit you." Her eyes narrowed. "I have some fabric that I bought today that would make a fabulous—"

"No!" Beth said sternly. "Do not make me one of those . . . those . . . schoolmarm outfits."

As she dodged through the canvas flap, she heard Helen call out, "Saloon girl it is. Make sure you wear a hat!"

Beth marched toward the RV, more determined than ever to ditch the calico. She might have been thrust into the realm of make-believe, but that didn't mean she had to play along. There were more than a few bystanders in modern dress.

But her irritation didn't last more than a few feet. She couldn't be mad at Helen. Not when the woman had been willing to give her a job—even if it was only for a few days. The money—any money—would be a godsend.

Refusing to let her thoughts veer in that direction, she wrenched open the door to the RV and climbed inside.

Within seconds, she was wrestling out of the high-necked blouse, then the voluminous skirt which Helen had secured with safety pins since the woman couldn't find anything small enough for Beth's frame. Clearly, pioneer spinsters were not flat-chested munchkins like herself.

Finally, Beth managed to free herself from the cumbersome clothing and replace it with her own. Black jeans, black tank top, black sneakers. She grimaced. The clothes would probably be hotter than hell in the blazing Wyoming weather, but the rest of her wardrobe wasn't any better. Black hid the dirt.

For a moment, she wondered if she could get away with staying in the RV. Although her stomach rumbled with hunger, she didn't want to eat. She felt uncomfortable dipping into Helen's supplies, and the concession prices would probably be sky-high. Not to mention that Beth needed every penny she could scrape together. It was time for another move, and for once, she was hoping for bus tickets. North. Where there were mountains. Somewhere where it would be cooler.

The thought was enough to bring all of her worries stampeding back, flooding her brain with what-ifs that threatened to bring her to her knees. But she clenched her jaw and shoved them resolutely away. It didn't do any good to worry about any of it. Not when there was nothing more she could do. As soon as she'd been paid, she would agonize about how much to devote to food, and how much to put aside for tickets. Until then . . .

She would do whatever it took to melt into the background. Beth glared at the stifling costume she'd folded on the bed. Even if it meant dressing up like Rebecca of Sunnybrook Farm. And if Helen wanted her to walk the row toward the food suppliers, Beth would do that too. That way, when she returned and lied about eating, her story would have more credence.

Beth was about to fling the door open and step outside when she caught a glimpse of her reflection in the mirror pasted to the refrigerator.

Hell's bells. Pay attention, Bethy.

Growling softly, she tore the straw hat with its sad silk flowers from the top of her head and threw it onto the bench. Then, mindful of Helen's warning to cover her head, she snagged a company ball cap from those Syd had tossed onto a nearby chair.

Flinging open the door, she jumped into the dust, then nearly stumbled and fell on her face when a long, lanky frame pushed away from the RV.

"Good. You're ready."

BETH'S reaction was priceless: shock; swiftly followed by guilt; then an inward *"What the hell is he doing here?"*

Bodey didn't wait for Beth to utter the words out loud. "Helen told me you were changing."

He used one finger to slide a pair of dark glasses down his nose so that he could get a better look of her frame now that she had ditched her outfit. She was finally free from her ill-fitting pioneer garb, and on the first pass, he was struck again by how small she was. Her body was lithe and slim, like a dancer's. But her posture was all wary biker babe. Taking more time to study her, he noted the black high-top sneakers, the black skinny jeans, black tank top, black baseball hat.

"Not too fond of color, are we?"

Her eyes narrowed. "What's that supposed to mean?"

He shrugged. "You're going to roast alive in all that black."

She crossed her arms—a particular piece of body language she was fond of using when he was around. "I hadn't planned on staying out in the sun all that long."

"Fine by me," he said, pushing his sunglasses back into place. "Let's go."

"Go where?"

"I came to replace Helen's Pepsi, and she asked me to show you around. She said you'd never been to a SASS event before."

He watched the wheels turn in her head and knew that she wanted to refuse. But she must have realized he wouldn't be that easy to ditch—especially since Helen had asked him to squire her around—because she scowled, slamming the door behind her.

"Shouldn't you be resting in the dark somewhere?"

"There's time for that. Right now, I'm feeling hungry, and that's a good sign."

"I'm not eating with you."

He nearly laughed aloud at her preemptive strike. For a moment she looked as bristly as a porcupine he'd once found cornered in the tack room by Barry's miniature goat.

"I don't remember implying that you had to eat with me. I believe I left that option open-ended when I made the invitation once before."

But even as he offered the words, he knew there wasn't a chance in hell that Beth would join him for lunch.

And that was too damned bad.

THREE

———•———

BODEY gave her a chance to grow accustomed to his company, matching her smaller strides, subtly leading her around the tent and onto the main drag. To the left was vendors' row, and to the right the shooting range.

"Has Helen explained the competition?" he finally asked.

Her arms were still wound tightly in front of her, but her gaze was fastened on the posses finishing up their practice matches. "A little."

Bodey gestured to the shooting bays which had been butted up against a natural berm. "There are twenty 'stages' in all—ten to the north, ten to the south. When the competition begins tomorrow, everyone will be assigned a group called a 'posse.' Each posse will shoot ten stages. Some begin in the morning, some in the afternoon. The next day they switch times and finish the second half of the course."

She nodded to show she understood.

He motioned to the fence that separated the dirt lane from the range. "Each stage will require the competitors to use single action pistols, a rifle, and a shotgun. If you look up and down the line, you can see how the stations are all different."

He motioned to one that had been decorated with a store-front. Contestants were moving through the course, shooting through the windows and doors at metal targets located on the other side. Next to that one was another area with a post office and stage coach.

"Each stage has a scenario which might have occurred during the Old West." He drew her down to the next section where false walls had been painted to look like the façade of a cabin. Several targets were lined up outside of the structure. A doorway led through to a "room" with more targets outside a false window and an antique hip bath.

"In this one, a miner is washing up when claim jumpers start a stampede to drive him out of his claim." She finally unfolded her arms to rest them on the fence rail. He leaned toward her, gesturing to the tub.

"Shooters have to begin in the tub."

"Sitting down?"

"As long as the person's body is inside it somehow, they can shoot." He pointed to the targets located on the other side of the window. "If you'll notice, each target is shaped like a different animal. The competitor has to shoot back and forth from moose, deer, moose, deer, until he or she has emptied both pistols. Then, the shooter moves through the doorway, hits the three antelope with a rifle, front to back, and a pop-up target with the shotgun."

"Pop-up?"

He touched her arm, drawing her closer. "See, there's a metal trigger near the ground. When it's hit by the shot, something will fly into the air—usually a can of soda or a charcoal briquette. The competitor has to hit that as well. As people work through the course, they're timed and awarded points for hitting the targets. If they miss, they either have to try again, amassing more time, or they receive a penalty. If any of the targets are shot out of order or a safety rule is breeched, the shooter receives a 'procedural,' which can cause another penalty or disqualify him altogether."

She pointed to one of the gun carts. "What's that?"

"Most of the competitors keep their weapons and ammo in something they can pull from stage to stage." He pointed to an ATV fashioned to look like a stage coach and a small wagon shaped like a coffin on wheels. "As you can see, a lot of the participants get a little crazy trying to outdo one another."

Beth regarded him with wide eyes. "It really is like redneck golf!"

He laughed, drawing her back onto the dirt track. "You've been talking to Helen." He grinned. "But don't let outward appearances fool you. Depending on how invested a person is in competing, it can get to be an expensive hobby. And even though the only reward is bragging rights, there are some who are incredibly competitive."

"Like you?"

Bodey opened his mouth to offer a stock answer, but then he nodded. "Yeah. I take it pretty seriously, although I can only attend a few of the matches each year."

"Why does it matter so much that you come in first?"

Again, he had to stop and think.

"I like to win," he said finally.

"Why?"

Why?

He'd been grilled about why he liked cow cutting and shooting before, but never why he felt driven to win. He stopped in his tracks to regard her but found no flippancy in her expression, merely a quiet assessment. So he thought things through before answering her.

"Maybe it's because . . . I'm the third of four sons. My older brothers are . . . incredible. Elam is athletic and fiercely loyal. Jace is talented and smart." He tucked his fingertips into his trouser pockets, wondering why he was telling this woman more than he would probably admit to the brothers in question. "Maybe I've wanted to stake my claim and prove I'm as good as they are."

Wondering if he'd said too much, he began walking again.

"What about the fourth brother?"

He glanced at her and she said, "You mentioned that you were the third of four sons. What's the fourth brother's claim to fame?"

"Ah," he said smiling at the mere thought of his little brother. "Barry's something else. He's the glue that holds the family together."

There was more he could tell her—that Barry had special needs, that since a brain injury as a child, he'd remained a child locked in a growing man's body. But it was probably more than she wanted to know.

"Hungry?"

The moment the word left his mouth, he knew he'd made a mistake. Where seconds earlier, Beth had seemed to relax, she instantly tensed up.

"Not really, no."

Yeah, right. He'd bet she hadn't eaten at all yet. But he knew better than to challenge her.

"Then come with me to the charity range. If you'll take a couple of practice shots, I'll leave you alone for the rest of the day."

The expression that Beth wore made it clear that she doubted he'd keep his promise, whether or not she agreed to a couple of practice rounds at the charity range.

"I really don't need to—"

"Come on, Beth," he urged. "You're in the middle of a marksmanship competition. You can't go away from here without shooting something at least once."

Her sigh managed to sound both impatient and long-suffering. "You are really getting on my nerves," she muttered under her breath.

He bent close to murmur next to her ear, "I know. But you like it more than you're willing to admit."

"And why would you think that?"

"Because it's clear to me that you need someone around to take over some of your decisions."

Crap. The moment the words came out of his mouth, he could have kicked himself. The phrase had come out wrong. Really, *really* wrong.

Open mouth; insert foot.

And, sure enough, she called him on it. "Excuse me?"

Bodey grimaced, knowing he was bungling this. Damnit, he usually didn't find it so difficult to talk to a woman. But, he found himself oddly flustered and tongue-tied. And in trying to be charming, he was coming off as an asshole with a capital "A".

"Okay, that sounded a bit 'male-chauvinist pig.'"

"A bit?"

"Totally." He sighed, forcing himself to think before he opened his mouth again. "What I meant to say, was that I think you'd enjoy a challenge to do new things every once in a while."

"I'd enjoy the challenge, huh?"

The way she repeated his words made it clear that she still thought he was a jerk.

"Look. I honestly didn't mean to be insulting or . . ."

"Misogynistic."

"That too. I just want you to have some fun while you're here."

"And you think firing a weapon is fun."

"Well . . . yeah."

He thought she would offer a searing retort—something against shooting altogether or him in particular. But when he began backing toward the charity practice range a few yards away, she followed, albeit reluctantly.

Knowing that she might change her mind at the drop of a hat, he quickly handed the volunteer behind the loading table a twenty-dollar bill. He didn't miss the way Beth's eyes narrowed—as if she thought his donation was far beyond the activity's worth.

If he were honest, he was hoping that she'd relax enough to let him teach her the mechanics of firing a single action revolver. He'd heard Elam say once that teaching P.D. to shoot had been one of the sexiest moments of their unusual courtship. Not that Bodey had any intentions of courting Beth—or anyone else. He merely liked the idea of having an excuse to wrap his arms around her.

But before he could even think of the best way to offer his services, Beth picked up the Ruger revolver, snapped it open, loaded the cylinder with the ammunition provided, then took the proper stance and emptied four bullets into a metal target shaped like a cowboy.

Each and every shot hit dead-center between the spot where the eyes would have been.

Then, after a quick glance in Bodey's direction, she fired the final shot. Right into the cutout's "family jewels."

Before Bodey could even react, she snapped open the cylinder, emptied her brass onto the loading table, and set the empty pistol beside them.

The entire process took her only a few seconds.

"Challenge met," she offered succinctly, then spun on her toe and marched back in the direction of Helen's tent.

Her footsteps crunched away in the gravel, punctuating the silence she'd left at the loading table.

"Da-amn," the volunteer behind the table finally drawled, a hint of envy coating his words. "A woman who can handle a weapon that way? That's pretty hot."

Oh, yeah.

That was definitely hot.

BETH couldn't prevent the burst of satisfaction she felt as she strode away from Bodey Taggart, knowing that his mouth was probably still hanging open in surprise.

Served the man right. What made him think that it was any of his business to offer her advice—or to presume that her life was so . . . so . . . *lacking*? And to imply that he believed that he could "fix" her?

Damn him. Damn him for looking down his nose at her.

Although . . . she couldn't honestly say he had ever done that.

In fact, when she'd left him, his eyes had echoed more than his surprise. They'd also smoldered with interest.

Interest that she couldn't afford to entertain.

Hell's bells, Bethy. That was a stupid, stupid, *thing to do.* A man like Bodey would probably interpret her one-upmanship as a Wild West version of tossing down the gauntlet. Either that, or he would get too, too interested in how she'd acquired her skills.

She skirted the tent before Helen could catch sight of her and stomped into the motor home. Since her face felt hotter than the short walk should have made it, she splashed cool water on her cheeks, refusing to meet her own glance in the mirror.

Don't think about that man. Don't think about what he looks like in his cowboy finery. Don't think about the way he makes you feel all tingly and alive.

Stop! There was no reason to dwell on Bodey Taggart at all. So far, he'd been rude, chauvinistic, and . . .

The quintessential naughty boy. Not a "bad boy" in the truest sense of the phrase. Just impulsive, charming, and . . . tempting enough to be intriguing.

Stop.

It.

Knowing that she had to get her mind off a person she'd known for only a few hours, she unlatched the fridge, taking out a bottle of soda and ignoring the sandwich fixings. She couldn't bring herself to make a sandwich—even if Helen insisted. She was feeling jumpy and anxious and her stomach was twisted into knots. No doubt, it was because she'd skipped breakfast. Not because . . .

Not because Bodey Taggart kept infiltrating her thoughts. Interrupting her day.

She supposed that any other woman might be thrilled with his attention. He was rather tall, good-looking.

Well-built.

Interesting.

Stop it! Stop it! Stop it!

She didn't have the time, the inclination, or the energy to deal with someone like that. Someone who was brash and bold . . .

And high-handed and nosy!

She already had more responsibilities than she could

handle to dabble in these inappropriate flights of fantasy. She was a grown woman, not some teenager ogling the lifeguard and fantasizing all the what-ifs. And Bodey Taggart wasn't some misguided knight in shining armor who'd come to save her from the evils of the world.

This was reality. Stark, unadulterated reality. And she'd be better off remembering that fact.

Realizing it was past lunchtime and she hadn't checked in yet, she dragged her phone from her pocket, quickly hitting redial. She waited impatiently as it rang once, twice, three times . . .

"Where are you, Eric?" she muttered to herself.

But the phone eventually switched to voicemail, causing her stomach to twist even more.

"Eric, text me back as soon as you can and let me know that everything's okay. I should be home about seven. Eight at the latest."

Then she hung up and took a swig of her soda, grimacing when she realized that she'd absentmindedly taken a diet root beer instead of her favorite diet cola. Ugh. Yet another reason to ignore Bodey Taggart. Now, more than ever, she couldn't afford the distraction that such a man would provide.

Even though Helen had told her to stay in the RV for an hour, as soon as she'd changed into her calico costume again and forced herself to down half of the soda, she headed back to the tent.

Helen smiled when she entered. "Feeling better?"

"Peachy." The moment the snarky comment was uttered, Beth regretted it. Helen had been nothing but kind to her—and she couldn't possibly know that Beth's recent brush with Bodey Taggart had left her out of sorts.

But Helen must have sensed that something was wrong because she eyed Beth consideringly. "Did you get something to eat?"

Beth opened her mouth, more than prepared to lie, but Helen's heavy sigh stopped the words before they'd even been formed.

"No. You didn't."

So Beth decided to put the blame where it belonged. "Bodey interrupted me before I could get that far. He insisted on going to the charity range."

Helen tried to remain casual about the information, but there was no disguising that her interest had been piqued. "Ohhh?"

Beth fought not to roll her eyes. She could all but see Helen's matchmaking antennae beginning to probe the air.

Thankfully, Syd, who'd been arranging Hopi jewelry in a case, chuckled, diverting Helen's keen gaze. "Judging by what I heard from Pistol Pete, Bethy here loaded, emptied, and cleared her brass in under five seconds. Every shot hit that old outlaw target right between the eyes." His eyes twinkled. "All except one, that is."

Helen must have guessed the trajectory of the last bullet, because her rich giggle soon became a hearty laugh. "Good for you! I bet that took Bodey by surprise."

Syd grinned. "Pete said it took 'em a few minutes to scrape their jaws off the floor. They were both expecting Bethy here to be a complete novice. Especially Bodey."

That made both Syd and Helen laugh even more—to the point that Beth was sure she'd missed the punch line.

"What?" When their laughter intensified, she said a little more forcefully, "What?"

A large group of women wearing SASS T-shirts and shorts entered the tent and began perusing the cases filled with cameo pins, earrings, brooches, and jeweled hair combs. Syd, as was his custom, slipped out the back after seeing there were no males in the group.

As she stood from her chair, Helen leaned close to murmur, "It's the oldest trick in the book. Teaching a woman how to handle a revolver is a lot like teaching her to handle a baseball bat. In a man's opinion, the best way to do it is by standing behind the girl and wrapping his arms around her."

In an instant, Beth imagined herself standing at the loading table and Bodey's arms encircling her, his chest pressed close to her spine. Her cheeks grew hot.

Her blush must have been evident because Helen grinned. "But then, you dodged a bullet with that one, didn't you?"

Had she?
Or had Beth lost a golden opportunity?
Sweet heaven above, stop thinking like that!

Helen started laughing again. But as she backed toward the customers, she warned, "You *are* going to go get something to eat—even if I have to make you a sandwich myself and force you to chew and swallow. Let me handle these ladies first."

Beth was about to respond when her phone pinged. She glanced at the screen to see:

Everything fine. Went to park with D.

True to form, Eric's response was overly brief. Yet another intransigent male.

But that didn't stop her from quickly thumbing the screen to type:

Love you. But stay in touch more often like I asked.

The screen remained blank for long minutes before she finally had her response—and despite the miles that separated them and the limits of technology, she could all but hear Eric's sarcasm.

Fine.

IT was late when, for the second time in a day, Bodey knew he'd made a mistake. After sleeping for most of the afternoon, he'd awakened grouchy, stir-crazy, and hungry as a bear. So when his buddies from the posse had invited him to meet them at a local bar, he'd willingly accepted.

But within minutes of his arrival, the pounding music and the drone of conversation had filled him with a sense of . . . emptiness.

What was the matter with him? Why couldn't he relax and enjoy the moment?

Heaven only knew that Miss Ima Ontop was willing to help him forget his cares. She'd shown up with several other women from Hell on Wheels nearly an hour ago. The ladies, he'd discovered, were part of a group called the Show Belles, and they were known for their fast shooting, larger-than-life personalities, and miniscule costumes. Even in their "civilian attire" they were a sight to behold—with a blonde, brunette, and two redheads—all of them clearly looking for some fun.

Normally, Bodey would have been at the head of the line to impress them. It would have been one more competition he would have been duty-bound to win.

But tonight . . .

He was just too tired.

Or too . . . bored.

Maybe he'd been around his brothers too much lately. Heaven only knew that he'd been invited to enough "pity" dinners over the past few months. Both of his sisters-in-law seemed to think that he was incapable of opening up a can of soup on his own. And he wasn't about to refuse the offer of a home-cooked meal—especially if P.D. or Bronte were cooking it.

But he'd absorbed more than food during those evenings. He'd been privy to warm smiles, bright chatter, rambunctious kids, and a sense of . . . belonging. Granted, he'd always felt that way with his brothers. They'd been a tightly knit group before the older Taggart siblings had married. But now that the women and their families had been folded into the herd, there was something deeper, warmer, and completely . . .

Wonderful.

Bodey yanked his thoughts away from that track. What the hell was wrong with him? He was still young, still eager to play the field. There was time for all that marriage and family life nonsense later.

But even as he tried to convince himself that the "nonsense" wasn't for him, the pounding music and high-pitched laughter of the bar wasn't tempting him to join the fun. It simply reverberated in his head in a way that threatened another migraine.

Pushing his beer away, half finished, he stood and scooped his hat up from the table.

"You're not leaving, are you?" Ima Ontop asked from the corner chair. She sat with her hands cupped around her beer in a way that squeezed her breasts together so that they threatened to spill from the leather halter top she wore. "Things are starting to warm up."

The last two words held extra emphasis but Bodey pretended not to notice. Instead, he offered her a practiced, "Sorry, darlin'. I've got another appointment back at Hell on Wheels."

Which was a nice way of saying that he was going back to his trailer to sleep. Alone.

"I could keep you company on the way back."

Her smile was warm. And she was pretty, damnit. Downright gorgeous. For all intents and purposes, she was his type personified—long dark hair, doe-like brown eyes, and legs from here to Denver.

But maybe he was still under the aftereffects of that migraine, because he felt . . .

Nothing. He could have been talking to one of Bronte's kids.

"Thanks, but . . . I've got something to take care of on the way. Maybe another time."

"Sure. You know where to find me."

He nodded and backed away. But as he strode out into the warmth of the Cheyenne evening, he felt nothing but relief.

IT was after dark when Beth let herself into the motel room. The lights were out and the television flickered from the corner, casting shadows onto the ceiling and into the corners of the room.

For a moment, her heart rocketed into her throat at the

unusual quiet. Normally, she would call out, but since the living quarters were only a few strides in either direction, she was able to see the jumbled shapes swathed in a nest of blankets on the couch.

Rolling her bicycle beneath the window, she made sure the drapes were firmly closed before leaning it against the wall. Somewhere, sometime, she needed to find a screwdriver to tighten the kickstand. But for now, the annoyance was so far down her priority list that it barely registered. Instead, she backtracked enough to check that the deadbolt and the safety catch were properly latched, then swung her backpack onto the floor.

Crossing to the couch, she felt a tugging in her chest as she saw her two siblings propped in the corner asleep. Noodle, their little mutt of a pet, had curled into a ball at their feet.

Eric was getting so tall. In a few months, he would turn sixteen. She couldn't help noticing that he'd had a growth spurt in the past few weeks. All the extra food he'd been craving must have gone to his legs, because his pants were already showing a good three inches of sock.

Beth sighed.

They'd bought the jeans at a thrift store less than a month ago. And with his waist so narrow, it was already getting difficult to find anything long enough without having them drop off his hips. Somehow, someway, she would need to scrape up a few extra dollars so he wouldn't stand out.

Her eyes drifted to Dolly. Unlike Eric, she appeared to shrink a little more each day—which made Beth worry. Her sister was eating well enough. And Beth wasn't the only one who'd begun to augment Dolly's diet with bites from her own plate. She'd seen Eric sneaking her little tastes as well. But the little girl was incredibly tiny. Although she was nearly seven, she looked more like a five year old.

At least Beth could take comfort from the fact that her sister had always been tiny for her age. But she couldn't help the niggling unease that the condition had been caused by malnutrition and neglect the first few years of her life. More than anything, Beth longed to ply her with meat and vegetables and whole grains to see if the little girl would catch up to her peers.

An image of the inside of Helen's fridge swam through her head. There had been a variety of lunch meats and three kinds of cheese, crisp lettuce and celery and carrots, juices and fruit.

One day—one day soon—Beth vowed that her little sister would find the same choices inside their own fridge.

One day.

As if pulled by that thought, Beth crossed to the tiny refrigerator supplied by the motel. Opening the door, she stared into the yawning void. Except for a few condiments and a half gallon of milk, the shelves were bare.

Tears pricked her eyes and she quickly closed the door again, her sweeping gaze taking in the empty cartons of Cup-O-Noodles in the garbage and the box of cereal on the counter. Two bowls sat in the dish drainer by the sink.

She took a deep gulp of air—*don't let me cry, not tonight, not here*—but rather than easing her emotions, it merely compounded them.

Things should be better by now.

Have I made a mistake? A horrible, horrible mistake?

Whirling away from their meager supplies, she saw that her brother was awake. He'd pushed himself into a sitting position so that he could meet her gaze over the back of the couch.

The gentleness that she saw there, the infinite gratitude, was her undoing and she sobbed out loud, then quickly scrubbed away a pair of tears that plunged down either cheek.

"It's okay, Bethy," Eric said softly. "We're together. And we're okay."

Okay?

They were one step away from homelessness. They were anything but okay.

Eric must have sensed her continued disquiet because he

wriggled free of Dolly, laying her back down against the pillows. Then he strode toward Beth in those man-boy strides that grew longer every day.

He reached out to pull her close—and as he did, she acknowledged that he was already inches taller than she was.

"We're okay, Bethy. Things will get better, you'll see."

Things will get better.

How many times had she offered her siblings that same promise? Probably too many to count if it was being quoted back to her. But as her brother pulled her close and awkwardly patted her back, she prayed that, at least in this instance, she would be proven right.

Because she couldn't bear to think of the alternative if she were proven wrong.

FOUR

———◦•◦———

THE next morning, Beth arrived at Hell on Wheels an hour earlier than usual, thinking that it would give her some time to straighten the racks and tidy the jewelry cases. But as she wheeled her bicycle into place beside the RV, she could see that Helen had already opened the tent and was busy with customers.

Beth hurriedly retrieved her costume from the motor home—a new concoction with puffed sleeves, a scooped neckline, and a ruffled skirt. But after throwing it on and tightening the skirt with a safety pin, Beth grimaced. The outfit was supposed to look like "Saloon Girl with a Heart of Gold," but on Beth's frame, the too-large bodice looked more like "Flat Chested Teenager Borrows Well Endowed Sister's Clothes."

Oh well.

When she entered the tent, Helen looked up in relief. But when her expression was marred with a crease between her brows, Beth knew that she'd been right. As costumes went, Pioneer School Marm and Saloon Girl had both been an epic fail. Even Helen knew it.

Thankfully, there was little time to worry about her own attire. There were too many customers to focus on in the next few hours. They came in spurts—with the tent growing crowded one moment, then thinning, then becoming crazy busy again.

By listening to the bits and pieces of conversation from the men and women who passed in and out, Beth was able to gather that the black powder portion of the competition would begin soon after lunch on a separate range, several hundred yards away. From where the tent stood, Beth could barely make out the metal buffalo targets that had been spaced at intervals across a nearby field. In the meantime, more practice posses were gathering in the stages that lined vendors' row.

Judging by the way that the parking lot was filled to bursting, more participants had arrived throughout the night. That meant there was an increased drop-in trade for Helen until well after noon. Since Helen had been busy with a couple who had come to order a "bespoke" wardrobe for an upcoming SASS cruise, that left Beth to field the walk-in trade.

Over the past few months, Beth had worked at a lot of odd jobs—pet sitter, waitress, landscaper, typist. But she was discovering that she liked working in retail more than she would have ever imagined. Or maybe it was because she was working with Helen and her fantasy-oriented goods.

It was after noon before the rush began to disperse— probably chased away by the increasing heat and the tantalizing smells drifting their way from the food concessions positioned in the center of the camp.

As her stomach began to rumble and the bright sun caused her head to pound, she realized that she'd been foolish not to eat breakfast that morning. Sure, she was accustomed to hard work—and she'd often skipped meals. But the sweltering weather, the sifting dust, and the blazing sun were draining her energy to the point where she was feeling a little shaky.

So when the tent finally cleared of everyone but the

"bespoke" couple—and Helen suddenly muttered "Fudge!" under her breath, it took Beth a moment to react.

Helen stood from where she'd been rummaging through bins of fabric hidden beneath the draped tables near the cash register and held up a pair of amber shooting glasses and what looked like a set of earplugs connected by a string.

"These must have dropped and been kicked under the table. These earplugs are custom made and expensive."

Beth tried to remember if she'd seen anyone wearing the protective eye gear or ear pieces when they'd entered the tent. If not, she and Helen would have little hope of getting them back to the owner unless they came looking for them. Beth couldn't imagine hunting through the current crowds, seeking someone who might fit the earplugs much like Prince Charming looking for the owner of the glass slipper.

Ew.

But just as quickly, Helen's expression cleared when she saw a small tag fashioned from masking tape hanging from the cord.

"'B.T.' They must belong to Bodey." Helen dropped both items into a small sack and held it out in Beth's direction. "Would you mind taking them back to him? I'd hate for him to be without his eyes and ears if he's competing in the black powder event this afternoon."

Beth wanted to say "no". She really, *really,* wanted to say "heck, no." But if she did, Helen might take that as a sign that Beth was bothered by Bodey. And hell's bells, that was the last thing she wanted anyone to think.

"I don't know where . . ."

"Go to the main gate of the car park. Bodey has his trailer situated there. It's a huge thing, white and blue—one of those horse trailer, living quarter combinations. You won't be able to miss it."

Beth resisted the urge to sigh. In the small universe of Hell on Wheels, she was doomed to cross paths with that man.

This time, she didn't bother to change out of her costume before venturing down vendors' row. What was the point? Maybe if she showed up looking like the poster child for

Dorks United, he wouldn't give her a second glance. He certainly wouldn't try to maneuver a way to get his arms around her. Because she hadn't known that's what he'd intended when he'd asked her to go to the charity range. And if she had . . .

For crying out loud!

"Make sure you eat!"

She barely heard Helen's instructions over the sharp *bang-pings!* of renewed shooting coming from the bays, and the deeper *boom booms* from the next ridge over where the black powder competitors were warming up.

Beth lifted a hand to show she'd heard but she didn't turn around. Maybe Helen was right. All of Beth's dithering and fussing was probably due to low blood sugar. Honestly, she didn't think she'd ever allowed a man to get under her skin this quickly. She was normally quite cool and level-headed.

Calm.

Lonely.

Good grief!

Angry at herself for allowing her thoughts to once again slide to Bodey Taggart, she wrestled her phone free of her pocket, then sighed. Eric was supposed to leave her a message every other hour. But so far there were no missed calls. No texts.

"Damnit, Eric," she muttered under her breath.

Don't worry. Not yet.

Moving out of the way, she quickly dialed his number. But she was sent directly to voicemail. So she texted:

Let me know you're okay, Eric.

Then, knowing there was nothing else she could do, she marched the rest of the way to the main gate.

Helen hadn't been lying when she'd said that Bodey's trailer would be impossible to miss. As she'd stated, it was one of the longest in the parking lot, with two sections, one for horses and the other for its human occupants. But even that wasn't what made it so distinctive.

To describe it as "white and blue" was like saying the Sistine Chapel had some color. Bodey's trailer proudly bore his name and a custom painting of Bodey on horseback, chasing a black cow through a field of scarlet poppies. To the side was a list of championships he'd won: cow cutting, calf roping, bull riding, bronco busting.

Good heavens, the man was more of an adrenalin junkie than she'd ever imagined.

Not willing to follow that avenue of thought—or to examine the way it made her pulse beat a little faster—she marched up to the door and rapped loudly.

At first there was no answer, no clue that there was even someone inside. Then she heard a muttered, "Give me a minute."

She waited impatiently, her toe tapping in the dust. Unaccountably, she wished she'd at least ditched the hat she'd been forced to wear.

But before she could think of a thing to say, the door swung open.

Sweet heavenly days in the morning.

Bodey must have been sleeping late. Because he braced his forearms on the doorjamb and leaned forward, blinking against the bright sunlight. His hair was mussed, poking up at odd angles in a way that made her fingers twitch to smooth it down. He rubbed his eyes with the heel of his hand and then, when he saw her, he offered her a slow, warm smile that started in his eyes as irresistible warmth before spreading to the rest of his face. It was an intimate smile. One that should have been reserved for early morning pillow talk not . . . not . . .

Not someone like her.

For some reason, that intimate, all-knowing expression caused a warmth to sink low in her belly, one that glowed hotter as she wrenched her gaze from the way his eyes crinkled in the corners and his hand tested the stubble on his chin. But that was a mistake, too, because once her eyes began to dip, she was confronted with the man's bare chest.

And lordy, the man had a lovely chest.

Bodey Taggart had broad, muscular shoulders and arms—probably from all that roping. But where other men might grow bulky from such strength, he was lean and honed, like a greyhound, his musculature tautly outlined—flat pecs with dark-brown nipples, chiseled obliques, rock-hard abs . . .

Breathe, Bethy. Breathe.

He had an "inny" belly button, and beneath it was a thin line of dark hair leading down, down, to twill trousers that hung low on his hips—even lower than they should have because he'd apparently dragged them on to answer the door and the button at his waistband was still undone. They were similar to the pants he'd worn yesterday, and the suspenders hanging loose at his thighs certainly weren't helping to keep his pants up.

Not to mention, if the man wore any underwear, she wasn't seeing any evidence of it.

The thought of Bodey going commando caused a heat to sweep into her face with such ferocity that Beth feared Bodey would guess her thoughts. So she held out the sack and abruptly said, "Helen found these in her tent."

Bodey straightened but didn't reach for the sack right away. Instead, he ran his fingers through his hair, locking them behind his head. Then, he stretched and yawned in a way that had her pulse beating in places where it shouldn't as she took in the rippling of his muscles, the taut exposure of sinew and bone. And heaven help her if his jeans didn't slip another inch.

But then—*thank you, thank you*—he reached behind him and snagged a shirt.

As much as she knew it was for the best that he cover up all that skin—sun-kissed skin, with no evidence of tan line—

For heaven's sake!

—she couldn't help thinking it was a shame to hide all that masculine beauty.

The shirt was like the one he'd worn yesterday on the range. Made of super fine handkerchief linen, the fabric lovingly clung to his frame. But as she watched him fasten the buttons, one by one, tuck the tails into his waistband, then loop the suspenders over his shoulders, she couldn't decide if he should hurry up or abandon the task altogether.

Finally, when she felt as if she might spontaneously combust, he reached for the sack and briefly peered inside before tossing it into the dark shadows.

"Thanks."

That's it? Just "thanks"? After she'd been forced to interrupt her day, march to his trailer, then endure a . . . a reverse striptease—one that was pretty heavy on the *tease*—all she got was a measly "thanks"?

But even as the thoughts raced through her head, Beth wasn't sure what she'd expected or ultimately wanted as a response. She found herself . . .

Unsatisfied.

Her fingers balled into fists and she realized that she should go. Now. Before her confusing reaction to this man could get any more complicated.

She took a step back but before she could go any farther, Bodey said, "Wait up. I'll go with you."

Damn. She definitely didn't want that.

But before she could get her sluggish brain to react, Bodey had stomped his feet into a pair of square-toed cowboy boots and closed the door to the trailer.

"Weren't you . . . uh . . . ." she pointed to his quarters. "Weren't you sleeping?"

"Yeah. But I was up at the crack of dawn. I was taking a quick nap to chase the beginnings of another headache away. If I sleep any longer, I'll wake up feeling worse instead of better."

He motioned for her to precede him, but she hesitated, knowing that if she appeared on vendors' row with Bodey and his severe case of bedhead, people would jump to conclusions.

"Don't you think you should—" She gestured vaguely toward his hair.

"What?"

Merciful heavens, how dense could he be?

"You've got some wild-child hair going on," she finally managed to say.

"Really?"

His truck was parked next to the trailer and he bent to look in the side mirror. Beth thought she heard a muffled curse. Then he combed at it with his fingers—which helped, but wasn't completely successful.

Sighing, he reached through the open door of the cab and snagged the same hat she'd seen him wearing the day before. Then he fastened that one last button, the one at his waistband that he'd nearly forgotten.

"Better?" he asked as he turned.

For a moment, her mouth grew so dry, she couldn't speak. *Lordy, lordy, she was a sucker for suspenders.*

"Uh . . . sure."

This time, when he gestured toward the path, she didn't hesitate.

BODEY was still reeling a little from opening his door and finding Beth there. After bungling things with his high-handedness at the charity range the day before, he figured she'd make sure their paths never crossed again.

But there she'd been, standing right outside his door.

And even though he'd been struggling to wake up, he'd felt her gaze like a hot hand trailing down his body.

Holy, holy hell. He couldn't remember ever having felt another woman's scrutiny so powerfully.

"Where'd you learn to shoot so well?" he asked, then could have kicked himself for reminding her that he'd been a jerk. Not only had he all but maneuvered her into participating, she'd probably caught on that he'd hoped for a chance to "help" her as well.

Judging by the look she shot his way, he was busted.

"I watched a lot of Westerns."

"Really?"

"No."

He laughed when he realized that she was making fun of his blanket assumptions.

"Then where?"

She rolled her eyes. "At a public gun range. With a *female* instructor."

Bodey absorbed the depth of meaning behind that explanation. First, she'd fathomed his secret motives for wanting to teach her. But even more tantalizing was the fact that most women didn't want to be within one hundred yards of live ammunition. Yet Beth's explanation indicated that she hadn't been taught by a family member. Which meant she'd indulged in some lessons—and some damned intense practicing—in order to be that good. Well, that was . . .

Hotter than hell.

Bodey couldn't help the satisfaction he felt in knowing that she hadn't let some other asshole wrap his arms around her shoulders to show her how to steady his weapon.

And didn't that thought sound incredibly dirty when it popped into his head?

Good thing he hadn't allowed his mouth to echo the sentiment.

They were near the center of vendors' row by now, but Bodey hadn't seen a thing. Instead, he'd been picturing Beth, her feet slightly parted, her arms lifted, a Ruger pistol in her hands . . .

He couldn't wait to see what other weapons she'd be willing to handle.

Knowing that he would either have to concentrate on something else—or find a way to subtly adjust himself . . .

Damnit.

Thankfully, he became aware of the crowds hovering in the center of the camp near the concessions area.

Food. He'd be more in control of himself with some food in his belly.

He caught Beth's arm, bringing her to a halt. "I still owe you lunch."

She opened her mouth and he knew that she meant to insist that she didn't need anything to eat and would return to Helen's RV. But at that moment, the breeze changed. As if on cue, the rich scent of smoked meats and BBQ wafted through the air. He nearly laughed aloud when her eyes closed and her chin tipped so that she could sniff the heady aroma.

"What is that?" she breathed almost reverently.

Rather than answering, he took her hand. "Come on. My treat."

Bodey ignored Beth when she tried to tug free, clearly uncomfortable with his offer—and with his touch.

"No, I—"

"Don't say 'no'." He faced her, forcing her to see he was completely sincere. "If you hadn't helped me when you did yesterday, I would have been incapacitated with the mother of all migraines—maybe for days. As it is, I got to some painkiller in time to tamp it down to a dull ache." He squeezed her fingers ever so softly—somehow knowing that if he did anything more, she would bolt. "I think that taking you to lunch is the least I can do."

He knew she still wanted to argue but he didn't give her the chance. Lacing their fingers together, he pulled her close beside him as he joined the line forming in front of a mobile smoker shaped like a pig. Within minutes, they both had a sandwich the size of a dinner plate nestled in a take-out container along with a mound of coleslaw and a package of chips. In the other hand, they carried cold, freshly-squeezed lemonade.

Mindful of the heat—and the weird striped outfit she was wearing which must have had ten pounds of ruffles sewed to it—Bodey led her into the shade of the event tent which had been filled with tables and chairs. He picked a spot near one of the entrances so they could take advantage of the breeze. From here, Beth would be able to see across the lane where a practice posse worked its way through a stage set up to look like the passenger car of a train.

But contrary to what he'd expected, Beth didn't even look at the shooters. Instead, she opened the Styrofoam container and stared at her food. A curious mix of awe and greed crossed her features but was quickly stifled by an overt restraint.

Bodey felt his breath hitch in his chest. He'd seen the blatant hunger for only an instant but it made him study her gamin features even more closely.

Beth's bone structure was delicate and well-defined. She had a heart-shaped face and high cheekbones that her spikey hairdo showed to its best advantage. But since her outfit had a scooped neckline and short sleeves, he could see the pronounced arc of her collarbones and the daintiness of her wrists. Somehow, he sensed her thinness was due to necessity rather than vanity.

"Eat up," he urged, then damned himself for the way his voice emerged with gruff undertones he hadn't intended. Geez, now more than ever, he didn't want to scare her off.

She began with the coleslaw, eating slowly at first, closing her eyes as if to savor it. The expression she wore was hedonistic and rapturous at the same time. She was so focused on the task, so intent on its possible pleasures, that he couldn't help but wonder if she enjoyed all of life's activities so intently. If so . . .

Imagine the kind of lover she'd be.

Crap. Those kinds of thoughts were going to get him slapped. Especially if they slipped from brain to mouth without a filter.

And Lord knew, he didn't have much of a filter.

Afraid of what she might find in his own expression if he continued to regard her so closely, Bodey dug a fork into the colorful mixture of cabbage.

Growing up on the ranch, he was accustomed to eating quickly—because there was always a more critical task awaiting his attention. During hay season or the grain harvest, an entire meal might be finished in less than five minutes—or skipped altogether. But mindful of the woman next to him, Bodey kept his pace slow, concentrating on the flavors and textures of the coleslaw, the crisp vegetables, the creamy sauce, the peppery seasoning, and the hint of vinegar.

"It's good," he murmured, chewing.

And even though coleslaw wasn't in his top one-hundred list of favorite foods, he had to admit it really was tasty. Either that, or his nap had left him starving.

Or the company had improved the black mood that had hung over him for weeks.

Beside him, Beth offered a self-indulgent laugh. "Oh, yeah. It's really, *really* good."

In that moment, she smiled—an honest, true smile that went straight to her eyes.

And, darn it, if he didn't find himself falling a little bit in love.

Again.

Trouble was . . .

He was pretty sure this wasn't the kind of woman interested in a little harmless fun.

And he wasn't the kind of man capable of offering her anything more.

BETH knew that Bodey was studying her but she would not be drawn in by his curiosity. Especially when there was food at stake. Glorious, glorious food.

She scooped another forkful of coleslaw into her mouth, refusing to feel guilty, knowing that such a dish would never keep for later. Honestly, she couldn't remember the last time that she'd had something so delectable, so . . . fresh. For months now, she'd subsided on peanut butter or noodles or mac and cheese—whatever she could get in large quantities without denting her pocketbook too much. There hadn't been many opportunities for crisp vegetables, let alone meat. Yet here, nestled in a Styrofoam clamshell container, was more food than she would usually eat in a week. Even better, the mix of carrots, onions, and cabbage was filling, which meant that she could save the rest for later.

But even as she licked the last of the creamy dressing from her fork, and her stomach felt deliciously satisfied, she found that she couldn't ignore the sandwich. Not when it was warm and fragrant and oozing with an extra drizzle of sauce.

Using the plastic utensils she'd been given, she cut off a small bite and scooped it into her mouth. The minute the tangy sauce and charred meat hit her tongue, she knew she'd died and gone to heaven.

"I'm glad to see you're not a vegetarian after all."

She looked up to find that Bodey was watching her, his broad hands wrapped around his own bun. He winked at her and said, "You don't have to be so ladylike. Go ahead. Pick it up and take a huge bite."

Was that a dare?

Beth eyed him closely, but he merely smiled and chewed, lowering his sandwich again so that he could wipe his mouth with a napkin.

She looked down, knowing that she shouldn't, knowing that she was already comfortably sated. But the temptation—and the need to meet Bodey's challenge—became more than she could resist. Using her knife, she carefully cut the huge sandwich into three pieces. Then, grasping the piece that she'd already begun to eat, she lifted the bun to her lips and took a bite.

Her eyes slammed shut in enjoyment and she couldn't prevent the moan that burst from her throat. The spices alone were enough to send her over the edge. But when they were combined with the tender chunks of beef, she was a goner.

"It's good, huh?"

She nodded, lowering her sandwich and quickly grabbing a napkin to wipe away a dribble of sauce that had landed on her chin.

Tensing slightly, she waited for Bodey to say something more but, to her surprise, he was content to eat in silence, his gaze straying to the outside world framed by the tent's awning. It was a strange sight—meandering couples in modern and Victorian garb, children darting in and out of the crowd, and the practice posses who continued to go through their paces, punctuating the air with the bright *bang-ping!* retorts of bullets striking metal targets.

Slowly, drawing out each possible taste as long as she could, Beth continued to eat her sandwich and sip her drink. And with each moment that passed, she felt a tingling energy flood her limbs and her spirits lift in a way that they hadn't done in quite some time. Maybe Helen had been right to nag at her the last couple of days. Maybe the best way to handle the heat was to sit for a few minutes in the shade, eat and drink, so that she had the fuel she needed to get through the rest of her shift.

But even as she insisted to herself that those were the only reasons for the upswing in her mood, her gaze strayed to Bodey again.

"Feeling better?"

She nodded, carefully lowering the lid on the two portions of her sandwich that remained and the bag of chips that she hadn't bothered to open. But this time, she felt no regrets because her stomach was stretched tight and unable to hold another morsel.

"It was really, really good. Thank you."

Bodey shrugged off her comment, tossing his own unopened bag of chips her way. "It was my pleasure. You saved my life yesterday."

"Hardly."

"No, really. Another few minutes in the sun and they would have had to scrape me up out of the dirt." He rolled his head as if to test his range of motion. Then he nodded in satisfaction. "This morning, I thought it was coming back, but now . . . I think I've chased the sucker away."

"So that's it? No more headaches?"

He grimaced. "Hopefully. But I'll have to be careful—dark glasses, stay out of the sun as much as possible, and wear a hat. But, knock on wood . . ."—he tapped the table top—". . . the worst is over."

Silence descended between them, somehow prickly and uneasy now that they didn't have food to occupy their attention.

He gestured to the bag of chips. "Put those away for later, too."

"You don't want them?"

"Nah. I'm not really a chip eater."

Beth hesitated, doubting his assertion, but then tucked the package into the box with the rest of her food. "I should probably head back and check to see if Helen needs my help."

Bodey nodded. "Sure."

Beth expected him to push more, to insist she stay with him longer—or at least let him accompany her back to Helen's tent. But when she stood, he rose to his feet, touching the brim of his hat. "I'll be seeing you around."

She didn't quite know what to say, so she nodded, then brushed past him. But when she turned, just before striding out into the sunshine, she found him watching her with a strange expression on his face.

And in that instant, she knew it was only a matter of time before she found herself tangled up with Bodey Taggart again.

FIVE

———•◦•———

THANKFULLY, Beth wasn't able to stew over that point—
or the reasons why it was imperative that she not get
involved with Bodey. As she neared the tent, she could see
that both Helen and Syd were busy again. Darting out back
long enough to stow her food in the refrigerator, she hurried
to help.

The next few hours were hectic as the practice posses
finished their stages and began meandering back to their
trailers. Beth and Helen worked together to help women try
on clothing or accessorize the perfect historic ensemble.
There were those who bought straight off the rack and others
who were measured for special orders to be made in their
own colors or specifications. Beth filled shopping bags with
jewelry, fans, stockings, and parasols. She boxed up boots
and hats and shoes.

So it wasn't until the sun had begun to dip in the sky and
long shadows stretched across the ground that Beth realized
that the noises from the range had completely disappeared,
replaced by the luff of canvas and soughing grass as the
wind grew stronger. From far away, thunder grumbled.

After seeing the last customer out, Beth lingered in the doorway, letting the breeze flow deliciously around her. Far off on the horizon, a wall of dark clouds rose like the prow of a ship, heavy and dangerous, even though the rest of the sky was clear.

Helen settled into a folding chair positioned under the awning. Sighing, she reached for one of the fans arranged on the table behind her and snapped it open with practiced finesse. "That was quite a run of customers!" she said with evident pleasure as she tried to cool her pink cheeks. "So far, we're doing much better than last year."

"I left a stack of trousers that need hemming behind the cash register."

"I saw them." Helen grimaced. "But they can wait an hour or two. I'll get them done tonight after the Dutch oven dinner. Will you be staying?"

Beth had seen Syd setting up the squat black pots in the parking lot next to the motor home that afternoon. According to Helen, she and Syd had asked "one or two people to drop by for a bite to eat." Judging by the number of ovens and the array of food, Beth wagered most of the camp was expected.

A part of her wanted to stay. It had been a long time since she'd been able to relax and idly converse with another woman. There was something about Helen's manner that soothed Beth's worries and made her feel as if she . . . belonged. But since she'd ridden her bicycle to work, she knew it wouldn't be a good idea to linger. As it was, it would probably take her the better part of an hour to get back.

Pulling her phone from the pocket of her striped skirt, she glanced at the screen. Still no messages. And even though she'd told herself that there were plenty of logical reasons why Eric hadn't returned her calls and texts throughout the day, she'd already gone through the stages of curiosity, frustration, and concern. Now, she was heading straight for panic.

"I wish I could stay, but with those clouds in the distance, I should probably head back home." She added hurriedly, "Unless you need me to help you with something else."

Helen snapped the fan shut and used it to offer a shooing motion. "We're done for the night. Syd and I will keep the tent open another hour or so to catch the stragglers, but I doubt we'll have more than one or two people drop by. Everyone's ready to put their feet up and enjoy the breeze." She stood. "Since you won't stay, let's ladle up some of Syd's cooking for your supper and you can take it home."

"Oh, no. I still have my sandwich from—"

Helen shooed away her objections. "Nonsense. You look like a good wind could blow you away."

Beth grimaced as she followed in Helen's wake. *Well, hell.* Judging by the way everyone was urging her to eat, she must look worse than she thought.

But there was no time to respond, because when she walked through the rear flap, she found that Syd wasn't tending his pots alone. In the shade of the motorhome, Bodey had stretched out in a camp chair. He half sat, half reclined, his hands clasped behind his neck, his long legs stretched out in front of him, languidly crossed at the ankles.

He must have showered and changed, because this time, he was dressed in tooled boots, soft black jeans, a glaringly white, button front shirt, and a black felt cowboy hat with a beaded band.

Damn the man. As soon as he saw her, he tipped his head and grinned, touching his finger to the brim of his hat as if he were Rhett Butler and she were Miss la-di-da Scarlett O'Hara.

And double damn the way her stomach flip-flopped in response.

After that brief moment of eye contact, he returned his attention to Syd and the two men continued to talk about reloading, rocket fuel, Rugers, and doping the Hindenburg. Having no idea what any of it meant—or how the disparate topics connected with one another—Beth concentrated on shedding her Saloon-Girl-Outfit-Gone-Wrong and stowing it in the motor home.

By the time she'd finished, Helen had filled several plastic containers with food and placed them in a grocery sack along with the leftovers from Beth's lunch. Too late, Beth realized that, since she'd ridden her bicycle to work, it was going to be difficult getting everything home.

But Helen must have anticipated the problem, because she opened the door and called out, "Syd, throw Beth's bike into the back of the Jeep and give her a ride back into town. After the long day she's had, the last thing she needs is another workout."

Beth froze when it wasn't Syd's familiar tenor that answered. It was Bodey's deep bass.

"No need. I'm headed that way. I've got to pick up some supplies in town and fill my tank with fuel. I'll give her a lift."

No.

No, no, no!

Beth quickly folded the rest of her costume and tossed it into a haphazard pile. If she hurried, she could climb on her bike and be gone before Bodey returned with his vehicle.

But even as she threw open the door and jumped to the ground, she heard the low rumble of a diesel engine.

Crap.

As soon as she'd made it outside to confirm her suspicions, Helen stepped from the motor home and handed her the sack full of food. Beth nearly stumbled beneath its weight.

"Helen, there's enough here for an army!"

Helen waved aside her comment. "Whatever you don't eat tonight will keep." She enfolded Beth in a quick hug. "We'll see you tomorrow morning. Once you're up and ready, give me a call on my cell, and I'll come pick you up."

"No, I can—"

"I insist. I know you like using your bike to get around, but tomorrow will be busy. Really, really busy."

Deciding that she could renew the argument in the morning, Beth nodded. "Goodnight, Helen. Syd."

She rounded the RV to see a large stretch cab pickup with a flatbed. Somehow, her bicycle had already been strapped in place. Bodey sat inside with one arm draped over the wheel, but when she approached, he leaned across the seat to open the door for her.

Beth set the sack on the floor, then hesitated. The truck was jacked up so high, she feared she was going to have to crawl inside.

Bodey held out a broad hand. "Hang on and I'll pull you up."

Seeing no other option, she allowed her palm to be swallowed by his. Then, as if she weighed nothing at all, he hoisted her into the seat.

"Looks like I'll need some running boards," he murmured as he released her and reached to put the truck in gear.

Beth felt her cheeks heat, even though there was no reason why she should feel embarrassed. It wasn't her fault that Bodey's truck was so blasted tall—and there was no need to be talking about running boards.

Even so, she gave more attention to her seatbelt than was necessary as Bodey maneuvered through the parking lot and turned onto the main road beyond.

"Where to?"

Where?

Beth panicked when she realized that Bodey was asking for her address. *Crap!* She'd insisted on using her bicycle for transportation because she didn't want anyone to know where she was staying. In a pinch, she might have relented to having Syd drop her off at her doorstep. Kind, empathetic, sweet-hearted Syd.

But this man?

No.

No, no, no.

Too late, she realized that she was trapped in a speeding vehicle with no way to stop the train wreck that was about to happen. Scrambling for an alternative to giving him directions to her home, she finally said, "I'm at the Red Fox Inn. Do you know it?"

"The one where they'll have the banquet?"

She nodded.

"Yeah, I know where that is." He signaled, then took the on-ramp to the freeway. "I thought you were local."

Damn.

"I-I'm staying there while I help Helen," she replied as nonchalantly as possible, hoping that he would buy her story and not ask too many questions. Because, if he really thought about it, he might wonder why she was paying more to stay in the Red Fox Inn than she could possibly make in wages over the next few days.

But Bodey nodded, keeping his eyes on the road.

"I can pick you up in the morning, if you want. I'm board-ing a horse at a friend's place outside town while I'm at the shoot, and I check on it at the crack of dawn. I could have you back to the tent in plenty of time."

And wasn't she popular today?

She opened her mouth to refuse. But the muted whine of the tires on the road, the steady stream of cool air blowing from the ducts, and a day spent on her feet left her curiously lethargic. Honestly, she didn't have the energy to argue— even though there was no way on earth that she was going to accept.

"I'll give you a call if I think that'll work," she said vaguely.

He appeared satisfied with her response. Lifting the top to the console that separated them, he rummaged through slips of papers, log books, and packages of half-finished jerky, fishing out a business card.

"My number's on the front there."

She glanced at the card with its heading: Taggart Enter-prises. Beneath it was a photograph of a green meadow studded with vibrant red poppies. A backdrop of jagged mountains framed the figure of a man on horseback gallop-ing full-speed after a black cow. Despite the smallness of the card and the minute details of the rider, Beth recognized the set of his shoulders and the strength of his arms as he whirled a lasso over his head.

"This is you. It's the same painting that you have on your trailer."

He grimaced. "Yep. I'm the poster child of the family."

She couldn't help smiling at his disgruntled expression. "Why you?"

"Probably because I'm the best looking member of the Taggart gang." His brows wiggled meaningfully but he quickly added, "Or because I'm the only one who will do it. Elam's not one for getting his picture taken. I think his wife had to threaten him to pose for the wedding photographer. Jace would rather be behind the camera."

"And the other brother?"

"Barry?" He snorted. "Oh, Barry would be more than happy to take over as cover model. But he's still young enough to enjoy mugging to the camera, so I don't suppose a thumb to the nose would give the right *professional* impression."

He painted such a vivid picture, she couldn't help laughing. In her opinion, more businesses could benefit from such an honest approach, but she could see Bodey's point. If the Taggarts were trying to make a stunning impression, Beth would be the first to admit that they'd succeeded. The photograph's setting was striking. The man in the center was hypnotic. Even in a two-dimensional representation, she could sense the speed of the mount and the innate athleticism of the rider.

Beth knew that she should throw the card away as soon as she returned home, but something prompted her to tuck it deep into her pocket. She didn't bother to question why she took such care with an insignificant piece of cardstock— she couldn't afford to analyze her answers.

The truck slowed as Bodey took the off-ramp. On the rise above them, she could see the imposing edifice of the Red Fox Inn. Her heart knocked insistently against her ribs as she realized that she was going to have to be careful over the next few minutes. The last thing she needed was for Bodey to offer to carry her things inside.

"Front or back," he asked.

"Back is fine."

He turned into the parking lot and drew up next to the rear entrance. "Is this okay?"

"Yeah. Thank you. I appreciate it."

"My pleasure."

He left the motor going as he stepped outside to free her bike from the length of rope that had been used to tie it to the bed. Beth breathed a tiny sigh of relief as she gathered her things. If the engine was still running, then he probably wouldn't bother to insist on escorting her inside.

By the time she'd managed to wrestle the bag into her arms and open the door, Bodey was there.

"Here, let me help you."

She thought he meant to take the bag, but he took her by the waist instead and lifted her to the ground. His grip was sure, steady—and for a petite woman who often despaired of being regarded as a child, there was nothing "childish" about his gesture. Quite the contrary. Long after her feet had met the pavement, his hands, broad and sure, lingered on her waist, causing her heart to adopt a curious bossa nova rhythm. His thumbs unconsciously moved in a slow circular motion and the air squeezed from her lungs as a delicious warmth began pooling in that spot, radiating outwards.

No.

No, no, no.

All day, she'd tried to ignore this man, and even more importantly, the sensations he aroused in her. But in that instant, she couldn't corral the sudden rush of want and need. Not for a man, not for sex. No, it was more than that. The caress was innocent and intimate. Soothing and arousing. It was human contact when she needed it most, but wanted it least.

"Stop," she whispered.

Instantly, his thumbs stilled, and he grimaced, as if only then realizing what he'd been doing.

Inexplicably, she regretted the loss of that silken movement. But if she'd thought the heady sensations would ease, she was wrong. Heat continued to seep through her body from the palms nestled in the lee of her waist. And his eyes . . .

Sweet heaven above, she'd never seen a man with such expressive eyes. She couldn't look away, drawn by the deep blue, the flecks of brown and green. But it was more than the exotic mix of colors. In their depths she felt a connection, a linking, humanity.

Had she ever experienced something like that before? If so, she couldn't remember. And for a moment, with Bodey so near, so warm, so vital, she didn't feel quite so lonely.

The thought hit her like a lightning bolt and she stepped back, immediately severing the invisible ties that had wrapped around them like vines.

She couldn't allow this to happen.

Her life was already incredibly complex and difficult. She didn't have the time or emotional energy for anything more. And she certainly couldn't indulge in a selfish moment of flirtation when so much was at stake.

But her skin still felt an echo of warmth from the spot where he'd held her.

Avoiding his gaze, she retreated even farther, praying that he wouldn't follow.

To his credit, he seemed to sense her confusion and allowed her to maintain her space.

"Do you need me to give you a hand inside?" He gestured to the bike leaned up against the wall.

"No. I'll be fine. Thank you for the ride."

She feared that she sounded awkward, like a child offering rote pleasantries to an adult after a party. But if he found her stiff manner odd, he gave no indication. Instead, he smiled—a slow rich smile that made his eyes light from within.

And that smile should be declared hazardous to a woman's health.

Thankfully, before she could relent and surrender to the temptation he inspired, he touched the brim of his hat.

"Until tomorrow morning, then."

She had to bite her tongue to remain silent. Much as she wanted to accept his offer of a lift—if only to feel this heady rush of femininity and awareness—she knew she couldn't. Spending any more time with Bodey Taggart would be a *bad* idea. In more ways than one.

So she dipped her head in a semblance of a nod and retreated toward the spot where he'd leaned her bike against the wall. Setting one hand on the door handle, she grasped the sack with the other, waiting until Bodey climbed into his truck. Then, with one last wave, he maneuvered the large vehicle out of the parking lot and onto the main road.

As soon as the rumble of his engine disappeared into the distance, Beth took a deep breath, willing her pulse to slow and the ache in her chest to subside.

She wouldn't dwell on the regrets. Not now. Not ever. Not when she had more than she had ever thought she would.

So she waited one minute. Two. Three. And with each ticking second, she strained to hear the low rumble of Bodey's distinctive engine. Finally, when she was sure she'd given him more than enough time to drive away, she grappled with the shopping bag, tying it to the handlebars of her bike. Then she headed around the hotel, carefully looking both ways to make sure that Bodey Taggart and his truck were nowhere in sight. Once she assured herself that he was truly gone from the area, she began the short ride home.

DAMN, damn, damn, damn, damn.

How could he have been so stupid?

Bodey sighed, watching the numbers on the gas pump flashing past with alarming speed. But for once, he wasn't paying attention to the cost of diesel. Instead, he was kicking himself for scaring the hell out of Beth.

He wasn't so jaded that he couldn't tell when a woman was shy. Inexperienced. Young.

Shit.

What had he been thinking? Lifting her down from the truck, letting his hands linger on her waist, stroking her with his thumbs?

Had he been chasing women for so long that he couldn't stop himself anymore? Was he so selfish that he'd convinced himself that time had slowed down so that he could concentrate on the hitch to her respiration and the warmth of her body beneath the thin layer of her T-shirt? Or was it absolute stupidity which had caused him to absorb the way his palms perfectly fit into the notch at her waist?

Geez. He'd already established that Beth wasn't his type—and not because she didn't match the Rodeo Queen mold that he'd always been attracted to before. This wasn't a "no strings" kind of woman. And if there was one rule that Bodey refused to break, that was it. No single mothers, no widows, no virgins. Absolutely, no one vulnerable.

Beth was vulnerable. He knew that to his bones. She might present a will of iron to the world—especially to him—but behind that strength was something . . .

Hell, he didn't know what was going on with her, but he sensed she had the weight of the world on her shoulders.

Which meant she was off limits.

Absolutely.

Unequivocally.

Off.

Limits.

Damnit.

A thump signaled that the flow of fuel had stopped. Sighing, Bodey replaced the nozzle, grabbed the receipt, and then turned to screw the tank cap back in place. Idly, he looked up, noting that the shadows were growing even longer and that traffic was becoming more congested.

He was debating if he wanted to take the time to check on his horse tonight or wait until morning when he saw a slight figure in black riding past him on a bicycle. Swinging from the handle bars was a bulging grocery sack.

For a moment, his brain grappled with the sight. Then he did a double take.

What the hell?

He squinted, sure it had to be a coincidence and he was watching a stranger. But as the woman looked both ways to negotiate the intersection, he knew he wasn't imagining things.

That was Beth.

Had she lost the key to her room or something?

But that was nuts. If she'd locked herself out, she wouldn't be riding down the street with her bicycle. She'd be talking to the front desk.

Keeping his eye on her, he climbed into the cab and started his engine. Then he carefully eased into the busy street.

Hanging back as far as he could, he followed Beth for another two blocks where, to his surprise, she turned into the cracked and weedy parking lot of a run-down motel. Sixty years ago, it had probably been a cute place for families to stop with their Packard station wagons loaded with kids. At one time, the U-shaped strip of domiciles, each designed with a cottage-like entryway, had probably been painted with crisp white paint and bright green trim. But now, the units surrounded an empty pool cluttered with leaves and dust and stray bits of garbage. Out front, a neon sign flickered wearily, advertising KITCHENETTES and REASONABLE RATES. But there was no hiding the fact that the once kitschy roadside stop had become cheap rent-by-the-day housing.

Bodey pulled to the curb, not daring to get any closer—and he was glad of his precautions when she hesitated at the door of a cottage in the far corner. Warily, she glanced over her shoulder as if she sensed his scrutiny. Then she knocked, still mindful of her surroundings. Bodey couldn't fault her for that. It didn't look like the sort of place where a woman would feel safe.

The door opened a crack. The person on the other side must have recognized Beth right away, because a tall male stepped outside to take the bag from her, then backed up again so she could wheel the bicycle inside.

Then the door slammed shut.

What was that all about?

Granted, Bodey had only known Beth for a few short hours. But what he'd witnessed didn't jibe at all with what he'd gleaned so far.

Since Syd and Helen had been short on space in their RV, Bodey had volunteered to pack their Dutch ovens to Cheyenne in his own trailer. Once he'd delivered the squat cookers this afternoon, he'd lingered to visit with Syd. In doing so, Bodey had done his best to subtly ply the man for information about his new employee. Although Syd hadn't known much himself, the other man had been under the impression that Beth was a college student on summer vacation, looking for a little cash.

But Bodey was beginning to piece together an altogether different picture. One of a woman who guarded her privacy, who probably hadn't had a square meal in some time, and was living paycheck to paycheck.

And she wasn't living alone.

Bodey wasn't sure why that detail ruffled his feathers. Even more, a purely primitive rush of possessiveness swelled in his chest, threatening to swallow him whole. But he finally managed to find the corner of his brain that still functioned properly. He pulled away from the curb and made a wide U-turn.

None of your business, he insisted to himself. *Absolutely, none of your business.*

If anything, he should be grateful for the insight he'd unwittingly been given. Clearly, Beth had a complicated life. One that was already more than she could handle. She had no interest in Bodey or in having a little fun.

She wasn't that kind of woman.

He grimaced.

So why was he tempted to meddle?

SIX

———•◆•———

As soon as the door closed, Beth was besieged with noise and chaos—Eric's demands to know what was in the bag, Dolly's squeals of welcome, and the sharp, ear-splitting bark of Noodle, the Heinz 57 mutt that had adopted them a few months ago in Fargo.

"Hey, hey, *hey!*"

Except for Noodle's excited yelps, the din eased.

Beth leaned the bike against the wall, then reached to give her brother a quick hug and a kiss. But her gentleness dissolved in an instant.

"Why didn't you text me back? I've been worried sick! I called you about noon and I've sent a dozen texts since then!"

Eric grimaced. "My phone ran out of batteries while I was playing games and Noodle chewed through my charging cord."

See? Nothing serious. No reason to panic.

But Beth had a hard time getting her pulse to slow from its rocketing speed.

Eric became immediately contrite. "Sorry, Bethy. Really.

It took me a while to get some tape from that grouchy lady at the front desk so that I could twist the wires back together."

Realizing that her brother was blaming himself for worrying her, Beth carefully schooled her features.

When had her brother become . . . almost a man? Overnight it seemed like his voice had dropped an octave and the peach fuzz on his face had become darker. It wouldn't be long before he'd be shaving in earnest.

"Are you mad at me?" he asked hesitantly. Still enough of the little boy remained that he could be upset by his older sister's foul mood.

She shook her head, pulling him in for another hug. "It's not that. I was thinking that you grew another three inches today."

When she released him, he blushed, but looked pleased. When he backed away, she realized he'd be passing the six foot mark soon. A shock of brown-blond hair hung over his forehead into his eyes, and with a jerk of his head, he forced it back into place.

"We need to give you a haircut tonight."

He scowled. "No one wears short hair anymore, Bethy. It's supposed to look like this."

She made a face. Granted, she wasn't one to offer fashion advice, but Eric's current "do" looked like he'd been standing too long in a wind tunnel.

He must have sensed that she was wavering because he added, "I want to keep it like this."

As much as she admired his bid for independence, she offered a noncommittal, "We'll see."

Dolly tugged on Beth's shirt hem and Beth immediately swept the little girl into her arms.

"You can cut my hair," she said seriously.

Beth leaned close to rub her nose against Dolly's. "I can, huh? Do you want a Mohawk?" But even as she teased, Beth knew that she'd never take a pair of shears to her little sister's hair. Not when it rioted around her face in natural curls so reminiscent of their mother's.

Dolly framed Beth's face in her small hands, forcing Beth to meet her gaze. "Can we go to the park? Eric an' me didn't go today," she whispered with utmost seriousness.

The query made Beth even more aware of their surroundings, the shabby carpet, the scarred furniture, the lumpy bed in the only other room. Even worse, the space was stifling, despite the chugging rattle of the swamp cooler mounted in the window.

"Mmm. Maybe."

More than anything, Beth wanted to keep her siblings inside, away from prying eyes, safely hidden. Especially since, only moments before, she'd had that prickling sensation of being watched.

But she also knew that Dolly and Eric needed fresh air and sunshine—as well as the illusion of freedom—if she were to keep things as normal as possible.

"Pleeeeease?"

Relenting, Beth kissed her sister's cheek. "I think that would be a great idea . . ."

Dolly beamed.

"But . . ." she added fatefully.

Her little sister's smile faltered.

"First I think we should eat. My new boss sent home all sorts of yummy things and there's a great big sandwich for you and Eric to share."

Dolly squealed and wriggled free, hurrying to the metal table in the "kitchenette" section of the room.

In truth, the advertised amenities were Spartan at best. A narrow counter held a vanity-sized sink, a microwave, and a mini refrigerator. With such limitations, their diet had begun to resemble the fare of a college student in a dormitory—cereal, peanut butter, noodles, and macaroni and cheese. But tonight, as Eric pulled the containers from the sack, Beth could see that they had a veritable banquet. Besides her leftover sandwich and the packages of chips, there were Dutch oven potatoes, macaroni and potato salads, homemade rolls, crisp cut up vegetables, Cornish game hens with stuffing, and gooey almond cherry chocolate cake.

Dolly's eyes widened at the dessert. "Can I have some of that?" she asked with such breathless anticipation that Beth laughed.

"Of course. After you eat some real food."

Eric was staring into the plastic tub containing the game hens with something akin to suspicion. "What is this?" He poked at one of the birds with a plastic fork. "This isn't a pigeon or something weird, is it?"

His expression was so patently horrified that Beth couldn't help reaching out to ruffle his carefully coiffed hair. "It's a Cornish game hen."

He poked it again. "Which is . . ."

"A miniature chicken. Honest. It's chicken."

At least, she hoped it was a chicken.

Eric gingerly tore one of the legs free. Then, still eyeing it with consternation, he took a small bite. But as he chewed, his suspicions were allayed because he hooked his ankle around the leg of his chair and pulled it beneath him as he sat.

"These drumsticks aren't big enough to fill anybody up," he muttered as he quickly stripped the bone of the succulent meat.

"You can have the whole hen."

"Really?"

"Sure. When you go to a fancy dinner, they put a complete Cornish game hen on your plate."

"Cool!"

While Eric claimed the rest of his bird, Beth prepared a paper plate for her sister, offering her a wing and some breast meat from the other hen, part of the leftover brisket sandwich, and the packet of potato chips.

Dolly clapped her hands. "Chips! I love chips!"

As she wrestled with the package, Beth leaned back in her own chair, watching her siblings as they sampled each of the dishes.

Even though she knew that she'd done the best she could for the past year, Beth couldn't prevent the twinge of guilt. Fourteen months had passed since she'd assumed custody of her siblings, and by now, she'd hoped to be able to give them so much more. She should have a steady job and regular hours. She should be able to offer them a permanent place to stay where there were bedrooms with real drawers for their clothes.

After this long, they shouldn't still be looking over their shoulders, living out of the backpacks that they kept stuffed with their meager belongings in case they had to leave at a moment's notice. Come fall, Dolly and Eric should be in school. They needed teachers who could help them catch up to their peers rather than Beth's fumbling attempts to tutor them.

Her gut twisted with the ever-present worries and she pushed aside the plate of vegetables she'd set in front of her.

Eric caught the movement and his brow creased. "You gotta eat, Bethy. You're getting too skinny."

"It's the style," she shot back at him, echoing his own words.

"You'll get sick if you don't eat."

And that, right there, was one of her biggest fears. That one of them might grow ill and need medicine, which would cause a whole host of complications.

"I had a late lunch, so I'm not all that hungry." She pushed her food toward Eric. "I'll eat again later on." She pointed a warning finger at Dolly. "So don't you dare gobble up all the chocolate cake."

Dolly giggled. "Can I have some now?"

Her little sister had already eaten everything she'd been given, and it hadn't escaped Beth's attention that she'd run her finger over the plate to catch every last drop of sauce, then licked the digit clean.

"Don't you want some more chicken? Or sandwich?"

Dolly's gaze zigzagged between the food, Eric and Beth's plate, and the cake. "No. We can save some for tomorrow."

Beth's heart twisted in her chest. It was obvious that Dolly was under no illusions that this sudden bounty of food would last. And if they were going to be back to noodles and peanut butter sandwiches, her little sister would rather put that moment off as long as possible.

Tears pricked the back of Beth's eyes but she forced them away. She would not be sad. She wouldn't be sad or guilty or filled with regrets. Their situation might be tough right now. But just as Eric had reminded her the night before, they were together. They were safe. They could pack their bags and go anytime they wanted. They could spend the day in their pajamas watching television or walk to the park and play. Right now, Beth had work, and soon she'd have enough cash in her pocket to buy a bus ticket to somewhere else where maybe they could put down roots long enough for her to get a job. A real job with real hours.

Wouldn't that be something?

Pushing aside the ever-present hammer of thoughts that repeated themselves over and over again in her head like an endless loop, Beth reached for the last container.

"Cake for everyone."

"Even Noodle?" Dolly asked, her eyes sparkling.

Noodle issued a short bark.

"No, not Noodle. Chocolate is really bad for dogs. But maybe she'd be happy with a little piece of chicken."

While Dolly tore a small piece off the remaining hen and bent to offer it to the dog, Eric's eyes met Beth's. He tipped his head, indicating the door. "Can I talk to you a minute?"

Setting a slice of cake on Dolly's plate, Beth stood. "Sure."

They walked to the door, Eric opening it wide as if allowing the breeze to enter the room. But he stood on the other side, far enough away where their little sister wouldn't hear.

"I don't know if I'm being paranoid, but . . ."

Panic skittered down her spine.

"But what?"

"I keep seeing this old red farm truck passing on the road out there." He gestured to the street opposite. "It could be nothing—maybe it's someone who lives around here. But it seems to . . . I don't know . . . slow down whenever it gets within a block or two. It circles around this neighborhood six, seven times a day."

Beth's eyes immediately scanned the area, looking for the telltale truck. "Maybe it's making deliveries or belongs to someone working in one of the nearby fast food joints."

"Yeah. Maybe."

Her brother didn't appear any more convinced by her explanation than she was. But they couldn't take off. Not yet. They had to postpone any plans until she'd been paid.

Surely, they could wait that long.

Dear heaven, don't let her make a mistake.

Beth's eyes were still darting over cars as they passed beneath the pools of light beneath the street lamps. A lump of lead lodged in her stomach when she pondered everything that could go wrong.

No.

She couldn't think that way. Not when so many things were going right.

"Stick inside for the next few days and keep Dolly away from the windows," she said slowly. "Hell on Wheels will be over Saturday night. On Sunday, I'll help Helen and Syd pack up their merchandise. Then they'll be heading back to Utah."

"Maybe we should go with them," Eric said wistfully.

If only they could.

SHE woke with a jolt, her heart threatening to pound from her chest, her lungs already burning from the way she gasped for air.

For long moments, she grappled with the darkness, wondering what had awakened her. Had it been her nightmare—the same reoccurring dream that plagued her night after night? Or was it something else? A sense that something, *someone,* was wrong with her surroundings.

She didn't move—didn't dare move. Keeping her eyes closed to slits, she scanned as much of the room as she could.

But with the television off and all of the drapes pulled shut, there wasn't much light. All she could do was listen.

Please, please.

Not now. Not yet.

She threw her silent prayer into the blackness, listening for the slightest noise that could reveal if an intruder was present. She strained to hear the soft sough of breathing or the rustle of clothing.

Then she heard it, a soft growl, coming from the far side of the room.

Noodle.

The dog had been with them for a couple of months now. Hurt and shivering, it had appeared at a different rooming house, a different doorway—yet one so similar to their current residence that it could have been yesterday. Beth suspected that the dog had been hit by a car—or perhaps had been thrown from a moving vehicle and abandoned.

From the moment her siblings had found it, Beth had discouraged them from even touching the animal, let alone bringing it inside. The canine had been filthy and bloody and yipping in pain—and Beth had known that if the pup needed medical attention, she couldn't afford to find a vet. She hadn't wanted her brother and sister to grow attached to something they clearly couldn't afford to keep.

But, true to form, Dolly and Eric had begged her to at least try to help the little dog. And, true to form, Beth had given in. There were so many times when she had to tell her siblings "no," so when she had the ability to indulge them, she caved.

In the end, Noodle had provided a bit of normalcy to their lives. Soon enough, they'd discovered that her wounds were superficial and her bedraggled appearance came naturally. In fact, the dog was a little off-putting with bulging eyes, a lolling tongue, and black and white patches of fur in varying lengths. But she was loyal and loving.

And protective. That, above anything else, had convinced Beth to let her stay.

The dog growled again and Beth slowly rose from the

couch. If someone were inside, the dog would have gone berserk. Whatever had alerted her, had come from outside.

Reaching for the backpack on the ground, Beth slid her hands beneath the neatly stacked clothing and wrapped her hand around the snub nosed pistol. Then, standing, she padded toward the door.

"What's wrong, Noodle?"

The dog offered a whimpering whine, but remained at her post.

Beth peered out of the peephole. A weak streetlight with a dying bulb flickered an other-worldly bluish gray so that it was difficult to discern much more than what was directly in front of her. But she was able to see that the parking lot was clear. The drinkers, smokers, and partiers who congregated in clumps on the cracked asphalt rather than their cramped and overheated rooms had all gone to bed. Which meant it must be close to dawn.

Crossing to the window, Beth nudged the fabric aside with her finger and searched again from another angle. For a moment, she thought she saw someone disappearing around the edge of the main office. Probably one of the managers making their rounds.

Noodle eyed her expectantly, ready to burst into attack mode, which—with her spindly legs and a body of a stout Chihuahua—would entail launching an assault at someone's ankles.

"You can stand down. I think it was the manager."

Sometimes, Beth could have sworn that Noodle spoke "people," because she instantly relaxed, then padded toward Beth, her tail whipping from side to side so enthusiastically, it gave her the weaving stance of a drunkard.

Resetting the safety on the pistol, Beth tucked it into the waistband—grimacing, when she realized that she'd fallen asleep in her clothes. Then, she bent and scooped the animal into her arms, burying her face in its fur and absorbing the dog's warmth and unrestrained affection.

"Just a false alarm," Beth murmured into Noodle's back

as the dog wriggled this way and that, trying to find the best opportunity to offer Beth a face licking.

Beth supposed she should shower and change into her sweats but as the adrenalin seeped from her body, leaving her trembling and exhausted, she sank onto the couch again, wrapping a blanket around them both. Then, she reached for the remote, knowing that sleep would prove elusive for some time.

But when the television finally flickered to life, she sighed when she found that it was tuned in to a classic Western channel and a rerun of *Bonanza*.

How many times had Beth watched Hoss and Little Joe with her father? In fact, how many times had she seen this particular episode?

During the last few months of her father's life, as he'd withered away from the cancer that he'd fought against for years, Jasper Tivoli had sought comfort in the memories of his childhood: *Bonanza; The Lone Ranger; The Wild, Wild West;* and old John Wayne movies. All of them visual representations of a time when men were men and women were reluctant damsels in distress who required saving—only to fall into the hero's arms at the end.

Clearly, the plots were based on fantasy rather than reality.

Noodle wriggled beneath the blanket, circling her lap for the perfect spot to settle down. As the dog made its bed, Beth heard a muted crackle. Reaching into her pocket, she withdrew several folded dollar bills, a handwritten note with Helen and Syd's phone numbers . . .

And a business card.

Beth couldn't account for the way that her thumb brushed over the raised lettering, then traced the flight of the black cow, the field of poppies, then, finally, the cowboy with the lariat.

Her eyes flicked to the television set, to Little Joe and Adam vying for a woman's attention at a dance, then back down again to the cowboy on the card.

She felt a soft nudging somewhere in the region of her

heart, but she ignored it. Granted, Bodey Taggart might look like the quintessential cowboy of old. But this wasn't the Wild West—despite the illusion being created at Hell on Wheels. And she wasn't a damsel to be saved.

Even though she knew she was on borrowed time.

Sighing, she leaned her head back on the couch and closed her eyes.

If real life were like the movies, she would find a way to write her own ending, one where everything turned out for the best and the characters rode happily into the sunset. But real life was never that neat. And even if she could do such a thing, she wouldn't know how to bring about such a finale. Especially not now. After more than a year of running, she was no closer to protecting her siblings from the effects of a bitter custody dispute than she'd been after her mother's death.

She only knew that she couldn't allow them to be returned to the man who claimed to be her mother's common-law husband. A man who had threatened to steal Dolly and Eric away, if necessary.

But she also didn't know how she was going to prevent it from happening for much longer.

Again, her gaze dropped to the card, to the man on horseback and to his expression of utter joy and abandon. Yup, if this were the movies, Bodey Taggart would be the kind of cowboy who would ride to the rescue of a damsel in distress.

But not this damsel.

This damsel was going to have to solve her problems all on her own.

SEVEN

———◆———

THE sun was already high and bright—and hot—the next morning when Bodey slid his arms into a cobalt cavalry tunic and began fastening the buttons. Reaching for his hat, he grimaced when his gaze was pulled to the window of his trailer. Again.

Damnit. He had to stop acting like a stalker. He'd only met Beth, what? Two days ago? Yet, he found himself thinking of her far too often.

It wasn't as if he was planning to pursue her. Far from it. He'd spent most of the night, reassuring himself that his attraction to her was all wrong and his preoccupation with her had to end. He was used to women who were tall and leggy. He wouldn't know how to act around someone so . . . so . . . dainty. No, not dainty. That girl had a stubborn streak that belied that description. And "short" didn't fit her either. She was small, yes, but she had presence to her. She stuck up for herself and—

Shit.

He reached for the hat that completed his uniform and settled it carefully over his brow. He needed to keep his mind on the matter at hand, shooting a clean set of stages.

Gathering his gloves and his dark glasses, Bodey threw open the door and jumped to the ground. He'd already packed his gun cart with ammo, water, his prescription meds, some power bars, and looped his holsters over the handle. Unlocking his truck, he flipped the seats up to reveal the locked cases for his long guns and pistols.

He was looping his holsters around his hips when he looked up to see a cyclist turning into the parking lot.

Beth.

She noticed him in the same instant because she skidded in the loose gravel and was forced to put her feet down.

"Morning," Bodey called out.

Beth hesitated, then swung her leg over the saddle and rolled the bike toward him.

"Good morning."

"You got here just in time. The match is set to start in about twenty minutes. Sure you don't want to sign up for one of the last minute posses?"

She shook her head. "I'm fine watching from the sidelines."

"Suit yourself."

"I'd better go check with Helen. She and Syd are competing this morning as well."

"Hold on for a minute and I'll walk down the row with you."

He slid his weapons into the custom made slots on his cart, locked his truck, then fell in beside her as they joined the crowd beginning to head toward the center of the camp. Each morning's events would begin with a recitation of the rules and safety precautions, then a raising of the U.S. flag. Food vendors were already busy with orders for pancakes, fried scones, eggs and bacon, and the main tent was full of early morning diners.

"You're wearing black again, I see," he remarked.

"It hides the dirt."

She'd said the same thing yesterday, but after seeing the rundown hotel, the words took on new meaning.

"You know it's going to be over a hundred degrees again today, don't you?"

She shrugged.

"So, did you sleep well in your hotel?"

The moment the words left his mouth, Bodey could have kicked himself. *Shit, shit, shit.* The last thing he wanted to do is give any indication that he knew she wasn't staying at the Red Fox Inn.

He kept his gaze on the path ahead of him, even though he felt the way she shot him a quick glance.

"As well as a person can in a hotel, I suppose."

Mmm. Interesting response.

"Do you have family in the area?"

Damnit. His brothers always complained that Bodey didn't have an EDIT button, that he didn't know when to stop. But the words popped out before they were even fully formed.

This time, her glance was more pointed. "Not really. Why?"

Not for the first time, the image of the tall male ushering her into the dilapidated motel room flashed into his head. Hell, he'd told himself a million times that Beth's private life was none of his damned business, but that moment stuck in his head like an old phonograph needle on a scratchy record. He'd been hoping there was an innocent explanation for what he'd seen, that maybe Beth really was staying at the Red Fox Inn, that she was visiting a friend or—

None of your damned business.

They had slowed as they reached the knot of people forming around the flagpole and Bodey came to a complete stop, knowing that he'd gone as far as he should—with the conversation as well as the walk with Beth. It was time to get his head back into the game. After all, he'd come to Hell on Wheels to forget the horrible summer he'd had already, to immerse himself in competition, and to push himself further and faster than he'd done before. He'd come to this event to win.

But as his gaze tangled with Beth's, he couldn't focus.

"I guess this is where we part ways," he murmured, stating the obvious.

She nodded, regarded the crowd, then met his eyes again. "Good luck."

"Thanks."

Awk-ward.

Hell. He couldn't remember a time when he'd found himself at a loss for words around a woman.

"Maybe I'll see you after the stages. We could . . . grab a bite to eat or something."

He sounded like a teenager asking a girl to meet him for a soda after school.

He thought she would refuse—he expected her to refuse. He could see the rebuttal forming in her head as if the thoughts were printed above her head in a comic strip balloon. But when she spoke, she said, "Yeah. Okay."

The words were uttered so softly that Bodey nearly didn't hear her over the growing murmur of the crowd. But he saw her reply form on her lips, saw the hint of panic that flared in her eyes the moment she spoke. He knew that she wanted to retract her response but he didn't give her a chance. Not when her acceptance eased the tension that had settled into his chest since the night before.

Touching his fingers to the brim of his hat, he allowed himself a small grin. "See you then."

AS she resolutely turned away from Bodey—away from the keenness of his gaze and the rife temptation of his smile— Beth inwardly kicked herself.

Hell's bells, Bethy. What were you thinking?

Hadn't she learned her lesson already? Hadn't she spent the night fretting and fussing over the fact that she didn't have the time or the energy to even *think* about Bodey Taggart, let alone . . . let alone . . .

Crap.

The whole trip to work, she'd vowed to herself that she

would keep her mind on her job, help Helen any way she could, then return home having as little interaction with this man as possible. She'd repeated that mantra to herself over and over again, until the sentiment echoed the whirling rhythm of her tires and she was sure that her resolve was unshakeable.

Then, the minute she'd turned into the parking lot, every precaution for self-protection had skittered out of her head. Apparently, she had as much control as the wild hare that had scampered pell-mell through camp yesterday, seeking a way out of the unfamiliar maze of tents.

She blamed it on the uniform. That damned cavalry uniform. She'd always been a sucker for a military man—and what woman wasn't? But sweet heaven above, when she'd rounded the corner and seen him standing there? Every line and plane sheathed in a tailor-made, cobalt blue, nineteenth-century cavalry uniform complete with gold braid, shiny brass buttons, leather gauntlets, and that . . . that . . . hat pulled low over his brow?

Gooseflesh raced up her arms.

Get a grip! You don't have the time or energy for this.

But her body contradicted her brain, the shock of awareness hitting her system like a jolt of caffeine. So much so, that she couldn't resist peeking over her shoulder, one last time . . .

Only to find that he'd been watching her.

Unable to help herself, Beth allowed her gaze to rake down his body. The blue of his uniform glowed in a sea of other Western-garbed competitors. But most of them had chosen practical colors—blacks and browns, dark greens and splashes of red. There were a few Civil War uniforms, but they were already faded from time in the sun—or from strategic attempts at distressing the costumes. Bodey's uniform appeared crisp and parade ready, the body beneath hard and fit and—

For heaven's sake, Bethy!

"God bless America!"

Beth started guiltily, realizing too late that she'd arrived at the Hendersons' tent and she'd nearly mowed her employer down with her bicycle.

At first, she thought that Helen's fervent murmur had something to do with the flag ceremony that was about to begin, but then she realized that her boss was looking in Bodey's direction as well.

When her brows rose, Helen chuckled. "God bless America for providing us with such a fine specimen of manhood."

A betraying heat began to seep into Beth's cheeks at being caught ogling Bodey Taggart so openly. But Helen grinned and said, "I might be married, but I'm not dead. And those Taggarts sure know how to fill out a uniform."

The warmth in Beth's face intensified but Helen's gaze was still trained on Bodey—which allowed Beth the luxury of one more peek at the way the wool coated his broad shoulders.

"If you think he's something," Helen murmured, "wait until you see the other brothers. When they're together, it's enough to give a body heart palpitations." Her boss didn't require a response from Beth, because she turned to call out, "Syd! We need to get to the ceremony!"

Syd's voice floated out to them from somewhere behind the tent. "I'm comin', I'm comin'."

When Helen faced Beth again, her manner was all business. "I've put change in the till. And the iPad with the credit card reader is in the drawer beneath—oh, and I left a pile of order blanks and the tape measure there as well. You should have plenty of bags . . . and . . . *Syd!*"

Syd rounded the tent corner from the outside, pulling a gun cart behind him. Today, he was dressed like a mountain man complete with buckskins and a hat that looked like it had been made from a skunk pelt.

Beth's eyes widened slightly at the sight, wondering if Flower *and* Bambi's mother had given up their lives for the ensemble.

But Helen leaned close to murmur, "It was his idea. No actual animals were used in the making of his costume."

Beth couldn't prevent a soft snicker.

Helen, resplendent in a stylish shirtwaist and bustle skirt, tugged a pair of lace gloves over her hands, then secured a straw hat to her head with an enormous jeweled hatpin.

"We're in Bodey's posse, praise the Lord, so we should have some fine shooting today. I've left some bacon and bread for you in the RV. Eat it before you start. It's going to be hotter than the hinges of hell itself again today. I left a cooler full of water bottles and sodas behind the cash register, so drink as much as you can throughout the day. I don't want you getting heatstroke." She paused long enough to wink. "Although, if you want to pretend you're going to faint, I could arrange for one of those handsome National Guard medics to come check you out."

Beth's mouth dropped, then she laughed, not knowing how to respond.

But Syd's low chuckle saved her from thinking of a quick reply. "Ignore her. She gets this way when the menfolk dress up."

"Yes, I do," Helen said with obvious enjoyment. "I have a rich fantasy life. And on days like today, I don't have to use my imagination."

Tension eased from Beth's body at the lighthearted banter, and muscles she hadn't even known had been held tightly in check began to loosen as her mood grew brighter.

How long had it been since she'd felt this way? So . . . buoyant, so . . . normal? She couldn't remember when she'd enjoyed a warm summer morning with friends or the fancifulness of a festival atmosphere. And if she found the thrum of excitement, the wonder of make-believe, and the good-natured teasing of this place a balm to her spirit, didn't her siblings deserve the same?

Unbidden came the image of Dolly adorned in pantalets and petticoats skipping up and down vendors' row and Eric dressed in buckskins—or trousers and suspenders. It had been so long since her siblings had been allowed a chance to play, really play. Not a few hours in the park carefully glancing over their shoulders, but plunging headfirst into a crowd, absorbing the festive spirit.

Maybe . . .

Since they'd be leaving Wyoming within a couple of days . . .

But as soon as the thought came, she shook it away. She'd insisted to Bodey that she had no family. She couldn't show up with two siblings in tow. Especially when their appearance would raise more questions than she would ever be prepared to answer.

"Is something wrong?" Helen asked. "Did I forget something?"

Beth wrenched her attention back to find that Helen was eyeing her with concern.

"No. I was . . . thinking."

Lame.

But after a moment, Helen accepted her cryptic answer. "We'll be shooting the stages on this end of the range, so you'll be able to see us. If you need something, come up to the safety fence. If it's a customer with specific concerns, arrange for them to come back in the afternoon."

"I'll be fine. Don't worry."

Helen reached to pat Beth's hand. "I know, I know. You've been such a help these past couple of days. I don't know what we would have done without you." Just as quickly as the words were spoken, she turned to Syd. "Ready?"

"I've been ready for some time. Soon as you quit yammering, we can be on our way."

"Nag, nag, nag," Helen replied good-naturedly. She snagged a frilly parasol from the gun cart, snapped it open, then offered Beth a wave. "'Bye, now!"

Beth watched the two of them hurry away, but they'd only gone a few yards when Helen turned and called out, "I left you a new dress hanging on the bathroom door in the RV. You needed something that wasn't being held up with safety pins!"

Great. Another dork outfit.

Beth grimaced, but waved to show she understood. She might not be thrilled about looking like a flour sack with a string tied around the middle—or a soiled dove in borrowed finery—but she understood the need. Helen and Syd were walking advertisements for their store, and as their employee, Beth needed to be in costume as well.

Even if it made her look like a grade "A" dweeb.

Sighing, she wheeled her bicycle through the tent to the RV where she parked it near Syd's camp chair. Then, she climbed into the motor home, her nose twitching at the scent of bacon that still hung in the air.

Her stomach grumbled, reminding her that she hadn't eaten much since lunch the day before. And since she was sure that Helen would notice if Beth didn't have breakfast . . .

That was all the excuse she needed. She reached for the bread wrapped in a plastic bag and noticed immediately that it wasn't a grocery store brand. The loaf was unsliced and obviously artisan made, with an unfamiliar label declaring it to be "Dilly Sourdough" from a place called Vern's.

Using a knife from the drawer, Beth cut a slice, then, after only a moment's hesitation, she cut another. Setting them aside, she placed the bacon on a folded piece of paper towel, warmed it in the microwave for a few seconds, then cut one of the slices of bread in half to make a sandwich. The other piece, she slathered with butter—*real* butter, *heaven!*—and set that on the plate as well. Then, knowing she needed to hurry back to the tent, she glanced around, looking for the next horror in calico that she would be forced to wear.

Her gaze did an entire circuit of the vehicle, found nothing, and then bounced back to the bathroom door.

"Oh." The word escaped in a tiny puff of sound. Because it wasn't a schoolmarm outfit that awaited her or a too-big saloon frock. It was . . .

"Steampunk," she whispered reverently.

How on earth had Helen known that Beth was a steampunk addict? Where other people surfed the net for ideas on gardening or fashion, Beth had Pinterest files on her phone filled with steampunk weaponry, vehicles, and paintings. When she and her siblings went to the thrift stores to augment Eric and Dolly's wardrobes, Beth couldn't leave until she'd checked the selection of books on the off chance that someone, somewhere, might have donated a steampunk novel.

She'd never stopped to analyze why she was so fascinated with the Vernian literature. She only knew that it spoke to her own brand of fantasy. She loved the intrigue, the adventure, and the kickass females who populated its pages.

And today, she would be dressed like one of those women.

The thought was barely formed before she was toeing out of her sneakers and shucking her clothes. As she reached for the costume, she could see that Helen was very thorough. There were black and gold striped thigh-high stockings, a crisp ruffled taffeta petticoat, an overskirt of gold and black striped silk, and a high-necked blouse with a black ascot. Topping it all was a black and gold paisley corset adorned with a series of buckles.

Wondering if she'd died and gone to steampunk heaven, Beth dressed as quickly as she could—even though she couldn't prevent the way her fingers lingered over the luxurious fabrics.

How? How had Helen come up with such a creation on short notice—and managed to make it fit like a glove? Beth couldn't remember any of these items being in the store stock that they'd unloaded from countless storage totes. Had she made all this? In a matter of days?

She was ashamed to admit that when Helen had shown her the sacks of fabric she'd acquired in town, Beth hadn't been paying much attention. But she was fairly sure that she would have remembered these combinations of black and gold.

As she stood in front of the full-length mirror bolted to the bathroom door, Beth couldn't account for the figure who stared back at her. She'd grown so used to the *sameness* she saw each day—same shapeless clothes, same dark colors, same pinched expression—that she'd long ago stopped paying much attention beyond ensuring that she had her "disguise" firmly in place. That meant dyeing her hair and wearing makeup more pronounced than anything she would have chosen a few years ago—even if that meant spending precious dollars on such non-essentials.

But the woman who stared back at her was so different, so . . . *exotic,* she felt as if she were looking at a stranger.

Her hand automatically ran down the boned front of the corset and plucked at the ornate draped gathers of her skirt. As a petite woman, she was often mistaken as a teenager. Because she was small, some people assumed she didn't have the brains God gave an ant.

But in this outfit, there was no denying that she was a woman. The skirts added fullness to her hips while the corset offered the illusion of a wasp-waist and more of a bust.

Wow.

Wow!

No wonder the SASS people liked dressing up so much.

A colored square caught her attention and Beth tugged a sticky note from the reflective glass to find the words *Get yourself a pair of boots from stock . . .* written in Helen's flowing hand.

Realizing that she'd already spent too much time in the RV, Beth whirled, a frisson of delight racing through her veins at the rustle of silk and taffeta. But as she shoved her feet back into her shoes for the dash into the tent and grabbed the paper plate with her food, she couldn't prevent the thought that popped unbidden into her head.

Wait until Bodey gets a look at this!

BODEY pulled a bottle of water from his gun cart and chugged it down, patiently waiting for the last two members of his posse to finish shooting.

So far, he was winning. He'd shot three clean stages with fairly good times. And, as it had a hundred times in the past, his body was zinging with the satisfaction of a good shoot and some friendly competition.

Unlike the pressure of the cow cutting circuit, where scores meant money, and money meant exposure for the ranch, the SASS shoots were more relaxed—if vying for the first place in his category could be called "relaxed." Since he wouldn't know any of the results of the other participants until the event finished late Saturday, he was competing more against himself, shaving a second off here, another few there. But it still had his heart pumping and his pulse racing.

Not for the first time, he acknowledged that he truly was addicted to the rush of competing. What had Beth called him? An adrenaline jockey?

If there really was such a thing, he supposed he would be president of the fan club. Because there was nothing, *nothing,* he loved more than reaching for something just out of his grasp, pushing himself a little harder, a little further, a little faster, until he could reach it.

Helen moved to stand beside him, her parasol casting some much needed shade over his face.

"How's the head?"

In truth, the heat had caused an ache to settle behind his eyes. But he'd come prepared, tucking some of his prescription medicine in his gun cart next to his power bars. He'd already taken one as a precaution and so far the symptoms had eased.

"I'm holding my own," he said, knowing there was no sense lying. It was as impossible to deceive Helen as it had been to fool his mother when she'd been alive.

"I slipped a few extra Pepsis into the cooler in the tent. Feel free to help yourself if you need one."

"I barely paid off the last one."

She waved that remark away. "Nonsense. What's mine is yours. I appreciate the way you gave Beth a lift last night. I don't feel comfortable having her cycle on those roads so late at night."

For once, Bodey thought carefully before saying, "I'll be heading out tonight to feed my horse again, so I'd be glad to give her another lift."

He thought Helen's brows lifted ever so slightly, but her tone was neutral when she said, "That would be a load off my mind."

The last shooter finished and the score keeper yelled out his time. Since the posse in the stage ahead of them was still shooting, his own group dawdled in loading up their weapons. A few crossed to the plastic tubs where bottles of water had been provided by the event organizers. Already, the heat had grown intense enough to melt most of the ice and a woman wearing an old-fashioned striped bathing costume was riding up and down the line on an ATV replenishing the supplies.

Helen dabbed at her upper lip with a lace edged handkerchief. "I know I could use one of those Pepsis about now."

Knowing a hint when it had been thrown his way, Bodey gestured to his cart. "If you'll keep your eye on this, I'll go get something for us both."

"And a root beer for Syd."

"Yes, ma'am."

Since it was already hotter than the depths of Hades, Bodey decided to throw historical accuracy to the wind and unbuttoned his tunic. "Mind if I leave this in your tent?"

"Not at all."

As he rounded the safety fence, he shrugged free of the woolen coat, sighing in relief when the breeze flattened against the linen shirt he wore underneath, chilling the sweat which had gathered along his spine. The loss of the wool and an infusion of cold caffeine were just what he needed to finish off the morning's round of stages.

Nearing the tent, he kept his eyes peeled for Beth's latest Little House on the Prairie outfit, but when he stepped inside, he could hear her low voice coming from the rear. He realized she was probably in the changing area with a customer. Not wanting to startle her by rifling around behind the cash register, he called out, "Beth? Helen sent me to get some drinks from the ice chest."

"I'll be out in a sec."

Although he knew he shouldn't linger too long, Bodey decided to stay. Only for a minute.

Squatting in front of the cooler, he lifted the lid and searched for two Pepsis and a root beer.

"Hey, you want anything while I'm looking?" he called out.

"Uh . . . sure. A diet cola. Thanks."

Diet. Like she needed a diet anything. But Bodey found her one nonetheless.

As he snagged the last bottle out of the ice, a woman in jeans and a T-shirt stepped from behind the changing curtain. She nodded and offered a smile in Bodey's direction, then strode from the tent.

"No sale, huh?" Bodey said.

"Actually, yes. She bought a ball gown for the banquet but it needs re-hemming, so she'll come back tomorrow morning with her shoes so Helen can make the adjustments."

The curtain rustled again and Bodey glanced over his shoulder, blinked, and then slowly pushed himself to his feet.

Holy, holy hell.

EIGHT

———◆———

T HE woman who stood in front of him had nothing in
common with those he'd met the last couple of after-
noons. Gone was the fussy calico school marm, or the uncomfortable saloon girl. In their place was a pint-sized pack
of trouble with laced up leather boots, striped hose, and an
outfit that was half Clockwork Princess and half dominatrix.
All she needed was a quirt to slap against her palm. Or his—
   Hell! Don't think like that!
   He prayed she hadn't read even half his thoughts. But she
must have sensed something, because her cheeks grew pink.
   "It's some outfit, huh?" she murmured self-consciously.
   "Oh, yeah," he said slowly, then could have kicked
himself.
   Shit, shit, shit. After all the stories Helen had been telling
her, she already thought he was a wild competitive jerk who
couldn't keep his pants zipped, he didn't need to add any
ammunition to the argument.
   But, sweet merciful heavens, she didn't seem insulted by
his reaction. Instead, she looked . . . pleased.
   He reached blindly behind him, setting the bottles of

soda on the counter. Then he stepped toward her, his eyes roaming hungrily over her frame. Yesterday, he'd mistakenly thought she was tiny. Fragile. But in that outfit, the blunt cut of her hair highlighted her high cheekbones and arching brows, making her eyes look incredibly huge. The crisp white shirt with its ornate cravat declared "prim," but the corset with its buckles and brass fittings screamed "madam."

Holy, shit!

Bodey couldn't help himself. He reached out to cup her cheek in his palm—and she nudged against the caress, her eyes flickering closed. And in that instant, he knew it wasn't the outfit that made her so beautiful. It was the confidence that lit her from the inside out. It was the sense of peace that chased away the haunting shadows in her eyes.

It was the way he felt being near her—strong, protective, possessive . . .

Unsure.

Bodey didn't think; he reacted. Reaching out, he snagged her around the waist and hauled her even closer. Then, before the whisper of conscience could tell him this was a bad, *bad* idea, he swooped down to capture her lips.

To her credit, her reaction was just as swift. She lifted on tiptoe, reaching to knock the hat from his head and plunging her fingers into his hair. And then, *hallelujah*, she opened her mouth.

Immediately, he slipped his tongue into her sweetness, plundering the soft folds, tasting her, tempting her. And she responded, measure for measure, her hands clutching at his shoulders so that he could wrap his arms around her waist and straighten, lifting her feet off the ground.

Damn, she was tiny. Tiny, but strong and eager and lush in all the right places and—

"Bodey! You're up next!"

The call startled them both. Bodey barely had the time to set Beth back on the ground and take a couple of steps away before Helen came striding through the front opening.

"You're going to miss your turn if you don't get a move on things."

"Yes, ma'am."

Damnit, even he could hear the garbled huskiness of his voice.

He saw the way Beth dipped her head to hide a smile.

Helen turned to adjust one of the mannequins and Bodey had enough time to snag the sodas and his hat. Then he leaned low to murmur in her ear, "Lunch."

Then, he was striding out into the sunshine with Helen hurrying to keep up.

And damned if the strangest thought didn't ricochet through his brain.

Scores be damned. Let's finish up these stages as fast as we can.

HE ended up being third in his posse. *Third.*

After his "break" in the tent, he'd missed three shots in the next round. And on the stage after that, the one located directly opposite Helen's tent, he'd been given a procedural. He couldn't even remember the last time he'd received a penalty like that. But damned if he wasn't aware of the way that Beth had settled into a folding chair in the shade of the awning and watched him shoot. He'd become so unaccountably self-conscious that he'd flubbed up the first few shots.

Normally, such an outcome would have had him fuming and stomping for the rest of the afternoon. But other than the good-natured ribbing he'd received from the rest of the group, he hadn't given it another thought. Not when he kept remembering the way Beth had looked in her steampunk dominatrix outfit.

As soon as he'd finished, he hadn't waited for the others. Instead, he'd headed back to the trailer where he'd locked up his weapons and his gear, then stepped into the miniscule bathroom for a quick shower. Ten minutes later, he was still dressed in Western regalia—a pair of twill pants, a loose cotton shirt, and a leather vest. This time, he was aiming for "railway road crew," rather than "dress blues cavalry officer" so that he could be as cool as possible in the blazing Wyoming heat.

He was still tucking his shirt tails into his waistband when he stepped out of the door and slammed it behind him.

"Three misses and a procedural," a low voice drawled from the direction of the camp chairs that Bodey had arranged in the shade.

Swearing softly under his breath, Bodey turned to find Elam slouched in one of the seats, his wife—and Bodey's best friend—Prairie Dawn, ensconced in the other. The two of them looked comfortable enough, their hands loosely linked. But they couldn't have been there that long.

"What's the rush? You're done for the day," Elam drawled, but the twinkle in his eyes convinced Bodey that he knew more than he was letting on.

"I'm hungry, that's all," Bodey said, immediately defensive. Whatever . . . *thing* . . . he was exploring with Beth was none of his brother's damn business.

"Uh huh." Elam sounded unconvinced. "How's the head?"

Bodey's eyes narrowed, his gaze ping ponging from his brother to P.D. and back to Elam again. "Why? What have you heard?"

Elam grimaced good-naturedly. "Not much. Just that my kid brother missed a couple of targets that were as big as a barn door. I thought I'd better come and make sure you weren't seeing double again."

So he hadn't heard about yesterday's headache. And if he didn't know about it, Bodey wasn't about to tell him— even if it would give him a logical excuse for shooting so poorly. Last thing he wanted was for Elam to start worrying again. Because, if he thought Bodey was still sick, he really would make Bodey ride Snuffles for the rest of the summer.

"Yuck it up, Elam. We'll see how you've done once you finish the afternoon stage."

Elam pushed himself to his feet, then held out a hand for P.D. Not for the first time, Bodey was struck by his brother's tenderness toward his wife. Especially now that they were expecting their first baby in November.

"You're not shooting, are you?" Bodey asked P.D., his own macho instincts pushing to the front.

"No." She beamed at him, palming the mound of her stomach beneath the frilly Victorian-pregnant-lady outfit Helen must have sewn for her. "I'm going to watch Elam for an hour or so. Then I'll spend the rest of the time chatting with Helen in her tent while Elam goes through his paces."

In the tent.

With Helen.

And presumably Beth once her lunch break was over.

Hell. If the stories had been flying before, Bodey could only imagine the tall tales that Beth would get this afternoon.

He felt his ears grow unaccountably hot at the thought of all those women.

Discussing him.

And his past.

Lord, have mercy on his soul.

"You sure you're feeling okay?" Elam asked again.

"I'm fine."

"'Cuz you're looking a little worried."

Hell, did it show?

Stay calm, real calm.

Or Elam will guess that you've found someone new. Someone . . . different. Someone . . .

Someone that Bodey didn't want hearing all the sordid details of his love life.

Elam eased toward him, his eyes narrowing, becoming so intent that Bodey couldn't help shifting like a guilty little boy. It was the same look he'd seen in Elam's eyes when they were kids, right before he went to rat him out to one of their parents.

"By hell, I think I know what's got you all twisted up inside," his older brother said softly.

Again, Bodey's gaze bounced from his brother to P.D. and back again. Even though he wasn't sure what he'd done, Elam had him feeling guilty.

For what? He hadn't done anything but kiss the girl!

Elam poked a single finger in his chest. "You're worried you're going to lose."

Lose? Lose what?

"To me."

Bodey blinked at Elam for several long seconds, uncomprehending. Then, it finally dawned on him that Elam wasn't talking about Beth at all. He was issuing a challenge.

Relief flooded through him like a cold wave and his breath escaped his lungs in a whoosh that he quickly disguised as a laugh.

"Oh, you think," he offered.

"I know."

"Fifty bucks says I win."

Elam grinned. "You're on."

P.D. rolled her eyes.

Elam laughed in obvious enjoyment as he grabbed his gun cart with one hand and slid the other around P.D.'s waist. "Come on, darling. I've got some shooting to do. Baby needs a new pair of shoes!"

THROUGHOUT the afternoon, Beth's gaze kept straying toward the stages opposite the dirt lane. Although she was kept busy, there were enough lulls between customers that she could track Syd and Helen's progress.

Yeah, right. Syd and Helen's progress.

Jerking her attention back to a woman trying to decide between a black cotton walking skirt and a black twill walking skirt, Beth tried to ignore that little inner voice that taunted her with the truth. Syd and Helen could have been throwing water balloons at the targets for all she knew. Every time her eyes had strayed to the competitors, they'd been sucked to a single figure.

No, no, no.

She didn't have time for this. She really didn't. Nor could she indulge in the luxury of flirtation, no matter how brief. The SASS shoot would be over in a few days. Soon after that, she would help Syd and Helen pack up their goods and dismantle the tent. Then, the Hendersons would be heading to the next SASS competition while she and her siblings . . .

Well, she didn't know where they would go. But she was certain that Bodey Taggart wouldn't be coming along.

Stifling a sigh, she once again yanked her attention back to the woman who wore a huge blonde wig and an Annie Oakley ensemble that must have skirmished with a bedazzling machine because the woman sparkled like a disco ball. Dimly, Beth remembered Helen telling her that there were several categories to the costume contests. One of them was a . . . what did she call it? A "B" Western group, whatever the heck that was. All Beth knew was that no self-respecting Western woman, "B" or otherwise, would wear that many rhinestones and crystals when the sun was pounding down and the temperature hovered near one-hundred-and-five degrees. She could probably nuke a burrito at fifty paces with the beams that radiated off her chest alone.

The thought caused Beth to snicker, which she quickly disguised as a cough.

"I don't know. I just don't know," the woman sighed, holding up one skirt, squinting at it, then repeating the process with the second one.

For crying out loud! They're both black!

Beth's gaze strayed to what she could see of the lane again. She knew Bodey's posse was finished because she'd seen some of the men from his group sauntering toward the food vendors. Even Syd and Helen had returned long enough to stow their gear and promise that, as soon as they'd had a chance to eat, they'd come relieve her.

So where was Bodey?

Stop.

It.

"Which one would you buy?" the woman asked.

Beth was tempted to retort, *"The black one."* But she stopped herself in time.

"That depends. The twill one has a nice drape to it and it's especially sturdy if you're doing a lot of active shooting." *Really? And you know this how?* "The cotton one is lighter, cooler and will flow better as you move."

Come on, Bodey. I must be hungry because I'm getting snippy.

Thank the stars and all the bright little angels, the woman

seemed to come to a decision because she thrust both skirts in Beth's direction.

"Wrap them both up. You can't have enough black clothing to choose from."

Truer words had never been spoken.

But even as Beth carefully wrote up the ticket and transferred the skirts into a bag, she was forced to amend her thought. A little color was nice, too.

Her hand unconsciously smoothed down the front of her corset. At that moment, a shadow fell over her and she looked up to see a looming figure stepping into the tent.

Bodey.

"Here you are. Thanks so much."

The woman beamed. "You've been very helpful. Make sure you tell Queen Helen that Flashy Flora said 'hello.'"

"I'll do that."

As the woman passed Bodey, she said, "Afternoon."

Bodey lifted his hat a scant inch from his head. "Ma'am."

Wow. When these people were in costume, even the manners were nineteenth century.

Bodey waited until the woman was well out of the tent before turning to Beth again.

"Hi."

The greeting was rife with remembrance of their last moments together and Beth felt a warmth climb up her neck, but she ignored it.

"How'd the shooting go?"

She wondered if he knew that she'd been watching him. Lordy, how the man could move. He had a fast draw that could rival any character she'd ever seen in movies. She'd watched him empty both pistols, a rifle, and a shotgun in a matter of seconds. All the while, he'd moved from point to point with athletic grace. And it hadn't hurt that, through it all, he'd been wearing cavalry boots, tight cobalt trousers, and a shirt with fabric so fine that she could see the muscles bunch through the linen.

Get a grip!

"You don't want to know. Today was . . . well, let's say I've done better."

She blinked, then remembered she'd asked about his shooting.

"I missed three shots and received a penalty for a procedural."

Beth waited for him to finish. "That's it?" she asked, one brow lifting. "That doesn't sound so awful. I've seen a lot of people doing worse today."

In the spurts of down time when she'd been able to study the competitors, she'd begun to sort them all into two groups. The ones who were completely focused on winning and . . .

Well, the ones who appeared to be having a lot more fun.

"I should think you could make up whatever mistakes you made today with tomorrow's shoot."

He opened his mouth to argue, then seemed to consider her point. "I suppose you're right. Still, I've got a bet going with Elam."

"Elam?"

"My brother. He's the oldest of the four of us."

"How much are you betting?"

"Fifty bucks. He's out there now, shooting the afternoon stages."

Beth couldn't prevent the way her eyes widened slightly. *Fifty dollars.* She couldn't remember the last time she'd spent that much on necessities. She couldn't imagine wagering it so frivolously.

"Is there a way to make him miss?"

Bodey laughed, then his eyes settled on her, warm and somehow more intimate now that they'd kissed.

"I like your way of thinking." He took a step forward, and another, and another. Then he reached out to touch one of the buckles on her corset. "Maybe we can come up with something." He hooked a finger beneath one of the straps, pulling her closer. "We'll have to talk about it over lunch."

The way he was looking at her chased "lunch" completely

out of her head and replaced it with altogether different thoughts. Those that strayed back to the kiss they'd shared.

No.

She shouldn't let it happen again.

And why not? If the outcome was going to be the same—and she was never going to see this man again—did it matter if she indulged herself for a few days? It could be her own Wild West fantasy. A souvenir. A memory that she could pull out any time things became too hard to bear.

But even as that thread of temptation played out in her mind, it brought an accompanying wave of fear. To allow someone else into her life was . . . complicated. Even worse, it required a certain level of trust that she didn't know if she could give. She was the only person who could possibly care for her siblings right now. And even though she loved Eric and Dolly with her heart and soul, the transition from independent single adult to caretaker hadn't been an easy one. Adding another person to the mix—however briefly—wouldn't be fair to them. Nor would it be wise.

Bodey was eyeing her expectantly and she unconsciously licked her lips. Immediately, his gaze zeroed in on that spot.

"Helen and Syd . . . they're not . . . I mean, they're eating right now, so I—"

You sound like a blithering idiot.

He must have understood the gist of her garbled statement because he smiled—and that smile filled her soul with molten honey.

You've got to tell him to go away. Nothing good can ever come of this.

But even though she willed herself to say the words, she couldn't form them on her lips. She was caught in a horrible tug of war between doing what was right and doing what felt good.

"I'm in no hurry. We can wait until they get back."

Beth was prevented from a reply when a trio of women decked out in Civil War hoops and ruffles stepped into the tent. Mouthing "sorry," she brushed past Bodey to help them.

As soon as she'd finished with the customers, she would

find a way to make it clear to Bodey that he was wasting his time with her. She owed it to Eric and Dolly.

But even as she tried to hurry the women through their purchases, another shopper arrived, then another, and another.

Since one set of stages was finishing up and the next still waiting to start, some unconscious call to arms must have been telegraphed for prospective buyers. Soon, Beth didn't have time to think about anything but writing up tickets for hats and stockings, fans and jewelry, until soon, she feared she would be overrun.

Looking up to see how many people still waited for her attention, she was startled to find that Bodey had stepped in to help her. She watched in amazement as he chatted with a pair of women trying on wide-brimmed hats. Like a born salesman, he teased and complimented them both until they dissolved into giggles.

Forcing herself to return her attention to the cash register, Beth tried to remind herself of everything she'd heard about Bodey Taggart. That he lived life on the edge. That he went through women and relationships like some women went through shoes. The way he acted with those customers was proof enough. Beth wouldn't be surprised if they decided to buy the whole selection of headwear.

All the more reason to stop this madness between them and focus on what was really important: earning enough money to buy three bus tickets to somewhere else.

But her inner voice couldn't summon up enough conviction to make the arguments stick.

Not when it had been so long since a man had looked at her with something more than dismissal.

And there was no denying, when she'd stepped from the changing cubical and he'd caught his first sight of her in her steampunk getup . . . Bodey Taggart had regarded her as a woman through and through.

IT was nearly an hour before Syd and Helen returned from their lunch—and even then, there were several customers waiting. So Bodey stuck around, offering his limited expertise—which amounted to standing around, looking like he knew what he was doing, and bullshitting his way through a sale with his best teasing smile. Unlike Beth, after a crooked grin, a compliment or two, and a hint of innuendo, Bodey usually had the females in the palm of his hand. But for once in his life, he found that having them concede so easily wasn't nearly as satisfying as it usually was. He was discovering that a shy tip of Beth's lips—one encouraged after earning her trust for a couple of days—was far more rewarding.

Finally, as the noise of gunfire resumed from the range, the rush of customers eased and Helen sidled close enough to murmur, "Take the girl to lunch, Bodey Taggart. She's earned a break. And keep her off her feet for at least a couple of hours, you hear?"

"Yes, ma'am."

He waited until the woman Beth had been helping decided to come back later. Then, before Beth could be drawn into conversation with someone else, he took her hand and pulled her out the rear flap of the tent.

"Wha—"

"Helen told me to carry you off and ravish you."

He heard her gasp.

"She did *not!*"

"I'm pretty sure that's what I heard."

"Then maybe you'd better get your hearing checked."

Bodey stopped in his tracks, and the inertia of her headlong dash sent Beth crashing into his chest. He didn't wait for her to react, merely wrapped his arms around her waist.

Her expression was so startled, so . . . panicked, that he hurried to reassure her, realizing that she probably didn't have much experience with sensual banter. At least not enough for her to realize he'd been kidding.

"Lunch, Beth," he said softly. Then, unable to resist, he bent toward her. "I'm taking you to lunch."

NINE

——◆——

B IT by bit, she relaxed in his arms, her fingers curling
into his biceps. Her eyes were dark but they burned with
an inner fire that relayed the moment when her alarm turned
to awareness.

Bodey hesitated, suddenly unsure. He was used to women
who were quick to pick up on his cues—and often match
his interest with their own eagerness to hook up. But
Beth . . .

He doubted if she'd ever played such games. He could
read her inexperience in the flush of her cheeks and the
ragged hitch of her breathing.

He lifted his brows, his gaze flicking to her lips, tacitly
asking her permission. When she lifted on tiptoes, he knew
he had his answer, and he closed the distance between them.

She was sweet and soft and willing. There was no pre-
varication for effect, no reluctance. Instead, she leaned into
him, her mouth parting, her hand slipping around his neck.

And dear heaven, she was enticement personified, her
lips warm and willing and eager. She sighed into his mouth,
that little puff of air so telling—letting him know that she'd

been holding her breath until that moment when their lips had touched. Then her mouth remained parted, tempting him even more.

Bodey had never been much good at resisting temptation, even in the best of times. And with a molten fire spreading through his veins, he didn't even think twice before succumbing to the invitation. His tongue slipped inside tangling with hers.

As he deepened the embrace, he was reminded again of how petite she was. Petite, but shaped for his exploration in all the right places. The corset made her breasts high and firm and her waist so tiny that he could probably span it with his hands. And she was slight enough that it was easy to take her weight, lifting her against him.

Her tongue teased his and Bodey couldn't prevent a soft moan of pleasure that eased from his throat as he followed suit, absorbing an echo of diet soda and . . . bacon?

He smiled against her at the thought, drawing back, fearing that if he surrendered to the hot wave of excitement plundering his veins that he might scare her off with the strength of his attraction. Hell, he was scaring himself with the hunger that swept through him like wildfire. He'd never been one to rush a romance. He liked to take his time and draw out the heady sensations, knowing that the newness would wear off too fast and then his ardor would flicker and die. But with Beth, he forgot everything he'd ever learned.

Resting his forehead against hers, he murmured, "What would you like to eat?"

Her mouth opened and he loved the way she searched for an answer, her lip caught between her teeth. "I-I don't know."

He kissed her again, quickly, then once more. "Do you want to stay here or head into Cheyenne?"

She shook her head. "You decide."

He was glad she deferred to him, because he suddenly had an idea.

"Okay. Let's go."

He pulled her past the motor home, making his way

through a parking lot that had filled to capacity while he'd been shooting.

"Where are we going?"

"I've got something good in mind."

She tugged self-consciously at the bottom of her corset. "Shouldn't I change?"

"Nah. You'll be fine."

"But . . ."

He stopped long enough to turn and stroke her cheek. "Don't worry. Where we're going, no one will give you a second glance."

BETH wasn't sure what Bodey had in mind but she couldn't imagine a place other than the Hell on Wheels compound where she wouldn't cause a stir. And the minute that thought entered her head, she realized that she'd made a mistake. She'd been so caught up in the storm of emotions that Bodey had inspired with a few quick kisses, that she'd allowed her guard to drop.

Again.

How could she have been so stupid?

Knowing her panic might be broadcasted on her features, she stared out of the window of Bodey's truck, watching the grassy pastures outside her window whiz past. She was only partly cognizant of the stands of antelope that bounded away as the vehicle approached. Instead, she was trying to formulate a way to keep Bodey from going somewhere public.

But when she'd screwed up her courage enough to tell him she'd changed her mind, Bodey pulled into the drive-through window of a mom and pop hamburger joint.

"Is this okay? They have really good burgers or sandwiches. Or would you like something else?"

Mystified why Bodey had brought her to the far edge of town for a hamburger—when they probably could have bought the same thing in camp—she opened her mouth to insist they return to Hell on Wheels, but she couldn't bring herself to say the words. Instead, she said, "A burger's fine."

Bodey ordered cheeseburgers, fries, and sodas for their lunch. Then, as soon as he'd collected the food, he was back on the road again.

When she saw that they were headed away from town, Beth began to relax. Soon, the fields grew green, stretching unabated into the distance. And the scents of the food Bodey had purchased wafted into the air, causing her stomach to rumble.

When was the last time she'd had a fast food burger? And fries? She honestly couldn't remember. She'd been pinching pennies for so long that she'd forgotten the enticing scents that could come from a paper sack full of convenience food.

"Hungry?"

"Mmm."

Bodey reached across the seat to take her hand. "You can start eating now, if you want."

"No, I'll wait."

He nudged her hand. "Come on. You've got to be starving. You've been working like a demon. I know I'm hungry. You could pass me my food while I'm driving."

Beth felt a twinge of guilt when she thought of her siblings. But since Bodey had purchased the burgers, she couldn't explain her dilemma. Instead, she promised herself that as soon as she'd been paid and the bus tickets purchased, she would see to it that Dolly and Eric had a similar meal.

Opening the sack, she snagged a small handful of fries, hissing softly when she found them still piping hot. She held them out for Bodey to take, but he seemed oblivious of the offering and opened his mouth instead.

For some reason, there was something . . . intimate . . . about giving him a fry, then another, and another. But when he accepted each offering with casual gusto, she told herself she was being silly. Obviously, she'd been out of the dating scene for some time if the mere thought of his lips so close to her fingertips caused a tightening within her.

So she continued to feed him, alternating one for him and one for her.

"Wish they had fry sauce in Cheyenne."

"Fry sauce?"

He grinned. "It's a Utah thing. I think it's ketchup and mayo mixed together with a little chili sauce. Or maybe it's that white salad dressing stuff. I don't know. I've tried making it myself when Barry's making a fuss, but I've never been able to get it to taste like the hamburger joint near the ranch."

"Barry?"

"My little brother. He's . . . picky."

Beth knew all about that. There had been a time when Dolly wouldn't eat anything but orange food.

"One of these days, I'll introduce you to this culinary delicacy. Being a Utahan, born and bred, it's hard for me to eat anything fried without it."

Beth felt a pang when she realized that Bodey would never have the opportunity to make good on his promise. Soon, they would part ways.

For a moment, her appetite dimmed, but she pushed the sensation of loss away. As much as she knew that she should call things off between them, she was forced to admit that it wasn't going to happen today. Not when he caught her gaze and grinned. Not when he drove with one hand draped over the wheel—so casually, so effortlessly, that her eyes were drawn to the dusting of dark hair, the long slender fingers, the network of veins that underscored the ropy muscles beneath.

Mentally, she raised the white flag, knowing that she might live to regret giving in to the temptation he inspired, but knowing that she couldn't insist he leave her alone. Not now. Not when his nearness warmed her from within.

And in that moment of epiphany, she realized that she didn't care what the consequences might be for this . . . brief interlude. These few days of normalcy were an unexpected gift and she couldn't waste a moment of them.

THEY had both finished their food when Bodey began to ease off the gas. Up ahead, Beth could see a long gravel drive with a gate marked by a lodge pole arch. When he turned into the lane and approached a security panel, she saw a wooden placard swinging from the upper beam proclaiming: ROCKING HORSE RANCH.

Bodey punched a code into the keypad and the electric gate slowly swung open, allowing him to drive through. After a few moments, the gate closed again.

"This place belongs to a buddy of mine. He lets me board my horse here when I come through Cheyenne."

They approached a neat, two-story farmhouse, but Bodey continued down the lane.

"He's not here right now?" Beth asked.

"Nah. He's on the cow cutting circuit."

There was a wistful note to his voice, reminding Beth that Bodey was "grounded." But before she could question him further, he stopped next to a barn that was three times the size of the farmhouse.

"There's my new toy."

He gestured toward rows of fencing that branched off from the barn. In one of the enclosures stood a horse with a flowing white mane and a body done in patchwork blotches of brown and white.

"She's a beauty, isn't she?" Bodey murmured in satisfaction.

Beth nodded. "Can we get closer?"

"Sure."

He opened his door and Beth needed no further encouragement. Unhooking her seatbelt, she hurried to catch up to him as he approached the fence. He offered a short, high whistle, then extended a hand and made a clicking noise with his tongue.

The horse's head bobbed coyly before the animal looked directly at Bodey. Then the filly ambled toward him with deliberate slowness—as if she knew the beneficial effects of "the tease." Finally, when she'd closed the gap, the animal cautiously sniffed Bodey's palm and sidled close enough for Bodey to stroke its long nose.

Beth hung back. Even with the fence between them, the

horse's size was intimidating. Beth was fairly certain that she wouldn't be tall enough to gaze over its back, let alone get on the thing. She'd need a ladder. And if she ever did manage to get on such an animal, the view from the saddle would be terrifying. It was a long way to the ground.

"She's a pretty little thing, isn't she?" Bodey murmured as he grasped her halter with one hand and continued to stroke the white patch on its head with the other.

"Little?" Beth croaked.

Bodey laughed, reaching out to Beth in much the same way he had for the horse. Except, this time, his palm was up, providing the perfect resting spot for her fingers.

As soon as her skin met his, a soothing warmth flooded from his body into hers, easing her nervousness.

"Come closer. She won't bite," he urged. He turned to murmur to the animal, "Will you, girl?"

Beth reluctantly took a step toward the fence, then another, and another, until she stood beside Bodey. When the animal didn't appear to mind, she whispered, "Can I touch her?"

"Sure. Hold out your hand first, with your fingers down and curled into a soft fist, so she can sniff you."

Beth did as she was told, catching her breath when the horse's warm breath puffed against her skin. Then, she tentatively reached out to touch it. She laughed softly when the horse nickered and moved closer. It nuzzled her with a nose as soft as velvet.

"She likes you, don't you, Willow?"

"That's her name? Willow?"

Bodey nodded, reaching up to scratch the horse behind its ears. "It's actually Willow-the-Wisp Walking On, but she and I think that's a little bit pretentious. So we've agreed on Willow. Just Willow."

Beth couldn't help smiling and adding, "One name. Like Cher."

"Exactly."

Bodey looked at her then, his eyes narrowing slightly. "Hey, you never did tell me your last name."

She could have told him that the omission was on purpose, a means of protection that she'd grown all too used to using. But she found herself whispering, "Tivoli."

"Mmm." He seemed to consider it. "Pretty."

And why did his simple phrase make her want to flush like a schoolgirl?

"Willow, here, is only two years old—still a teenager by horse standards. So she's a bit flighty, quick to make friends, but her feelings are easily hurt."

Beth was sure that Bodey was teasing her with such a statement, but his expression was absolutely serious.

"Willow is also the first animal I've ever had that wasn't a purebred quarter horse."

"What's a quarter horse?"

"It's a breed. They're sturdy, hard workers." He patted Willow's neck. "But this beauty . . . she's an American Paint. Delicate, made for speed and elegance."

Beth grew braver, inching closer so that she could reach up to the animal's ears. There was such a contrast in textures to the animal's hair—fuzzy and velvety near its mouth, short and crisp up its nose, coarse at its mane, and teddy bear soft at the ears.

"She's amazing."

"That she is. She likes you, you know."

"How can you tell?"

"Horses are intuitive animals. They read people and their emotions, and they react to them. She wouldn't be this close, this accepting of you, if she didn't know she could trust you." He rested a boot on the lower rung of the fence. "I've got some friends back home who have a ranch that uses adopted mustangs for horse therapy. A lot of veterans with PTSD go there for treatment. They also host a summer camp each year for kids with special needs."

"And the horses help them?" Somehow, Beth couldn't wrap her head around that concept.

Bodey rested his arms on the top rung.

"There's something about a horse that is large and intimidating."

Beth wouldn't argue with that point. It was only the fence between them that gave her the courage to be so close.

"But like I said, they're sensitive to human emotions. You might be able to fool people with your 'I feel fine and there's nothing wrong with me' bullshit, but not a horse. So the horses help a person strip away all pretense, live in the here and now. To get a horse to bond with you, follow your commands, accept your touch, accept you as a rider, you've got to tap into your own emotions and let go of the bad stuff." He shrugged. "At least, that's my theory. I know it's helped my brother."

"Elam?"

Bodey laughed. "No. Although, come to think of it, when he was going through a really hard time, I didn't see him ride much. Maybe he knew the horses would throw it all back at him or something. But I'm talking about my little brother Barry." He paused, reaching again to pat Willow. "He was in a car accident when he was about seven. It killed my parents and Barry's twin, Emily. Barry . . . well, he sustained some brain damage that was irreversible."

"I'm so sorry," Beth whispered, thinking of her own siblings and the bond she had with them. How much harder must it have been for Bodey to suffer such a loss?

"He's good now, really good. That kid does more than the doctors ever thought he would. But when he first came home from the hospital, it was tough. Not only were Mom and Dad gone, and Emily, but suddenly everything was impossibly difficult for him. He had to learn a lot of things all over again, walking, reading, even feeding himself. He'd always been so stubbornly independent, it was frustrating."

Bodey offered a wry grimace. "He spent months in the hospital and even longer in a rehab facility—and we kept him there because we were told it was best for him. But he'd get into these . . . rages. I think when things got really difficult, he didn't know any other way to react."

Bodey leaned into the horse, fussing with its mane.

"Finally, Jace—my other brother—had reached his limit of Barry's crying and pleading every time we had to leave him alone there at night. He'd scream and flail around—his temper tantrums worse than anything he'd had as a baby. Probably because he was bigger by then. Stronger. So Jace pulled the plug, told the doctors he was taking Barry home."

Bodey shook his head. "They tried to talk him out of it—told him that Barry's progress would be stunted for good. But Jace packed up his things and brought our little brother back to the ranch."

"Did that help?"

Bodey laughed. "No. He still flew into the rages, but now it was because his soup was too hot or his clothes were too scratchy. Looking back, I'd say we were partially to blame. We were still hovering over him, a bunch of dumb men who didn't know what to do with any kid, let alone one with medical issues. Then Jace got to the point where the ranch work was piling up and none of us could afford to be at the house night and day—and Barry was worse when we tried to hire someone to take care of him."

He grimaced. "One afternoon, Jace completely disappeared. I was only about nineteen at the time and I'd been left alone with Barry. He'd been pitching a royal fit for hours and hours and hours—to the point where I thought I'd lose my mind."

"You're exaggerating."

"Not by much." He grimaced. "I tell you, he screamed so loud, he was growing hoarse. It was enough to put me off having kids for the rest of my life. Then suddenly, I hear this rumble of an ATV, and when I go outside, I see that Jace has taken a gardening cart and welded a contraption together that would safely hold Barry's wheelchair. Without a word, he comes striding into the house, scoops Barry up— his screaming, writhing, pajama-clad body—dumps him in his wheelchair, then rolls him out into the cart. Then, just like Jace, all he says is: 'Somebody's got to get some work done today.' And he drives off with Barry."

"Then he calmed down."

Bodey laughed. "No. Not right away. Jace was repairing irrigation pipes on one of the pastures, so he left our little brother on the cart in the middle of a pasture full of mares with new foals. It didn't take Barry long to see how he was frightening the animals, especially the little colts and fillies. So within a few minutes, he got quiet. It took a while but some of the mares who knew him finally came close enough so he could pet them."

Bodey grinned. "By this time, Jace had caught on as well. He knew he could nag and beg and plead and order Barry to stop the noise but nothing would work unless Barry wanted to do it himself. Now, Jace isn't one for talking a whole lot, so we've learned that if he opens his mouth, you need to pay attention. In typical Jace fashion, as soon as he'd finished his work, he went back to Barry, looked him in the eye and said: 'You can fool me, you can fool Bodey, but you can't fool those horses. If you're tired of people treating you like a baby and wheeling you around in a chair, then those animals are your ticket to freedom. That means you're going to have to work hard so you can sling a saddle and get yourself onto the back of one of our ponies. Once up, you can go anywhere you want on this ranch. But these animals won't put up with any of your nonsense. Long as you behave, I'll bring you out to them any time I can until you can get out here yourself, but I won't have you riling up these new mamas, understand?'"

"Did it work?"

"Oh, yeah. Barry had been on a horse since he could sit up—had his own pony from the time he was three. But it wasn't the promise of getting around that got him out there. Like I said, a horse senses everything boiling inside of you, even when you try to hide it. But they're patient and they're kind, and they'll give you all the love and friendship you want as long as you give it back."

Bodey eyed her as if he'd said too much—and maybe that would have been the case an hour earlier. But as she stroked Willow's nose and scratched behind her twitching ears, she could feel the emotions that Bodey referred to. There was an unfathomable, unnamable sense of . . . *acceptance* radiating from the animal. And that sensation soothed parts of her soul that she'd thought she'd managed to bury.

Uncomfortable that Bodey might somehow sense her emotions, she asked, "How is your brother now?"

Bodey pushed away from the fence, grinning. "Wait until you see him. He's a firecracker. He still has some limitations—he'll always be a kid in some respects—but he doesn't let anything or anyone get in his way. He's got his first job this summer."

"On your ranch?"

"No, it's his first 'real' job, according to Barry. He's always helped where he could on the ranch, but this summer"— Bodey moved to a large plastic barrel and lifted the lid—"he's working as a camp counselor with the horse therapy ranch I told you about. They have two separate summer camps, one for kids with disabilities and one for kids with cancer. Barry helps them with the riding sessions."

He scooped what looked like dried oatmeal flakes into a bucket, then dumped it into a metal feeding trough hooked to the fence.

"Jace recently married. His new wife, Bronte, has two kids of her own, a teenager, Kari, and a girl who's barely turned eleven, Lily. Jace and Bronte didn't have a chance for much more than a weekend away when they married. Since Kari is working at the same therapy ranch as Barry, Lily stayed with her great-grandmother so that Jace and Bronte could take a three week trip to Europe as a belated honeymoon."

Three weeks. In Europe.

Beth couldn't even imagine what it would be like to take such a trip. Such thoughts were the stuff of dreams in her world. She doubted that she'd ever have the resources to even consider such a thing. But oh, how she'd love to be proven wrong.

"So who's watching your ranch?" she asked curiously.

Bodey shook his head. "That's the amazing thing. Jace has always had an iron control on the place, ever since he took over after my parents' deaths. Until Bronte came along, I don't think he slept a night away from the ranch since the accident."

He grabbed a pitchfork from where it had been impaled in a huge bale of hay, tore off a scoop, and dumped it into a rack above the trough. "But this summer, he decided that the hired men were trained well enough to take over and he ordered Elam and I to take a vacation as well. Jace said it was the only way he'd feel good enough about leaving for Europe. So Elam took P.D. up north to Yellowstone and circled down through Cheyenne for the shoot. And I"—he stabbed the pitchfork back into the hay—"went to pick up this little filly in Colorado Springs."

Sensing that it was time they headed back to the shoot, Beth offered a last caress to the animal. "'Bye, Willow." Then, she reluctantly backed away.

The horse bobbed its head as if offering its own farewell.

"Look, she's sad you're going," Bodey said as he took Beth's hand.

Beth glanced over her shoulder to see Willow hadn't moved.

"How can you tell?"

"Are you kidding? She has a trough full of grain. Normally, nothing would come between her and her dinner."

For some reason, the thought—no matter how farfetched—caused a warmth to settle in Beth's chest.

If only . . .

If only she could stay a little longer. If only she could bring her brother and sister to see this. If only . . .

No.

It was useless to dwell on the could've, would've, and should'ves of life. Beth's responsibilities might be hard right now. Really, really hard. But when she thought of the alternative . . .

"Hey," Bodey said softly, coming to a halt and forcing her to look up at him. Too late, she realized that moisture had begun to gather in her eyes and Bodey must have caught a glimpse of the sheen.

She blinked the telltale evidence away, hoping he would attribute it to allergies. But Bodey wasn't put off that easily.

Instead, he slipped his arms around her waist and drew her tightly against him.

Although she knew that she should resist—if only to offer a façade of strength and invincibility—she found she couldn't do it. Maybe it was as Bodey had said and Willow's gentle strength had stripped all pretense away. Or maybe, just maybe, she was tired. Tired of being alone, tired of being the strong one, tired of pushing her fears and worries to the side and ignoring the way they had begun to grow in size and intensity until she felt that she would be buried in an avalanche of despair.

Unbidden, her arms wrapped around Bodey's waist and she rested her cheek against his chest, absorbing the warmth of his body, the faint scents of laundry soap and Old Spice, the comforting *ba-thump* of his heart.

She knew that Bodey wasn't the answer to her problems. In a few days, he would be gone and she would still have the same troubles she had now. But right now, today, this moment, she would draw from his strength.

TEN

FOR the first time in his life, Bodey felt himself at a loss for words. Since meeting Beth, he'd grown used to her stubbornness and her stoic deadpan refusal to show her emotions. But this . . .

This was a single moment of unguarded honesty. A glimpse of need and fear unlike any that he'd ever witnessed before. And just as he'd begun to wrap his head around the emotions reflected starkly on Beth's features, she reached out to him.

She reached out to *him*.

"What's wrong?" Bodey murmured, tucking her more tightly in his arms. She was so tiny that, again, he had the sensation of her being like a bird, trembling and unsure.

She didn't answer. Not that he'd truly thought that she would. So he held her tightly, not knowing what else he could do.

Confused, he waited for her to burst into tears—wondering if he'd done or said something to offend her. But for the life of him, he'd thought she'd been having a good time. She'd bonded with Willow in an elemental way. Not that he was surprised by such a thing. He'd seen people take to animals and vice versa that quickly before. But this . . . this didn't seem to have anything to do with the time she'd spent with the horse.

Eventually, he realized that he wouldn't piece together the seeds of her mood unless she volunteered them herself. And since she didn't appear inclined to do so, he turned his attention to comforting her instead. He ran his palm up and down the delicate sweep of her spine, wondering again if she'd had training as a dancer. She moved elegantly, economically. And now that he held her, he could feel the evidence of strong, lithe muscles. There was a gracefulness to her frame that the exotic steampunk ensemble underscored. But for the first time, he damned the stricture of her corset and layers that covered her body. He wished he could see and feel more of her to confirm his suspicions.

But when she lifted her head, his thoughts scattered to the four winds. Rather than finding misery in her expression, he witnessed stark, uncensored need. It was there in the dark intensity of her eyes, in the way she gripped his arms. Her breathing was sharp and shallow, her body trembling in a way that had more to do with anticipation than with fear.

And in that moment, time hung suspended—as if warning him to tread carefully. Her vulnerability was a tangible thing, filling his chest with a strange aching need. It didn't seem to matter that he was breaking his own rules, that he was becoming more deeply involved with the kind of woman that he'd sworn he would never date.

As much as he might tell himself that he was making a mistake, that there was a very real danger of hurting this woman—or of being hurt himself—he couldn't deny that holding her like this felt oh, so right. So he grew still, curiously hesitant to disturb the moment, knowing that whatever happened next would cast the die. Either he would step away and keep things casual, or move closer and . . .

Conscious consideration scattered altogether and he reacted instinctively, knowing that any choice had been an illusion. He could no more step away from Beth Tivoli than stop breathing. And when she reached to grip his shirt, pulling herself up to meet him, he cursed himself for waiting this long.

Their lips met in a crush of need and stark unrelenting desire, and he found himself eager to explore everything about her—her taste, her scent. The willow slim line of her back. The sweet fullness of her breasts. But even as he tried to get closer, to imprint her body against his own, he moaned in frustration. She was so small, so slight, he couldn't quite . . .

Reacting instinctively, he scooped her up and strode blindly to his truck, setting her on the flatbed platform. Her eyes widened in surprise but immediately she spread her legs open so that he could stand between them. Finally, finally, they were chest to chest, their lips about even, their hands able to move more freely.

He gasped as she began wrenching at the buttons of his shirt, unfastening them nearly to his navel so that she could reach inside, spreading her fingers wide and palming his abs, his ribs, moving up, up, until she cupped his pecs, her thumbs sweeping across the sensitive beads of his nipples.

To his amazement, she smiled against him, and for an instant, he drew back enough to see that her eyes sparkled with joy and . . . and *hunger*. A shimmering aching need so raw and uncensored that he could scarcely believe that it was aimed at him. Then, she raked her nail across his nipple and he had no wherewithal to think at all. He swooped in to taste her, again and again. He wasn't entirely gentle—and neither was she, nipping and biting, wrenching free to trail hungry kisses across his jaw, his neck, leaving a trail of love bites in her wake. And when she continued to move lower, lower, until her tongue could circle his nipple, he almost came unglued.

Dear sweet heaven above. He wasn't an innocent man. He'd been a hell-raiser for as long as he could remember—lost his virginity at sixteen. He would have thought that there wasn't a whole lot left that he hadn't tried at least once. But this woman made him feel as if he were as new and untried as an unbroken colt. A single lick was enough to send blood pounding to his groin with a ferocity that he hadn't experienced in a very long time. And her hands . . .

Holy, holy, hell. Her hands made him hot and cold, leaving a rash of gooseflesh in their wake.

Unwilling to let her be the only one to taste and explore, he bent to kiss the elegant arc of her neck. When she gasped, he realized that she was even more responsive than he had at first supposed. He glanced up to find that her eyes had slammed shut. Her chest heaved in her efforts to draw breath in her tightly laced corset.

Then she was thrusting her fingers through his hair, drawing him down for another kiss, another melding of tongues and minds and emotions so powerful that he feared all common sense would be swept away.

It was only that tiny shred of awareness for his surroundings that finally prompted him to pull back.

They were both breathing hard. He could see where her cheeks were red and slightly abraded, even though he'd shaved well that morning. And her mouth . . .

Her mouth looked well and thoroughly kissed.

He didn't know what to say, didn't know how to explain himself. He wasn't even sure why he'd stopped. With any other woman, he would have continued on, bringing this frantic embrace to a happy conclusion. And he could see in her eyes that she was confused that he hadn't done so, that she would have been willing to throw caution to the wind in favor of drowning herself in the passion that had flared up between them.

But even though he knew she would be a more than willing participant if they made love, here, in the grass, on the truck, or anywhere else for that matter . . .

He couldn't do it.

Not like this.

So he drew her tightly into his arms, whispering, "Not yet. Not yet."

He felt her clutch at his shoulders as if he were a life raft and she were caught in a raging flash flood that would swallow her whole. But he didn't relent.

Not like this.

Not hurried and quick in the dust and the dirt. Not knowing that people were waiting for her to return to work.

Not for their first time together.

So he wrapped his arms more tightly, rocking slightly from side to side as if she were in need of comforting, until the trembling of her body stilled and she grew quiet in his arms.

It was some time later when he drew back and murmured against her ear. "We'd better get back. Helen will be wondering what I've done with you."

She nodded against him, and again, he found himself wondering why this woman was so different. It wasn't only that she'd been slow to warm up to him or that there was an innocent air about her. Hell, if nothing else, the last few minutes had been evidence that she wasn't completely a novice at seduction.

But there was still something that made him hold back, that warned him to take things slowly, cautiously. Even though he wasn't sure why his gut insisted such a thing wasn't merely important, it was crucial.

Kissing her one last time on the top of her head, he stepped away, helping her to jump to the ground and fix her skirts. Then he ushered her to the passenger door. "Lift up the console in the middle. There's a seatbelt underneath. That way you can sit next to me."

She didn't demur. By the time he settled into his own place, she had her belt clicked so that as soon as he started the engine and turned the truck around, she could settle beneath his arm.

As he pulled her more tightly against him, he marveled again that, despite their disparate heights, she fit against him as if she'd been tailor made for his frame. But what struck him even more, was that after the storm of emotions she'd endured, she appeared relaxed. Even . . . happy.

Had it only been a couple of days since he hadn't even been able to get her to smile?

"What's happening here?" Beth whispered.

He didn't pretend not to know what she was talking about. This . . . relationship they'd started was moving at warp speed.

"I don't know," he said honestly. His hand moved up and down her arm.

She was quiet again and he figured he could guess her thoughts—that neither of them was in a place where they could truly pursue this attraction. Hell on Wheels was a bit of a fantasy—one which could have been the impetus for this attraction. Would the excitement they feel fade as soon as the Wild West tent city disappeared into the dust? And if what they felt did survive, in a few days Bodey would be returning to another state and Beth . . .

He didn't know what Beth would be doing. Truth be told, he didn't know much about her at all. He'd only learned her last name today. And he still didn't know why she'd lied about staying at the inn. Was it a matter of pride? Or something darker?

Hell. In the past, Bodey hadn't invested a whole lot of thought in his relationships. He'd followed his gut—or, more to the point, his dick. But with Beth, he found himself proceeding more carefully.

Why?

He wasn't exactly sure.

But he also found that he didn't want to dwell on his doubts. For the first time, he was willing to fly by the seat of his pants.

"Whatever is going on," he murmured, "I refuse to worry about it."

She offered a self-deprecating laugh. "You're talking to the queen of worriers."

He detected a darker note to her voice and wondered briefly if her response had anything to do with the rundown motel. The male who'd welcomed her inside.

"What exactly do you have to worry about?"

He felt her sigh against him.

"Everything."

"Such as?"

She didn't immediately answer but he could feel the tension seeping back into her muscles and he couldn't let that happen. Not when only minutes before she'd been boneless in his arms.

"You're not a closet bigamist are you?" he asked teasingly.

"Wha—No!"

"A collector of cats?"

"No. I have a dog. A single dog. And she wasn't my choice, actually. She's a stray that refused to leave."

"Ah, now we're getting somewhere. I've been thinking about getting a dog myself," Bodey admitted. "We've had lots of them on the ranch through the years and they're actually pretty handy."

"And any man worth his salt needs a dog."

He looked down again, seeing only a glint of humor, so he grinned.

"That's right. I've been checking into a few of the breeds, trying to narrow down what I want. Since I'm grounded for the summer, I don't have to worry so much about trying to train a puppy while I'm on the cow cutting circuit."

"What *is* cow cutting?" Beth asked.

"It's a sport similar to something you might see in a rodeo. But in this particular competition both the rider *and* his horse are being judged. The object of the event is to separate a cow from a herd and keep it on its own for a certain length of time. At one point, the rider loosens the reins—it's called 'putting his hands down'—and the horse has to take over."

"Is it dangerous?"

Bodey laughed. "Not usually. Despite what Helen's told you, I don't have a death wish or anything. In cow cutting, you usually only have a few minutes to show off your and your horse's skills. The horse moves quickly, changes directions, dodges from side to side, so you have to be ready for anything. But the sport isn't as prone to injury as rodeo riders." He nudged her. "How about you? Are you into anything dangerous? Martial arts? Cage fighting?"

He saw her lips twitch.

"Hardly."

"You can sure as hell shoot. Is it to keep the men away?"

"No, the men usually stay away all on their own."

The remark held a rueful note, so he leaned over to kiss the top of her head.

"I find that hard to believe."

"Let's say my life is . . . complex."

"In what way?"

There was a beat of silence, then, "I've had to move a lot lately."

The answer was vague and telling at the same time. Bodey wanted to probe for more information, but contrary to his nature, he tamped down his curiosity, sensing she wasn't ready to share anything too personal yet. But that was okay. Especially, since she wouldn't say much at all to him only yesterday.

"Ah. I can relate to that. Being on the road has its challenges." He paused a moment to pass a slow moving tractor, then said, "But for me, that's normal. For me, being home has been more . . . 'complex.'"

"How?"

This time, it was his turn to confess something personal—and he realized that it was easy to share the happy stuff. Not so easy to let someone in on the heavier bits. But he felt compelled to give her whatever she asked.

"There's been a lot of . . . changes around the ranch in the last few years. Most of it has been great. But . . ."

He could only meet her gaze for a moment before he forced himself to return his attention to the road. It was easier to be honest if he didn't meet those dark blue eyes. He hadn't even said anything, damnit, and she was already looking at him with a wealth of understanding.

"Like I said, I've got nothing to complain about. Elam? He's been through hell and back. He was in Afghanistan when his first wife died. Soon after, he was injured. Honestly, until P.D. burst into his life, I didn't think we'd have him around for much longer. He was so angry and . . .

grief-stricken. P.D. literally brought him back from the brink. But until P.D. and Elam became an item, she was probably the best friend I ever had—still is, of course, but she's busy and . . ."

"And being her brother-in-law changes things."

"A little. Yeah."

"Then there's Jace's wife, Bronte." Bodey couldn't help a smile. "She's amazing. Since our parents' death, Jace has done so much to keep this family and the ranch together. But I think he was burning out. Bronte helped him find the joy in his life again. And she had kids, which ended up being really great for Barry. As far as he's concerned, they're his sisters."

He paused, knowing that this was the tricky part. With all the good that had come from such additions to the family, how could he complain without coming off like a total jerk?

But it was Beth who explained it all with, "It's tough when everything around you changes and you're left wondering how you fit in."

Bodey felt a rush of relief at her words—because she'd said them before he could force them out of his mouth. And there was a wistfulness to her tone that told him that she not only understood, but she'd experienced something similar.

"Yeah. Yeah, that's it. I mean, I'm not complaining. All these new additions have been great, and . . . I want to give my brothers some space with their new families . . ."

"But you were used to having them all to yourself."

He nodded. "But that's not the crux of it. Some time ago, Elam built a cabin for P.D. and him on the hillside. And once Jace and Bronte married, they moved into the family home that we call the Big House. Taggarts have lived there for generations."

He glanced down in time to see her wince.

"Yikes," she murmured. "That had to be awkward. Sharing a house with a newlywed couple—and didn't you say she had kids as well? After living in an all-male, all-sibling household, you must have felt like you had to be on your guard all the time. You wouldn't dare walk into a room unannounced or wander around the house in your underwear."

Bodey couldn't account for the relief that someone—finally—understood his reasons for moving out—and didn't think he was a jerk for doing it so abruptly. "Yeah. I didn't want to give the impression that I found them a bother. I was afraid I'd hurt Bronte's feelings—or she'd think that she and her kids had chased me out somehow."

"Especially since it was your childhood home."

"Exactly. But, honestly, it wasn't a big deal. I probably spend as much time in the trailer as the Big House during a normal year. There's a small cabin on our ranch that was built by one of the original Taggarts. It didn't take much to fix it up so it was livable. I had to add a bathroom onto the back. I still have the plumbing to connect, but I've been able to use my trailer for showering and such."

"But now, instead of being around your brothers all day, you're alone a lot of the time."

"Like I said, I'm not complaining. I kind of like having my own place."

"But it's different," she supplied.

"And then when you factor in the injuries, the down time, and being grounded from all my competitions . . ."

"You don't know who you are any more."

Her voice held such a note of empathy that he sensed he'd touched on something that echoed her own "complex" life.

A crease appeared between her brows and she looked down at the hands she'd locked together in her lap.

"So with all that, it's crazy to add anything more to the mix," she murmured.

He knew what she was thinking. That the attraction they'd begun to explore would only make things worse.

"Actually . . ." he reached for one of her hands, bringing it up so that he could brush his lips against her silken skin. "For the first time, something feels right for a change."

She met his gaze, clearly unsure.

"Really?"

"Really."

When he lowered her hand again, he set it on his thigh—and thank you, *thank you*, she didn't resist. In fact, her fingers curled toward his inside leg, instantly sending his thoughts skittering away from his own self-indulgent problems to the woman beside him.

She melted into him, conveying that—for once—he'd said something right. And that was a miracle. Normally, he sucked at expressing himself without catching a major case of foot in mouth disease.

Again, he bent to brush his lips over the top of her head, absorbing the silky texture of her hair and the faint clean, crisp scent of her shampoo. He loved that about her. After so much time with women who fit the Rodeo Queen and pinup mold, with lacquered curls and tons of makeup, he loved the way that Beth's beauty was so . . . honest. Yeah, she had an edge to her look. But even the blue hair was beginning to grow on him.

He smiled when she melted into him, her fingers making idle circles on his leg. Her body grew relaxed, nearly boneless.

It was only when they were driving through town, passing the spot where only the night before she'd turned on her bicycle to ride to that horrible motel, that he felt the tension return to her frame. As Bodey eased to a stop at a red light, her gaze shifted and she stiffened. But when he glanced down to see if she was looking in the direction of the run-down establishment, he was surprised to see that she wasn't even facing that direction. Instead, she watched intently as a battered red pickup made a right hand turn at the opposite corner, then sped away.

For a moment, her attention was so intent that Bodey wondered if she'd recognized the driver. But the vehicle was gone before Bodey could get a good look.

"Someone you know?" he asked.

She answered quickly. Too quickly.

"No. I don't think so."

"You're sure? We could try to catch up to them if you want."

"No! No, it's nothing."

She settled back against him, her hand resting on his thigh once again.

But the tension had returned to her frame.

THE moment Bodey's truck rolled to a stop behind the tent, Beth unclicked her seatbelt and muttered a quick, "Thank you." Then she opened the door and fled toward the canvas structure.

Away from the strength of Bodey's arms.

The promise of his smile.

And the fear of what would happen if she confided in him.

She was still a few feet from the rear entrance when she heard, "Hey!"

Knowing she'd lost her chance to escape, she turned to find that Bodey hadn't followed her, merely rolled his window down.

"Did I say or do something to tick you off?"

She bit her lip. Then, knowing that she couldn't shout at him from several feet away, she reluctantly returned to the truck.

"No. I'm not mad."

He had one arm draped over his window and she was struck again by the ropy musculature of his forearms, the broad hands, the long slender fingers. If the simple sight of his bare arm could do that much to her, how much more of an effect would there be if she were to see his whole body?

Lordy, lordy.

She wasn't in denial so completely that she couldn't admit to herself that if Bodey hadn't stopped things between them, she would probably still be lying in his arms.

"Look—" he swept his hat off his head and threw it onto the seat beside him. He seemed to choose his words carefully, then said, "I don't know what's going on here, okay? I know that Helen's probably told you that I've . . . well, I've entertained a woman or two."

Beth couldn't help the snort that burst from her throat.

Bodey offered a rueful grin. "All right, I'll fess up. I don't have much of a track record for long term relationships."

She didn't know why he felt the need to tell her that since anything going on between them would be over in a matter of days.

"All I can say is that this . . . whatever this is . . ." His hand waved between them. "It feels different, okay? It feels good. So none of my usual moves seem . . . right." He grimaced, rubbing at a crease between his brows. "Wow, that sounds cold, doesn't it? What I mean is—"

"I know what you mean," she interrupted, hugging her arms. "I simply don't know how anything can come of this. In a couple of days, you'll be gone."

He rested his thumb against his upper lip. "Logically, I know that. Then I keep thinking I could hang around a little longer."

She shook her head. "It would only prolong the inevitable."

"Maybe. Just don't . . . don't shut me out, okay?"

Beth knew she was making a mistake, knew she should cut things off now while neither of them was invested in anything more than an afternoon of fun. But she nodded instead. "Okay." She hitched her thumb toward the tent. "I've got to get back to work."

"Maybe I'll see you later tonight?"

Say no. Say no.

Say no.

"Okay."

He waved to her then, and knowing that she'd already said too much, she turned and hurried into the canvas structure.

ELEVEN

———•◦•———

O NCE inside the tent, Beth quickly took stock of the
interior. Seeing that Helen was busy with the only customer, she hurriedly took her phone from her pocket and
dialed her brother's number.

Although most of the luxuries she'd once enjoyed had
been abandoned, the phones weren't among them. It had
been imperative that she be able to contact her siblings at a
moment's notice.

Eric answered on the first ring. "What's wrong?"

"Nothing, I . . ." She forced herself to take a deep breath
so that she wouldn't sound as panicked as she felt. "I wanted
to check in. Is everything okay?"

"Mostly. I think the swamp cooler's dead. It started making a rattling noise, then stopped blowing air at all, so
I turned it off. It's hot in here. Really hot. Dolly wants to go
to the park and she wasn't happy when I told her she'd have
to wait until you came home. She started crying. I tried
putting cartoons on but it didn't help. She cried herself to
sleep."

Guilt twisted in her gut like a serpent, reminding Beth

that she was on borrowed time. If something didn't change soon . . .

She couldn't think about that now. Not now.

"Tell her that when I get home, we'll . . . we'll go for some ice cream," Beth said, saying the first thing that came to her head.

There was a long silence, then Eric asked, "Bethy, are you sure we're doing the right thing? Maybe Dolly and me—"

"Don't you say it, Eric Tivoli. We've hit a rough patch, that's all. It won't be like this forever."

The silence told her more than words ever could that Eric was beginning to doubt her. Squeezing her eyes closed, she prayed that she was doing the right thing.

"Eric, have you seen that red truck again?"

"Yeah, a couple of times. Why?"

"No reason. I merely wondered. Does it stop or slow down at all?"

"No, but I've been careful to make sure I stand behind the curtain."

"Good. Good." Knowing that if she said anything more, she would put Eric even more on guard, she said, "If it comes any closer, text me, okay?"

Again, there was a long pause, then, "Bethy? Do you think it's someone from the Farm?"

She forced herself to laugh, but the sound sounded false even to her own ears, so she decided she wasn't doing any favors by prevaricating. "Just have the bags ready, Eric. If you see something, hear something, bug on out of there. Once you're safe, you can call me and I'll come get you."

"You need to be careful, too, Bethy. If anyone is likely to be recognized, it's you."

"I'll be fine. Trust me, this isn't the kind of event that anyone from the Farm is likely to attend."

But as she ended the call, she no longer felt so sure.

UNLIKE that morning, the afternoon proved to be slow for customers. Ominous clouds began to pile up on the horizon and the heat was augmented with a sticky humidity. After tidying up the jewelry cases and the changing area, Beth joined Helen and a pretty pregnant woman on the chairs under the awning.

"Beth, this is P.D. Taggart, Bodey Taggart's sister-in-law."

Beth shook hands with the woman, remembering that Bodey considered her a close friend and an asset to the family. She could see why. P.D. fairly glowed with happiness—and Beth suspected that it wasn't only her pregnancy that was its cause. If Elam was anything like Bodey. . . .

Don't think about that now. Not when you know, deep down, what you have with Bodey will be over in a heartbeat.

The thought was more painful that she could have ever imagined. Regret lodged in her chest like a lead weight and her throat grew tight. Since both P.D. and Helen had borrowed elaborate lacy fans from the counter behind them, Beth did the same, hoping that she could create enough of a breeze that she could breathe. As much as she loved her steampunk corset, it was quickly becoming a silken prison.

"I haven't seen you working with Helen before," P.D. remarked.

Beth shook her head, but it was Helen who supplied, "Ellie had to head back to Bliss before we even set up. Her sister went into premature labor, and with four little ones at home, she and her husband needed Ellie's help. Beth, here, answered an ad I put up at one of the convenience stores in town, and she's been a godsend." She snapped her fan shut and pointed it in Beth's direction. "If I could get her to move to Bliss, I'd hire her full time and take her on all the shoots."

Move to Bliss.

The words stirred something within Beth, but she pushed them away. As much as she would love to follow Helen to Utah, to have a job with a woman she already admired, to live near Bodey, see the ranch he'd spoken of . . .

The idea was a fantasy. A fairy tale. One of those pipe

dreams that you know, deep in your heart, will never come true.

Besides, she and her siblings had made it this far by keeping to themselves. If they made attachments, the likelihood of their being discovered would multiply.

"How about it, Beth? Would you consider coming to Bliss?"

There was enough of a teasing note to Helen's tone that Beth was able to answer with her own less than convincing, "You name the day."

After the brief exchange, the heat sapped them all of what little energy remained, and they slipped into silence, until P.D. sighed and set her fan back on the counter. "I think I'm cooked on both sides. I'm going to head back to the trailer, strip to my underwear, and turn the AC up to high."

And didn't that sound like heaven?

P.D. snorted, then started to laugh. "That is if someone can help me out of this chair."

Beth jumped to her feet and extended a hand. After pulling P.D. from the camp chair, she asked, "When are you due?"

"The first part of November." P.D. smiled and a gentle light warmed her blue eyes. "Another Taggart boy, I'm afraid."

"Do you have a name?"

"Not yet. We've got a few rattling around but I have a feeling we'll need to meet the little fellow before we come up with something definite." She rolled her eyes. "So far, the only one to stick is completely inappropriate."

Helen's brows rose. "Oh?"

P.D. laughed. "Barry suggested Antman because Elam explained that the baby was still really small. Since then, whenever he talks to the baby, that's what Elam has been calling him."

An image flashed through Beth's head of a man looking very much like Bodey speaking softly against the mound of P.D.'s belly. And in an instant, the mental picture morphed into Bodey himself. And her.

No.

A pang centered in her breast and she pushed it away.

This was why she had insisted on no entanglements. It took her head out of the game and diverted her attention. It made her start daydreaming and wishing and thinking of things that could never happen. *Would* never happen.

Geez, she'd only known Bodey for a matter of days and already she was mooning around like a lovesick calf. She'd be a fool to think that this was anything more than a quick fling. And she needed to remember that she'd probably be experiencing the same emotions if any other man here at Hell on Wheels had given her a few moments of attention. It had been so long since she'd had anyone even take a second look at her, let alone take the time to batter down her defenses.

Once P.D. had left, Beth scanned the crowd that milled past the tent. Now that the competition had begun in earnest, there were lots of spectators—some in costume, some in regular clothes. There were children and women pushing strollers and dozens of little dogs dressed up in various versions of cowboy attire. And there were men. Lots and lots of men. Men dressed as preachers and gunslingers and Civil War veterans. There were family men with beer belly paunches and National Guard medics with tightly honed bodies. Any one of them could have inspired the same butterflies in her stomach as Bodey Taggart if she'd given them the slightest bit of encouragement.

Any.

One.

Of.

Them.

A man dressed in boots, a ten-gallon hat, and a long canvas trench coat was making a beeline for the tent. He carried a stack of trousers in his arms that probably needed hemming. He had a nice enough face, looked to be about Bodey's age and height. Sizing him up in a glance, Beth decided to give her theory a try. If she smiled at him and he smiled back, she was sure that she would feel the same giddiness that Bodey inexplicably inspired.

"Helen, Helen!" he called out. "I need your help." He held up the pants. "Can I tempt you to do a rush job for me?"

This was it. Her chance to prove, once and for all, that Bodey Taggart had no real hold on her emotions.

"When do you need them, Slick?"

"What do you think?"

The man reached for his coat and whipped it open, revealing a bright red union suit. And nothing else.

Whatever "come-hither" maneuvers Beth had been about to employ vanished as she stared, open-mouthed, at the Victorian version of a flasher with his skinny body clad in saggy red drawers, ornately tooled boots, and too-large hat. But her shock quickly wore off beneath Helen's robust chuckle.

"Are you still doing that old gag?" Helen said, standing to take the proffered pants.

"It never gets old, Queenie. It never gets old."

As the two of them disappeared toward the back of the tent so Helen could take his measurements, Beth felt her bravado seep away like air in a pricked balloon. Because, like any other red-blooded female, she'd unconsciously taken a pretty good look at "Slick" in his droopy red drawers—and there hadn't been a whole lot left to the imagination. Other than being startled, then amused . . .

Beth had felt nothing.

Absolutely nothing.

Damn that Bodey Taggart. She was a goner.

BODEY was slouched in a camp chair under the awning of his trailer nursing a Pepsi and damning the fact that ache was forming behind his left eye again.

Hell.

He didn't have time to nurse a migraine, didn't have the energy. It was taking everything he had to curse the heat and the wind and the Wyoming weather while he watched a wall of storm clouds heading his way.

But even as that thought appeared, he pushed it aside. What was sucking up his energy was the inner battle he was fighting not to march down vendor's row and plant himself on a chair in Helen's tent.

Shit. He had to get a grip on himself.

Maybe Jace had been right, not so long ago, when he'd given Bodey a "come to Jesus" talk. Maybe by going from woman to woman, Bodey was slapping a Band-Aid on a bigger problem.

In the short time since Jace had known Bronte, Bodey had seen his brother's solemn, stoic features come alive. Always laid-back, slow to talk, slow to show emotion, Jace had been the one to step into the breach left by their parents' deaths and take over the bulk of the responsibilities. With Elam deployed so much, it had been Jace who'd assumed the business aspects of the ranch, Barry's care and rehabilitation, and all the day-to-day crap like shopping and cooking and laundry. Hell, he'd even managed to keep Bodey in line during his wilder years. He'd become so adept at hiding what must have been an enormous burden that Bodey had taken it for granted that his brother had always been stoic and sober.

Until Bronte had driven into town.

Bit by bit, Bodey had seen his brother transformed. And the change had been as dramatic as that made when P.D. had brought Elam out of his grief and misery.

Suddenly, Jace was taking time off and smiling like he knew some sort of guilty secret. Even more astoundingly, he'd returned to the art that he'd once loved so much—to the point that the ranch welding bay had pretty much become Jace's private studio because he kept hauling home scrap iron and bits of junk and fashioning them into these amazing, larger-than-life sculptures.

So one night, when Bodey had been nursing a bruised ego because his latest flame had decided that she and Bodey should "be friends," his brother had sized up the situation in a single glance and, rather than offering comfort, he'd said, "One of these days you're going to have to take a good hard look at what's really going on. Maybe it's not the women or your ability to stick things out. Maybe you're blindly slapping a bandage on a bigger problem that you still haven't figured out yet."

And Bodey had to concede that Jace might be right. But if he was, Bodey didn't have a clue what his "bigger problem" might be. He jumped from woman to woman, relationship to relationship, like he jumped from one venue of competition to the next. He couldn't explain it—and he sure as hell couldn't stop it. Sometimes it felt like something was eating him alive, pushing him to show he was better, faster, more popular. Even the need to prove he was equal to his brothers only satisfied part of the explanation—because there was no pressure on their part.

So what the hell was driving him so hard?

Hard enough that he'd consider breaking one of his cardinal rules.

Don't ever get involved with someone who's vulnerable.

Bodey took a quick swig of soda, then nearly choked to death when someone pounded him on the back. Coughing, he glanced up to find Elam grinning at him.

"I'll take that bet in crisp ten dollar bills," he said, sinking into the chair on Bodey's right.

Bodey's voice was rough from the sting of carbonation at the back of his throat when he offered, "I take it you had a good set of stages?"

Elam's dark eyes sparkled. "I had a perfect set of stages. No misses, great times," he paused and added with extra emphasis, "and no procedurals. Ha!"

Bodey grimaced. "I'll make it up tomorrow."

"Maybe. Maybe not." Elam slouched in the chair, lacing his fingers over his taut stomach. "So what's got you looking like someone kicked your puppy and deflated your basketball? Is it your terror at being beaten by your older brother?"

The words were offered in jest but Bodey didn't rise to the challenge as he usually would.

"Can I ask you something?"

Elam's eyes narrowed slightly. "Sure."

"Is there something wrong with me?"

That caused a bark of laughter but Elam's humor disappeared when he realized the question wasn't a joke.

"What do you mean?"

Bodey shifted in his seat, wondering how to put the roil of emotion he was feeling into words. "I don't know. Maybe having to slow down this summer has left me with too much time on my hands or . . . too much time to think. But . . ." He waved dismissively. "Never mind. I'm in a bad mood, I guess."

Elam squinted into the distance, regarding the encroaching clouds. But when he spoke, it wasn't about the weather.

"It's been a rough couple of months for you. Two concussions, health problems, and a complete disruption of your usual routine. Add to that the fact that your home life has shifted the last couple of years with Jace and I getting married and your move from the Big House to the Little House—a gallant gesture on your part, I might add."

Bodey grimaced. There was no way that he'd admit to Elam that his move from the huge ranch house he'd lived in all his life to the refurbished cabin hadn't been that much of a sacrifice. Besides the reasons he'd given to Beth, he'd considered it a matter of self-preservation so he wouldn't have to watch Jace and Bronte casting goo-goo eyes at each other across the table or snuggling up with one another on the couch.

But Elam wasn't finished.

"Seems to me, with all that upheaval, it wouldn't be unusual for a man to take stock of himself."

Bodey grimaced. "And find himself lacking."

"How so?"

"I don't know, I . . . sometimes I feel like I'm stuck in a rut, going round and round in circles, doing the same things, making the same mistakes."

He expected Elam to give him a list of those mistakes, even if he was only joking. But to his credit, Elam merely looked thoughtful.

"I've been there a time or two. Or three." He regarded the thunderheads again, but Bodey doubted his thoughts were on the weather. "Most times, I thought I was doing the right thing—and maybe I was. It usually took a kick in the pants or an unexpected gift to get my head up enough to see that I'd just been handed a way out of my misery."

Misery. Elam had suffered through the death of his first wife and injuries that had brought an end to his naval career. If anyone had suffered through that emotion, it was Bodey's eldest brother. But even as that thought surfaced, Bodey realized that it had been a while since Bodey could remember being happy. Sure, he'd had some great times . . . but happy? Satisfied, yes. Fulfilled, yes. But that deep-seated contentment that settled deep in your gut and gave you a reason to see everything shaded with its own special glow?

He couldn't remember feeling that way in a very long time. It was as if there were something hollow in his soul that he kept trying to fill up with mindless distractions, but as soon as he'd won a competition or reached another goal— or seduced another woman—it all drained away like sand in an hourglass.

"So how do you know when you've been offered a way out?"

A rueful bark of laughter escaped from deep in Elam's chest. "Sometimes you don't know. Sometimes it whacks you over the head like a two-by-four. Other times, it sneaks up behind you and you don't know what's going on until you realize that you're having fun again."

Fun.

Was that his problem? Had all his competing become a chore? Heaven only knew that he hadn't been having any fun for a long time. But then again, had it ever been "fun"? Or had it only been a diversion?

Maybe Beth had been right. He'd become an adrenaline junky, searching for the next rush, all the time forgetting the original purpose behind it.

"So was P.D. your gift?" he asked quietly.

"You know it."

"Did she sneak up on you or hit you like a two-by-four?"

Elam laughed. "She was a bit of both. Still is. Every day

she challenges me to get out of my rut and try something new. Not for me, but for her. There's nothing I wouldn't do to make her smile."

There's nothing I wouldn't do to make her smile.

Was that the litmus test? Because Bodey had done everything he could think of to make Beth smile, and once he'd succeeded, he'd wanted to make it happen again and again.

Elam slapped Bodey on the back again and pushed himself to his feet. "Just keep your eyes open, little brother. Sometimes the things we think are impossible are the ones that are meant to be."

THUNDER rumbled ominously overhead and Beth took a moment from straightening the displays to peer outside, frowning.

Huge black clouds had shut out the sunshine, forming an artificial dusk. In less than an hour, the sultry breeze which had done little to alleviate the heat had grown stronger, so that now, it kicked at the sides of the tent and tore at the canvas awning.

Except for the competitors on the range, most of the traffic on vendors' row had dried up as people returned to their trailers or took shelter in the event tent near the food booths.

Beth took her phone out of her pocket and glanced at the time. With the sudden darkness of the skies, she'd been sure that it was getting late, but it wasn't even five yet. There had been no unusual texts from Eric—which was a good sign. Merely cryptic messages every other hour.

Fine.

Hot, but fine.

Really hot, but fine.

Each time Beth had grown nervous and antsy and texted him outside their usual arrangement, he'd been a little more expansive: Dolly was in a better mood since her nap; their rooms were cooling down now that the storm clouds had rolled in; they'd finished up the last of the chocolate cake.

Beth, on the other hand, was in agony. Every instinct screamed at her to get back to their rooms, pack up their bags, and get the hell out of Cheyenne.

But she wasn't quite sure what she would be running from anymore. The need to keep hidden, or the need to outrace her tumultuous emotions.

A clap of thunder made her jump, the sound coming from right outside the tent. She looked up in time to see the competitors at the stage opposite whipping out rain ponchos and umbrellas as a flash of lightning and another deafening rumble ripped the clouds open.

In an instant, a deluge of water came rushing down, the ferocity of the storm like nothing that Beth had ever seen before. A solid sheet seemed to roar from above, even as the wind grew worse, lashing the rain against the canvas walls. The drumming moisture became nearly deafening. To her horror, Beth could see that the gusts were driving through the front opening, beginning to soak the first few racks of clothing.

Beth was at a momentary loss for what to do. Helen and Syd had taken the motor home into town, saying something about gray water levels and emptying the tank. Since Beth hadn't had a clue what they were talking about, she'd merely nodded. But now, she realized she was going to have to make some decisions on her own.

Running to the front, she hauled Virgil inside, tugging with all her might when the sculpture proved to be heavier than she'd imagined. She gathered up the folding chairs and set them in the center aisle. Then, braving the weather, she stepped outside and began untying the canvas strips that held the awning in place.

By the time she'd finished the first side, she was soaked to the bone and shivering. The flap she'd freed whipped and snapped in the wind as she rushed to the second side. But she'd only gone halfway when she felt something strike her back, her arm. Looking up, she realized that the rain was swiftly turning to hail.

Hunching her shoulders as the stinging balls of ice rushed to earth, she finally managed to get the last strip free— which meant that, because the tent had been built to mimic those found in the Old West, there were no zippers to seal her in tight, only another series of ties.

Numbly, she set to her task, her fingers trembling with cold as the temperatures dropped as suddenly as the hail. She'd managed to tie up one side when the hail finally stopped. But what she'd thought was a break in the storm was only a momentary lull. The rain came down again, harder and faster than before, until the ruts in front of the tent became rivulets, then mini-streams that rushed past in their efforts to cause more mayhem. The wind whipped against the canvas, causing the large center poles to shimmy and sway.

Just when she'd begun to fear that the rain and the wind would tear the tent ropes free, the corner of the tent which had been roped off as a changing room collapsed—proving that her suspicions weren't so far-fetched.

Dear sweet heaven above, what am I going to do if the whole tent falls down around me?

The center pole began creaking, moving from side to side, testing its boundaries now that one of its supports had come loose—and not knowing what else to do, Beth ran to steady it. But as she fought to keep it upright, she could feel the true power of the storm and knew it was only a matter of time.

Closing her eyes, she prayed that Helen and Syd would return—or the storm would blow itself out. But with the half open flap still snapping in the wind and letting in bursts of rain, she feared that neither would happen in time. Either the tent would fall down, ruining Helen's stock or . . .

Or I'm going to be blown clear to Oz.

For a moment, with her lashes squinched shut and the pounding of the rain on the canvas, she thought she heard her name being called—causing her to issue a bark of laughter that bordered on being hysterical. But when she heard it again, she opened her eyes.

"Beth!"

The tent flap lifted, and for the life of her, she thought she was hallucinating. How else could she account for the huge shape that loomed in front of her, one that was so out of time and date that she had to blink to convince herself that she was focusing on something that was really there? A man straight out of the Wild West in boots, a gunslinger canvas duster, and a black hat peered at her from under the flap. Then, a burst of lightning lit up his features.

TWELVE

———◆———

"BODEY!"

More than anything, she wanted to rush to him and the strength he represented, but she didn't dare let go of the pole.

He held up a hand in warning. "Stay there! I'll tighten the rigging and reset any pegs that have come loose."

Lightning flashed again and he was gone, making her wonder if he'd ever been there at all. But then she began to hear the sharp *ping, ping* of a hammer striking metal. The noise worked its way around the tent, the collapsed corner bloomed back into place, and bit by bit the center pole grew steadier so that finally she could release it altogether.

Resting her hands on her hips, she fought to get air in her lungs.

The flap lifted again and Bodey stepped inside. Water ran from the brim of his hat, down the canvas duster and into a puddle at his feet. But she'd never seen such a wonderful sight.

"Do things feel steadier?"

Still catching her breath, she nodded.

Bodey quickly tied up the last flap, then tore the hat from his head, swiping the moisture beading his face.

"You all right?"

"Y-yes, I—" But she couldn't catch her breath.

Swearing softly, Bodey strode forward, tearing off the leather work gloves he wore. After shoving them in the deep pockets of his duster, he reached toward her.

"Come here."

Quickly, deftly, he unbuckled the fasteners on her corset, then unhooked the busk. Then wonderfully, miraculously, she was able to take a deep gulp of air.

"Better?"

"Uh-huh."

She didn't need to say anything more. Without another word, he unbuttoned his duster, then pulled her tightly against the warmth of his chest before wrapping her up again.

"You nearly blew away."

"I know!" She laughed.

If Bodey hadn't come when he had, the tent and all of Helen's beautiful things could have been ruined. But even as she opened her mouth to thank him, she found him watching her with such a strange expression that the words died. Instinctively, she wiped her face, then pushed her wet hair out of her eyes, realizing that she must look like a cat pulled out of a well. "What's wrong?"

He shook his head. "Not a damned thing. I was wondering . . ."

He took so long to finish that she finally prompted, "What?"

"I was wondering if you were a gift or a two-by-four."

Huh?

Beth opened her mouth to ask him what he meant, but she wasn't given a chance. Instead, he swooped down for a kiss, and the minute their lips met, every thought, every warning, every reason she'd had for not getting involved with this man exploded like a flash of lightning. Then, she was lifting on tiptoe, matching his ardor with her own. Her arms wrapped around his neck, and just like that, he was lifting her against him so that they were eye to eye, mouth to mouth.

Lordy, lordy, what this man did to her. He sucked, he nibbled, he explored in a way that filled her body with heat and an energy to rival the storm outside. Even through her damp clothing, she could feel his warmth seeping into her, chasing away the chills. And his hands . . . they were strong and secure, broad, hot against her waist, making her believe that he could hold her this way, hour upon hour, and never grow tired.

No, no, no! She couldn't fall for him. She mustn't!

But deep down, she knew it was already too late. Somehow, in only a few days, Bodey had stormed through defenses that had been years in the making. He'd stripped her of her usual reticence and reserve and left her wanting him more than she would ever have thought possible.

Even though it couldn't last.

And she knew it couldn't last.

When she finally managed to tear free, they were both panting. But as she looked up into his eyes—those eyes with their shards of green and blue and brown—she realized that she wasn't the only one perplexed by the strength of the emotions raging through them.

"What are you doing to me?"

The words were low and deep and echoed the uncertainty that she herself was feeling. Not knowing how to answer that question, she merely shook her head.

"This isn't how it's supposed to be," he continued.

Her brows creased. "How what is supposed to be?"

"When I meet someone that I'm . . . well, I'm interested in . . . I like to take things slow and easy." He set her down so that his palm could cup her face. "But this . . . this is like a wildfire."

Again, not knowing how to respond, she nodded.

"Surely, anything that rages so white-hot from the beginning is bound to burn itself out just as quickly."

The thought hurt, but she forced herself to whisper, "Yes. Probably so."

His brow creased and his expression became fierce. "But I don't want it to end at all."

The words brought equal measures of joy and sorrow.

"It has to end," she reminded him.

"Why?" The set of his jaw grew stubborn.

"We don't even live in the same state, for one thing."

We don't live in the same world, the same universe.

"But—"

Although it was one of the hardest things she had to do, she placed a finger against his lips. "Shh." She drew him down to replace her lips with her finger. "Shh."

Then, she was in his arms again, swept up in the magic of his embrace. Even though she knew it would have to end soon. She allowed the last barriers to her defenses to fall, knowing that it was useless to try to keep this man out of her heart. Like he'd said, what was going on between them was a wildfire of emotion and sensation, sweeping over her with a power and heat that she could no longer resist. And in the wake of its destruction came new sensations, fragile green shoots of hope that reached out, seeking the warmth that he offered.

She didn't know how, she didn't know why, but Bodey Taggart made her feel safe. And she hadn't felt that way in a very long time.

Maybe it was the strength of his arms as they drew her against him. Or the rock hard planes of his body. Maybe it was the driving purpose of his lips, or the wave of passion that plundered through her veins. Or maybe, it was the way, when he lifted his head ever so slightly, that he regarded her with such a wealth of wonder and tenderness, that the breath was literally stolen from her body.

No . . . no . . .

If there was one thing that she wouldn't be able to defend herself against, it was that unguarded moment. An instant when she wasn't a sister or a protector, an employee or an outcast. For several heart-pounding seconds, she could see herself reflected in his eyes as a woman.

A wonder.

A treasure.

Unbidden, her throat tightened and tears prickled. But she pushed them away, grasping Bodey even tighter, straining for his kiss, trying with all her might to block out the inevitable wave of despair.

Because nothing could ever come of her time with Bodey. To think that anything ever could would lead to more despair. For all intents and purposes, she was a woman on the run and Bodey would never be safe as long as he was with her. And with her siblings needing every ounce of her concentration, she couldn't allow herself to be swept away into this wave of madness.

Even if being in Bodey's arms felt like the closest thing to salvation that she'd experienced in a very long time.

He must have sensed something was wrong, because Bodey drew back far enough to search her features.

"What's wrong?"

She shook her head, knowing that there was no way that she could put her fears into words even if she could safely do so.

"You're trembling," he said, pulling her even more tightly against him.

Her arms wound around his back and she pressed her ear to the center of his chest. She could hear the rapid *ba-thump* of his heart and the strident rasp of his breath. And she marveled at the fact that she had done that to him.

She had done that to him.

"Bethy? What's wrong?"

Bethy. Her siblings called her that sometimes, but the nickname sounded so much sweeter coming from Bodey.

"I'm afraid," she whispered, the words slipping free before she could stop them. But even though she damned herself for uttering them aloud, she couldn't retrieve them.

Bodey's arms tightened around her. The heat of his body chased away some of the chill which had settled into her bones long before the storm.

"Why are you afraid? Is it the storm?"

She reluctantly shook her head, knowing that the storm trying to tear at the canvas was nothing compared to the tempest of emotion buffeting her from within.

"I'm afraid of . . . of *this* . . . of what I'm feeling."

She squeezed her eyes shut, fearful of saying too much. But even more worried of saying too little.

She felt him bend over her, his lips pressing against the top of her head.

"You don't have to be afraid," he murmured.

But she did. There were bad people out in the world. Bad men. And some of them were looking for her and her siblings. And if those people found them . . . Beth wouldn't merely lose contact with what was left of her family. She would be putting them in danger.

And she would never be able to live with herself if something happened to them.

You need help. You can't do this on your own anymore.

But even as Beth absorbed the strength of the arms that surrounded her, she shied away from her own thoughts.

Ask Bodey for help? Out of the blue? First of all, she didn't know if she could even trust the man. She'd known him for such a short time. How could she even think of confiding in him? She'd survived this long by keeping her problems to herself.

But as he rocked her softly from side to side, the need to unburden her fears and allow someone else to share her worries was almost overwhelming.

"Bethy? What's the matter?"

Too late, she realized that she'd begun to tremble. And this time, it wasn't from the cold, but the way her heart warred with her head.

You can trust him.

No. You can't trust anyone.

BODEY felt a shift in the tension that gripped Beth. Somehow, things had altered between them—from passion, to tenderness, to aching vulnerability. He didn't completely understand what was happening. He only knew that Beth was wrestling with something—something important. And he couldn't rush her. It was imperative that he didn't rush her.

A wave of possessiveness rolled through him, quickly followed by an almost overpowering need to protect. Normally, Bodey would shy away from such intense emotions. He'd become a master at skipping through life on the surface, shying away from the deeper currents. But for the first time in memory, he couldn't retreat from the tacit distress of another human being.

"What is it? Tell me so that I can help."

For a moment, she looked up at him, her eyes wide and turbulent, and in a flashing montage he saw the rundown motel, the male at the door, the battered red farm truck—and he knew they were all connected to the fear he saw buried in her expression.

But before she could say anything, he heard the distinctive rumble of the Hendersons' motor home pulling into its parking place.

In an instant, the moment was shattered and he watched as Beth emotionally re-erected the barriers that he'd been butting his head against since he'd met her.

"Bethy?"

She shook her head, wriggling free of his embrace. But rather than taking only a few steps back, it was as if she'd placed miles between them.

"That's Helen and Syd," she stated needlessly. "They'll want me to help take care of some of these wet things."

Feeling a little desperate to reestablish the connection they'd just experienced, Bodey said, "Can I see you later tonight?"

He saw the doubt race across her features, and with it, what looked like a curious flicker of resignation. But the impression was so fleeting, he wasn't sure if he'd imagined it.

"I-I don't know." She cast her eyes around the tent. "I don't know what I'll need to do here. Helen said she'd be closing up about five because there's something going on later."

Bodey nodded. "Casino night. They set up a few gaming tables in the main tent and the proceeds go to charity. Why don't you come? Either that, or we could head into town and get something to eat. Maybe go dancing."

Again, he saw the way she hesitated, a flare of regret, a spark of longing—and, once again, he had an image of a male stepping aside to let her into that rundown motel. Maybe she wasn't free to openly step out with him.

Step out with him.

What the hell? This wasn't the nineteenth century and he didn't really care what anyone thought. They weren't characters from those books P.D. liked to read, where a breath of scandal would ruin a couple's reputation. Bodey's reputation probably couldn't get any worse than it already was. It wasn't like the two of them were going to cause a flurry of outrage if it became public knowledge that they were—

Were what? Dating? They hadn't even done that yet. Unless he counted today's lunch.

But something was holding her back—and he sensed it had to do with the figure he'd seen at the door.

Damnit. He couldn't start second guessing things now. It hadn't been so long ago when he couldn't even get her to smile. He wasn't going to push her. If she needed time to get used to what was developing between them, he'd give it to her.

The back flap began to rustle as a muffled voice called out, "Beth? Are you okay?"

Helen.

"Look," Bodey said quickly, quietly. "If you can't come to Casino Night, then give me breakfast. I'll pick you up at the inn and we can go somewhere and talk. Just talk."

She offered him a shy, crooked smile. "Just talk?"

He stroked a finger down her cheek. "Unless you decide that you want more."

"Beth?"

"I'm in here, Helen! I'm fine!"

Bodey took a few steps away, reaching for the spot where he'd left his hat. He was settling it over his head when Helen stepped in.

"Landsakes, that was a storm! And it's still coming down.

Luckily the wind . . . has died. . . ." Helen's comment faltered a bit when she saw Bodey, but she quickly caught
herself. "Bodey Taggart. I sure seem to be seeing a lot of
you this trip. Were you watching out for our girl?"

He nodded. "I was afraid she might have some problems
getting the flaps closed. Good thing I came to check. The
wind pulled a few of the pegs out and it had already collapsed in one corner. I was able to get things tightened up
again before you had a real problem on your hands."

"Thank goodness. There's a half dozen vendors who were
blown over. One of them has merchandise spread from here
to the far fence, poor thing." She returned her attention to
Beth and gasped. "But heavens, look at you. Wet to the bone
and probably chilled through. Can you believe we've gone
from blazing hot weather to cold in the space of a few
hours?"

Beth plucked at her sodden skirts. "I'm so sorry that your
beautiful outfit has been ruined."

Helen waved a dismissing hand. "It'll dry. But we've got
to get you out of those things before you catch your death.
Head back to the motor home and change into your own
clothes. Bodey, do you think you could take her home? We'd
be fools to open up again after this. I'd rather put my feet
up until it's time to get ready for Casino Night—if they can
even hold the event in this weather. And you"—she pointed
to Beth—"need to go home to a hot shower that's more
powerful than the grasshopper spit we have in the motor
home."

She stopped in her speech long enough to glance at
Bodey and he nodded.

"I'd love to take her home."

"Leave your bike here," Helen added. "I'll send Syd for
you in the morning."

"No, I can get her. I'll be heading out at the crack of dawn
to take care of my horse, so I can pick Beth up on the way
back."

"That sounds like a really good idea." Helen's gaze
bounced consideringly between the two of them, and Bodey

had seen that look before. It was the same expression she'd worn when Jace and Bronte had tried to pretend they weren't seeing one another. A bit concerned and a little devious. And that's the last thing he needed: Helen donning her matchmaking persona.

But, thankfully, her gaze bounced back to Beth. "Go on, now. Change your clothes. By the time you're done, Bodey will have brought his truck back to the motor home so you don't have to get wet again."

Beth moved to the flap with obvious reluctance. Maybe she'd sensed the Yenta vibes as well, but she finally ran to the RV.

The moment her squelching footsteps faded, Helen prowled toward Bodey with deliberate steps. Extending a warning finger, she poked him square in the chest.

"Now you listen to me Bodey Taggart, and you listen good. I love you like a son. I always have. But I'm sensing there's a world of hurt buried in that woman and I won't have you toying with her, you hear?"

Bodey held up two hands in surrender.

But Helen wasn't finished. "I've come to care for that girl. An awful lot. If I had my way, I'd bring her home with me, wrap her in cotton batting, and let her catch her breath from whatever demons she thinks are chasing her." She stabbed him in his chest, again and again, her sharp nail forcing him to back up. "So if you hurt her, I'm warning you now. I'm a middle-aged woman short on estrogen and patience, and I've got enough guns and ammunition to change you from a stud to a gelding in the blink of an eye, so watch out!"

Bodey couldn't help laughing, even though he knew she was serious. Backing up, his hands still held high, he promised, "I will be a gentleman. You have my word."

When she continued to stare at him with disbelief, he allowed his guard to drop, knowing that when he did, Helen would probably see at least a hint of the confusion that he himself was feeling.

"The last thing I'd ever want to do is hurt Beth. But if I'm honest, I have to admit that I can't promise I won't. Because

I don't know what I'm doing here. And I don't know enough about her yet to avoid any emotional landmines she might have." He thought again of the tall male who had met Beth at the door. "But I can't . . . stop."

He wasn't sure if he'd managed to explain his own confusion. But something he said caused Helen to grow calm again.

"You get her some dinner before you drop her off."

It wasn't a request.

Bodey smiled and touched the brim of his hat. "Yes, ma'am. You have my word on that as well."

AS soon as she saw a pair of headlights slice through the rain, Beth waved goodbye to Syd and Helen and rushed out to the truck.

Since Helen had given her an umbrella to use, she was able to go most of the way without getting too wet. But it took her a few seconds to wrestle it closed again before she could shut the door. When she turned, however, she was momentarily struck dumb.

Since meeting Bodey Taggart, she'd seen him in a variety of western costumes—cowboy, cavalry officer, gunslinger. But there was nothing old fashioned about him now. He wore faded jeans that hugged his thighs and hips, a T-shirt that had probably seen a thousand washings, a loose leather jacket, and a green baseball cap with the words TAGGART ENTERPRISES embroidered with white thread.

The effect of the casual dress was like meeting him all over again. The cap made his jaw more angular, his nose blade thin. For the first time, she noticed that he had a faint cleft in his chin that was accented by the beginnings of stubble which gleamed in the dome light.

"Ready?"

"Yeah."

He flipped a switch, plunging the cab into shadows, then began to navigate the muddy parking lot.

Looking out at the still falling rain and the gusting wind, she was grateful that she didn't have to make the trip home on her bicycle. But there was no escaping the fact that she would be getting wet all over again. Once Bodey dropped her off at her supposed digs, she would still have to walk several blocks home.

"Helen made me promise that I'd stop and get you some dinner."

Conflicting emotions see-sawed in her stomach at the pronouncement. Much as she would like to spend more time with him, she worried that the storm had upset Dolly. And Eric was a good kid, but he needed to be relieved from his role of babysitter.

Bodey gestured to the clock on the dashboard. "I'll take you somewhere quick. Then, you'll still be back long before you would have been if the storm hadn't washed out vendors' row.

She opened her mouth, ready to refuse. But heaven help her. She couldn't. Not when her time with him was already so limited. And she *would* be back early. Eric and Dolly wouldn't be watching for her yet. If she stayed, maybe she would have a chance to talk to Bodey. Really talk.

No.

She had to remember that this man could never be more than a brief, casual flirtation. After everything that had already happened between them, she really needed to throw on the brakes. Otherwise, she was bound to do something that she would later regret. Because, so far, they'd kissed, they'd flirted, they'd succumbed to heated moments of passion.

But she honestly couldn't handle anything more . . . emotional or binding. And she couldn't have him thinking that she might.

Even though she wanted to surrender to anything he might offer her. More than she would ever willingly admit.

"I really shouldn't. I've been gone so much that—"

Stop! Stop before you say too much.

"I need to get caught up on some things."

Too late, she remembered that she was supposed to be staying at the Red Fox Inn which would rule out any excuses like laundry or cleaning.

Unsure what to say next, she remained silent, biting her lip until it stung as a reminder to choose her words carefully.

Silence ticked between them for several long seconds. It was clear that Bodey wasn't used to having his invitations refused—yet another reason why she should keep her distance. But he recovered quickly, rubbing her arm in a way that caused a rush of gooseflesh.

But not from the cold.

No. If she were honest, she would have to admit that what caused the chill to race through her veins was the evidence of how far Bodey had battered through her defenses. A week ago, she would have prided herself on remaining aloof and detached with those she met along their journey. She'd developed independence to an art form. She'd learned the best ways to camouflage herself in a crowd or to keep herself emotionally detached.

But Bodey represented everything that scared her. Everything that tempted her. She wanted to wallow in the light shining from his eyes any time he looked at her. She wanted to bask in the warmth of his arms. Even more, she wanted to embrace the emotional lifeline he held out to her—one that would allow her to give up her secrets and know that the person she'd entrusted them with would not use them to hurt her.

Bodey leaned over to say against her hair, "So . . . what about dinner?"

It was one of the hardest things she'd ever done to say, "I-I really shouldn't. I'm so . . . tired."

Lame. So lame.

But damned the man, a gentle expression settled over his features. The glow from the dash limned his features, accenting the blade of his nose, the blunt shape of his cheekbones, the square edge of his jaw.

"Geez, I'm being an asshole again," he muttered.

"No, Bodey, I—"

He wrapped his arm around her shoulders, pulling her tightly against him. "Helen's right. You need to get back to your hotel room where you can take a hot shower and put your feet up. Working in that tent all day can't be easy.

You've been wearing those period boots the whole time—and judging by some of what I saw today, you probably alternate between slow spells and bursts of complete panic."

"It's not that bad. In fact, I've really enjoyed it."

Bodey grinned. "Maybe you should make a career of it."

He couldn't know how much she would love such a thing—to work for Helen permanently would be heaven on earth at this point. But it was a pipe dream. There was no way that Beth could settle in one place. And there was no way that she would drag anyone else into her problems.

They were nearing the Red Fox Inn and Beth couldn't prevent the way her fingers curled into Bodey's thigh, absorbing the strength to be found there.

"So . . . do you want me to drop you in the front or the back?"

For a moment, she debated telling him the truth. The last thing she wanted right now was to walk nearly a mile in the other direction. Not with the rain still falling. Not when she longed to linger by his side, absorbing the warmth of his body.

But he would ask too many questions.

Questions she couldn't answer right now.

"The back is fine."

The words coated her tongue like dust.

He didn't respond, merely turned on his blinker and maneuvered the truck as close to the door as possible. But when she would have slid across the seat, he stopped her.

"I just—" He broke off, reaching to cup her cheek with his palm.

It took every ounce of self-control she possessed not to lean into that caress, to soak up the heat from his skin, to deepen the sensation of his skin. His fingers were slightly callused, evidence of hard work—or perhaps the result of time spent in the saddle and controlling the reins of horses that could single out a cow from the middle of a herd and swiftly cut it from the group.

And was that what she was? Another woman cut from Bodey's group?

The thought was more painful than she could have

imagined, because he reached to stroke her forehead, smoothing away the crease between her brows.

"What?"

She shook her head, not knowing how to voice her fears without appearing incredibly pathetic. Finally, after constructing and discarding a dozen questions, she asked, "What are you doing here with me, Bodey Taggart?"

It was his turn to look puzzled. "What do you mean?"

"Why me? I mean . . . there are dozens of women at Hell on Wheels who—"

He placed his thumb on her lips before she could even finish the question. "Why wouldn't it be you? Geez, you're so beautiful."

She shook her head. "No, I—"

Again, he stopped her. "You're beautiful." His voice was so earnest, so urgent. Even more startling was the way that those same sentiments were echoed in his expression. "Sometimes you scare me with how beautiful you are. Your eyes are like nothing I've ever seen—so blue, so deep, they remind me of the night skies over the ranch because they're so dark that they're almost black. But they sparkle and shine like they're loaded with stars."

"Oh." It was a bare puff of sound, but Beth couldn't have prevented it. She didn't think men really talked like that. Certainly not any men she'd ever known.

"And I swear, sometimes you scare the hell out of me, you're so tiny."

That caused her to grimace.

"But you're strong. And fierce."

"You make me sound like a Chihuahua."

He offered his own quick laugh. "No." He cupped her face with both hands. "No, you're all woman, Beth." His voice faded to a mere whisper while his head dipped. A mere hairsbreadth away, he said, "A beautiful, beautiful woman." He brushed her lips with his own, so softly, so briefly, she could have imagined it. "And I am so glad I met you."

THIRTEEN

———•◦•———

AND I am so glad I met you.

Unaccountably, as the words reverberated through her soul, Beth felt tears pricking at her eyes. But she pushed them away, refusing to spoil the moment with feminine hysterics. Not when she wanted to absorb every second with Bodey.

His kiss was feather light, whispering over her lips, once, twice, three times. When she would have increased the pressure, he smiled against her.

"Uh-uh."

His thumbs stroked her cheeks as he continued to explore her face—his mouth slipping over her temples, skimming her cheekbones, tracing the curve of her jaw. And then, finally, he returned to her lips.

She reached out to grab fistfuls of his shirt to steady herself as he nipped and sucked. At long last, he allowed her to increase the pressure, to open her mouth to him. Then, as if a match had been touched to kerosene, there was no more hesitancy, no more restraint. He pulled her tightly against him, hard to soft, male to female.

In an instant, she became incapable of coherent thought as she was stormed with sensation, her body submitting to a rush of heat that warmed her from within, licking at parts of her core that she hadn't realized had lain dormant.

"You have no idea what you do to me," he whispered as he wrenched his lips away and began tracing a fiery trail down her throat.

"If it's anything close to what you're doing to me . . ."

She released her grip on his shirt, tugging on the hem until she could reach beneath it to the warm flesh beneath.

Sweet heaven! Was this how a man was supposed to feel?

His body was like iron sheathed in silk and velvet. Ridges and valleys carved through taut muscle, hinted at the strength of bones and sinew. A classical statue come to life in a way that combined art and form with hot flesh and wisps of hair on his sternum, then again below his navel, moving down, down.

She couldn't help tracing the path with a single finger, absorbing the gooseflesh that sprang up in her wake. Then, needing to explore more, she circled the oval shape of his buckle, then followed the line of his fly.

He made a sound that was half laugh, half gasp against her lips.

"If you keep that up, I'm going to have a hard time stopping."

She hesitated only an instant, knowing that she was playing with fire once again. A hot, western wildfire. But she couldn't prevent what was about to happen any more than she could tamp down the inferno with her bare hands.

She could only whisper, "Then don't stop."

Bodey drew back enough to search her features—and Beth could scarcely believe the stark desire that she saw shining from his eyes. But even more than that, there was a sense of wonder and disbelief—as if he couldn't quite believe what was happening between them. The emotions were so raw, so honest—and echoed hers so exactly—that she felt a beat of uncertainty.

Could she do this? Was she strong enough to handle such a wealth of passion and truth without buckling beneath its weight? Heaven only knew it had been years since she'd had any kind of relationship with a man. And she'd never experienced anything as powerful as this. Beneath his regard, she felt as if she were being consumed by the heat of a hunger unlike anything she'd ever known.

But she couldn't back away.

She didn't want to back away.

Her fingers rubbed against his fly once more, firmly, intently. His body—which had already begun to react—swelled even more.

"Don't stop," she said again.

"Hell. Hold on," Bodey rasped.

He pulled away from her long enough to put the truck in gear and move it to the far side of the car park behind a copse of scrubby trees. There were no other vehicles around them. And with an empty field nearby, there were no lights spilling into the darkness. Instead, the drumming rain and condensation soon obscured the view and gave a sense of privacy—one that Beth knew was an illusion. But she didn't care. It had been so long—if ever—since she'd felt this way. And with this heady rush of passion came a bravado that only heightened the sensations she was feeling.

When Bodey cut the engine and turned to her, she felt a surge of power, a recognition of her femininity. Because even in the limited light, she could see that Bodey wanted her.

He. Wanted. Her.

She pushed away all thought of what the future might bring. In that instant, she surrendered to the moment, twisting so that she could face him. Then she grabbed for the hem of her T-shirt and swept it over her head.

Much like the rest of her clothing, her brassiere was black as well. Lacy. Nearly sheer.

She heard him suck in his breath. Then he was fighting with his seatbelt and his own shirt, shedding it as quickly as she'd done hers. He shifted, resting one leg on the bench seat so that he was half-reclining, his back braced against the door. Then he was pulling her in between his thighs so that she was draped across him, stomach to stomach, breast to breast.

And it felt good, oh, so good, that first meeting of flesh to flesh. She watched as his gaze dipped, taking in the way her breasts plumped against his chest. The heat that flared in his eyes, the expression of worship he wore, was her undoing. Thrusting her fingers through his hair, she reached to kiss him, all of her pent-up loneliness and frustration, denial and hunger naked in the embrace.

Rather than questioning the source of her desperation, he met it with his own storm of need, until they were locked so tightly together that she couldn't remember where her body ended and his began. Like a sponge, she absorbed his strength and his passion—and yes, a little of his wildness. Heaven only knew that she'd never been so out of control, so . . . reckless.

But it felt good. Oh, so good.

She wrenched away to pepper kisses over the square line of his jaw, into that faint hollow in his chin, then down to where she paused, sucking at his Adam's apple, before moving lower, to the hollow at the base of his throat, then lower still.

His chest shuddered as she used her nose to feather a light caress over the crisp hair that she'd found there—and she loved that about him. That he had a touch of masculine unruliness to him rather than being completely man-scaped. Then her lips roamed sideways, finding the hard nub of his nipple.

He grasped her then, his strong fingers tangling in her hair.

"Should I stop?" she said against him.

"Hell, no."

His garbled answer made her laugh—and even she was surprised how it emerged from her throat in a way that was husky and low. The sound of a temptress.

She took his nipple between her teeth, nipping, holding, while her tongue circled the sensitive tip.

Bodey bucked against her, his hands shifting, moving with lightning speed to circle her hips, bringing her tightly against him so that she was intimately aware of the bulge pressing against her.

She shifted to increase the pressure and he gasped, releasing her long enough to reach between them for his belt buckle.

For a moment, he hesitated, catching her gaze—probably wondering if he was going too far, too fast. But at the moment, she could only think that he wasn't going far or fast enough. So she smiled, afraid that he would see the stark want in her gaze . . .

And afraid that he wouldn't.

He unhooked his buckle and reached for his zipper—and she let him, enjoying watching him, watching his strong fingers manipulating the fastenings. But then he paused, taking her hand and setting it low on his belly.

Obviously, he was giving her a choice, allowing her to set the pace. Meeting his gaze, she could see that he had no agenda, no ultimate goal. He would follow her lead.

The thought was nearly as heady as the skin beneath her palm. And she had no hesitation. Leaning forward for his kiss, her fingers slipped beneath the edge of his jeans, skin to skin, until she encountered the hard hot length that offered her the proof of his arousal.

"Mmm," she murmured, unable to hide her pleasure.

He laughed. "What?"

She couldn't prevent the smile that spread over her lips, even as she kissed Bodey. Wrapping her hand around him, she freed him from the stricture of his pants. She felt herself trembling—with excitement and a little bit of fear. She was still unable to voice her chaotic thoughts, but she did manage to murmur, "Lucky, lucky me."

She couldn't be sure, but she thought that he blushed in the darkness, muttering, "Shit." But then, he was pulling her close for a passionate kiss that left her in no doubts of his desire for her.

For her.

Pulling back, she whispered, "Why?"

His brow creased. "Why, what?"

"Why me?"

His smile was slow and rich and settled into her chest like sweet, hot molasses. "Why not you?" He framed her face with his hands. "Don't you see what I see when you look in the mirror? It hurts my heart if you don't. Geez, I find myself staring at you sometimes, not wanting to miss a single instant. Your face is so . . . so . . . damnit, I'm not very good at this. I'm a stupid man and I don't know how to explain it. But sometimes you look innocent as a Sunday school kid and I swear butter couldn't melt in your mouth. Then, seconds later, I've got a temptress on my hands." His voice dropped to a whisper. "Like now."

A temptress.

Definitely not a term that had ever been applied to her. At least out loud.

No. Never. Not even in her wildest dreams.

Temptress.

Wow.

But then, she'd never had anyone make her feel the way Bodey did. She couldn't analyze why—she couldn't even wrap her head around the fact that she was here, in a parking lot, with a man she'd barely met. On the whole, she'd never had much luck with men, especially not sexually. Most often, she'd found herself disinterested or . . . overwhelmed. Smothered.

With Bodey, she felt . . . safe.

She didn't know why. She'd begun to believe that it was her size that was the problem, or she was too timid, or repressed, or just too damned tired to deal with men.

Until now.

Now, she couldn't get enough. She wanted to absorb everything about him in an instant, yet savor him for hours. She wanted to feel his hands on her, his body next to her. She loved the fact that he'd instinctively offered her control, yet, she felt out of control as well.

"This is nuts," she whispered.

"Uh huh."

"But I suppose you—"

He shook his head. "Never this fast."

She regarded him suspiciously. "I doubt that. Wild Bodey."

He swore under his breath. "Damnit, I'm going to have a talk with Helen," he muttered, then leaned toward her to say against her lips. "*Never* this fast. *Never* this intense. Call me old fashioned, but I knew my mother would haunt me if I indulged in a string of one night stands."

Until now.

But then, they still had a little time. It didn't have to be a one night stand.

In that instant, she knew that she didn't want to waste another minute. Somehow, Fate had seen fit to bring this man into her life. Even though they would soon part ways again, she had tonight . . . and maybe another night after that.

And maybe another . . .

Then there was no time for coherent thought. She reached for him, hungrily, greedily, and he met her half-way, his broad hands roaming over her back, her hips, pulling her against him so that she could feel the strength of his body. There was a flashing moment of doubt as she wondered how on earth she would be able to accept such a big man. But rather than scaring her, the thought caused her body to pulse with such aching need that she knew she couldn't wait any longer. If he was determined to let her control the pacing of their love-making, then she didn't plan on delaying another instant.

Balancing on one knee, she fumbled with the button to her jeans. For a moment, Bodey's fingers were there, stopping her.

"You're sure? You're sure this is how you want to—"

She didn't even let him finish the words. She shucked off her jeans. Then she was straddling him, reaching for him.

"Wait," he gasped. "Wait a second." His hips lifted, bringing her in even closer proximity to the part of him that had her wild with need. He wrestled with something in his pocket, withdrawing his wallet. While he searched for a condom among the bills and receipts, she peppered kisses down his throat, turning her attention to his nipple again.

"Shit, shit, shit," he whispered, gasping and bucking against her. Then he readied himself, still struggling for breath—hissing sharply when she bit him.

The moment he'd sheathed himself in the condom, she lifted up. And he was there, guiding their joining.

Her eyes closed as she savored the stretching, the fullness. She'd been so sure that she wouldn't be able to accommodate him at all, but he let her take control of the movements, his own breath coming in rough soughs that caused a frisson of gooseflesh to race down her spine. A low moan slipped from his throat, the sound one of such utter pleasure, that it turned her on even more, driving her, igniting her very being until, unbelievably, she felt herself beginning to climax hard and fast and hot, the pulsations rushing through her body with such force that when she lay quivering in his arms, she was deliciously exhausted and flush from pleasure.

But Bodey wasn't finished. As she caught her breath, he kissed her neck, her shoulders. Then slipped the bra strap down, revealing the plump curve of her breast and a nipple so taut and aching that she knew the only thing that would ease the pain was the warmth of his mouth, the velvety softness of his tongue.

As if her thoughts had been telegraphed to him, he dipped his head, his lips closing around her.

Her eyes slammed shut and she was riding him again, wrapping her arms around his neck, plunging her fingers into his hair to keep him there.

She was gasping for breath, her body suddenly alive with energy and electricity, all of it centered in her core. Until, miraculously, she felt herself reaching the precipice again, felt herself letting go.

This time, as she surrendered to the ultimate pleasure, he joined her, wordless noises of passion and elation bursting from his lips until she bent to capture them in her kiss, rocking against him, absorbing every nuance as he came within her.

And in that moment, there was no fear, no worry, no regret.

There was only joy.

Something she hadn't felt in a very long time.

BODEY sucked air into his lungs, trying to gather enough brain cells together for coherent thought.

Holy, holy hell.

He couldn't ever remember making love with such abandon, such utter . . .

Geez.

Beth had literally detonated in his arms—and she'd made him feel the same way. True, he'd had a checkered past, but he hadn't been lying when he'd told her that he'd never had sex with a woman within a few days of meeting her. But with Beth . . .

It hadn't seemed like he'd known her for such a short period of time.

And it hadn't felt like just "sex."

"You have no idea what you do to me," he said into her hair, not knowing why he said the words aloud. He only knew that he couldn't hold them in.

He felt her smile against his chest.

"I think I have a fair idea . . . because I feel the same way."

She would never know how her response caused something warm to settle in his chest. And rather than seeping away as his heart rate returned to normal, it took root and lingered.

For the first time in as long as he could remember, he felt something ease within him. A bit of the tense need to prove himself time and time again faded beneath a curious sensation of peace.

Normally, after making love to a woman, he wasn't one to linger. He found himself looking for a quick way out or hoping that his partner would fall asleep soon so that he could head back into the cool mountain air where he could clear his head.

But this time, he found himself basking in the moment, praying that the steamy windows would remain opaque a little while longer so that he could wrap his arms around Beth and draw her head into the spot beneath his chin. As his fingers drew invisible swirls across her back, he closed his eyes, concentrating on the way he could feel the rapid thump of her heart against his ribs.

She shifted slightly against him.

"I should—"

He stopped her with a, "Shhh . . . shh . . . not yet. Not yet."

And for once, she didn't argue, but allowed him to have his way, settling against him with her slight weight.

Rain drummed against the roof of the car, adding a poignant tattoo to the rough cadence of their breaths. But, bit by bit, he felt her relax.

"You are a dangerous man, Bodey Taggart," she murmured against him.

Glancing down, he saw that her eyes were closed. But a crease had formed between her brows and he longed to smooth it away. He didn't want her to worry. He wanted her to be happy.

"Why's that?" he idly asked.

She propped her chin on her hands, looking up at him.

"No one has ever made me lose control like that."

His smile unfurled from a spot deep in his chest.

"But you liked it." There was a slight questioning edge to the pronouncement.

Thankfully, she erased his concern with a soft, "Oh, yeah."

She reached to trace his lips and he lifted his head to snatch her finger into his mouth and suckle it.

He loved the way her eyes fluttered closed as she absorbed the sensation. Loved the way she sighed in a way that was half release, half anticipation.

"In a few days, this will be over."

He almost didn't catch the words. But when they seeped into his mind, he shook his head.

"Don't talk like that."

She shook her head in patent disbelief. "Why not? It's the truth."

He thrust his fingers into her hair, forcing her to look at him. "We don't know what the truth is yet. We'll make our own truth."

Even in the dim light of the truck, he saw a faint flicker of hope touch her eyes. But it was extinguished just as quickly by doubt and a wary acceptance. Briefly, he wondered who had let her down in the past. Who had made her believe that hope was a fairytale?

"I won't let you down, Bethy." The words slipped from his lips without conscious thought. And even in the dappled lighting caused by the rain streaming down the windows, she saw the sheen of moisture that suddenly appeared in her eyes.

"You don't even know me, Bodey."

He cupped her face in both hands now, forcing her to meet his steady gaze, knowing instinctively that if he couldn't get her to believe him—to believe that what he felt for her was different and unique and special—he would lose her completely.

"I know what I need to know," he said urgently. "I know that you're strong and stubborn and feisty and gentle. I know that you have a heart capable of unfathomable emotion. I know that you're passionate and smart and loyal."

Her lower lip trembled and her breath caught in a soft sob.

"I know that I'm a better person for having met you, Beth Tivoli." He stroked her cheeks with his thumbs. "And I know that you've made me feel things that are new and . . . a little bit scary."

She bit her lip, and for an instant, he caught a moment of recognition in her gaze—as if she'd felt the same mix of hope and uncertainty that warred within him.

"I know that Helen's been talking. Hell, she couldn't tell you anything that I don't know myself. I'm a bad gamble. I've dated a lot of women."

She snorted and again he prayed that Helen had only hit the tip of the iceberg with her recitations. Because he had nothing in his dating history to recommend him as a good bet.

But he didn't want Beth to think of him that way. He didn't know what he would do if she felt that she couldn't trust him with his heart.

"Just give me a chance, okay. We'll take things a day at a time. See where they lead."

He waited, his heart wallowing in his chest, unable to beat again until she finally nodded.

"One day at a time," she repeated.

He could hear the doubt in her tone. Clearly, she didn't think that anything could come of their brief association. She couldn't know that, to Bodey, there was nothing that motivated him more than a challenge. If he set his mind on something, come hell or high water, he would do his best to make it happen.

And this, he sensed, was probably one of the most important battles he would ever win. Proving to Beth Tivoli that he was worthy of her trust.

"Give me a chance," he whispered again, bending to brush a soft kiss against her lips.

She didn't respond at first. He could nearly see the gears working in her brain as she tried to weigh all the ramifications of his offer. But then, she finally nodded, some of the tension seeping from her body as she settled back against his chest again, her arms wrapping tightly around his waist.

"All right."

The words were so soft, he might have thought he'd imagined him.

But the warmth that spread through his chest, assured him that they'd been real.

THAT same inexplicable emotion was still nestled under his heart much later when Bodey pulled his truck into the parking lot of the same gas station where he'd filled his tank only the night before. Carefully positioning his vehicle so that the distinctive flatbed would be hidden between a delivery van and a Suburban, he turned off his lights and waited.

Only moments before, he'd dropped Beth off at the back door to the hotel again. After they'd dressed, he'd insisted on making good on his promise to take her to dinner by hitting the drive-through of a Mexican place across the street.

Throughout the process, Bodey had dawdled—loathe to

leave her. He kept hoping that now—after they'd shared an evening that was so intimate, so mind-blowing—that she might consider opening up to him, telling him what the hell was going on with the other motel. Hell, if she was trying to save face, she needn't bother. He didn't care if she couldn't afford to stay at the Red Fox or if she was living paycheck to paycheck in whatever digs she could find. And he knew, sure as hell, that the man he'd seen couldn't be someone she was intimate with, or she wouldn't be making love to Bodey. She wasn't capable of being so . . . cold.

His gut pinched a little at that thought, reminding him that he didn't know anything about her. Worse, she didn't seem to be inclined to tell him more.

He pushed that thought resolutely aside as well. He knew enough. He knew enough to have a little faith. He had to believe in his first impressions of this woman. And he had to believe in his own instincts as well. A niggling little voice inside him kept insisting that something was going on— something that had nothing to do with the relationship that they were beginning to build.

And it must be some serious shit if Beth was being so careful.

He glanced at the glowing clock on the dash. At least the rain had tapered off to a drizzle and the windows had become a little less steamy.

He grinned at that. Holy, holy hell. They'd managed to fog them up pretty good.

His body was still thrumming at that thought when he saw a familiar figure turn onto the sidewalk only a few yards away. Beth's head was down beneath her umbrella and she still clutched the sack of tacos left over from their meal.

Bodey had purposely ordered more than either of them could possibly eat. He'd remembered yesterday when Beth had looked at her sandwich and coleslaw as if she'd died and gone to heaven. He remembered the way she'd eaten the coleslaw first, savoring each bite as if it were a delicacy. He could personally take coleslaw or leave it, but she'd acted as if it were manna delivered from heaven. Then, when he'd challenged her to eat her sandwich . . . she'd carefully cut it into three pieces.

Three pieces.

He waited until she crossed the street at the corner. As soon as he figured she was out of earshot, he started the truck, easing out of the parking place.

Avoiding the bright lights under the pumps, he circled around the back of the convenience store, losing sight of Beth for several minutes until he could reach the cross street.

But he was forced to wait until an old pickup eased closer to the stoplight before he could turn onto the road.

A red pickup.

Bodey frowned, remembering the odd way Beth had reacted when she'd seen that same truck earlier in the day.

His gaze flicked to the driver. But the rain streaked windows and a layer of dust that had turned to grime kept him from seeing anything but a hazy outline.

Automatically, his gaze flicked to the plates. He immediately recognized the familiar pine tree in the center.

Oregon plates.

What the hell?

Why was Beth worried about a pickup driven by someone from Oregon?

He caught only a glimpse of the series of numbers and letters stamped onto the metal before another car eased up to the light and blocked his view.

Not wanting to catch the driver's attention, Bodey waited until two more cars fell into line and the light turned to green before easing onto the road. He barely cleared the corner before the light changed again.

He automatically scanned the sidewalk, looking for Beth, but it was as if she'd vanished.

Bodey muttered a curse, more worried that Beth would see that he'd been following her than he was about the red pickup. So he took the next off street, making a wide circle around the area until he could double back to the old motel. Parking several blocks away in an apartment complex, he doused his lights and his engine. From here, he couldn't see much, but at least he could see the corner unit she'd entered once before.

Bodey waited there for what felt like hours—even though the dash clock confirmed it was only about twenty minutes. He was about to give up, telling himself that what he'd seen the night before was an isolated incident and Beth had only been taking a bike ride to clear her head. But then she strode into view between some parked cars, her umbrella missing despite the rain, her shoulders hunched. She slipped in and out of the shadows with practiced ease—her movements so cloaked by darkness, he wouldn't have noticed her if he hadn't known where to look.

Over and over, she kept glancing over her shoulder as if she feared she were being followed, and Bodey felt a stab of guilt, wondering if she could sense his gaze. Geez, he didn't want to scare her—and he didn't want to come off as some kind of stalker. He merely wanted to know what the hell was going on. And now, more than ever, he needed to know that if she were staying in the Trailblazer Motel, she arrived there safely.

She knocked on the motel door and it cautiously opened.

For one stark moment, Bodey was offered a brief, startling tableau illuminated by the interior light—a tall, thin male. No. Not a grown male. A teenager. Judging by his narrow chest and rounded features, he was probably a couple of years younger than Barry.

Relief thundered through Bodey's frame.

It was a kid. A kid!

But even as Bodey congratulated himself on his master detective skills, another shadow broke away from the interior and a little girl with golden ringlets launched herself into Beth's arms.

A shaft of stunned surprise pierced through Bodey's chest, and the jubilation whooshed from his body as quickly as the outrush of air from his lungs.

Shit.

Beth had a kid.

A kid.

FOURTEEN

———•———

BETH held her sister tightly—probably more tightly than was necessary—as she stepped inside so that Eric could close the door behind them. For a moment, she closed her eyes and breathed deeply of the faint scents of baby shampoo and peanut butter. Then Dolly wriggled against her grip.

"What did you bring us tonight?" she asked, jumping free and grabbing the sack of take-out food.

"Tacos."

Dolly's eyes widened. *"Tacos!"* Her tone held a reverence that made Beth laugh.

"Yes, and there's plenty of hot sauce for Eric."

Dolly ran to the table and began pulling out the paper-wrapped packages. But when Eric would have followed, Beth caught his elbow and pulled him back.

As soon as she was sure Dolly was distracted, she asked, "Did you stay inside all day?"

Eric frowned. "Yeah."

"You didn't go out at all. Not even to . . . . I don't know . . . go get ice or something."

Eric snorted. "That old ice maker in the breezeway hasn't worked for days."

"So you haven't even gone out of the door?"

Eric's features grew grim and Beth felt a pang. A boy his age shouldn't have to know that kind of seriousness in his life. He should be worrying about making the sports' teams, talking to girls, and getting good grades—things that Eric had never had a chance to experience.

When Beth was only five, and her parents had divorced, her mother had taken her to Oregon "Where the air is clear and a person can re-commune with nature," Francis Tivoli proclaimed.

But it had soon become apparent that their mother hadn't been as interested in nature as she'd been with Leroy Vonn, an anti-establishment survivalist who espoused the virtues of living off the land and off the grid.

At first, it had been an adventure. Beth had been spirited away to a spot deep in the woods where they'd lived in a small cabin in a compound of similar structures. There'd been no formal schooling—merely "organized play," as her mother had called it. Beth had learned to fish and hunt, gather berries and nuts for food, and collect water from a nearby artesian spring.

Beth had been so sure that she and her mother were "camping," and that once the summer was over, she could return to her *real* home where her mommy and daddy would live together again.

But when the leaves turned and frost cloaked the ground, it had soon become clear that leaving the Oregon woods wasn't going to happen any time soon—not while her mother remained enthralled with Leroy Vonn. So autumn stretched into winter. A year passed. Then five. When Eric was born, Beth had been content to stay a little longer. But it soon became apparent that Eric was special—because he was a boy—and Beth was soon shunted to the side.

With each subsequent year, Leroy became more fanatical in his views, attracting a cadre of followers who were equally sure that the End of Days were near and the U.S. government would lead the way to the Apocalypse.

Before Beth quite knew what had happened, Leroy Vonn had a hand in every decision made in their camp—and especially every decision concerning her. He determined what she was allowed to eat, and wear, and do—until she feared he wouldn't be satisfied until he could control her thoughts as well.

Then, on her fifteenth birthday, he decided that it was time for her to marry.

To a man who was thirty years her senior.

Luckily for Beth, her biological father got wind of what was happening. Having barely been diagnosed with cancer, he'd finally appealed long and loud enough to the local authorities that he was able to convince one of the sheriffs to accompany him to Vonn's compound. Armed with legal documents that proved he had been awarded sole custody of his only child, he'd taken Beth away.

But he hadn't taken Eric.

He couldn't take Eric.

And even though a part of her was old enough to understand the legalities, Beth had never forgiven him for not fighting harder to get Eric the same help that her father had been willing to give her.

By the time she was twenty, Beth was on her own. But she hadn't even been able to mourn her father's passing because, within the space of a month, she'd discovered that her mother had given birth to a little girl.

From that moment, Beth had been filled with a consuming need to liberate her siblings from the Vonn compound—which had grown even more isolated and poor in the intervening years. In all that time, Beth had only been allowed to visit Eric, Dolly, and her mother three times. Each time, she'd begged her mother to leave with her.

But Francis Tivoli had become a hollow shell of a woman with sunken cheeks and blank eyes. Beth could see that a part of her mother wanted to escape. But she'd spent so long under Vonn's thumb, having him make every decision for her, that she would simply shake her head, silent tears rolling down her cheeks as she gripped Beth's hands.

Until Vonn forced Beth to go.

It wasn't until eighteen months ago that Beth had discovered that her mother's misery had hidden a streak of strength. Somehow, in the intervening time, she'd found a way to sneak into town and see a lawyer—probably under the guise of working in the farmer's market to trade the compound's produce for necessary cash and staples. So when her mother passed away from complications caused by diabetes, Beth had been named her siblings' sole guardian.

Vonn had clearly been unaware of the arrangements. So much so, that when Beth had appeared—with the papers in hand and a sheriff and deputies in tow—he'd pulled a gun. An action which had resulted in his being arrested.

Beth hadn't been so stupid as to think Vonn wouldn't fight back. Not through the courts. No, he would never deign to work with a government he refused to acknowledge. Vonn would take the children by force.

So she'd packed up their things and they'd left in the night. And the three of them had been running ever since— paying only cash, never staying anywhere more than a few weeks, living in cheap motels or campsites—at least until her car broke down somewhere near Fargo.

But they couldn't keep running like this. Moving from place to place, always looking over their shoulders . . . that was no kind of life for anyone, let alone two kids.

Beth's eyes grew moist when she realized that, one way or another, she was going to have to find a way to bring an end to this. She'd been so sure that she could handle the situation on her own, that eventually Vonn would stop looking for them.

Obviously, that wasn't the case.

Someone had found them here—*here*—in Cheyenne.

"Bethy, what is it?"

She hesitated, not wanting to burden her brother. He'd already shouldered far too much of the responsibility of their flight.

But she could tell by the stubborn jut of his chin that he wouldn't be satisfied until she told him the truth.

"I saw that red pickup today, the one you've been telling me about, when I came through town during lunch."

"On your bike?" Eric asked, confused.

"No," she hesitated, "no, I was with a friend that I met at Hell on Wheels."

"Your boss?"

Again, Beth was forced to carefully choose her words. She'd already told so many lies—even if most of them were only lies of omission. The weight of them on her spirit were nearly unbearable. So she decided to tell her brother the truth.

"No. It's a man I met there. He's from the same town in Utah as Helen and Syd. They're good friends. He's in the competition."

For a moment, Eric blinked at her, uncomprehendingly. "You made a friend with some man?" Then, before she could answer, he quickly said, "Oh, it's a *man.*"

She rolled her eyes. He made it sound like she'd formed an acquaintance with a gigolo selling his wares on the street corner.

"It's not like that, Eric. I just . . . like him."

"You like him? Or you *liiike* him?"

And how was she supposed to respond to that? Eric was fifteen and came from an extremely sheltered lifestyle. But he was a teenage boy, for heaven's sake.

Nevertheless, she didn't think that the storm of emotion that Bodey had inspired in her over the past twenty-four hours could ever be corralled into the little word "like." And since assuming custody of her siblings, Beth had never entertained the attentions of a man. *Ne-ver.*

Even so, she could feel a heat seep into her face when she admitted, "A little of both, I suppose."

Her brother's features remained expressionless for so long, her pulse began to pound in her ears. But then, he suddenly grinned and held up his hand. "Well, all right!"

Rather than giving her brother the "high-five" he expected,

she grabbed his hand and pulled it down. Dolly was unwrapping one of the tacos but she would soon wonder why Beth and Eric weren't joining her.

"Forget about Bodey for a minute."

"Bodey, huh? Bodey what?"

"Taggart. Darn it, Eric, you're off the point. I saw the pickup. And I saw it again tonight on my walk home."

"Walk? Where's your bike?"

"It's a long story, but . . ." She checked Dolly again. The little girl sat with her food suspended in front of her mouth, eyeing them curiously.

Pushing her emotions aside, Beth threw her a reassuring smile. "We'll be there in a second, Dolly. Go ahead and start."

As soon as Dolly returned her attention to her food, Eric asked, "Did the driver see you?"

Beth shook her head. "I don't think so. I ducked into a doorway and stayed there until I was sure it was gone. But the truck made a couple of sweeps before the driver gave up. I was able to see it had Oregon plates."

The color leeched from Eric's face and he whispered, "Then we've got to get out of here!"

No. Not now. Not when she had so many reasons to stay.

A part of her wanted to heed Eric's advice and pack up their things. But there was another part that clung to everything which had made her so happy over the past few days: her association with Helen and Syd; working at Hell on Wheels; and Bodey.

Especially Bodey.

Then there were the practical details. They couldn't leave now. She needed her paycheck. Her bike.

And she couldn't go without saying goodbye.

A giant, invisible hand squeezed around her throat as regret bloomed inside her. *This* was why she didn't form attachments. It made it so much harder to leave.

Tomorrow was the last day of the shoot. The day after that, Helen and Syd would pack up and go. Surely, if she and her siblings were careful, they could last that long.

"Have everything ready in the bug-out bags—and I mean everything. I've only got two days left with the Hendersons. As soon as I've been paid, we'll leave. Until then, you and Dolly have to stay inside."

When Eric looked anxious at that thought, Beth said, "We'll talk to her about it tonight, after the two of you have eaten. This time, we won't be keeping any secrets from each other."

He looked relieved at that detail.

"If you see anything—or anyone—that makes you think it isn't safe here—"

"I know, I know. We grab the bags and climb out the back window. Then we go somewhere safe like the park."

She shook her head. "No, this time I want you going to a place with lots of people. That way, you can scream and get the attention of a security guard if you need one. I'd rather sort things out with the police than let someone from the Farm snatch you up without a peep."

He nodded. "There's a Walmart about five blocks west."

"Perfect. If anything happens, you go there. Go to the toy department. That will keep Dolly distracted until I can get there."

Eric's features were pinched and pale. But this wasn't the first time that they'd rehearsed an exit strategy—nor, if worse came to worse, would it be the first time they'd used it.

"And if we get separated, what's the code word?" he asked grimly.

Beth thought for a moment, trying to think of something happy. Peaceful.

For a moment, she was flooded with images—Bodey's smile, the strength of his arms, the intensity of his passion. She thought of the rain pouring off his hat and duster when he'd come to rescue her from the collapsing tent. And that single moment of tranquility when a part of her had decided to trust him with her emotions, if not her heart.

"The code word is 'Willow,'" she said softly.

"Willow?"

Immediately, she remembered the way Bodey had told

her about the intuitive nature of horses and how their gentle natures were often used as a means for healing.

But in her case, it wasn't the animal who had given her the courage to face her demons.

It was the man behind the horse.

BODEY slouched in a chair he'd pulled into a dim corner of the event tent. He probably shouldn't have come to Casino Night. He wasn't in the mood for the noise and laughter. Around him, women of the SASS club were strutting their saloon girl finery, while the men were dressed like gunslingers and cowboys, bankers and bank robbers. Only Helen had gone out of her way to break with the stereotypes. While the tables around her were filled with people playing poker and roulette, she'd arrived wearing a snow white Temperance outfit, complete with hatchet. She'd sunk the blade of her weapon an inch into the wooden table she'd chosen and then proceeded to host what she called "Dueling Tea."

Her table didn't have a single empty chair and there were dozens of people waiting to play.

From what Bodey had been able to piece together, she poured each of the contestants a steaming cup of tea from the urn that Syd had carried and left on the table. Then, she offered each person an English biscuit—which looked a hell of a lot like a cookie to Bodey. Helen was clearly acting as some kind of referee, because, on her mark, the duelists dunked their cookies into their cups. Then Helen counted to five, and as soon as she'd finished, the contestants hurried to consume their cookies. The first to finish raised a hand, and Helen would shout out "Nom!" So far, he'd also figured out that a "Splodge" was called if the sodden cookie fell into the person's lap, "Splash!" if the cookie fell back into the teacup, and "Splatter" if it fell pretty much anywhere else.

Currently, it was drawing more attention than any of the other charity games, so Helen had set up an empty saucer to collect donations for the scholarship drive.

"You look uncustomarily modern."

Bodey looked up to find Elam looming over him. Blinking, he realized that P.D.—also dressed in Temperance finery—was taking her place at the tea table. Elam had shied away from the primarily feminine participants at Helen's table, but he hadn't gone so far away that he couldn't keep his eye on P.D. He'd readily admitted to Bodey that since P.D. had become pregnant, Elam's "caveman" instincts made it hard for him to let her out of his sight.

Which was a shame. Because, right now, Bodey could use a heart-to-heart talk with his old friend. Even if he didn't know what he would ever say to start the conversation.

When Elam continued to look at him expectantly, Bodey finally muttered, "I didn't feel like dressing up tonight."

Elam nodded but thankfully he didn't ask any questions. "Where's the little shopkeeper?"

Bodey blinked, yanking his attention back to his brother. "What do you mean?"

"P.D. said that Helen had a new girl helping her in the tent. I thought she'd be here tonight. P.D. said she liked her."

He settled into the chair next to Bodey and handed him a mason jar filled halfway with a clear liquid.

"This isn't the moonshine that Wiley Jack was distributing, is it?"

"Nah. P.D. has been nagging me about not being 'hydrated' enough. So it's water."

Bodey took a sip, then coughed when it burned the back of his throat.

"Steeped from her own special concoction of ascorbic acid, ginseng, lemon, and other assorted horrible hippie remedies passed down to her from her parents. I wouldn't be surprised if kerosene was one of the ingredients. I've been tempted to see if it will burn."

"Oh . . . my . . . hell . . ." Bodey coughed again and Elam pounded him on the back. "And you drink . . . this stuff?" he wheezed.

"Nope. Whenever she has her back turned, I pour a little onto the ground so it looks like I've been sipping it. Then, when we meet up, I hand her the empty jar and tell her how 'rejuvenated' I feel."

"How long has she been feeding you this crap?" Bodey's voice still sounded like sandpaper.

"Only the last few months. She's been a little on edge with the baby on the way."

"She looks so happy."

"She's over the moon." Elam shrugged. "But her nervousness is to be expected. Her own childhood was . . . sheer hell. Even though she won't say it out loud, I think she's worried that because she didn't have much of an example of sterling parenting skills, she might be a bad mom."

Bodey snorted. "That's ridiculous. You and I have both seen her with Barry—and with Bronte's kids."

"You know that. I know that. I've tried to reassure her, but I have a feeling that until the baby comes, she's going to be in hyper-protective mode. Once Antman comes—"

"Antman?"

"Long story. But once he comes, I'm pretty sure she'll be able to relax. I've learned with P.D. that—much as I'd love to rush in and fix things—sometimes I have to let her work things out for herself. That's why it took so long for us to get married. P.D. had to get to the point where she believed the fact that I didn't plan on looking at any other woman but her."

Bodey thought of Beth, of the horrible hotel, of the teenager at the door. Maybe, she wasn't trying to deceive him. She merely didn't know him well enough to trust him with the important stuff in her life.

"And what if P.D. doesn't work things out? What happens then?"

As if sensing she was the subject of conversation, P.D. looked their way and smiled.

Elam smiled back, lifting his mason jar in a silent toast, and Bodey quickly followed suit.

"Then God help us all," Elam said. His face maintained his loving smile, but his voice held a note of dread. "Because she'll probably find some other 'hippie remedy' to try."

Bodey laughed when, as soon as P.D. had turned away again, Elam poured a good inch of liquid out of his jar. Bodey did the same—wondering if the matted grass would spontaneously combust.

"I think you're the only one in any real danger," Bodey murmured, distracted enough from his own troubles to laugh at Elam's.

"Oh, no, little brother. She's decided that you're looking a little too pale and skinny." He shot Bodey a look rife with warning. "Whatever you do . . . do *not* eat anything she brings you that looks like peanut brittle."

IT was Syd who called Beth before dawn the next morning. They'd found a broken window in the bathroom of their RV, probably due to the hail the previous night. A shop in town was willing to fit them in before business hours if they would come in right away, so they were going to drop the Jeep off at the Red Fox Inn for Beth to use to return to Hell on Wheels.

Even though the shoot wouldn't begin for a few hours and she wasn't expected to open the tent for business until nine, she decided to go to work early.

But even as she gently shook Eric awake enough to remind him of his instructions, she knew that there was another reason for going so early. She would be leaving Cheyenne soon. And she didn't want to waste a moment that she might be able to spend with Bodey.

The horizon was barely tinted with pink when she pulled into the parking lot. She drove the vehicle to its customary spot near the tent, then walked back to Bodey's trailer.

The air was still cool after yesterday's storm and the ground was muddy and dotted with puddles, but there was a hint of heat already, so much so, that the air felt humid. Steamy.

But it wasn't the promise of another hot day that had her body growing boneless and warm. It was what lay on the other side of the door.

Knowing that she might lose her courage if she debated for too long, she reached out and knocked. She grimaced when she realized that it was a timid knock—probably inaudible from the other side.

She waited, hearing nothing to signal that Bodey was even there.

Did she have the guts to knock again?

She slipped her phone from her pocket, grimacing when she saw it wasn't even seven o'clock yet.

Go. You can see him later.

But at that moment, the door squeaked open and she saw Bodey squinting down at her. The moment he realized it was her, he opened it even farther and held out a hand to help her up the steep steps.

She had barely reached the top when he slammed the door shut again. Then she was in his arms—and, lordy, lordy did the man smell good first thing in the morning. The faint scent of soap still clung to his skin as well as the crisp tang of sun-dried linens.

"You smell good," she murmured as he bent toward her.

"And you taste good."

Then his mouth claimed hers and she didn't have the wherewithal to think of anything except sensations that plundered her as completely as his mouth.

Man, oh, man, Bodey could kiss.

She didn't wait for permission or even an invitation to deepen the embrace. He'd come to the door with no shirt again, only hastily donned jeans. Immediately, she reached for the snap, then tugged at the zipper.

He grinned.

"What's the rush?" he whispered as his lips trailed down her throat.

The rush?

That she would be leaving him and would have no way of telling him where she had gone. That she would never see him again.

"I don't want to waste any time."

If Syd and Helen weren't depending on her, she would

spend the whole day with Bodey. As it was, she would be lucky to have a few hours.

"I'm on the afternoon shoot," Bodey murmured against her lips. "I don't have to be anywhere until noon."

"Helen and Syd had to take the RV into town to have a window fixed. So I have to open up this morning."

"Shit."

This time, it was Bodey who reached for her, helping her to pull her T-shirt over her head. Then, while she wrestled with her jeans, he shucked free of his own.

For a moment, she stilled, knowing that she had to burn this memory into her brain.

"What?" Bodey asked.

"You're beautiful."

He shook his head, his cockeyed grin returning.

"Not as beautiful as you."

The deep tones of his voice, the huskiness, were as powerful as his hands stroking her bare flesh.

She reached behind her to unhook her bra, tossing it aside. His eyes burned from within, the pupils growing large. And for the first time in her life . . .

She *felt* beautiful.

Within an instant, she had shed her shoes and pants as well. Then Bodey was hauling her against him.

The first time they'd made love, there had been clothing between them—Bodey's pants, her bra. But this time it was flesh to flesh—and it felt so good. Not only because he was a powerful man—lean and muscled. But because of the way he held her, like some precious thing that he intended to protect and claim as his own. No man had ever made her feel that way. No man had ever made her feel . . .

Sheltered.

Her fingers curled into his shoulders and her eyes slammed shut when his foray of her neck continued, moving down, down, before he took her nipple in his mouth and explored it with the tip of his tongue.

How could this man have turned her life upside down so quickly? How could he have made her abandon all of the rules that she'd once set in place for herself: no attachments, no men, no distractions? And how could she ever go back to the way she'd once been, knowing what she was missing?

Her breath emerged in a soft sob and Bodey immediately straightened to frame her face in his hands.

"Did I hurt you?"

"No!"

"Did I do something you don't like?"

"No. Absolutely not." Seeing the bed behind him, she took his hand and lay down, pulling him with her.

He cupped her cheek. "You'd tell me if I did?"

"Uh huh."

She ran her palm over the stubble at his jaw, loving the way that it made him look disheveled and wild and incredibly masculine.

"What do they call it again when you separate a cow from the herd?"

His brow creased. "Cutting. You cut the cow from the herd."

"Mmm. Somehow that doesn't sound very good."

"What?"

"That you've cut me from a herd of women."

He shook his head—even managing to look a little angry. "You were never part of a herd, Beth."

"According to Helen—"

"I've known Helen since I was a little boy—and in a lot of ways, she's been a bit of a second mother to me. I love her dearly, but this time, she's got it wrong. Yes, there have been a lot of women in my life. I don't know . . . I've always liked women."

Beth couldn't help laughing but Bodey took her chin and forced her to look at him.

"No. You didn't hear me right. I said 'I've always *liked* women.' And I have. I've felt passion, lust, and affection. But no matter what I did, within a few months they all became my friends—a fact that has been a source of amusement for my brothers." His fingers skimmed over her jaw, her cheek, then carefully swept the hair out of her eyes. "But I never felt anything like this, Beth."

"Like what?"

"Reckless. Wild." He kissed the corner of her eye, her cheek, her lips. "You make me feel new and untried, willing to abandon every rule I've set up for myself in regards to women."

The words so echoed her own that her throat grew tight with emotion.

"You've made me realize that when the person is right, there isn't a whole lot you're not willing to do to be with them."

FIFTEEN

———•———

B ODEY kissed her again, deeper, more powerfully, leaving her in no doubt that he meant what he'd said. Through it all, Beth could barely think coherently, let alone speak. The honest way he'd revealed his feelings still left her reeling.

"I haven't cut you from any sort of herd, Beth."

He was looking at her lips and her body felt as if it would burst into flames from the stark desire she found there.

"I think, instead, that I was the unruly one, a stubborn maverick determined to do his own thing. Until you singled me out and brought me home."

Home.

But she didn't have a home. Didn't even have a hope for one in the foreseeable future. Nor could this . . . fling with Bodey ever become something permanent—even if he was thinking somewhere along those lines. She couldn't give him that. She could only give him the here and now.

Knowing that her expression would give her away if she thought about it anymore, she closed her eyes, kissing Bodey with all the pent up desire she had for everything he represented. A future. A commitment. A companion. Someone to share her burdens. And when he would have allowed their lovemaking to take a slow and leisurely pace, she didn't allow him that luxury. She wanted all of him—his mind, his body, and his soul. Even if it was only temporary.

So when he grabbed a condom from a drawer and readied himself, she drew him down on top of her—something she'd been loath to do in the past. Bodey was a big man and she feared his weight, since she didn't like the sensation of being crushed. But she needn't have worried. He was instinctively careful, propping his weight on his elbows, allowing her to control their lovemaking with her hands on his shoulders and her legs wrapped around his thighs.

By the time he drove into her, again and again, she knew she could trust him not to hurt her.

Now if she could only trust herself enough to keep from begging him to find a way to help her stay by his side.

"WHAT'S wrong? You're awfully quiet."

Although she knew it was growing close to nine, Beth lingered in Bodey's arms, loving the way he made her feel. Warm. Desirable.

Safe.

Why did she keep coming back to that word? It wasn't as if anything had altered in her predicament. She was still alone in her responsibilities—and she would have to remain that way.

Tell him.

No.

She couldn't bear it if something she said made him look at her differently. Vaguely, she remembered when he'd told her about his little brother. At one point, he'd stated that dealing with Barry had been enough to put him off having children for the rest of his life.

Did he still feel that way? Because, God willing, she would have her siblings with her until they were old enough to live on their own. She came with a ready-made family—

one of them a teenager. Most men would start running at that combination.

Somehow, she couldn't see Bodey Taggart—admitted adventurer and a man with a reputation for moving from woman to woman—willingly stepping into the role of guardian. Not when it would tie him down—or even curtail some of his activities. And it wouldn't be fair of her to ask it of him.

Yet, even with that forewarning, she couldn't help wishing that she could be someone different. Someone who had what it took to tame this self-avowed maverick.

But she'd never been enough. Why would she think that anything could change now?

"Beth?"

She started, realizing that he'd asked a question.

"What? Nothing's wrong."

"You suddenly look like you have the weight of the world on your shoulders."

She was resting her head low on his chest, facing him so that she could memorize the angles of his face, the untamed mess of his hair.

"No. Just enjoying the view."

He must have realized that she was focused on his hair because he cursed under his breath and tried to smooth it down with his hands.

"You're making it worse."

"I need a shower to tame it. I take after my mother. Her hair was really curly. When it's humid—"

She placed her finger over his lips. "I like it. It makes you look a little . . ."

"Slobby?"

"Uh-uh. Well-ridden."

That caused a slow smile but it faded far too quickly. He reached to trail his fingers over her back in sweeping circles.

"You'd let me know if there was something wrong, wouldn't you?"

She quickly searched his expression.

What did he know?

Had she somehow slipped up?

But he was regarding her with such tenderness that she decided that he was speaking about their lovemaking.

But before she could reassure him, he shifted. "Where's your phone?"

"Why?"

"Give it to me."

Still curious, she reached for her jeans and slipped it out of her pocket. After unlocking the display, she handed it to him.

"I'm going to put my number in your contact list. If you ever need something, you call me."

She offered him an indulgent smile, knowing that she would never do it.

He must have sensed her thoughts because he said, "I mean it. This isn't one of those offers people give but they never really mean." He handed it back to her. "Now call me."

"Why?"

"So I can store your number in my phone."

Beth hesitated, wondering if he'd somehow known that if he'd asked for her number, she would probably have put him off or given him a false one. But since she was essentially cornered, she had no real choice.

She pushed the call button and within seconds the theme from *The Good, the Bad, and the Ugly* came from the cellphone he'd left on the counter.

"Really?" she asked with amusement.

"What did you think I'd have as my ringtone? *It's Raining Men*?"

He reached to grab the phone and quickly tapped on the screen, saving her number. Then, he placed it back on the counter.

"Can I call you if I'm in trouble?"

His question was lighthearted, but it plunged into her breast like a sliver of ice.

"Absolutely." Her answer was barely more than a whisper. But even as she assured him that he could call day or night, she knew there would be a time when she would have to change her number.

Because she couldn't drag this man into the ugliness of her world.

BODEY wanted to walk Beth to the tent, but because of the size of his shower—and the fact that they might choose to linger if they shared—he'd let her go first. By the time he emerged, she was gone.

He didn't worry too much about her absence. She'd been in a good mood when they'd switched places in the shower. And a glance at the clock showed him that it was only a few minutes before nine. He appreciated the way that she took her job with Helen so seriously. It spoke well about her character and her relationship with Helen.

Even though he would be shooting with the afternoon posses, he didn't want to have to come back to change, so he dressed in woven pants, a red bib front shirt, a tan bandana, button suspenders, and an old tan hat. Then, he stamped his feet into a pair of work boots.

At the last minute, he decided not to bring his weapons and gun cart. He could come back for those later. Maybe that way, he'd be able to spend some time with Beth in the tent.

He grabbed his dark glasses and slid a couple of his prescription pills into his pocket, just in case. Then he headed outside.

Already, the moisture from yesterday's storm was beginning to evaporate under the morning sun. So far, it was still cool, but the wind blowing in from the west was hot. By the time it was his turn to shoot, it would probably be in the high nineties again with the intent of breaking a hundred. But that was normal for the Hell on Wheels competition, which was usually held over the Fourth of July Weekend.

Idly, Bodey wondered if Beth had any plans for the Fourth. He was sure there would be at least one fireworks show in town, maybe more. If he could figure out where, maybe he could see if one of them was visible from his friend's ranch. He could arrange a picnic, throw out a blanket, and he and Beth could lie down and watch the show. Then they could make a few fireworks of their own.

"You're in a good mood today."

He started, looking up to find P.D. heading toward him. Mindful of her condition, he stopped and waited for her.

It still shocked the hell out of him to see P.D. preggers. They'd been friends for a half dozen years—long before Elam had come home from Afghanistan. And she was the one woman he'd never been tempted to date. Because they'd started out as friends, good friends, he'd never wanted to spoil the arrangement. Not that she would have gone out with him anyway. P.D. had been too wrapped up in starting her restaurant to date much.

Until Elam came along.

"How's little Antman."

She grimaced. "Elam told you."

"Yeah. It's going to stick, you know."

She rolled her eyes. "That's what I'm afraid of."

They continued toward vendors' row, but Bodey kept his pace slow. Sensing that P.D. was headed toward Elam's first stage, he altered their trajectory. The safety meeting was finished and the flag was already atop the pole, so that meant Bodey was only a little bit late. Most of the competitors were still heading toward the shooting bays.

"Are you feeling okay?"

P.D. grimaced. "At least I'm not puking anymore." She patted her stomach and her smile was gentle and slightly secretive. "We've come to an understanding. I'll let him continue his acrobatic routines and he won't make me sick. The last few weeks, that seems to be working."

"Any word from Jace and Bronte?"

"I got a text from Bronte last night. They're in Venice."

"Has she seen anything but museums yet?"

P.D. grinned. "Actually, they haven't been to many at all. Europe has proven to be . . . very romantic."

Only a week ago, Bodey might have been irritated at the

news that Jace was getting even more loving—when he and Bronte seemed to get plenty of it at home. But now that he'd met Beth . . . he could understand why Jace enjoyed the company of the woman in his life.

"Way to go, Jace."

"And Bronte. After all, they went for the 'art.'" P.D. grinned. "So far, I don't think they've seen much more art than the hotel room ceiling."

"They deserve the time alone. Heaven only knows, with three kids underfoot most of the time, they don't get much of it."

They had reached the shooting bay and Bodey looped his arms over the safety fence.

They watched the posse getting ready in silence for several minutes. Then P.D. said casually, "Helen says that you've taken an interest in her new employee."

Bodey opened his mouth to mutter that Helen needed to mind her own damn business but he supposed that would be churlish since she was only stating the truth.

He wasn't sure how to respond, so he dug the tip of his toe into the dust. "Her name's Beth."

P.D. nodded. "I know. I met her yesterday." She regarded Bodey with quiet eyes for a moment, then remarked, "She's not your usual type."

Again, he searched for the best way to respond. With anyone but P.D., he would be flippant or sarcastic—or cut off the first hint of prying. But he knew P.D. was merely opening the avenue for conversation. If he wanted it. If he didn't want to talk about it, he would only need to say so and she'd drop the subject.

"I guess you could say that my interest isn't the same either," he finally admitted.

P.D. knew enough not to comment. She merely nodded.

"She's . . . different," Bodey added, not explaining the myriad ways that Beth was unlike any other woman he'd dated. It wasn't only her physical attributes. It was the way she listened so intently. The way that she was so guarded with her emotions one minute and so honestly open the next.

It was the way she made his mind jump to meet her verbal challenges and the way she made him feel passion, tenderness, joy—and, yes, that inner caveman protectiveness that Elam often spoke of when he referred to P.D.

"She was quiet yesterday," P.D. said. "But that might have been because I was new to her. Helen is really impressed with her work. She told Beth that she'd take her home and hire her full time if Beth were open to the idea. I'd guess that Beth thought she was kidding, but I'm sure Helen was serious." P.D. waited a beat before adding, "Helen believes she needs some TLC."

Bodey nodded. "Yeah. I think so, too."

P.D. beamed at him, clearly pleased that he wasn't being as dense about such things as he usually was.

"Maybe you can talk her into coming to Utah."

Bodey shrugged. "I'm sure as hell going to try. I think she feels like she's fighting all of her battles alone."

P.D.'s lips twitched. "Then maybe you could convince her that she's got some powerful backup behind her. With you, me, Helen, and the rest of the Taggart males, seems to me she can do just about anything—*Ow!*"

The cry of distress was so sudden, so loud, that Bodey automatically reacted, reaching out to steady P.D. But she suddenly smiled and waved to Elam, who'd been midway through his round of shooting.

"Sorry, sweetie! I stubbed my toe."

As soon as Elam returned his attention to the range, she grinned and said under her breath, "There you go; my gift to you. At least one miss and a procedural. From here on out, it should be a pretty fair fight for the highest shooter."

Bodey laughed. Now that was a true friend.

UNACCOUNTABLY, Bodey didn't linger around the gun range to see how his brother fared after that. Nor did he pause to watch the participants—many of whom had become close friends to Bodey over the dozen years he'd been a member of SASS. Instead, he made his way into one of the nearby tents to make a purchase, then wandered down vendors' row toward the familiar shape of Virgil the Cowboy as he swayed in the wind, beckoning customers to step inside the Hendersons' store.

It didn't escape him that there had once been a time when the sight of so many racks displaying ruffled pantalets and embroidered corsets, ribbon bedecked parasols and lace adorned garments would have sent him in the opposite direction. Now, he didn't even give them a second glance as he rounded the corner and searched for Beth.

She was standing near the back corner—and she was alone. One by one, she took a garment down from the rack, straightened it on the hanger, then put it back again. From what he could see, she was sorting the clothing back ino a semblance of order again, grouping jackets, shirts, and skirts together, then moving on to complete ensembles.

For once, she wasn't dressed in costume. Instead, she wore the same clothes she'd had on this morning—black T-shirt, black jeans, black lace-up boots.

By now, he knew her choice was practical since a cheap motel like the Trailblazer didn't offer an in-house laundry room.

Somehow, she must have sensed his approach, despite the way that he'd tried to be quiet so that he wouldn't disturb her work. She glanced over her shoulder, recognized him, then offered him a smile that landed like a sucker-punch in his gut. Never in his life had a woman looked at him with such a rife mixture of pleasure and awareness, shyness and pure feminine allure.

"Hi there, handsome."

Her words took him off guard.

Handsome?

Elam was handsome. Jace was handsome.

Bodey knew he was pretty much ordinary.

But the way she was looking at him made him feel like he'd been named one of the sexiest men alive. Unaccountably, he felt his ears and his cheeks grow hot—and he feared he was blushing like a kid at his first dance, because she laughed in delight.

"Where's Helen?" he asked, hoping to draw her attention away from his reaction.

"They pulled up in the motor home a few minutes ago. Helen's inside getting some sewing done and Syd's out watching some buddies on the range." She hooked a shirt in place on the clothing rail.

"No costume today?"

She grimaced. "My steampunk outfit is still drying out. I've got it hanging in the sun. I told Helen I'd stick to my own clothes until it was ready."

"Well, then." Bodey prowled closer, one arm snaking around her waist. At the last minute, he remembered the far corner. "Anyone in the changing cubicle?"

"Nope."

"That's what I was hoping to hear."

He dragged her into the cubicle, partially closing the curtain.

"I brought you something." He held up the sack. "Maybe you can wear this instead of your costume.

He saw the way she hesitated—as if accepting a gift was much too personal, even after everything they'd shared. But there was also a glint of pleasure in her eyes.

"What is it?" Her words held only a hint of suspicion.

"Take a look."

She finally took the bag, reaching inside to remove a bundle wrapped in tissue paper. With the carefulness of a person who wasn't accustomed to presents—and who wanted to prolong the anticipation—she carefully unwrapped the layers and shook free the bright yellow fabric.

For several seconds, she looked at the T-shirt—and Bodey could have kicked himself when he saw that the size he'd chosen was too large. But then she began to laugh.

"Do you like it?" he asked tentatively.

"Oh, yeah," she breathed. "I like it. Help me put it on."

He didn't need to be told twice. Shielding her from being

seen from inside the tent, he helped her sweep her own black shirt over her head. Truth be told, he didn't complete the chore as efficiently as he could have done. His fingers kept straying to her bare skin, the lee of her waist, the strong indentation of her spine. But after kissing and stroking and wasting as much time as possible, he finally managed to help her pull the hem into place.

Emblazoned on her chest was an old-fashioned photograph of a group of wizened, gap-toothed women from the nineteenth century. Underneath were the words: THE ORIGINAL WILD BUNCH GANG.

Beth looked down at her chest again and laughed.

"Thanks. It's priceless."

He looped his arms around her back, pulling her snuggly against his hips. "I actually bought it for the color. It'll be cooler than all that black and . . ." He kissed her cheek, the spot beneath her ear. "That's how you make me feel, all sunny and warm."

"Warm . . . or hot?" she asked, her tone rife with desire.

"Both."

He bent to offer her a soft, lingering kiss—and her response was rich with memories of the hours they'd already spent in one another's arms, as well as a promise for the next time they could steal a few private moments.

Bodey loved the way that Beth leaned into his embrace and lifted as high as she could on the balls of her feet. Even more, he loved wrapping his arms around her, taking her slight weight so that she could concentrate on the delicious things he wanted to do to her with his tongue.

"When do you have to get ready for your shoot?" she murmured when he finally drew back.

"I don't have to be to my stage until one. But I was hoping I could convince you to join me for an early lunch—say, around eleven?" He whispered next to her ear, "Somehow, I missed my breakfast this morning."

This time, Beth's cheeks grew pink, probably because she was remembering, as he was, how they had spent those delicious hours rather than getting a meal.

"So, do you think Helen would mind?" he asked as he lowered her to her feet again.

"I don't think so. She's usually lecturing me about not eating enough."

Her words were nonchalant, but the look she gave him was rife with want—and that was enough to cause his body to respond even more. He was used to women who played it cool and coy—or who were openly obvious about being into him for the sex. But Beth was a beautiful mixture of the two—at once innocent and honestly passionate, curious and adventurous.

A tall woman dressed head to toe in green gingham stepped into the tent and Bodey wished that he and Beth had been given more time to finalize their plans. But even as the thought ricocheted through his head, two more women—dressed in modern jeans and T-shirts—made a beeline for the jewelry counter.

"I'll leave you to your customers," he said lowly so that the women at the far side of the tent wouldn't hear him. He took a step back, then another, but couldn't bring himself to break the connection. Not yet. So he said, "How about if I bring something to the tent? That would give me enough time to eat and then get ready for the shoot, and you wouldn't have to worry about leaving if you get mobbed with customers."

Her smile was shy. "Sure. That sounds good."

"What do you want?"

She shrugged. "Surprise me."

He couldn't resist walking back toward her and bending low to murmur next to her ear. "You might not like the surprise."

He saw the way her eyes widened, ever so slightly. Her voice was husky when she responded, "I don't think there's anything you could dish out that I wouldn't like."

He felt an immediate response to the words but knew there wasn't time to do much about it, so he leaned down for a quick kiss. "See you later."

He strode toward the tent flap, then turned before going out into the sunshine.

"Oh, I forgot to mention something."

Her brows rose and her gaze skipped to the customers. Apparently, she was expecting a ribald comment, which made him laugh. "Nothing like that. You know that battered Ford pickup we saw yesterday?"

She regarded him blankly.

"The red one."

She stiffened. "Yeah?"

"Was the driver someone you know?"

"I . . . no, I don't think so. I thought he looked familiar, but . . . no." Bodey would have to be blind not to see the way she became infinitely still and wary. "Why?"

"I've seen it driving past here a couple of times this morning. I didn't know if I should mention it or not."

The color leached from her skin. He waited for her to explain what had upset her but she donned a plastic smile. One that told him as well as a flashing neon sign that something was wrong, really, really wrong. But she couldn't bring herself to confide in him.

He couldn't blame her. After all, the attraction they shared might be overwhelming, the passion, out of this world. But she didn't really know him—good hell almighty, he was beginning to believe that he didn't know himself anymore. He would have sworn he was a trustworthy sort, but looking back, he had to admit that, to date, he'd been wrapped up in his own concerns. He'd skated through most of his twenties like a rock skipping a pond, jumping from woman to woman, contest to contest, without bothering to plumb any deeper than surface emotions. And now that he was tempted to delve into something more?

He was truly out of his depth.

So, when the silence went on too long and she still didn't speak, he finally resorted to old habits, touched the brim of his hat with his fingers, and said, "See you later."

Sixteen

———•—•———

AFTER Bodey's innocent pronouncement, that he'd seen the red pickup with the Oregon plates, a trembling began in Beth's extremities, moving inward as if she'd suddenly caught a fever, until she feared that she wouldn't be able to stand.

She barely noticed as the women murmured something about coming back later and left the tent. She flashed hot, then cold, her pulse pounding in her teeth until finally, she fought to drag herself from the tar-like fear that held her in its grip. She rushed to the back counter where she'd set down her phone. Grabbing it, she quickly dialed her brother's number.

It was answered on the second ring.

"Hello."

"Eric, is everything all right?"

"Yeah, why?"

Her breath escaped in a shuddering wheeze. "Nothing, I . . ."

"Beth, what's going on?"

"Nothing. But I want you to be really careful today."

"Beth?"

"I'm just jumpy. Stay in the motel; keep the curtains drawn."

"Bethy, what's going on?"

"Nothing, I . . . I've got a bad feeling about that red truck, you know? I'll talk to Helen as soon as she and Syd are done shooting this afternoon. Maybe I can get my wages and we can be on our way that much sooner. In the meantime, be careful. Okay?"

"Yeah."

"You remember our plan don't you?"

"Bethy, I know what to do."

"Sorry. I'm . . . I'll talk to you later, all right?"

"We'll be fine, Bethy. No one will be able to see inside and we're not going anywhere. Don't worry. I promise to answer on the first ring if you need me."

But as she ended the call, Beth knew that she couldn't do anything *but* worry.

BETH felt a presence long before she consciously registered that someone had entered the tent. She didn't look up at first, supposing it was Bodey since it was almost eleven o'clock. But then, the hairs at the nape of her neck prickled, the sensation sweeping down her spine in a chill that robbed her of breath, forcing her to turn and confront the one person she was so sure that she would never see again.

John Joseph Connolly.

He looked different—not surprising, since she hadn't seen him since she was fifteen. He'd been a heart-breaker then, a tall lanky boy with the soul of a poet. She'd fallen for him hard, even though she'd known that such a thing was forbidden and she was doomed to marry another man.

"Hello Mary Grace."

The old name, the one that had been assigned to the girl that she'd once been, washed over her in waves of memories, some sweet, most bitter.

"That's not my name." The retort burst from her lips before she had a chance to think twice.

He had the good grace to grimace. "I never knew your real name."

"Beth. My name is Beth."

He didn't comment but she could see a little muscle in his jaw. One that made her aware of the fact that he was too thin for a man his age. She could see the sharp angles of bone sheathed in little more than muscle. He had a whipcord lean physique that was barely softened by dark twill pants and a white shirt he wore buttoned up to his Adam's apple. Even the severe haircut—shaved sides, military flat top—was hard and angular.

The uniform of the Farm.

Severe, staid, form-covering. If it weren't for the hair and the buttons, he could have been a participant of Hell on Wheels, passing as an Amish farmhand.

Of all the people from the Farm that she'd expected to ultimately confront her, face to face, John Joseph would have been the last person on her list. She was so sure that he would never want to see her again, let alone that he'd try to drag her back to the life she'd once led.

"You look good," he commented softly.

She could still tell when he was lying. He disapproved of her. She represented everything he'd been taught to abhor—a worldly, painted woman displaying her wares to the world.

"What do you want, John Joseph?"

She didn't know why she bothered to ask. She knew he hadn't come here for her. She was too late for redemption. Too "tainted" by the capitalist world and a corrupt government.

He shook his head, a gesture that conveyed disbelief at her supposed naiveté and her unwillingness to state the obvious.

"Where are they? You know it's only a matter of time before we find them as well. You'd be better off returning them to us now, than prolonging this . . . flight."

The shock of seeing John Joseph was quickly wearing off. In its place came a roil of emotion so powerful that Beth began to tremble all over again—this time with rage and frustration. For more than a year, she'd been dodging the long arm of the Farm's leadership and she wasn't about to give in so easily.

"I don't have them. I took them to live with friends."

John Joseph shook his head, making a *tsk*ing noise. "You and I know that you don't have any friends, Mary Grace."

"Beth. My name is Beth."

He advanced toward her, the boy she'd once known fading beneath the fervor of a man embroiled in a lifestyle of fanaticism and aggression.

"You'll never be Beth. Deep down, you know the truth but you're too weak to face up to it. You've strayed from the right path, been immersed into a culture that believes in nothing but self-gratification and oppression—"

"Oppression? Isn't that what the Farm is all about? Surrendering your rights, your needs, your own self-dignity to the will of a select few?"

John Joseph's eyes narrowed. "Listen to you. You even sound like one of the Outsiders."

"Outsiders!" she scoffed. "If that's what you want to call being just like everyone else, I'll gladly wear that label."

"You've allowed yourself to be assimilated into a culture of—"

"Assimilated? I'm a person with my own wants and needs, John Joseph. And since leaving the Farm, I've lived like a human being! I have a home and a family of my own. I'm allowed to live and love the way I want!"

Spots of color appeared on his cheeks and she knew that he was remembering that there was a time when John Joseph had proclaimed to love her enough to run away with her, to leave the Farm so that they could be together no matter what the group's leadership might say.

"So come back with me," he said softly. "You could still have all that within the Group Collective. I'm a Lieutenant now. We could be together."

A Lieutenant.

Within the Fundamentalist Army—or "The Farm" as it was sometimes called—there were only two groups with power. The Commanders, who made all of the decisions, and the Lieutenants, who enforced those decisions. The rest of the members were part of the Collective, those who were called upon to respond with utmost obedience to any of the directives handed down from their leaders.

Only the Commanders and the Lieutenants were allowed the privilege of procreation, picking their "brides" from the young girls among the Collective.

"I'm not going back," she said forcefully.

"Then give me Mary Catherine and John Jacob."

The false names her siblings had been given by Leroy Vonn grated on her ears. Her mother had given them names unique to themselves.

"Go to hell."

Her low pronouncement severed what control John Joseph had because he suddenly sneered at her, lunging across the aisle to grab her by both elbows.

"Do you think this is a game? When Vonn got wind of where you might be, I volunteered to find you myself. I thought it would make this easier for you. But if you don't hand those kids over, you know what's going to happen. I won't be the worst of your nightmares. They'll send one of the platoons out and take them by force—maybe even hurt you in the process!"

An invisible fist squeezed her heart—the sensation more painful than John Joseph's fingers gripping her arms. The thud of her pulse knocked so painfully against her skull that she feared it would crack in two.

John Joseph wasn't telling her anything that she didn't already know. It was why, after her mother's death and Beth's being named the children's guardian, she'd gone on the run—why they'd been dodging the Farm ever since. She'd known that—even with the law on her side—if Leroy Vonn managed to abduct her siblings, getting the children back would be nearly impossible. And Beth couldn't live with herself if her brother and sister spent another day locked in the compound without even the most rudimentary opportunities such as socialization and an education.

Free will.

"Back away from her. Now."

The low command vibrated through the tent. The words were simple but their tone resonated with barely concealed menace.

Beth looked past John Joseph to see another man looming in the entrance to the tent. This time, she had no doubts who it was. She would know the shape of Bodey's body anywhere.

John Joseph glanced at him in confusion and Beth could understand why. It was hard to believe that the dark silhouette was real. Bodey loomed over John Joseph, every inch of him the classic cowboy. He wore a dark felt cowboy hat with a beaded band, an ebony tab-collared shirt with arm garters, a black leather vest, ebony twill trousers, and soot-colored boots. Everything about him screamed the part of a Wild West villain. But what set him apart as a person to be reckoned with was the way he stood with his palms held loose and at the ready on the pistols strapped low on his hips.

Beth had seen that stance before—mere moments before Bodey emptied his weapons on the range. She knew that he could draw before John Joseph could even blink. She just prayed that John Joseph wouldn't know that Bodey's pistols weren't loaded.

At least, they weren't supposed to be loaded.

Were they?

John Joseph must have feared the possibility as well because he slowly released her, lifting his hands to show that he was unarmed.

But his slight retreat wasn't enough for Bodey, because his eyes narrowed and his fingertips brushed the pistols.

"You need to leave."

At that, John Joseph bristled. "This is a private conversation."

"Not anymore. Beth doesn't want you here."

"We have business to discuss."

"From what I overheard, she's made it clear that she

doesn't have anything else left to say to you, so it's time for you to go." His fingers twitched, as if he was eager to draw a bead on the other man.

"I don't—"

Bodey smoothly interrupted him. "Beth, do you have anything else left to say?"

Her heart was pounding in her throat, but she forced herself to say, "No."

"Do you want him to leave?"

John Joseph bristled, looking to Beth as if he expected her to smooth things over with Bodey so that they could continue their conversation. It was exactly what would have been demanded of her as a member of the Farm. Bowing to authority. Kowtowing to the established male leadership.

In a flashing montage, Beth saw the myriad times her mother had given in to Leroy Vonn. And each time; she lost a little piece of herself. There had been no partnership with her longstanding lover, no mutual respect, no give and take. It had been the role of master and slave. And Beth had been expected to follow suit.

But she'd escaped.

And she wouldn't be going back. Not now. Not ever. Neither would Eric and Dolly.

"I want him to leave and I don't want to ever see him again."

The words emerged from her mouth, slowly, deliberately, each syllable adding power to the next. She looked at John Joseph again, her chin tilting with pride and determination, leaving no doubt that the decision was hers.

That seemed to be all the confirmation Bodey needed, because he began to close the distance, taking his place behind her shoulder. She was grateful for the way he literally watched her back, yet made it clear that she was the person in charge.

"You can't do this, Mary—"

"Beth! My name is Beth!"

A muscle flicked in John Joseph's cheek. "You have no

idea what you're doing—the host of troubles that you're about to unleash."

Bodey took a half a step forward, so near now that Beth could feel the heat of his body. Yet, there was no disguising the smooth rasp of his pistol being pulled from its holster. For the moment, the weapon remained at his side, but he made it clear that he'd be willing to use it at any time.

"And you aren't going to stand here and threaten me! I'm the legal guardian of the children in question. If you try to interfere with that—you or the Farm—I will use every means in my power to protect them!"

The click of a hammer being locked into place punctuated her remarks.

"You need to leave. Right now."

John Joseph hesitated, only an instant, his fingers opening and closing in impotent fists. But after one last glance at Bodey's gun, he stormed from the tent.

Beth waited, counting her heartbeats. Then, when she was sure that John Joseph would be out of earshot, she allowed her pent-up breath to leave her lungs in a whoosh.

For a moment, her body radiated with power—the results of having stood up for herself once and for all. But then, John Joseph's pronouncement echoed in the stillness.

You have no idea what you're doing—the host of troubles that you're about to unleash.

"No, please, no," she whispered.

Beth ran to the back of the tent where she'd left her phone near the cash register. Her hands were trembling so badly, she fumbled as she snatched it up and tried to unlock the display.

"Beth?"

Bodey came up beside her, touching her on the shoulder—and his steady strength calmed her enough that she could dial her brother's number.

It rang once, twice, three times.

"Pick up, pick up!"

Four, five, six.

The phone kicked over to voice mail.

"No, please, no."

She quickly redialed. But it rang again and again with the same result.

Hanging up again, Beth quickly moved to the texting feature.

Bug out. Now!

She waited for a response but there was no answering text.

Damn it.

Frantic, she searched the confines of the tent as if it could offer a clue to what she should do next—but it only reminded her that Helen and Syd had gone to the range. She knew she couldn't leave the tent unattended, but she had to get back to the hotel. Now.

She began to tremble, feeling as if the canvas walls were growing and growing like some eerie photo with a telescopic lens.

But then she heard Bodey's voice and clung to it like an anchor.

"P.D., I need you to come to Helen's tent. Do you think you could take over the store for a little while?"

The words pulled Beth back, back, falling into her consciousness like rocks into a pond. At long last, their meaning began to coalesce and she realized that as Bodey spoke into his phone, he was offering a ray of hope.

"Thanks. My gun cart is sitting out front, keep an eye on it until you can get here."

He ended his own phone call and took Beth's hand. "P.D. is only a few yards away. She'll take over watching the store as long as it takes."

Beth scrambled to think. "Can I borrow your truck? I know I need to explain what—"

He took her elbows, his grip firm, but much gentler than John Joseph's had been. And when she looked up into his eyes, she saw no recrimination for the lies she'd told, no disappointment for her lack of faith in him, merely a fierce protectiveness.

"You don't need to explain anything and you're not going anywhere alone. I'll drive; you tell me where to go."

As much as she wanted to leave, *right now,* there was still a part of her that remembered that Bodey should be taking his place on the range. He had a bet to win. If he didn't shoot, he would probably have to forfeit.

"But you have a competition—"

He bent so that she could see the fierce light in his eyes. "Do you think any of that means a damn thing? You need help. That's all I need to know."

She sobbed—a sound that was half-joy, half-terror. Then she followed him as he strode out the back of the tent, pulling her along behind him.

Within a few yards, they were running at breakneck speed toward the spot where his truck was parked next to his trailer.

Using his key fob, he had the engine running before they even reached the vehicle. Opening the driver's door, he lifted her into the seat, then slid in beside her.

"Where do you need to go?"

AS Beth gave him directions to the rundown hotel, Bodey kept his silence, knowing that this wasn't the time to tell her that he already knew where she'd been staying. Instead, he backed out and maneuvered through the crowded parking lot. When he was finally able to turn onto the main highway, he gunned the engine, going as fast as he dared on the country highway.

While he drove, Beth returned to her phone, dialing again and again and again.

"They aren't answering!"

"Stay off the phone for a few minutes in case someone is trying to call you."

She nodded, holding the phone in her lap and watching it much the same way she might if it were a poisonous snake and she had to be ready for the slightest eventuality.

"So, I take it you knew that guy really well."

Shit, shit, shit.

Now wasn't the time to pump her for answers—but the words popped out before he could stop them, and once they'd been uttered, he couldn't unsay them.

She took a gulp of air—one that was ragged with emotion—and he could have kicked himself again for his insensitivity.

"Yeah . . . I, uh—" She pressed a finger to the crease between her brow. "He was part of the group I lived with when I was young."

Group? Odd choice of words.

Clearly unable to help herself, she touched the text button on her phone and began typing a frantic message.

Bodey waited until she hit SEND before prompting, "Group?"

A sound that was half laugh, half sob escaped from her lips, and he reached over to take her hand.

"My parents divorced when I was . . . uh . . . five? Six?"

He could feel the way her whole body trembled violently.

"My mother fell under the spell of a man named Leroy Vonn."

"The survivalist guy?"

She glanced at him in surprise. "You've heard of him?"

"Hell, yeah. I've got buddies on the circuit who are from the northwest. They've been complaining about the way he's been gobbling up land and expanding his trucking empire all under the guise of being a non-profit religious organization."

"That's him. But when my mother first met him, he didn't have nearly so many followers. It was a half-dozen families living in the woods, trying to live off the land."

"Sounds tough. Especially for a kid."

Her eyes closed for a minute—as if she were reliving a scene from her childhood. "You have no idea. Maybe there are other people who are cut out for existing that way but I wasn't so good at surrendering my own will to another person—even when I was little."

"So that guy back there—"

"John Joseph. He's the oldest son of another one of Leroy Vonn's followers." She hesitated, glancing up at Bodey with something akin to guilt. "He was my first crush, first kiss, first . . ."

He squeezed her hand to show her that he didn't fault her for such normal adolescent experiences.

"First lover?"

She nodded her head.

"I was only fifteen."

Bodey fought the urge to swear. Granted, he'd lost his own virginity as a teenager, but the thought of Beth surrendering her body to that bastard at such a young age made his skin crawl. Even now, years later, she gave off an aura of innocence. What would she have been like at fifteen?

But he didn't want Beth to misinterpret the tension that suddenly radiated through his body, so he lifted her hand to kiss it, showing that he understood.

"Looking back on it now, I know how foolish I was. We were both . . . stupid." She made a soft, bitter moan. "I didn't even know that there were risks involved. Neither of us were . . . protected."

The blood that boiled through his body suddenly turned to ice.

"Did you . . . I mean . . ." He didn't know how to ask it. Was the little girl he'd seen her daughter?

"No, no I . . . I was lucky. I didn't get pregnant, but . . . but Vonn was furious that I'd broken one of the group's rules. Sex isn't allowed unless it's sanctioned by him. So he decided it was time for me to be married. To a man who was nearly fifty years old."

"Damnit," Bodey whispered.

"Luckily, my biological dad found out about it. He was able to get emergency custody and he took me away."

The statement was filled with such sadness. Bodey didn't understand. Leaving the survivalist group should have been a relief.

But then he remembered the male at the hotel room door.

"But you couldn't bring anyone with you."

She nodded, her eyes filling with tears. "My brother and baby sister were left behind. And it wasn't until my mother's death—when I was made their legal guardian—that I was able to get them out of that place."

"But Vonn isn't willing to give them up."

"No. He's been pounding it into the group's heads that this is another instance of the government's interference into a person's liberty and self-determination. He's got them all brainwashed into thinking Eric and Dolly *want* to come back—when it couldn't be further from the truth!" She began to cry then. Huge tears that slipped silently down her face. It was all the more heartbreaking for the lack of noise. As was the look of utter despair that slid over her face.

Bodey released her hand to pull her close. "Nothing's happened yet."

"But Eric isn't answering the phone."

Eric. Finally. A name to attach to the face.

"There could be dozens of reasons why he hasn't called you back. It can't be the first time you've had to wait for him to respond."

She bit her lip. "No. But he promised. He promised he'd answer on the first ring."

"We'll be there in a minute. Then you can chew him out in person, okay?"

His attempt at humor fell flat, so he eased the truck onto the onramp, then pushed the speed even more—praying that there weren't any Wyoming Highway Patrol officers eager to chase down someone going nearly twenty miles an hour over the speed limit.

Thankfully, there were no flashing lights in his rearview mirror as he took the off-ramp again.

Now that he no longer needed to pretend that he didn't know where Beth was staying, it was nearly a straight shot to the access road. Only a couple of turns and . . .

He pulled to a sharp stop, twisting the wheel so he could skid to the side of the road and sandwich his truck between a moving van and a Range Rover parallel parked kitty corner from the motel.

Even from that distance, it was easy to see that there were more vehicles in the parking lot than normal. Most of them were older models, spattered with mud and sporting gun racks in the rearview windows. The familiar pine tree in the center of the license plates had been the first clue to Bodey that extra caution was needed.

"Do you recognize anyone there?"

Although most of the drivers had remained in their vehicles, a few of the men were milling around the parking lot.

"I-I don't know. Maybe?"

He squeezed her hand again.

"You can't go up to the front door. Judging by the way they're hanging around, either your siblings are playing possum or those guys already know they aren't in there."

Beth nodded. "There's a window around the back. Can you get me there?"

"Hold on."

Bodey did a quick U-turn and headed around the block, cutting through the parking lot of an electronics store to an access alley. But before he could even negotiate the turn, he came to a halt. He could see the half-open window of the corner unit, but two men were peering inside, deliberating which one of them should go in first.

Beth gasped, a small noise of panic that was half sigh, half cry of distress.

"Wha—"

The phone in her lap beeped and Beth snatched it up. "Eric?"

Bodey heard a garbled staccato response but judging by the way Beth sagged, he figured it was her brother.

Beth glanced up, still holding the phone. "Walmart. It's—"

"I know where it is."

SEVENTEEN

B ODEY backed the truck up slowly, knowing that the diesel engine could be overly loud if pushed. As soon as he felt he was a safe distance away from the Trailblazer Motel, he picked up the pace, carefully making his way through the side streets until he felt he was far enough away to join the main thoroughfare.

From there, he fought the streetlights, pushing to close the distance as quickly as he could. In reality, it probably took only a few more minutes to reach the huge shopping complex but it seemed like much longer before he could make his way through the mouse maze of inlets and parking lanes so that he could approach the front entrance.

"We're driving up now," Beth said into the phone. "No. Stay where you are. I'll come in and get you." She looked up at Bodey. "Can you drive around the parking lot once while I'm inside? We'll be watching for you, make sure you haven't been followed, then we'll run out as soon as you pull up."

Judging by her expression, she expected him to protest the precautions, but Bodey nodded. "If you see anything that worries you, call me." He offered her a quick grin. "I promise to answer on the first ring."

She flashed him a grateful smile—one that made him wonder how long she'd been on her own. He couldn't even begin to imagine what she'd been through. She'd been on the run through no fault of her own—and the legal protection which should have been hers hadn't been enough. If the same situation had happened to Barry . . .

He'd be out for blood—as would his brothers and probably half the community of Bliss.

But Beth, his sweet Beth, had been forced to do it all alone.

All that was going to change.

Bodey's fingers tightened around the steering wheel so fiercely that the plastic creaked.

From now on, she would have an army at her back if she wanted one. He'd see to it personally.

The truck hadn't even come to a complete stop when Beth scooted close to the door. Then, as he tapped the brakes, she jumped out and ran inside.

More than anything, Bodey wanted to stay at the crosswalk. Damnit, he didn't want her out of his sight. He needed to make sure that he could be there if she needed his help. He'd willingly go inside for her and take the brunt of any repercussions if they'd been followed. But he knew that Beth's instructions had been sound, so he rolled forward again, keeping an eye on his mirrors.

Rather than doing a broad circle, he made an irregular circuit through the parked cars, backtracking on his own trail, looking for suspicious farm trucks with Oregon plates, hoping that the other vehicles would hide his progress if anyone from the Farm was tailing them. By the time he made it back to the main exit again, his heart was beating so hard that an outsider might have thought that he'd run the whole way.

As he pulled up to the crosswalk again, Beth dodged out of the automatic doors. She was carrying the little girl with the curls that he'd seen once before. Behind her, a tall, teen-aged boy lugging several backpacks struggled to keep up.

As soon as the truck had rolled to a stop, they yanked open the doors. Beth struggled to get inside. The little girl she held sobbed and gripped her around the neck. So Bodey held out a hand, all but yanking them both into the front seat. In the rear section of the cab, Eric threw the backpacks onto the seat, then jumped in.

The moment Bodey heard the door shut, he gunned the engine, heading through the parking lot as quickly as he dared without drawing attention to himself.

"Is she all right?" he murmured as soon as Beth was able to disentangle her sister enough to draw a seatbelt around them both.

"Yeah. Dolly's just scared."

"We only had a couple of minutes to get out of there," Eric said, out of breath. "We nearly didn't make it down the alley before a couple of guys showed up." His face was flushed and beaded with sweat. "I need a drink."

Dolly's sobbing increased in volume.

"You're sure she's not hurt?"

Eric shook his head. "She's upset because we had to leave Noodle behind. He ran under the bed when I started gathering up the packs and I didn't have time to coax her out."

A glance in the rearview mirror made Bodey realize that Eric was no less upset; he simply managed to hide it better.

"You did the right thing," Beth said. Then she bent over her sister. "We'll go back for Noodle when it's safe. Okay, Dolly?"

But it was clear from her tone that Beth didn't really believe her own words.

Again, Bodey looked in the rearview mirror, catching the way that Eric surreptitiously wiped his eyes.

"I'll drop the three of you off somewhere safe, then I'll come back for Noodle."

Beth opened her mouth, meaning to argue, but Bodey shook his head, cutting his eyes toward the back seat. As soon as she glanced behind her, Beth's chin began to wobble as well.

"You can't," she said unsteadily. "I can give you the key, but if you're seen by those men in the parking lot—"

"I've got an idea. But I can't do it while you're around. Okay?"

She nodded, her jaw clenched. "But if John Joseph—"

He took her hand and squeezed it, murmuring, "I'll be careful. Trust me."

He knew how much it cost her to put her faith in anyone as far as her siblings were concerned, but she finally nodded. "Okay."

Bodey wove in and out of traffic, taking side roads, doubling back. He supposed he was probably being a little paranoid—after all, there had been no sign of anyone tailing them. But Beth's caution was contagious—and he did it as much to reassure *her* as anything else.

Finally, after taking the on-ramp to a freeway heading south, he wrestled his phone from his pocket and handed it to Beth.

"Go to my contact list and find Keagan West."

Beth was still trying to comfort Dolly but she managed to do as he asked, then handed the phone back to him.

He hit the CALL button. It rang twice, then was answered by a rough, masculine voice that was nearly indistinguishable from the background noise: the rumble of the crowd, a distant announcer, the whinny of a horse. In an instant, Bodey was mentally transported to the arena, waiting tensely for his turn. But even as the familiar emotions swam around him, he pushed them aside without a second's hesitation—or even, surprisingly, a twinge of regret.

"Keagan. How's it going?"

"Good. Good. I'm sixth in the rankings so far."

"Knock 'em dead."

"I'll do my best."

Bodey swerved in front of a Winnebago, taking the off-ramp onto a freeway heading west. "Hey, bud, I need to borrow your house."

"Trouble with the trailer?"

"No. But it's a bit of an emergency."

"Knock yourself out. Can't say there's much in the fridge but you're welcome to anything I've got."

"Thanks, man."

"No problem. Spare key should be hanging in the tack room unless . . . shit. I'm not sure if I put it back after the electrician let himself in."

"I'll let you know if there's a problem."

"With the door or your latest conquest?"

"It's not—"

Keagan interrupted him with a laugh. "Atta boy, Bodey." Then he disconnected.

Bodey felt the heat settling into the tips of his ears but he ignored it, hoping that Beth hadn't overheard the last bit of the conversation. But luckily, Beth was more concerned with Dolly, who had settled into hiccupping sobs.

"Who was that?" Beth asked.

"A friend. He's the guy who owns the Rocking Horse Ranch." He caught her gaze. "You can't go back to Hell on Wheels."

She sagged a little—obviously relieved that he wouldn't be suggesting such a thing.

"So I'll take you out to Keagan's place." At her blank look, he added, "Where Willow is stabled."

For a moment, there was a flash of raw gratitude in her eyes, and it humbled him.

"As soon as we've got you settled, I'm going to head back into town, get us some supplies, and pick up your dog. Then I'll be back."

"Syd and Helen—"

"I'll get word to them that you won't be coming back today."

"But—"

He stroked her hand with the backs of his fingers.

"Let me take care of it. Okay?"

There was only a beat of silence, then she breathed, "Okay."

*   *   *

DOLLY had fallen asleep in Beth's arms by the time they arrived at the Rocking Horse Ranch. Beth continued to hold her tucked under her arm, stroking her back when little shuddering sobs punctuated her dreams.

Bodey pulled the truck up to the barn and said, "Wait here while I get the key."

She nodded, watching as he disappeared through one of the side doors.

"Is that the Bodey guy you were talking about?" Eric asked quietly.

She twisted to face her brother. "Yes. Sorry. I should have introduced the two of you."

"It's okay." Eric shifted, looking out the window. "Is this his place?"

"No. He lives in Utah, like Syd and Helen. This belongs to one of his friends. But there's a horse, a brown and white Paint horse, like Little Joe has in those *Bonanza* reruns you like. It belongs to him. He's been keeping it here while he's been participating in Hell on Wheels."

Eric looked down at the backpacks, fiddling idly with one of the straps. But Beth knew there was nothing idle about his mind. She could all but see the cogs grinding away in his brain.

"Can we trust him, Bethy?"

She didn't hurry to dismiss his concern, but gave his question her own careful consideration.

They'd been on the road together for so long that they'd begun to believe that the only people they could count on were one another. And that had served them well for over a year. But they were at an impasse now. Beth knew they couldn't run forever. They were all growing tired. Tired and evidently careless.

But the only way to stop running was to bring an end to the chase. And she honestly didn't know how to make that happen.

Which meant that she needed to rely on someone enough to help her find a solution.

"Yeah. We can trust him."

"What makes you think that? You've only known him a few days."

She nodded. "That's true. But of all the people we've met over the past couple of years, he's been one of the first I've felt . . . comfortable enough to confide in like this. I didn't even have to ask him to help us. He just . . . stepped in when I needed him most."

His jaw clenched. "We don't need anyone else. We can just disappear."

Beth took a steadying breath. Yes. They could leave. As soon as Bodey had returned to town, she and her siblings could use that time to head to the main road. They could chance hitchhiking or hide and start walking the back roads after dusk. It wasn't anything that they hadn't done before.

But she couldn't run anymore.

She honestly couldn't run anymore.

She was tired of constantly looking over her shoulder, of living as if they'd done something wrong. For months now, the urge to provide a home—a real home—for her siblings had been preying upon her. Eric and Dolly had already lived in virtual isolation at the Farm, away from the opportunities that mainstream America could give them. And had she offered them anything better?

Not much.

Which meant that somehow, she needed to involve the authorities.

Sweet heaven above.

Hadn't she been through all this already? Hadn't she come to the same decision a dozen times? True, the authorities could enforce her legal guardianship. They could even issue a restraining order.

But a piece of paper wasn't going to keep the Farm from waiting for that one moment her guard was down. And she didn't think the authorities could keep Leroy Vonn's henchmen from trying to take the kids by force. If they managed to succeed and spirited the children into the woods . . .

Getting them back could be well-nigh impossible.

Eric was still waiting for an answer, so she said honestly, "You're right. We could run. But it's getting harder and harder to keep them from finding us. Maybe, Bodey can come up with a way for us to bring all this to an end, once and for all."

Eric looked skeptical and she couldn't blame him. But he couldn't know what she knew. That Bodey had made her feel hope for the first time in years. And once she'd seen that glimmer of a brighter future, she was willing to do anything to make it come true.

Before her brother could challenge her assertion, Bodey dodged out of the barn again and ran to the truck.

"Did you find the key?" she asked as he slid inside.

"No, but I know how to get in."

He maneuvered the car near the back door, then killed the engine. "Do you need help with the backpacks?" he asked, glancing back at Eric.

Eric's chin lifted a notch. "No, I can do it."

Bodey moved around the car to open the door for Beth. "Want me to take her?" he asked softly.

"No, she'll wake up if I hand her over, and then she might be scared."

"Okay."

They moved to the back door and Bodey motioned for them to wait. Then, turning slightly, he punched the window inset with his elbow.

Beth gasped—especially when it was clear that the jagged pieces had punctured his skin.

After clearing the rest of the shards away, he reached inside and unlocked the door.

"Careful now," he said, swinging it wide.

Eric moved in first, his boots crunching on the broken glass. Then Beth followed.

"Are you sure you're not going to get in trouble for that?"

"It's fine."

They'd stepped inside a simple kitchen decorated with warm wood cabinets and speckled marble counters, but Bodey led them through to a large family room with a television set bigger than anything Beth had seen outside of a stadium and an over-stuffed sectional couch that marched along three of the walls.

Eric whistled softly under his breath.

"Yeah, Keagan likes his football. But, other than beds and dressers, the furnishings are fairly sparse."

He led them down a short hall. "Guest bedroom's there and the room next to it is the bathroom."

Beth stepped into a simple set of sleeping quarters with two twin beds made of lodge poles. Both of them were covered in matching quilts featuring bears and pine trees.

Pulling back the covers to the nearest mattress with one hand, Beth lay Dolly down. The little girl sighed in her sleep, rooting her head in the soft pillow, before becoming still again. Eric set the packs next to the other twin bed, subtly staking his claim.

Bodey slid his fingertips into his pockets, gesturing behind him with a roll of his shoulder. "There's another room across the hall with a double bed—you'll probably want that one, Beth. I'll use the one in the master suite upstairs."

Beth couldn't help flashing him a faint smile for being mindful of Eric. Her brother fairly bristled with pissed-off sibling over-protectiveness, but once Bodey made it clear that he would be sleeping "elsewhere," Eric calmed slightly.

Bodey flicked a thumb toward the back of the house. "You guys settle in. I've already made a call to my brother and Syd to explain what's going on. They should be here in about five minutes at the most. As soon as they arrive, I'll see what I can do about retrieving your dog."

At that pronouncement, Eric sagged even more, his bravado seeping away. "Noodle will be scared," he said. "So she'll probably be hiding."

"If I don't find her right away, I'll look everywhere I can think of, okay."

"I could go with you and—"

"No," Bodey interrupted gently. "I'm counting on you to watch over your sisters. Elam and Syd will guard the area outside but I need you to stay inside and keep an eye on the windows and doors."

At that, Eric's chest swelled with pride and he stood straighter, his shoulders growing erect again. "You can count on me."

Beth's chest hurt with a mixture of satisfaction and gratitude as she watched the interaction between Bodey and her little brother. Instinctively, he'd known that her brother didn't want to be shunted to the side as a "child." Even more importantly, he'd given Eric something to do, an active job, so that he didn't have to feel so helpless.

"Good. Keep the doors and windows locked. I'll bring something back to replace the broken pane, but see if you can find a broom and sweep up the broken glass before I get back with the dog. We don't want it getting shards of glass in its paws. Stay away from the windows as much as you can. In the family room, you can pull down the blinds and draw the curtains. Keagan's got blackout liners, so no one can see through them. I really doubt that anyone from the Farm could have followed us but I don't want to take any chances. I'll be back as soon as I can. Think you can do that?"

"Yes, sir."

"Good boy."

Bodey backed into the hall.

Beth smiled reassuringly at her brother and then followed Bodey.

"We should probably see to that elbow before you leave," she said.

Bodey lifted his arm and stared at the blotches of red that were seeping through his shirt. Obviously, until she'd said something, he hadn't even realized that he'd been hurt.

"I'm fine."

"Bodey."

He reached out to cup her cheek. "Honestly. You can take care of it when I get back."

"But—"

He glanced behind her, ensuring that Eric couldn't see them, then leaned forward to brush his lips over her own.

"I'll be back soon. Check the cupboards and the fridge and make a list of everything we'll need for a few days. Text it to me and I'll hit the store before I go get the dog. That way we can hunker down until we decide what we're going to do."

What we're *going to do.*

She didn't miss the way that he included himself in the situation. But as much as she didn't want to do so, she had to give him an "out."

"You don't have to do this. If you want, you could drop us at the bus station or—"

He stopped her with a finger on her lips. His expression became fierce.

"You're not going anywhere and neither am I." He grimaced. "Except to get your dog." He made his way to the door, then turned. "What's its name again?"

"Noodle."

"Noodle. I hate to ask how it got the name."

"She likes to eat noodles."

"Of course. Is she prone to biting people?"

Beth fought a grin. "Only if she's afraid."

"Great. Just great."

Bodey tamped his hat a little tighter over his head then said, "Lock the door behind me."

"Why? Someone else can reach inside and unlock it as easily as you did."

"Just . . . do it. For me."

His features were such a mixture of emotion—irritation, worry, gentleness—that she couldn't resist reaching up to touch his cheek.

"I promise. For you." Her voice grew tight with emotion. "I still can't believe that you'd be so willing to do all of this for us. For me."

He glanced toward the bedroom again, then slid his hands around her waist. "I'm not the only one willing to help, you know. Syd and Elam, P.D., and Helen. They're waiting in the wings."

Tears stung the backs of her eyes. "I don't want anyone to get hurt—"

He cupped her cheek. "Don't you worry. We can take care of our own. And you're part of us now. You're family."

"No, I—"

He held her face up to him so that she couldn't escape the fierceness shining from his eyes. "Yes." He leaned down to offer her a quick, hard kiss. "Now lock this door behind me or I might change my mind about going after your mutt."

EIGHTEEN

———•◆•———

B ODEY met Elam and Syd at the gate to Rocking Horse
Ranch.

"Mind if we switch trucks?"

"Not at all. What's going on?"

"I don't have time to explain everything right now. I'll
do that as soon as I get back. Right now, I've got to go gather
supplies and Beth's dog. With any luck, I'll be back in under
an hour. I need you two to keep a close eye on the house.
Beth's inside with her younger brother and sister."

Syd made a *tsk*ing noise. "I didn't know she had any other
family."

"She's been keeping things pretty close to her chest. She's
had some trouble with that survivalist group headed by
Leroy Vonn."

Elam whistled under his breath. "I saw that piece they
did about him on the news."

"Yeah, Beth barely escaped the group when she was a
kid. She was fifteen when Vonn tried to marry her off to
one of the older men in the group."

Elam swore.

Syd's eyes burned beneath his brows.

"To make a long story short, he's decided that Beth's younger siblings belong with him, even though her mother named Beth the legal guardian. He's been trying to take them by force, so Beth's been doing her best to fly under the radar." He shook his head in disgust. "Nobody should have to live that way."

"What do you want us to do?" Elam asked. He'd slipped unconsciously into military-mode, his eyes already scanning the area.

"Just keep watch for now. Make sure no one gets onto the property. As soon as I get back, we'll sit down with Beth and figure out what she wants us to do."

DESPITE the fact that Bodey had told them to stay away from the windows, Beth found herself standing behind one of the curtains in the family room. As she watched the cloud of dust marking the progress of Bodey's truck down the dirt track, her heart wallowed in her chest.

Over and over again, the little voice in her head chided her for being a fool, for trusting a man that she'd known for only a few days. Heaven only knew that she didn't have a great track record with the male sex. Her first relationship had been a disaster. At fifteen, she'd been sure that John Joseph was the love of her life. But it hadn't been too long before she'd realized that she was in over her head. He'd been a product of his environment far too long. In his world, the male was law and the female nothing more than the means to his own pleasure. He'd felt no need to offer her any tenderness—or even much respect, for that matter. Yet, she was expected to worship him and be at his beck and call.

Then, there had been her father. In all fairness, the man had been battling cancer and he hadn't had much energy to deal with an adolescent girl who was severely behind in her education and social development. Even so, there'd been an aloofness to his personality. A sense that, because he had liberated her from the Farm, she owed him. She'd become his nurse, cheerleader, housekeeper, and cook. Yet, she'd never really felt like his *daughter.* Nor had she felt completely comfortable with him or in his house. Unconsciously, it seemed as if she'd transferred from one form of servitude to another. Even so, she'd grieved when her father had died. For all his faults, he'd loved her. He just hadn't known how to show it very well.

After that . . .

It had been odd at first, being on her own. By then, she'd graduated from high school. Her grades hadn't been the best—not after the educational neglect she'd suffered at the Farm. But she'd excelled in other areas, especially gymnastics—enough so that she'd been able to get a partial scholarship at a community college. She'd only been able to complete a couple of years before her mother had died and Beth had been forced to leave school, but she still had her associate's degree. And one of these days . . .

One of these days.

Less than a week ago, the thought of a future other than the one she was living would have been as intangible as a mirage, a hopeless dream for the future that would never come true. But somehow, in the space of a few days, things had changed.

No.

Her situation was exactly the same.

She'd been the one to change.

Beth wasn't really sure how such a thing had come about. But by confiding her problems in someone—in Bodey—in allowing him to shoulder some of her fears, she felt . . . lighter. Calmer.

More optimistic.

Dear heaven, she hoped she hadn't made a mistake.

BODEY drove as quickly as he dared into Cheyenne, stopping to gather the things he needed to repair the window on Keagan's door from a glazier that he'd located on his phone directory. Then, he made his way to a grocery store, grimacing when he saw the list that Beth had sent.

Milk, bread, peanut butter.

It was obvious that she didn't want to burden him with their needs and it pissed him off a little. But then, he supposed that if he were in the same position, his pride would have kicked in as well. So, he picked up the milk, bread, and peanut butter. But he also picked up apples and bananas, celery, carrots, and radishes, and lunch meats and cheeses. Then, figuring that Beth and the kids had been on a limited budget for some time, he channeled his little brother Barry and hit the junk food aisles as well, choosing packages of chips, animal crackers, and cookies, and some little squeeze packets of applesauce.

After tucking the sacks into the rear portion of the cab, he checked the dash clock, then began making his way back to the hotel.

He was hoping that, by now, the men from the Farm who'd been waiting in the parking lot would have realized that Beth and her siblings were gone and they weren't coming back. That way, if he was lucky, he'd be able to check for the dog.

Noodle.

What the hell kind of dog had a name like that anyway?

A dog belonging to a couple of kids.

Kids who were counting on him to bring their beloved pet back to them.

Forcing that thought away, Bodey concentrated instead on the roiling thoughts and emotions that gathered like thunderclouds. He was trying to grapple with everything that he'd learned since this morning but his head was still reeling. Beth and her siblings were running from Leroy Vonn. Leroy . . . frickin' . . . Vonn. Geez. Bodey was about to match wits with one of the country's most notorious anti-government, survivalist groups in order to help a woman he'd only known for days.

But none of that mattered. The only thing that really counted was his overriding need to protect Beth at all costs.

Hell, what was happening to him? He'd never been so . . . obsessed with a woman before. Sure, he'd been overwhelmingly attracted, eager for the next encounter. But for the most part, bastard that he was, he didn't really tend to think of the woman in his life when they were apart. He had too many other things on his mind—competitions, ranch work, sponsors. That didn't mean he didn't care for the woman he'd hooked up with, it simply meant he was able to compartmentalize.

But with Beth, each hour that passed flowed through his veins like a fever, until he was consumed by thoughts about the rarity of her smiles, the moments they'd been together, when they'd be together again.

And over-arching all those worries was his need to ensure that she was safe.

As he took the exit and headed toward the motel, Bodey bent to retrieve the pistol and back holster stashed beneath the center seat. Shifting, he tucked the clip into his waistband, then pulled the tails of his shirt over the weapon.

Elam had been the first person to insist that Bodey needed to get a concealed carry permit since Bodey was on the road a lot. Most times, he traveled lonely highways with hours of driving between cities. And even once he hit civilization, some of the arenas where he competed were in dodgy areas and the possibility of an encounter with someone who was drunk, high, or angry was pretty steep. But Bodey couldn't remember the last time that he'd found such precautions necessary.

Now, he was glad that he'd come prepared.

He didn't drive directly to the motel. Instead, he took a circuitous route around the block, checking for any sign of pickups sporting bright green Christmas trees on their license plates. As he'd hoped, the parking lot had cleared of the out-of-state vehicles. And as far as he could tell, there didn't seem to be anyone watching the door.

Even so, he didn't plan on taking any chances. After he'd reassured himself that he'd checked things out as best as he could, he made another circuitous route—this time to the businesses behind the motel.

Once again, he approached the area with utmost care, searching for anything that looked out of place. He couldn't be sure that no one was watching the back window of the motel room but he didn't see anything obvious—and he wasn't about to let anyone prevent him from what he'd come here to do. Those kids had been through enough. The very least he could do for them was to bring back their dog.

He turned into the parking lot of the electronics store behind the motel, carefully circling toward the rear.

So far, so good.

Seeing an access lane to a furniture store next to the motel, he parked under a pair of scrubby Ponderosa Pines and then stepped from the truck.

For a moment, he wished that Elam had come with him. After so many years in the military, Elam had a sixth sense for trouble. Bodey? He was more accustomed to obvious threats—tanked up cowboys who were too far from home and men suffering from a losing streak. Skirting through the bushes, he kept sweeping the area with his eyes, looking for a shadow out of place, a figure that appeared a little too vigilant. But the only movement he saw as he passed the loading docks and empty pallets was a cat sunning itself on the crumbling cinder block wall that half-heartedly separated the properties.

Keeping his right hand near the small of his back, just in case he felt the need to draw his weapon, Bodey slowly vaulted over the stacked blocks and edged his way toward the window to Beth's room. After glancing over his shoulder and ensuring that he was still alone, he removed the Ruger pistol from its resting place.

Bodey knew the chances that someone from the Farm had decided to wait inside for the occupants to return was pretty high, so he used his free hand to lift the wooden sash as high as it would go. He winced when it stuck and then jammed into place with a muffled screech.

His pulse knocked against his throat as he waited, one minute, two, straining for the slightest sound that would tell him he'd alerted someone inside. But he heard nothing.

Leaning his head inside, Bodey offered in a loud whisper, "Noodle?"

Nothing.

So he tried a little louder, "Noodle! Come here, boy. Girl?"

Damnit, he couldn't remember if he'd been told that the elusive Noodle were male or female—didn't even know what kind of dog it was. Why hadn't he stayed at the Rocking Horse Ranch for a few more minutes? Just long enough to get some more information?

But Bodey knew that if he'd stayed even a little longer, he would have been tempted to remain there for good. It had taken everything he possessed to leave Beth and her siblings beneath Syd and Elam's protection.

Still cursing under his breath, Bodey carefully swung one leg into a cramped bedroom, ducked his head under the sash, then followed suit with the other foot. Since the blinds had been pulled down in this room—and in the one beyond—the window he'd used to get inside was the only real source of light. But he could hear muffled voices, music, and boisterous sound effects—cartoons?—and he wondered if the children had left the television set on when they'd bugged out or if the noise were coming through the paperthin walls from another unit.

Holding the pistol at the ready, Bodey carefully made his way around the cramped quarters, easing open the closet door. Except for the faint jingle of the empty wire hangers, the space was completely barren.

He moved toward the doorway to the main room. Hesitating, he allowed his gaze to sweep over the miniscule kitchen area before he eased around the corner, covering himself with the weapon, eyeing the threadbare couch with its crumpled blanket, the flicker of the television with Wylie Coyote dropping an anvil off the edge of a cliff.

Knees slightly bent, sighting down his pistol, he edged around the sofa, thinking that someone could be out of view if they were lying down.

Nothing.

The pounding of his heart eased slightly but didn't completely slow. With no other visible closets or cupboards large enough to hide a man, he was able to breathe a little easier, but he didn't completely drop his guard. Not when the hotel room had an other-worldly feel. With two bowls of cereal half-eaten, the kitchen faucet *drip, drip, dripping*, the refrigerator door ajar to reveal a half gallon of milk and a jar of grape jelly, it looked as if the occupants had been fixing themselves a snack one minute, then had disappeared into thin air the next. And the fact that there were no personal items—no mislaid shoes, no stray socks, no towels on the floor—was testament to the fact that Beth and her siblings had become extremely self-disciplined about keeping their belongings at the ready so that they could leave at a moment's notice.

What the hell kind of way was that to live?

The thought that Beth and her siblings had been brought to this because Leroy Vonn had refused to relinquish his control filled Bodey with more rage than he could ever remember experiencing. From what Bodey knew, Vonn had several hundred followers. Why would he be so single-minded about keeping a couple of kids who would be of little use to him for years?

And where the hell was the damn dog?

Bodey sought the corners of the room, poked through the half-dozen cupboards in the kitchen, even checked the fridge, for hell's sake. Wandering back into the bedroom, he opened the drawers in the single dresser and knelt to peer under the bed.

Nothing.

Which meant the dog had probably found its way out of the half-open window. Or maybe the men they'd seen sneaking in had exited through the door and Noodle had seen a chance to escape.

Bodey felt a twisting in his gut when he thought of having to return empty-handed. Even worse, he supposed that it would be up to him to break the news that their pet was gone.

He knew full well what that could mean to Dolly and Eric. The dog had probably been one of their few tastes of normality. They might be on the run, they might be looking over their shoulder. But they had the unconditional love of their sister and their pet.

Shit.

Bodey reached out to turn off the television. After the forced frivolity of the cartoons, the silence made the room even more dismal and shabby. Lowering the gun, Bodey sighed.

What the hell was he going to do now? He could go back into the alley, he supposed, and see if there was any evidence of a dog. Barring that, his only other option was to drive around the block and call the animal's name. Bodey would be more than willing to holler from here to Denver if he thought it might do any good. But such an obvious search and rescue could bring the kind of attention that Beth couldn't afford.

Bodey dropped onto a chair, reaching to holster his weapon, but at the same time, the blanket which had been covering most of the sofa began to move.

He reacted automatically, whipping the Ruger into position even as his finger curled around the trigger. But then a head poked from the rumpled folds, a pair of bulbous eyes, a sharp snout, and a lolling tongue.

"Shit, damn, and hell!" Bodey quickly lifted the gun when he realized that he wasn't looking at some horrible medical experiment. Instead, he stared straight at the ugliest animal that he had ever seen in his life.

The dog came to a similar, distasteful conclusion about Bodey, because its lips drew back to reveal a row of sharp, pointed teeth. Then he growled low, his body beginning to tremble in a way that could have been fear, anger, or palsy.

Bodey's hands automatically lifted in surrender before he even realized what he was doing. The animal was beyond being a mutt. Its fur was clumped in patches of black and white, some of its hair long and wiry and coarse, while other parts were short and wavy. It had the delicate chicken-bone legs of a Chihuahua, the body of a stout dachshund, and a head and ears more reminiscent of a Doberman.

And it didn't like Bodey any better.

"Hey, boy . . ." Bodey said slowly, then, after a quick glance, ". . . girl. Hey, girl."

The dog growled even harder, its body shaking from the warning, its little legs threatening to give way to its barrel-shaped body. It barked then, causing it to bounce from the effort, its eyes protruding even more, its tongue flapping up and down through a gap in its teeth.

Geez, Bodey wouldn't have been surprised if Franken-stein himself had pieced him . . . her . . . *it* . . . together from the proverbial hounds of hell.

"Noodle?" Bodey tried again, slowly moving his hands until he could holster his weapon.

The sound of its own name gave the dog pause—either that or it had grown out of breath from its outburst because it panted loudly, then began to cough.

Knowing that this might be his only chance, Bodey reached out, ready to throw the blanket over its body so he could pack the canine back to the truck. But when Bodey said, "We gotta get you back to Beth," the dog's ears pricked up and Bodey could have sworn that the animal grinned. This time, the yelp that came from its throat was a short yip of joy.

"Yeah? You want to go see Dolly and Eric?"

Again, the short yelp. The dog trembled again but the swipe of its scruffy tail whipped its butt from side to side so swiftly that it could barely stand up.

"Let's go find them, huh? Beth, and Dolly, and Eric?"

When he reached out, the dog met him halfway—then all but scaled his body, wriggling enthusiastically, until it had wedged itself underneath Bodey's chin. Then that over-sized tongue began to lick every exposed inch of flesh it could reach.

"Aaagh." Bodey pushed to his feet, grimacing. Despite the wriggling dog and its rough little tongue, Bodey couldn't be upset. Not when he was filled with an overwhelming relief. He honestly didn't know how he would have survived the experience if he'd had to tell Eric and Dolly that their pet had been lost.

Since carrying the dog, negotiating the window, and having his weapon handy proved unwieldy, Bodey finally tucked the mutt into his shirt. With only its head and that monstrous tongue peeking out, he dodged through the opening and then closed it behind him as best as he could. Then, he walked as nonchalantly as he could back to his truck.

His heart was thumping in his ears as he unlocked the door and slid into the cab. But when he tried to set the dog on the seat, Noodle scrambled deeper into his shirt. Bodey could feel the animal trembling against his waist. As he cranked the engine, he wondered if the dog were picking up on his tension or if she disliked riding in a vehicle. In any event, after a minute, Bodey gave up and let the animal cower there, even though its sharp little nails were biting into his skin.

Before heading back to the ranch, Bodey drove in circles again, backtracked over his own trail, then headed miles out of his way where he found a knot of fast food restaurants. Not knowing what the kids liked to eat, he played it safe, buying several large pizzas with various toppings and one made with nothing but cheese. Then, remembering the half-eaten cereal he'd seen on the tables and the meager contents of the refrigerator and cupboards, he added several orders of breadsticks and a selection of two liter sodas. He was about to swing out of the parking lot when he saw a drive-through window to an ice cream shop. There, he ordered several different varieties of hand-packed tubs.

By the time he got back on the road, Noodle had ceased trembling. Too late, Bodey realized that he hadn't thought to check the motel for dog food. He swore under his breath until he realized that Keagan had a couple of Australian Shepherds on the ranch, so there had to be some kibble around the place. If not, Bodey was sure that Keagan—who was an avid hunter and fisherman—would have a freezer full of something. Bodey could reimburse him for anything he used—hell, he'd be happy to send him some replacements from his own freezer if Keagan would prefer.

He'd do anything to see the haunted look in those kids' eyes disappear.

For the first time, Bodey understood why Beth had been so prickly during their first encounter. Hell, he was surprised she'd decided to talk to him at all. He must have seemed like a total prick. After the stories she'd heard from Helen, then the way he'd been so insistent that she assimilate into the SASS competitive culture . . .

He must have come off as a man looking for reasons to make himself feel important, while she'd been doing her best to put food on the table and provide her siblings with as much normalcy as possible.

Hell.

In that instant, Bodey was flooded with a thousand different images from his past: the women, the drinking, the bars, the rodeos. Cow cutting competitions. SASS.

Women.

And then, bleeding into them all, driving the rest of the pictures from his head, was the sight of his father's Bronco dented and scorched, upended in an icy river on a cold winter day.

For years, Bodey had tried to drive that memory from his head. He'd been the one to find the accident that had claimed his parents and little sister. He'd been the one to call for help. He'd been the first person to desperately try to wrench open the doors on the upended car—knowing already that his parents were gone and his little sister had probably broken her neck. With the distant alarm from the firehouse summoning the volunteer rescue brigade, he'd been the one to pull Barry from the icy river and begin CPR.

He could still remember the helplessness, the utter sense of *aloneness*. Elam had been deployed in the Middle East and Jace had been wandering Europe. So in that moment of terror, there had been no one to lean on. He'd only been nineteen—and a hell-raising teenager at that—when, in an instant, his family had been nearly cut in half.

For three days and two nights, he'd been virtually alone at the hospital, keeping a vigil on Barry, who remained unconscious. It had taken that long for Elam to get home on an emergency leave. Another two days to track down Jace in Europe and bring him back. Although the hospital waiting room had ebbed and flowed with friends of the family who stopped by to help, the medical professionals had looked to Bodey to make most of the decisions until his older brothers could get there—and he'd been so afraid that he would do something wrong. Even more, he'd blamed himself for the accident, thinking in that crazy, convoluted way of a kid, that if he'd agreed to go with his parents when they'd asked him to join them for dinner, he would have delayed their departure for a few more minutes. Long enough so that the deer they'd hit would have already moved through the area.

Enough years had passed for him to realize that there wasn't anything he could have done. His family members had been taken away by a cruel twist of fate, not by his refusal to eat fish.

But as he drove toward the Rocking Horse Ranch, the smell of pizza filling his senses, the warm twitching body of the ugliest dog in the world close against his skin, he suddenly realized that all this time he'd been deceiving himself. He thought that he'd put that long ago trauma behind him by pushing his misguided guilt aside. But he hadn't dealt with the deeper issues.

Mistakenly, he'd thought that the competitions, the thrill seeking, the drinking, the women, had been a means to prove that he was as good as his brothers, that he could knock things out with the best of them.

But when he compared his lifestyle to the one Beth had been living for the last couple of years, it shed a harsher light on his actions, revealing them for what they were: a means to divert himself from the aching inside.

Damn it all, he missed his father more than he would have ever thought possible. And his mother . . . how many times did he find himself closing his eyes and remembering the way that he'd once rushed home from school and banged through the screen door, dropping his book bag in the hall so that he could run into her arms? And little Emily . . . the way she'd followed Bodey around as if he were the sun and she a greedy sunflower. To this day, he remembered the way she would sneak out of bed, dragging her blanket behind her, and climb into his lap while he sat watching TV. She'd snuggle beneath his arm and within a few minutes she'd be fast asleep again. His parents had tried to warn Bodey that he shouldn't indulge her, but secretly, he'd looked forward to those moments with his little sister.

Then, in a freak combination of frightened animals, icy roads, and a split-second of terror, all of that had been torn away from him and from his brothers.

His throat grew tight, his breath growing raspy to his own ears as the truth crashed down on him like a million pound weight. He'd never wanted to feel such fear again. He'd never wanted to feel such utter helplessness and devastation.

Bodey suddenly realized that, all this time, he hadn't been *seeking* something, he'd been doing his best to run away, to divert himself from emotions that he'd never truly acknowledged.

It had taken Beth, with her lack of artifice and her laser-honed instincts for what was true and honest and *important* to strip his soul down to its core, remove all the crap and the endless diversions, until he could see what mattered to him most.

Love.

Sure, there would always be a part of him that would want to compete—and there wasn't a thing wrong with that. But none of that mattered a hill of beans if at the end of the day that was all there was to fight for.

A sound that was half-laugh, half-sob burst from his throat—startling Noodle. But he barely noticed. Suddenly, Bodey grasped what Elam had been talking about when he'd tried to describe his relationship with P.D., how she'd come to him as a mixture of a gift and a two-by-four over the head. He understood what Jace had tried to tell him about trying to slap a Band-Aid on a deeper problem.

And suddenly, Bodey knew what it meant to battle for something that was truly important. Beth and her siblings had fought long and hard to stay together, and by hell, Bodey was willing to throw his own weight into the fray. But he didn't want to engineer another narrow miss with the Farm. As far as Bodey was concerned, they deserved a normal life, not one of fear.

But he also knew enough about the group to discern that they weren't too fond of outside interference—which meant threatening them with legal action wasn't going to do much good. Somehow, Bodey was going to have to come up with some leverage that would convince Leroy Vonn to leave them alone—now, and in the future.

Which meant that this wasn't merely a battle of brawn. It would be one of wits as well.

And this was one competition Bodey couldn't afford to lose.

NINETEEN

———•◦•———

A S he let himself through the gate and drove up the gravel drive to Keagan's ranch house, there was no sign of Bodey's truck, Elam, or Syd. But Bodey knew well enough that the empty yard didn't mean the two men weren't watching. He flashed the truck lights and sure enough, within a minute the large double doors on the barn slid aside far enough for him to pull Elam's truck inside so that he could park it behind his own.

Bodey slid out of the cab and gestured for Elam to come help him.

Elam carried a rifle—only one of several weapons that Bodey was sure were stashed on his body.

"I brought some groceries and a few pizzas for our dinner. Give me a hand carrying them into the house."

Elam nodded. "Did you find the dog?"

Sensing she was being discussed, Noodle roused from where she'd begun to doze. Her head popped out of Bodey's shirt and Elam visibly started.

"Good hell! Is that a dog or a science experiment?"

At Elam's sharp exclamation, the dog burrowed beneath

Bodey's shirt again, doing its best to scramble toward the small of his back.

Bodey grinned. "Apparently a bit of both."

They gathered up the food and quickly strode toward the house.

The whole way Bodey felt his senses twist into hyper drive. His eyes scanned the area for the slightest hint that something was out of place, a shadow misaligned, a faint trace of dust on the horizon.

So far, everything was quiet, but despite his precautions to keep from being followed, Bodey didn't allow himself to believe that they were in the clear. He wouldn't feel that way until the threat had been permanently removed.

They were several feet from the door when it opened, allowing them to pass through unhindered. Then, once they were cleared, Syd closed it again, automatically locking it.

"Beth! I'm back!" Bodey called out as he set the boxes of pizza and breadsticks on the table. Elam followed suit with the materials they'd need to fix the window and the sacks full of groceries.

Bodey heard the soft patter of footsteps racing down the hall, then a reverent, "Pizza!"

Dolly hung motionless in the doorway, her eyes wide, her features a study in unguarded delight. Then she bounded into the kitchen, followed by Eric, and finally Beth.

Eric tried to act a little cooler at the sight of the feast, but the flare of hunger and excitement in his eyes made Bodey's throat threaten to tighten up again. Was there anything more normal than a teenage boy and a box of pizza?

"There are paper plates, utensils, and cups in the bag with the breadsticks. You guys have got to be starving."

Surprisingly, the children didn't move, despite the aromas filling the kitchen. Too late, Bodey remembered that getting some food hadn't been his only reason for heading back into Cheyenne.

"Oh, and I found something else along the way."

He quickly began unbuttoning his shirt, making it only halfway before Noodle—who had roused again at Dolly's voice—scrambled free, freefalling to the floor in an ungainly sprawl of arms and legs. Then, scrabbling against the slippery tile, she fought for footing, before finally gaining purchase and racing toward the children with a series of high-pitched barks.

This time, the joy on Dolly and Eric's faces was contagious as they knelt to accept the dog's adoring yips and yowls. The poor thing was nearly beating itself to death with the excited whipping of its tail. It darted to Dolly, jumped excitedly, then ran the scant distance to Eric, then back again.

Bodey began looking through cupboards. "I'm pretty sure she's hungry and thirsty. I found her hiding under the blanket on the couch—Aha!"

He found a huge bag of dog kibble in the same cupboard as Keagan's brooms and cleaning supplies. "Eric, bring me a paper plate."

The boy hurried to do as he was told and Bodey scooped a big handful of food onto the plate and put it on the ground. But the pup was so excited, it merely skated over the tiles from the food to Dolly to Eric, moving with such heedless abandon that it made Bodey dizzy watching it.

"Maybe you two had better get your own dinner. That way, Noodle might know you're not going to leave her and she can take the time to eat her own."

Dolly and Eric needed no further bidding. While Syd opened the boxes to display their choices, Elam began pouring their sodas into the cups, allowing Bodey the opportunity to join Beth where she stood in the doorway.

There was a sheen of tears in her eyes when she looked up at him. "Thank you. You probably don't know how important Noodle has become to them."

Bodey drew her into his arms for a gentle hug. "I think I can guess," he said against her hair.

He felt the shudder of her sob against his chest and held her tightly until the tension seeped from her body. Then, knowing that she would be self-conscious of any further displays with Elam and Syd present, he urged her toward the table.

"Come on. Let's get you something to eat and drink. Then, after we're all stuffed to the gills, we'll put a movie on for the kids or plug in the Xbox so that we adults can have a war session."

Her brows creased. "War session?"

Bodey couldn't resist reaching out to smooth away the line of concern with the pad of his thumb. "Yeah. We're going to come up with a way to get Leroy Vonn and the rest of the Farm off your backs for good."

THE television was playing low in the background, the glow providing the only light, but Bodey wasn't paying attention—even when the ginormous screen was filled with sports highlights.

For the past two hours, Bodey, Beth, Elam, and Syd had scoured their brains for a way to free the Tivolis from the long arm of the Farm. But try as they might, they couldn't even come up with a reason why they were so bent on keeping the children.

Other than pure, unadulterated spite.

And that wasn't the kind of thing that could be reasoned with.

Sighing, Bodey tried to relax. He kept feeling like he was missing something. Some key to the puzzle that would give him the upper hand. In the past, when he'd come up against such challenges, he'd only had to force himself to be a little tougher, a little faster, a little stronger. He would push himself mentally and physically—sometimes to near breaking point—but he always managed to figure it out. That doggedness was probably one of his best weapons. But damned if he could figure this one out.

"Are you mad at us?"

Bodey started, his gaze latching onto the tiny figure in the doorway. If Goldilocks could have stepped from the pages of a storybook, she would have looked like Dolly: long blonde ringlets; a heart-shaped face with bright blue eyes; and dimples in her cheeks when she smiled.

Judging by her solemn expression, she didn't feel much like smiling right now.

"Hey, darlin'. No, I'm not mad. Why would you think that?"

She lapped one foot over the other as if the tile floor were chilly against her bare feet and tugged the blanket she was holding until the corner touched her lips. She was dressed in a pair of worn pajamas with ruffles on the butt and a picture of some kind of princess on her chest. Bodey was pretty sure that the cartoonists could have found a better study of the perfect princess in Dolly rather than the insipid redhead they'd chosen.

Dolly studied him carefully, then shrugged. "We're nothing but trouble."

The stark words coming from such a little cupid's bow mouth was tantamount to sacrilege in Bodey's opinion, and he wondered where she'd heard the phrase. Not from Beth, he was sure. He'd seen enough of Beth's interaction with her siblings to know that love shone from every word, every glance—even when she reminded them of their manners or they made a mess. The phrase had to have come from someone along their way.

"Why would you say that, punkin'?"

Bodey leaned forward, resting his elbows wide on his knees, hoping the relaxed stance would put Dolly at ease.

It must have worked, because she suddenly grinned. "I'm not a pumpkin!"

Bodey laughed. "No, you're not."

She took a few steps forward as if drawn to him out of curiosity. "Then why would you call me that?"

Bodey shrugged. "I don't know, exactly. My daddy used to call my little sister punkin'. It was his pet name for her because she was cute and sweet and always smiling."

Dolly's eyes grew wide and she forgot her reticence, because she padded closer. "What's your sister's name?"

Bodey's throat grew tight. His little brother Barry was always talking about his twin. Her name would pop into casual conversation without hesitation. But Bodey couldn't remember the last time he'd said it out loud.

"Emily," he said huskily. "Her name was Emily."

Dolly's forehead creased. "Did she change her name?"

Bodey didn't understand the question at first. Then he realized that Dolly had picked up on his use of the past tense.

"No, uh . . ." he cleared his throat, hoping to ease the tightness that gripped him like a fist. "No . . . she died when she was a little older than you. She was in a car accident."

Dolly's eyes dimmed. "Oh."

She was close enough now that Bodey could smell the scent of laundry soap clinging to her clothes and the sweetness of baby shampoo that clung to her skin.

"Then, I guess I can't ask to play with her." Her voice was filled with such wistful melancholy. But her expression remained resigned. With a jolt, Bodey realized that the little girl had probably had dozens of kids her age on the Farm but no one but her older siblings when she'd left.

"I've got a niece, though. Her name's Lily. She's a little bit older than you."

"How old?"

"Let's see. I think she just turned eleven."

Dolly wrinkled her nose. "That's probably too old then. I'll be seven soon."

Seven.

Shit, Dolly looked no older than five. If she was seven, she was tiny for her age.

"Do they have a school where you live?"

Bodey nodded. "Yes."

"Is it the kind of school that would let me come?"

His heart twisted in his chest. "I bet they'd love to have you."

When Dolly scooted a little closer, Bodey scooped her into his lap, then leaned back, pulling her blanket around her shoulders and over her bare feet. He thought that she'd remain stiffly sitting but she snuggled against his shoulder, and in that instant, he could have closed his eyes and been holding his baby sister, so familiar was the sensation of a tiny body still sweet-smelling from her bath, her hair slightly damp, her warmth seeping into his skin. Even the way two of her fingers slid into her mouth—a habit left from baby-hood, he supposed—was reminiscent of Emily.

She removed the digits long enough to ask, "Are you sure they'd take me? 'Cause I've never been to school."

Seven years old and she'd never been to school. Bodey remembered how excited Barry and Emily had been before entering kindergarten. They'd been nearly delirious with joy as they'd waited with Bodey at the bus stop for their first day. Bodey doubted they'd given their teary-eyed parents a parting glance as they'd clambered up the steep steps.

How sad that this little girl had been denied that rite of passage because of the fanaticism of a group that spouted freedom but was devoted to oppression.

"I think they'd love to have you there."

"They wouldn't have to catch me up. Bethy has taught me how to read and do my numbers. I even know some of my times tables."

"Your sister sounds like a good teacher."

"Yeah, but I still want to go to a real school."

"Tell you what. Once we get things sorted out, I'll talk to your sister about coming to Bliss. If she says yes, I'll drive you and your sister to the school myself to see that you get signed up."

Dolly's mouth formed a perfect O. One that was nearly as wide as her eyes.

"I'd like that. I'd like that a lot."

"You could ride the bus with Lily."

"And Eric?"

"He might be on a different bus. When I was younger, the big kids and little kids used to take the same bus, but now they go at different times."

"When can I go?" she asked eagerly, her head popping off his chest.

Too late, Bodey realized that he might be promising things that he couldn't deliver. "School doesn't start until the end of August. Right after the Fair."

"Whatsa Fair?"

"It's when everyone in the county brings all the things

they've been working on or growing throughout the year—animals and crops and flowers and sewing—and they show them off and have them judged. Those with the best products get a blue ribbon and a two dollar bill."

Dolly yawned, settling back against his chest. "Is it fun?"

Bodey wrapped his arms around her, checking to make sure that her blanket was secure again. "You bet. They play music all the time and people come to sing and dance. There's a rodeo every night and good food and rides."

"What kinda rides?" Her voice was growing softer, sleepier.

"There's a big huge slide and a Ferris wheel and sometimes a roller coaster shaped like a dragon. My brother Barry likes the cars best because he's always wanted to drive. Then there are games, too, and a bouncy house for the kids."

"An' fireworks?"

"No. Usually the fireworks are on the Fourth of July—or again on the twenty-fourth, since that's Pioneer Day in Utah."

"I wanna see some fireworks. Roy-roy promised I could see fireworks when I turned seven."

Roy-roy? Was that someone from the Farm?

Bodey grew still.

Did she mean Leroy Vonn?

"Maybe that's why he's been tryin' to find me so hard. So I could see the fireworks like he said I could."

Bodey felt a prickling at his scalp.

"What kind of fireworks, Dolly?"

She shrugged her shoulders again, yawning widely. When she spoke, her words were slurred. "The ones I sawed him making in the basement of his house. I wasn't supposed to be there but I was lookin' for my mommy . . . an' she was down there. When I found her, she was . . . mad at me and I started to cry. But she lifted me up and took . . . a picture of us that she sent to Bethy. Then . . ."

Bodey waited, knowing that Dolly was on the verge of sleep. But there was something there, something in the fractured scene that she was painting that was important.

He nudged her ever so slightly. "Then what, Dolly?"

Again, she yawned. "Then Roy-roy started coming down the steps. Mommy wanted me to hide in the cupboard but Roy-roy came down too soon." Dolly twisted her head into a more comfortable spot beneath his chin.

"What did Leroy do?"

"At first . . . he was yelling at Mommy. An' . . . he hit her." Her voice grew incredibly sad. "Then . . . she told a fib an' said *I* was the one to come down . . . all by myself . . . an' she was comin' to get me . . ."

Not yet, not yet, not yet. Don't fall asleep yet, Dolly.

Bodey lifted his shoulder enough so that she roused. "Then what happened?"

"I asked him why . . . his basement was so smelly." She lodged her hand under her cheek. "He said they were makin' fireworks for my birthday . . . but they wouldn't use 'em 'til I was seven when the . . . present came . . . to shyin' . . . for the . . . party . . ."

This time, when she fell asleep, Bodey didn't bother to wake her. Her words were already becoming completely unintelligible. And what he'd thought might be a piece of insight into the group was only more nonsense to clutter the facts.

Sighing, he leaned his head against the back of the couch. He was exhausted. The past few days had been a roller coaster of emotions and passion, fear and apprehension. And there was no end in sight. Since Elam had decided to take the first shift at the gate, Bodey knew he should surrender to his own weariness and get at least a couple of hours of sleep before it was his turn.

But when the floorboards squeaked, signaling that Beth had finished her shower and come to find him, he opened his eyes and smiled.

She was watching him indulgently. "I see Dolly tried to get you to let her watch some more cartoons.

Bodey shook his head. "Actually, she came to talk." He couldn't prevent himself from smoothing the riot of curls that spilled down the girl's back. "She was telling me how much she wants to go to school."

Beth's gaze grew shadowed. "I know. That's about all she has on her mind, lately. That and her birthday."

Again, Bodey felt a prickling at his scalp. "When's her birthday?"

"Tomorrow. She was born on the Fourth."

The Fourth of July.

"He said they were makin' fireworks for my birthday . . . but they wouldn't use 'em 'til I was seven when the . . . present came . . . to shyin' . . . for the . . . party . . ."

Bodey's gaze skipped from Beth, to the last few minutes of the news flickering on the television set, to the little girl in his lap.

Good hell, Almighty.

Very gently, he transferred Dolly onto the couch, then stood.

"Dolly said that your mother sent you a picture with her phone. One with the two of them together."

Beth frowned. "Yeah, sure. Mom wasn't supposed to have a phone of her own, but she had one they let her use every now and then to take orders for the goods they sold at the Farmer's Market. She sent me pictures whenever she could. It was about the only way we could communicate once we were separated."

"Do you still have them? On your phone?"

"Yeah, I think so. Why?"

"Go get it. I need to see if there's a photo taken of Dolly and your mom in Leroy Vonn's basement."

Beth backed into the kitchen and Bodey followed hard on her heels. He watched over her shoulder as she dug into her backpack, retrieved her phone, then began fingering icons until she could scroll through the gallery of photographs saved onto her SIM card.

"It must be one of these. The walls in the background look like something out of his cabin."

There was a picture of a younger Dolly looking up at the camera, tears running down her face. Another of Dolly reaching up to her mother. Then, there was a classic selfie of Dolly being held in the arms of a woman that looked faintly like Beth, but taller, thinner, older. Lines of stress carved through her face on either side of her mouth and tugged at her features, making them sag.

Why would she send these heartbreaking pictures to Beth? Why?

And why would she tell Dolly to hide?

Unless . . .

This time, Bodey focused on the background—a typical basement with unfinished walls made of logs, a concrete floor, rows of shelves containing bottled fruit and packs of toilet paper.

And backpacks.

Dozens and dozens of backpacks lined up on the shelves and work tables. Beside them were piles of wires and cellphones. And what looked like gray bricks.

"Shit, damn, and hell," Bodey whispered, reaching for his own phone. He punched a couple of buttons, then waited impatiently.

"Geez, Bodey," Elam growled. "I told you to get you some sleep so you can take the next watch."

"I'm going to send you a picture from Beth's phone. It was taken in Leroy Vonn's basement. Don't look at Dolly and her mother. Look at the background behind them."

Bodey quickly punched his brother's number into Beth's phone and forwarded the image. Almost immediately, he heard a sharp *ping* in the background.

"It's here now. Hold on a sec."

There was a moment's silence, then Elam came back with, "Holy shit. You think he knew Beth had that picture?"

"Either that or he knows Dolly was an unwitting witness. You still got buddies with the ATF?"

"More than one. Give me fifteen minutes to make a call."

"In the meantime, I'll call the FBI. They need to know about it *now*."

"What's the rush? If the Farm obviously hasn't done anything yet—"

"I know the target, Elam. Those bastards are planning

to bomb the stadium. There's a huge concert and fireworks display to celebrate the renovations they've made. The President of the United States is slated to attend. He'll be staying through the week to host that Governors' Summit they've been talking about on the news. The whole thing has been in the works for more than a year—about the same time that Leroy Vonn began making his fireworks."

"No wonder he was so eager to get those kids back. I'll start calling on my end, you take care of things on yours. As soon as I've finished, I'll head back to the house."

TWENTY

WITHIN an hour, a pair of black Suburbans navigated the gravel driveway. Beth stood at the window watching them approach, her body trembling uncontrollably.

If Bodey and Elam were right, Beth finally had some of the answers that she'd been seeking. For months now, she'd thought that Leroy Vonn had been pursuing them out of sheer spite and that he'd been determined to bring the children back under his control for no other reason than to show he was in charge. But after the last hour, she'd begun to see there was so much more to the situation than that. Somehow, Dolly had become the unwitting witness to a planned terrorist attack.

As soon as Bodey and Elam had explained what they'd seen in the background of the photos her mother had sent, tiny details began to click into place—her mother's suspicious death, her hasty funeral, Leroy's insistence that the children—children that he probably hadn't even known by name—must stay at the farm. And then, the relentless pursuit.

All the while, he had been covering his tracks.

Just in case.

Even John Joseph's actions suddenly made sense. Beth hadn't seen him for ten years and she'd chalked up their brief fling to a typical adolescent crush. Yet, once she and the children had been located, he'd been the first to approach her. Leroy Vonn must have thought that if she saw her childhood sweetheart, John Joseph would be able to play on her long-forgotten emotions—as if she'd been pining for John Joseph all these years.

What utter rot.

And what hubris the men of the Farm continued to display, thinking that a woman would surrender everything—her body, her mind, her will—because she'd been told to do so.

It left her humbled and shaking to think what kind of life she would have had if her father hadn't insisted that she live with him. She would have become a mindless automaton like her mother.

No. Not like her mother.

In the end, Francis had tried to free Eric and Dolly from the strictures of the Farm. Even more, she'd tried to get a message to the authorities in the only way she knew how. Through Beth.

Beth took a shuddering breath, not wanting to think what could have happened if Bodey hadn't somehow managed to piece together all of the disparate clues. Even now, with the FBI pulling around the house and Elam and Syd watching the perimeter, she knew that she should be terrified. In the space of a few hours, more people had become aware of her situation than ever before. For months, she'd insisted that there was no one she could trust and her battles were her own. But now . . .

Now, it seemed like an army of help was waiting in the wings. And she wasn't sure how to respond to that. She'd been alone for so long . . .

"Beth?"

Distantly, she heard her name being called.

"Beth!"

She jerked, staring blankly at Bodey. When had he come into the room?

She blinked once . . . twice . . . before her brain kicked in. "I uh . . . I need to . . ."

Her thoughts scattered before she could pin them down. What? What had she been about to do?

Bodey took her hand, lacing their fingers loosely together. "Come on."

He started to draw her toward the bedrooms but she dug in her heels. The FBI agents would be coming into the house any minute and she needed to be there when they woke Dolly.

"I can't . . . those men . . ."

"They can wait a few minutes. Come on."

He pulled her into the room where she'd stowed her backpack, then closed the door.

Before the latch had even snicked shut, he'd drawn her into his embrace.

The moment she felt his arms around her, she clutched at him with both hands, huge sobs tearing from her chest as she lost control.

"Hey, hey," he whispered. "It'll be okay."

"Oh, my god, Bodey. My sister . . . she . . . she could have . . ."

He bent, pressing his lips against her hair. Then he rocked her as if she were no older than Dolly, one of his hands cupping her head to hold her against him so that she could hear the conviction in his voice rumbling from a spot near his heart. "You got Dolly out of there—and you've protected her all these months."

"But—"

"We figured out what was going on in time to protect Dolly—and you, and Eric. Trust me. The worst of it is over. All we need to do now is explain everything to the Feds. Elam spent his time in the Navy as an EOD specialist. He's been studying the photos and he's pretty sure that he has a handle on how they are assembling the bombs and how they plan to detonate them."

She shuddered against him.

"They may not even need to talk to Dolly at all. She's

probably too young to give them any real information. You and Eric can help them more with the workings of the Farm and Leroy Vonn."

She nodded against him, breathing deeply of his scent—leather, soap, and a salty male tang.

"I'll be with you the whole time. Elam, too. Syd's gone back to Hell on Wheels to help Helen take care of the tent. He's got his phone so he can be back here in twenty minutes if we need him."

Again, she could only dip her head. How did this happen? How had she gone from being completely alone in seeing to Eric and Dolly's safety, to having her own personal phalanx of men and women backing her up?

She looked up, meeting the dark concern in his gaze, and instantly knew the answer to that question. Somehow, someway, Bodey Taggart had stormed into her life like a cowboy in a white hat. Sweeping all other concerns aside—even his need to win—he'd come to her rescue like a gunslinger of old.

"Thank you, Bodey."

He bent to kiss her forehead with such exquisite tenderness that she could scarcely credit that it was aimed at her.

"You don't have to thank me, Beth."

"I've had those photos for months and never even dreamed that they could hold such important information. If you hadn't pieced everything together . . . I never would have known why Vonn was so determined to find us." She shuddered. "And all those people at the stadium . . . what are they going to do about that? Finding so many backpacks in a flood of—"

Bodey touched a finger to her lips. "Shh. The FBI is full of smart people. They'll figure it out. If nothing else, they've been given enough warning to cancel or delay the celebration. Let them worry about that. The only thing you need to concentrate on is answering their questions. After that, your job is done."

He framed her face with his hands and she felt herself growing stronger from the gentleness she saw there. But that

wasn't all. Radiating in their depths was a fierce protectiveness, a vibrant possessiveness. And strength, so much
strength—as if he could will it from his heart and mind into
her own.

"I know this is hard. And stressful. But focus on what
this could mean. If all goes well, Leroy Vonn and most of
his henchmen will be arrested. Then, you've got your life
back. You can go where you want, do what you want. Even
better, Eric and Dolly can be normal kids again." He offered
her a crooked grin. "Dolly can go to school."

That thought alone was enough to cause Beth to burst
into tears. How long had she been wishing, hoping, praying
for such a moment? She knew more than anyone how much
her siblings had been denied. She wanted them to have
everything every other kid took for granted: friends, home-
work, and dreams for the future.

"Shit, did I say something wrong?"

She wrapped her arms as tightly as she could around his
waist. "No. Everything right."

He held her tightly, folding himself around her as best as
he could—and she couldn't remember a time when she'd
felt so nurtured. So . . .

Loved.

Beth looked up at him then, seeing him with new eyes,
seeing a face that was as familiar to her now as her own
reflection in the mirror. He was so much more than a friend,
so much more than a lover.

How had it happened?

Why?

But even as the questions ricocheted through her brain,
she knew the reasons didn't really matter. What mattered
was that she saw the same tentative emotions shining from
his eyes.

She lifted on tiptoe, drawing him down, and the kiss they
shared was soft and sweet. In that caress, there was strength
and comfort. But there was also a hope for her own future.
One where she wouldn't have to be alone.

The moment that thought appeared, she shied away from

allowing it to go any further. Even without the Farm on her heels, her life would be complicated—more so than most men would ever want to accept. Who would want to remain involved with a woman with a readymade family? Then, there were even more practical matters that would need her attention—a place to live, a job, maybe even the completion of her college degree. She didn't really have time to indulge in a relationship.

Bodey cupped her cheeks with his palms. "Uh-oh. You look like your brain is racing a million miles an hour."

She couldn't help a rueful grimace. "There's so much I need to plan. So much I need to do!"

Bodey bent to kiss her again. "But not tonight."

Beth opened up her mouth to argue but he stopped her with another kiss.

"Not tonight," he whispered against her lips. "Right now, you'll answer the FBI's questions. Then, you're going to get some sleep."

He prevented her protest with another kiss.

"You're exhausted—mentally and physically. I'd bet that you haven't had a really good night's rest since you spirited your brother and sister away. Right now, you've got plenty of people keeping watch over your family, so you can afford to let yourself indulge in a really deep sleep. If I have my way—and I usually do—you'll stay in bed until noon or later. Then, and only then, will we decide what needs to happen next."

She wanted to argue—if only for pride's sake. But then she realized that she didn't have to put on a brave face. Bodey had already seen everything her life had to offer— literally. From the crappy hotel room, to their dormitory-like diet, to John Joseph confronting her in the tent. Bodey hadn't gone running yet. In fact, he acted as if he planned to stick around.

And that, more than anything, made her fall a little more in love with him.

More?
More in love?

No. It wasn't possible. It wasn't even feasible. A person couldn't fall for someone that swiftly, that completely. Not in only a few days.

But even as she tried to talk herself out of her own feelings, she realized it was no use. She cared for Bodey. A lot. And it wasn't a mere crush. So what if it felt a whole lot like love? Like Bodey had said, she didn't need to think about that now. She didn't even need to decide what to do about it. She just needed to accept what she felt in the moment.

Beth heard her name being called and reached for Bodey's hand. "Will you stay with me while the FBI is here?"

"Absolutely."

IN the end, she was flanked on either side by Taggarts—and Bodey had been right in his assessment. The FBI didn't bother to wake Dolly. Instead, under the glow of the kitchen lights, they huddled around the table, first listening to Elam's assessment of the materials he could see in the background of the photo. It was clear from his debriefing that his military expertise was extensive and his information would prove a boon to their own explosives experts.

Next, they asked Eric a few questions—most of which pertained to the everyday workings of the Farm and the layout of the facility in Oregon, names of members, and whether or not he'd heard anything of Leroy Vonn's followers spending any time away from main properties.

By the time they began questioning Beth, she'd managed to tamp down most of her tension. They asked seemingly innocuous questions. Had she overheard Dolly or Eric talking about bombs or particular threats against the government? Could she draw them a map of the compound that they could compare to Eric's version? A diagram of Vonn's house?

Since the facility had appeared unchanged when she'd gone there for her mother's funeral, it hadn't been difficult to provide them with what they needed. She could even supply the make and model of Vonn's truck and the business van that her mother had often driven to the farmers' market. As long as the vehicles hadn't changed in the last year, the FBI might have a few leads.

Beth wasn't sure what she'd expected of the interview—more of an interrogation of sorts. In her mind, the FBI was synonymous with men in dark suits and sunglasses grilling their witnesses until they broke. And perhaps her fear came from her own stint at the Farm and the incessant negative indoctrination she'd received about the government and all of its agencies.

Bit by bit, she began to realize that her background might have been part of the reason for the way that she'd refused to believe that anyone would be willing to help her. She'd been certain that no one would battle the Farm—especially on behalf of two kids.

But Bodey had changed that for her. As she gripped his hand under the table, she realized that he'd given her the courage to take that last hurdle—one she hadn't even seen—to trust in the help of others. She didn't have to fight this battle alone. There were plenty of people who were willing to come to her aid.

Dawn was beginning to touch the hills with gold when the men in suits stood, shook hands with everyone, then headed to the door. After warning them to take normal precautions—stay close to the ranch, lock their doors, be mindful of strangers—they disappeared in a cloud of dust.

"Now what?" Beth asked, her body thrumming with weariness.

"Now, you go to bed. I wasn't kidding when I said that you needed to sleep until noon—although, judging by the fact that it's already past five o'clock, make that until three."

She shook her head. "Dolly will be up in an hour or so. I'll take a short nap—"

Bodey sighed and grasped her shoulders. "No. You'll sleep. We've got enough people on hand that we can all take turns resting. You go first."

"But you and Elam have been up as long as I have."

"Elam's a soldier. He's used to combat naps—which is

actually pretty spooky when you see him in action. Instantly asleep, fifteen minutes later, he's awake and too damned alert. Syd will be back around eleven, and knowing Helen, she'll be tagging along. As soon as they get here, I'll bed down. And there's Eric, too. He's already used to watching Dolly during the day. Now he can do it in style with an Xbox and movies. Downstairs, there's a game room and a workout room—there's even an exercise pool."

"Your friend must be loaded."

"No, he's a bachelor. He has no one to spend his prize money on other than himself, so his house is full of gadgets. All that stuff can certainly entertain your brother and sister for a couple of hours."

Beth had a feeling that the exercise pool would account for most of the time. Eric and Dolly had bemoaned the fact that the motel pool had remained dry and littered with debris during the Wyoming heat.

"Come on. I'll go lie down with you for a few minutes."

Bodey slipped an arm around her waist, subtly leading her inside.

"You make it sound like I'm a two year old that you have to entice into taking a nap."

"Is it working?"

She looked up into his eyes. In the shadowy hours before dawn, they were a study in blue with shards of green.

"Yeah," she breathed. "I think it is."

He drew her down the hall and into the bedroom.

"What about Elam?"

"Already on his way to guard the gate. Window's fixed. Doors are locked. Everything's fine, Beth. You can go to sleep."

He drew back the covers on the bed. The lodge pole frame was tall—so much so, that she wondered if she would be able to climb inside without looking like a child.

But she wasn't even given a chance to try. Bodey swept her into his arms, setting her on the side. One by one, he unlaced her shoes and drew off her socks. Then he toed off his own boots and threw his hat onto a nearby table.

"Scoot over," he said softly.

She did as she was told and Bodey slid onto the mattress beside her. Within moments, she was tucked beneath his arm, her head on his chest, the covers drawn up to her chin. Beneath her ear, the familiar *ba-thump* of his heart was already lulling her into a safe place.

"Bodey . . ."

"Shh. Whatever you have to say can wait until later."

She smiled against him but insisted on giving voice to her thoughts.

"Thanks," she whispered.

She felt his lips on the top of her head.

"No thanks necessary, Beth. If anything, I should thank you."

"Mmm, for . . . what?"

She was slipping deeper into a warm, comfortable place and it was growing increasingly difficult to concentrate. But she thought she heard someone say,

"For showing me what happiness really means."

BETH was still asleep and the sun was high when Bodey had slipped from the bed. He'd heard the engine to Elam's truck approaching and had known it was his turn to stand guard.

Elam looked remarkably fresh when they switched places, damn his hide. But then, Bodey supposed that he'd had plenty of practice in Afghanistan at getting a job done on little to no sleep. Bodey couldn't even imagine adding bombs and IEDs to the mix.

"How'd it go?" Bodey asked.

Elam squinted against the hot sun. "Quiet."

"The FBI thinks we're in the clear and that Vonn won't make a move on Beth and the kids any time soon."

Elam grimaced.

"So, do you think I'm paranoid to keep a watch on the place?"

"Nope. My gut's still acting up like a son of a bitch."

Bodey sighed. "Mine too." He put the truck in gear. "Have you heard anything from the Feds?"

His brother shook his head. "No, but I don't expect them to keep us in the loop. It's not their style." His lips twitched. "But I've got a couple of old buddies from EOD who have promised to let me know if they hear something. The minute I get a call, I'll pass on whatever information they can give me."

Bodey felt his throat tighten. He'd always known his brothers would be there to back him up. But this . . . This was above and beyond the call of duty.

"Thanks, Elam." He cleared his throat when it emerged with a husky note. "I . . . I appreciate everything you and Syd have done to help Beth. I know she's all but a stranger—"

"Not quite a stranger," Elam interrupted. His expression was deadpan, but his eyes held a wealth of mirth behind them. "And somehow, I think she'll be even less of a stranger in the next few weeks."

Bodey felt a heat tinge his ears. But rather than giving him grief, Elam offered him a crooked grin.

"So what is she? A gift or a two-by-four?"

Bodey rubbed his nose self-consciously. Normally, he'd go on and on about his latest "amour du jour" as Elam called them. But with Beth . . . he found himself curiously reticent.

Elam seemed to understand, because he slapped the side of the door and backed away.

"Enough said."

"But I didn't say anything."

"And that tells me everything I need to know," Elam said with a wave. Then he turned and headed toward the house.

IT was less than twenty minutes later when Bodey's phone vibrated in his pocket, letting him know that a text had arrived from Elam.

Scuttlebutt from ATF. Farm compound raided hour ago. Turn on news.

Bodey was reaching for the ignition switch when the door to the truck suddenly opened. He reacted instinctively, grasping the pistol at his side and whipping his arm out to stare down the sights.

"Whoa!"

The figure outlined in the doorway raised his hands and in an instant, Bodey recognized Jace's lean, craggy face.

"Shit! Do you want to get yourself shot?"

His brother slid into the cab and slammed the door. "I tried calling you but you didn't answer."

Bodey dug his phone out of his pocket, swearing again when he realized that he'd left the ringer off. After turning on the sound, he set his pistol back on the seat.

"What the hell are you doing in Cheyenne? I thought you and Bronte had another week in Europe."

"Yeah, we did."

"See many museums?" Bodey asked, tongue in cheek, knowing full well that Jace hadn't been to nearly as many as he'd planned.

"Actually, no." Rather than appearing embarrassed to admit the fact, Jace looked positively smug.

"I'm guessing that you saw your fair share of hotel room ceilings," Bodey continued, not able to resist goading his elder brother. Elam wouldn't put up with his shit but Bodey could occasionally get a rise out of Jace.

This time, Jace didn't indulge him. "Yeah, I'll admit I saw some pretty nice millwork." He chuckled as if enjoying a secret joke. "Bronte, on the other hand, saw more of the plumbing. She wasn't feeling too good."

"That bites." Bodey couldn't imagine how disappointed they both must have been to spend all that time, money, and effort planning the perfect honeymoon, only to have to come home early.

"Was she sick before you left?"

Jace's lips twitched and he rubbed his lips with his thumb. "Not sick. Pregnant."

It took a moment for the news to sink in—and when it

did, Bodey immediately reached over to pound his brother on the shoulder.

"You lucky dog. But I thought the two of you had decided to wait a few years?"

"Yeah, well, nature had other plans."

Bodey slugged him hard in the arm. "Atta boy!"

Jace joined him in a round of laughter, then quickly sobered. "So what the hell is going on with you? Bronte and I were on our way back when we got word from Elam that the two of you had left Hell on Wheels early because you were in some sort of trouble. That's why we decided to change our flights and land here in Cheyenne."

"Geez, Jace. You didn't have to do that. Bronte probably wanted to get straight home."

Jace shook his head. "We had a lot of turbulence on the way back, so I don't think she could have taken another minute in the air. She and P.D. are going to help Helen pack up her tent, then, the two of them are going to head back to Utah in the motor home. They'll both be more comfortable that way."

Again, Bodey felt a twinge of guilt. "Even so, I hate to put all of you out like that."

"No bother. Sounds like you could use the help."

Bodey saw the concern in Jace's gaze—and he was reminded again of the way Jace had stepped in to run the family business and more after their parents had been killed. He'd kept Bodey from going completely off the deep end.

"But you've got others to think about. Bronte and her girls . . . Barry . . ."

"And you," Jace said firmly. "What's going on?"

The afternoon sunlight was beating down on the truck and the distant road, causing a mirage-like rippling effect. The alien shimmer seemed to inspire confidences, so Bodey began at the beginning, telling Jace about the inauspicious way that he and Beth had met. And with each secret shared, it opened the doorway to more, until everything had been laid out on the table: Bodey's overwhelming attraction to

Beth; his obsession with helping her find a way out of her situation; and his fears that he wasn't up to the challenge of her siblings.

When he finished, the cab pulsed with silence. Jace didn't immediately speak—which was something that Bodey had always liked about his brother. He thought things through before he opened his mouth. And when he decided to talk, he didn't pull any punches.

"Sounds like you've got it bad." The words might have sounded discouraging but there was a pleased note to his tone.

Bodey didn't know how to respond so, for once in his life, he remained silent.

"What does Elam think of your . . . sudden interest in Beth?"

"He's here, isn't he?" Bodey retorted defensively, ready to defend the fact that, this time, his interest in a woman was different. Hell, if he'd known that his lifestyle would require him to justify his actions so much now . . .

He probably still would have done the same thing, damnit. He'd been an idiot in his younger years, but it had been those wild years that had taught him to truly appreciate the promise of what he could have with Beth.

"You and I both know that Elam would come to the aid of any woman in trouble. I'm asking what he's said about Beth to you."

"He said she could be a gift or a two-by-four," Bodey mumbled reluctantly.

Jace laughed out loud. "A what?"

"When I asked him how he knew that P.D. was the woman for him, he said that he started having fun again. That she came to him like a gift and a two-by-four up the side of the head."

Jace's teeth gleamed bright when he grinned. "That's our Elam. Still, he must think pretty highly of Beth if he's willing to share something so personal with you. Sounds like he's under the impression that you're pretty serious about this girl."

Bodey relaxed ever so slightly. "What about you? How did you know Bronte was the one for you?"

Jace laughed again. "Honestly?"

"Yeah."

"I probably knew it the second I drove up to her grandmother's house that night and found her standing in the rain. It was as if a part of me recognized that she was everything I needed. But I knew for sure when you started asking all those questions about her. It made me pissy as hell. At that moment, I would have pounded you into the ground if you'd so much as looked at her cross-eyed."

Bodey grinned, knowing instinctively how his brother must have felt. If anyone dared to look twice at Beth, he would have the same reaction.

"So what do you think, Jace? Am I crazy for thinking that, this time, my interest in a woman is different?"

"Hell, Bodey, you've already proven that point, haven't you?"

Bodey blinked at his brother in surprise. He'd expected an argument, not . . . an agreement?

"You've always loved the ladies. There's no denying that. But you've always had some strict rules. Your women were tall, thin, and stacked. No single mothers, no complications, no one vulnerable." Jace's gaze was direct and keen. "You proved your intentions were different from the moment you broke all your own guidelines." He shifted, as if needing to study Bodey more directly. "But more than that . . . you're happy. Despite everything that's going on and the fact that this must have you tied up in knots. You look really, really happy. Nothing else matters."

And in that instant, Bodey knew that Jace had hit the nail on the head.

He was happy.

For so many years, he'd been skating through life, looking for the next great diversion, the next great contest. But it had all been a distraction, keeping him from admitting the truth to himself—that he missed his parents and his little sister, that he'd been forever changed the moment he'd found their vehicle upended in the river.

For a time, he hadn't ever wanted to feel that much again. He hadn't wanted to worry that by loving someone, by completely giving himself over to them, that he could open himself up to that kind of pain ever again. But he knew now that he'd been kidding himself. He'd been living half a life, and that was no life at all. Because now that he'd met Beth—and he realized the utter devastation he would feel if anything happened to her—he'd also discovered that the only thing worse than losing her . . .

Would be wasting another moment he could have spent with her.

"So," Jace said slowly. "I guess the only question that remains—if you're really serious about the girl . . ."

Bodey's brows rose.

"Where the hell are you going to live? Because the Little House could be awfully cramped, especially without a working bathroom." He grinned, his pale blue eyes twinkling. "And Bronte and I will need your room in the Big House for a nursery."

TWENTY-ONE

———•••———

WHEN Beth woke, the house was quiet.
Too quiet.

A prickling ran up her spine and she hurriedly pushed the covers away. Her gaze bounced from the clock on the bedside table, to the window, and then to the floor.

Bodey's belongings were gone.

She scrambled to get out of bed, her feet tangling up in the covers before she managed to kick free. After rushing into the connected bathroom, she took one of the fastest showers on earth, changed into her usual jeans and then, unable to resist, the yellow T-shirt that Bodey had given her. Then, after jamming her feet into a pair of shoes, she whipped open the door and dodged into the hall.

But as soon as she came in sight with the kitchen, she skidded to a stop. Bodey and Dolly had their heads bent over the counter where they were making sandwiches—or rather, Bodey was making sandwiches and Dolly was giving each of them a healthy squirt of mustard before slapping the top piece of bread into place.

Eric, on the other hand, was slicing chunks of watermelon

and placing them in a plastic container already half full of grapes, cantaloupe, and strawberries.

When they saw Beth, Dolly looked up at Bodey and said in a stage whisper that could have been heard a block away, "It wasn't me. I didn't wake her up."

Bodey laughed. "No. You didn't wake her up." He leaned down to offer in his own stage whisper, "I think it was Eric."

Eric looked up, sputtering, then caught Bodey's wide grin.

Beth was at a loss for a moment. The scene was so domestic, so . . . normal, she didn't know how to react.

Thankfully, Dolly didn't notice her awkwardness. "Bodey said we're going to ride a horse, then have a picnic, then watch the Fourth of July fireworks. He says we can see 'em from the hill behind the barn."

Beth's gaze flew to Bodey's, and much as she didn't want to disappoint her sister, she said, "I don't know, Dolly. We might have to stick close to the house."

Dolly's joy instantly evaporated—and she quickly said, "Oh. 'Kay."

The fact that her sister had so quickly surrendered to caution tugged at Beth's heart.

Bodey reached out to pat Dolly on the shoulder. "Don't worry, Dolly. Beth's been asleep, so she doesn't know. Why don't you put all those sandwiches in those bags there? Eric can help you shut the zipper thingies, okay?"

"'Kay."

Bodey grabbed Beth's hand, drawing her into the T.V. room. The television was on but the sound had been muted. As Bodey reached for the remote, she could see that it had been turned to a twenty-four hour news station.

"Wait'll you see this," Bodey said, pointing the remote and hitting the VOLUME button.

Almost immediately, Beth was assaulted with a volley of information. But she was only able to pick out scattered phrases:

. . . raid on the Fundamental Army commonly known as the FARM . . .

. . . stash of weapons . . .

. . . Leroy Vonn arrested . . .

. . . new security measures in Cheyenne . . .
. . . celebration will continue as planned . . .

Finally, she turned to Bodey. "What does this all mean?"

He drew her into his arms. "The FBI and ATF raided the Farm early this morning as well as a half-dozen hotels here in Cheyenne. They've rounded up at least sixteen of Vonn's lieutenants and commanders and ordnance for twice that many men." Bodey bent to look her directly in the eye. "You, Eric, and Dolly are safe now."

She stared at him for several long moments, trying to digest everything that he'd told her. "But . . ."

"You don't have to worry about Vonn or his men trying to track you down anymore. The authorities rounded them up before anyone could be hurt. Granted, the Feds aren't taking any chances. Anyone going to the stadium tonight will encounter some pretty hefty security measures—scans, searches—just to be safe. But now that their plot has been discovered, there's no reason for anyone from the Farm to come after Dolly any more—or you and Eric, for that matter."

A shudder ran through her body. "I . . ."

But Bodey seemed to understand the emotions storming her body because he pulled her close whispering, "It's over, Beth. It's all over."

BODEY used the tack from Keagan's storeroom to saddle three horses. From past experience, he knew that Keagan's mares were docile and easy to manage. Even so, before they left the confines of the ranch, he instructed Beth and Eric on the basics of riding and had them circle the animals around the paddock before mounting Willow.

"Are you ready, Dolly?"

"Ready!"

"How about Noodle?"

"She's ready, too."

Ideally, Bodey had been hoping that their outing wouldn't include the dog. But Eric and Dolly had worried about leaving the animal behind, so he'd agreed to tuck the pup down his shirt again. And he couldn't help thinking, when he'd considered getting a canine to accompany him on the ranch, Noodle wasn't exactly what he'd had in mind.

Bodey had left Dolly standing on a half-ton bale of hay, so it was easy to reach down and grasp the dog. Noodle must have sensed what was about to happen—or she was spooked by the horse—because she quickly settled to his waist, then lay there trembling.

"Are you sure you're ready?" he asked Dolly.

She clapped her hands in delight, jumping up and down. "I'm ready, Bodey!"

He maneuvered Willow close to the bale, then reached out to scoop Dolly into the saddle.

"Hold onto the horn, okay."

"Mmm hmm."

Now that she was up on the horse, her enthusiasm dimmed slightly as she contemplated the distance to the ground, so Bodey wrapped an arm securely around her.

"Don't worry. I've got you. Relax and enjoy the ride."

He twisted in the saddle to regard Eric and Beth. Both of them were nervous but it was also clear that they were relishing the new experience.

"We'll take things at an easy walk. If the horse tries to speed things up more than you're comfortable with, pull back on the reins. You can bring the animal to a dead stop, if you want. I'll circle back and come help you, okay?"

They both nodded.

"Let's go."

Although Willow was a fairly inexperienced mount and was eager to show off, Bodey kept her in control with a tight hand, maneuvering them to the gate, where he leaned down, released the catch, then allowed everyone to pass through before shutting it again.

In front of him, Dolly nearly hummed with an overwhelming excitement as they headed away from the house to a slight rise in the distance. There were trees there—probably planted by an original settler—as well as the tumbling remains of a cabin and a green patch of pasture. It would be the perfect spot for a picnic. Not too far away for a first ride, yet interesting enough to entice a couple of kids with exploring.

Within a few hundred yards, Bodey could feel his body responding to the familiar exercise. The tension began seeping away, replaced by the heat of the late afternoon sun and the rocking motion of the saddle.

Glancing behind him, he could see that Eric and Beth must be experiencing a similar reaction. Beth's eyes were half-closed, her head tipped up to the sunlight, soaking up the warmth like a greedy flower.

Bodey could tell that she still hadn't come to terms with everything that had transpired in the last few hours—and he couldn't blame her. She'd spent so long looking over her shoulder, it must be hard to accept that the need wasn't there anymore.

"You've got a natural talent for riding," he remarked, unable to completely keep his surprise from feathering his remark.

But then, he supposed her natural athleticism shouldn't surprise him. He'd often thought that she must be an athlete or a dancer. She had an easy grace to her movements and an unconscious control. More than that, she'd shown she was game for any sort of challenge or new experience. It was one of the things he loved about her. Now that she didn't have to spend so much energy being cautious, he had no doubts she would be attacking her next new goal.

She smiled at him and he nearly forgot to breathe.

Dear sweet heaven, she was beautiful—with the sun picking up the blue highlights in her hair and her eyes wide and free from shadows. She was so full of life, it hurt to look at her. He couldn't wait to see what she would look like in a month, a year, when she'd had a chance to truly embrace her freedom and the possibility of her future.

But even as the thought raced through his head, Bodey knew that there would be no guarantees that he would witness such a thing. As soon as they had a few minutes alone, he intended to press his case and try to persuade her to come back to Bliss. After all, it was the perfect spot for kids—good schools, plenty of fresh air, and room to roam. Even more importantly, she would already have a support network behind her: Syd and Helen; Elam and P.D. Even Jace and Bronte were ready to hop on board.

And Bodey. More than anything, he wanted to be there, waiting in the wings, offering her any backup she might require.

But after Beth had endured a lifetime of being told what to do, he didn't want to appear as if he was corralling her into his own agenda.

"Can you make him go faster, Bodey?"

Torn from his thoughts, he looked down at Dolly's earnest face.

"You're sure?"

"Yes, please."

Bodey twisted in the saddle again. "Dolly wants to pick up the pace. Are you two on board?"

Beth's smile was instantaneous. "Let's do it."

"Heck, yeah," Eric chorused.

Bodey nudged Willow into a trot, then, when he saw that the other two were holding their own, he urged her into a lope.

As the jouncing gate leveled out, Bodey heard Eric making a whooping sound, and that made Beth laugh. The noise was so sweet to Bodey's ears, that he longed for a time when he could hear it a dozen times a day.

Please let her agree to come to Utah.

Because, if she didn't . . .

The thought gave him pause. His roots went deep into the Utah soil. Although he'd traveled extensively, he'd lived his whole life on the ranch. Several generations of Taggarts had built their home through sweat and sacrifice and privation. To leave it would be like ripping a part of his heart out. At any other moment in his life, if a woman had suggested that he move, it would have been a deal breaker.

But now, as he thought of abandoning these new, fragile ties that were forming between Beth and him, the decision wasn't so cut and dried. She'd been through so much already, he didn't really feel like he could dictate any terms. Instead, he found himself considering the alternatives.

He would miss the ranch—and he'd miss his brothers even more. He couldn't imagine working with anyone else.

But he also couldn't envision a future without Beth.

To a person who'd always been gun-shy about commitment, the thought should have been frightening—or at least sobering. Instead, he felt something akin to . . . eagerness unfurling in his breast.

So was that it? Was that what it meant to truly care for someone, not for the moment, but forever? Was it a warmth under your breastbone that wouldn't go away? A comfort in knowing that you'd never be alone? The security of living with someone who wasn't just a lover, but a friend?

Unbidden, he began to laugh along with the others, a rush of effervescence slipping through his veins. The thought of tying himself to a single woman—a woman who was everything he'd sworn to stay away from—should have scared the shit out of him.

But all he felt was . . .

Pure joy.

"What are you laughing 'bout, Bodey?" Dolly said, looking up at him with utmost earnestness.

"I'm laughing because it's a beautiful day and I'm having the time of my life."

She grinned. "Then I'm glad, too."

As soon as they reached the top of the rise, Bodey drew to a stop on the far side of the trees. He swung down first and set the dog in the grass. Then he helped Dolly to dismount. The moment her feet touched the ground, she was scampering away toward the ruins, Noodle barking and scuttling after her. He supposed that all of the time spent indoors had given Dolly a raging case of cabin fever, because the little girl didn't "walk" anywhere. She ran, she jumped, she skipped, she hopped.

Eric appeared no less exuberant. He brought his mare to a halt, then jumped down, quickly tying his horse to a branch the way that Bodey had taught him while they were safely inside the paddock.

Bodey didn't mind the kids' quick getaway. It gave him the illusion of privacy with Beth. So after tying his mount near Eric's, he approached Beth. He was glad that the horse shielded them from view, because when he looked up to find her eyes sparkling with delight, he couldn't wait to kiss her.

"How was your first ride?"

"Wonderful!" She bit her lip, then giggled. "But this horse is too high up."

He reached for her then, glad of the excuse to touch her. Wrapping his hands around her waist, he helped her down, slowly, allowing her to slide the length of his body. And, dear sweet heaven above, the feel of her, the shape of her, the scent of her, filled his body with such yearning. Not just to hold and be held, not just to love and be loved, but to watch her blossom and come into her own.

"What?" she asked softly.

"You're so beautiful it makes my heart hurt."

She looked stunned at his pronouncement, so he framed her face, leaning down so that she could see that he wasn't offering her a line. He needed her to know how much he'd grown to care for her.

"I can't wait to see what you do with your life."

Her brows creased.

"I-I haven't even thought that far ahead."

Using only his fingertips—because he was afraid that if he touched her more, he wouldn't be able to stop—he stroked her temple, her cheek, then asked, "So you don't have any plans about where you'll go next?"

She shook her head. "I never allowed myself to plan more than a day or a week in advance. And—"

He waited for her to gather her thoughts, knowing that he would have to tread carefully over the next few minutes. Her future was up to her and he wouldn't be yet another man who forced his will upon her.

"To be honest, I'm afraid to think of anything beyond the here and now. I'm afraid to believe that Leroy Vonn is no longer a threat. I'm afraid I'll jinx everything if I dwell on it too much."

Bodey's mouth grew as dry as the Nevada desert. He licked his lips, hoping he could summon enough spit to speak.

"Can I offer an idea—merely an idea. I'm not trying to influence you or anything, I just—" He sighed. "Damnit, I'm making a mess of this."

"Say it, Bodey."

She looked so nervous, that he realized he'd probably made her think something was wrong.

"It's no big deal. I just wondered—if you really don't have any specific place that you'd like to settle down—if you'd consider Utah. Northern Utah. Bliss, as a matter of fact. It's a really beautiful place, with mountains and clear rivers and green fields. It's mostly a ranching and farming community, but it's only a short drive away from several major cities and colleges. If you came there, you'd already have people you know—Helen and Syd, Elam and P.D.—"

He stopped abruptly, realizing that he was beginning to sound like a full-pressure sales pitch. All that was missing was for him to shout: "But wait, there's more!"

"Would you be there?"

"Well, yeah, I'll . . ."

She started to laugh and he realized that he'd left that part out.

Damnit. He was making a total mess of this.

Beth suddenly sobered. "Are you sure, Bodey? We've only known each other a short while. What if this . . . *thing* we've got going on between us fizzles out? What if you get tired of having me around?"

Bodey hated that she would even think such a thing was possible—but she'd probably been told enough stories about his dating history to think that he had the amorous attention of a gnat.

"I may not have the best track history in the world. I'll be the first to admit this. But what we have is different. More important. *Real.*"

She gripped his wrists. In her eyes, he could see a perfect echo of what he was feeling—a wonder at what their relationship had already become, and a fear that if they tested it too deeply, it could fall through.

"Are you sure?" she whispered.

"More sure than I've been of anything."

"My life is still . . . complicated."

"And mine has been shallow and purposeless. It could use some complication."

She grimaced. "But you said yourself that you'd sworn off children after taking care of your little brother—"

"That was when I was nineteen and stupid." He took her hands. "I know full well what's entailed with raising a sibling. Granted, Jace has stepped in as Barry's brother-father, but Barry . . . well, Barry is . . . Barry. He's important to me. I wouldn't wish away a minute spent with him. And maybe because we lost our parents or because Barry has some special needs, I understand a little of what you're going through. I'd do anything to protect my little brother—and I'd be tempted to kill anyone who threatened him."

He squeezed her hands. "So I get it. I get that their needs will come first, that everything you do is for them. I get how you ache when they hurt and celebrate when they succeed. Even more, I know how lucky they are to have a sister with a heart as large as the Wasatch Mountains and a spirit to match."

"Yes."

He blinked at her uncomprehendingly.

"Yes?"

She laughed softly, inching closer so that she could wrap her arms around his waist. "I think you've sold me on your idea, Bodey Taggart."

"Really?"

"You pretty much clinched the deal when you suggested Utah as my next stop. There's no other place I'd rather go."

His breath rushed from his lungs in a sound that was half-relief, half-sigh.

"You're sure?"

"Yeah."

"And it's something you really want. You're not merely humoring me."

"No. I'd like to go to Utah." She frowned. "But I'm staying there under my own steam. I'll get my own place, my own job."

"Of course."

"And there will probably be an adjustment period when I'll have to concentrate on Dolly and Eric."

"Undoubtedly."

"But . . . I wouldn't mind a helping hand."

Yes!

"And a friend."

Just a friend?

He waited, hoping she would go on. When she didn't, he quipped, "'But wait, there's more?'"

At that, she cracked up—and how he loved that sound. Mere days ago, he couldn't get her to smile. Now, she was free with her emotions—and the effect hit him in the gut like a full-fledged aphrodisiac. He could only pray that there were more descriptors on her list.

Like *lover.*

If that's what she wanted.

Please, please, let that be the gist of her thoughts.

As if she could read his mind, she looped her arms around his neck and lifted on tiptoe to whisper into his ears.

"Oh, there's more. At least a half dozen ways, a half dozen fantasies."

And, sweet heaven above, if that didn't hit his bloodstream and shoot straight to his groin. But before he could even react, she was kissing him. Not a shy, testing kiss, but a full-on, devour-me kiss that was a turn-on in its own right. It was a no holds barred display of emotion and passion that caused every nerve in his body to flare to life.

His arms whipped around her waist. A part of him wanted to hold her so close that he absorbed her into his very soul, while at the same time, he needed to feel her differences, soft to hard, pliant to angular. It seemed as if it had been years since he'd held her this way. She tasted of her own natural sweetness and a hint of minty toothpaste. She smelled of baby shampoo and lavender soap.

But all of that paled compared to the way she made him believe that, for her, he could have battled the world or leapt buildings in a single bound. He wanted to ravish her, yet savor each moment with exquisite gentleness. When he was with her, he was . . .

Alive.

Complete.

Invincible.

"When can we eat, Bethy?"

The two of them sprang apart, breathing heavily.

It took a moment for Bodey's gaze to focus, and when it did, he found Dolly peering at them. She peeked around the edge of the tree as if patently curious about what they were doing but not really sure whether or not she should intrude.

"Um . . . now, I suppose," Beth said, her voice husky with passion.

An effect which made Bodey want to strut like a peacock. But for once, he refrained. Prick though he occasionally was, he didn't want Beth to have irrefutable proof of the flaws in his character.

"Can we eat, Bodey?"

"Uh . . . sure." He went to take a step, then realized that the kiss he'd shared with Beth had inspired his body to greatness as well. So he said, "Go get Eric and spread the blanket out on a grassy spot by the cabin. We'll be there in a minute."

"Oh-kay!"

Dolly skipped away and Beth smiled in a way that threatened to delay his recovery.

"Good save," she murmured.

"I might need to spend a few minutes taking care of the horses."

She reached to cup the part of him that ached for a more complete joining.

"Take all the time you need." Her eyes sparkled with mischief and desire. "Until later. Then, you'll be on my time."

He felt himself grinning—probably a big idiot grin, but he didn't care.

"Yes, ma'am."

TWENTY-TWO

———•◦•———

BODEY honestly couldn't remember a time when he'd felt so relaxed, so content, so . . . *peaceful* as he did when he lay on the grass, Beth's head pillowed on one arm, Dolly's on the other, Eric and the dog lying only a few feet away. Near the horizon, fireworks bloomed in the sky like brilliant wildflowers and the stars glistened like chips of ice in the blackness.

"Was it worth the wait, Dolly?"

"Mmm hmm."

"I hear it's your birthday today."

"Is it my birthday, Bethy?"

"Yes, it is."

Too late, Bodey realized that in their rush to cooperate with the authorities, they hadn't remembered that Dolly was turning seven.

Beth shifted at his side and he knew she was thinking the same thing, so he hurried to say, "The fireworks are only the first part of your birthday. Tomorrow, if Beth doesn't mind, we'll go to a bakery so you can pick out a cake."

When Beth squeezed his hand, he knew that he'd done the right thing.

"Then, I'd like to take you all out to lunch."

"Where?"

"Wherever you want. You tell me the kind of food you want to eat, and we'll find the right place."

Dolly jumped to his knees and reached to frame his face with her small hands. "Can we go get ice cream?"

"Sure, but what kind of food do you want?"

"Ice cream *is* food."

Bodey struggled to keep a straight face. "Yeah, but if that's all I fed you, Bethy would be mad, so how about a hamburger first? Or chicken? Or maybe spaghetti?"

Dolly's eyes widened. "We can go get pasghetti?"

"You bet. Then we'll go to a toy store and you can pick out a present from me and Beth and Eric."

She launched herself at him, wrapping her arms so tightly around his neck that he could barely breathe. And in that instant, Bodey felt as if she held his heart between those tiny little hands.

Vaguely, he remembered a time when a girlfriend had declared that he could never be more than a "buddy" to children. That he couldn't keep a hamster alive. But in that moment . . . hell, he wasn't sure how—maybe he grew up at long last—because he knew he would do anything to keep Dolly and Eric safe and happy.

Dolly bounced away as quickly as she'd hugged him but Bodey wasn't able to switch gears that quickly. For a moment, a betraying moisture flooded in his eyes but he blinked it away.

But Beth must have sensed what he was feeling because she squeezed his hand and settled even closer against his side.

"Beth, is it Noodle's birthday too?"

"I don't think so. We don't know when Noodle was born."

"Then how come she got a present?"

Beth propped her chin on Bodey's chest. "What are you taking about, Dolly?"

"Noodle's new collar."

Beth frowned.

"What new collar?"

"She had a red one before. It's still red, but now it's new."
She clapped her hands. "C'mere, Noodle."

The dog bounded to its feet, its tail beating the air. It
jumped first on Bodey's stomach, punching the air from his
lungs, then scrambled over to Dolly.

"See?"

She held the wriggling animal, parting the fur at its neck
so that the collar was revealed.

Beth frowned, then slowly sat up, reaching for the dog.
Although there was barely enough moonlight to examine the
collar, she fingered the red nylon braid, scrolled it around the
dog's neck, and then said, "Bodey, I didn't buy this collar."

The twinge in his gut that he'd never been able to
completely push away suddenly bloomed into a full-fledged
ache. Sitting up, he reached for the collar, damning the lack
of light. It didn't help that the dog thought Bodey was trying
to pet him and began writhing in delight. In exasperation,
Bodey unclipped it altogether. Then, pulling his phone from
his pocket, he thumbed the flashlight icon.

At first, he couldn't see anything wrong. It looked like a
five-dollar band purchased from any discount store in the
world. But upon closer inspection, he could see that one of
the ends was slightly frayed and glued over on itself.

The ache in his gut began to burn—especially when he
could feel something stiff sandwiched between the cord.
Taking his knife from his belt, he slit it open so that he could
get a peek at what was inside.

The moment he saw the hard black piece of plastic, he
swore.

"Get on the horses," he said lowly, eyeing Beth so that
she could see the seriousness of his expression.

"The food—"

He ruthlessly snapped the circuit in half, sure that the
chip was either a bug or a tracking device.

"Leave it. Get on the horses and head for the barn. Don't
even tie them up when you get there. I'll do that. Elam left
his truck; the keys are in the ignition; my hat is on the seat.

I want you to make sure that Dolly and Eric are crouched low so they can't be seen. Wear my hat and hunch over the wheel so your silhouette is obscured. I want you driving like wildfire for Hell on Wheels. I'll call Elam and Syd to let them know that you're on your way. As soon as you get there, they'll take you somewhere safe, but I don't want you to be alone, okay?"

"Our things—"

"I'll bring them later."

Eric jumped to his feet and ran to catch Noodle. "This time, I'll put Noodle in my shirt," he said, then he strode toward the horses with purposeful strides.

Beth hesitated. "Later? You're not coming with us?"

Bodey stood and helped pull her up. "Only for a little while. Damnit! I should have thought things through. When we were trying to find the kids, we went around the back of the motel, remember?"

She nodded.

"We got there in time to see a couple of guys trying to get in through the window."

Her eyes widened.

"When I went back, I was sure that there would be someone waiting inside but there was no one there. Nothing but the dog. They must have planted the bug or the tracker— or whatever the hell it was—in the collar, then waited."

"But . . . they rounded up everyone from the Farm."

"Maybe, maybe not—and maybe I'm being paranoid. But if there's still one of Vonn's men here in Cheyenne that they haven't arrested . . . hell, I don't want to take any chances. I want you out of here and somewhere safe. I'd go with you, but I've got to close up Keagan's house and the barn. Jace still has his rental car, so I'll have him swing by and pick me up, then I'll meet you wherever Elam has stashed you. It shouldn't be much more than an hour or two."

He could see the way she trembled, but damnit, she lifted her chin and said, "Okay."

He paused long enough to swoop in for a quick kiss. "Promise you'll be careful."

Her tremulous smile nearly brought him to his knees. "Promise. You too."

By this time, Eric had pulled the horses close. Bodey helped Beth into the saddle, then checked Eric's grip on the reins. "Go as fast as you can, but not so fast you feel scared," he said lowly to Eric. "And keep an eye on your sister, okay? I'll bring up the rear. If there are any problems, anyone falls off, I'll take care of it."

Eric nodded, and for a moment, Bodey saw an echo of Beth's defiant tilt of the chin.

"Yes, sir."

Bodey scooped Dolly into his arms and hurried toward his own mount. For the first time, he wished that he hadn't decided to ride Willow. She was a new mount and Bodey feared that some of his urgency would be transferred to the filly and make her skittish. But it was too late to worry about that.

"I'm going to put you on first, Dolly."

She nodded, her cheeks pale in the moonlight. And the blatant fear in her expression filled Bodey with a potent fury. Who the hell did this to a child?

As soon as she was settled, he swung onto the saddle behind her.

"Hold on tight to the horn, Dolly. I'm going to ride fast, really fast, but I won't let anything happen to you."

"O-okay."

Bodey turned the mare and clicked his tongue, urging Willow forward.

He waited until they had reached the bottom of the hill to urge the mount into a gallop. Normally, he wouldn't chance riding so quickly in the dark. There were too many unseen obstacles that could trip up an unseasoned mount. But he wanted to close the distance between him and the other two riders.

He was proud of the way that Beth and Eric were riding at a hard trot toward the barn. Both of them clung to the horns of their saddles, letting the animals head, by instinct, toward home. For their second time on horseback Beth and Eric were both doing amazingly well.

It felt like eons before they reached the pale circle of light being cast by the lamp near the paddocks. Eric and Beth brought their mounts to a shuddering halt, then sat for a moment, breathing hard, giving Bodey enough time to bring Willow up beside them.

Even before the horse had come to a complete stop, he swung to the ground and reached for Dolly.

"You did great, Dolly. Run into the barn now and get into the truck."

The fact that she instantly obeyed him without a question was a further sign of what the past few months must have been like for them.

Bodey helped Beth dismount.

"Remember what I told you. Keep the kids down and wear my hat."

She nodded, then ran to slide the huge double doors out of the way.

Bodey grasped the reins, then moved to Eric, who was already on the ground. "Take care of them."

Eric nodded. "I will."

Bodey moved the horses out of the way and waited until the engine grumbled to life. Then, damning the fact that he couldn't go with them, he watched them ease out of the barn.

Beth briefly lifted her hand as she drove past.

As soon as she'd hit the gravel road that led to the main road, Bodey took his phone from his pocket and hit the speed dial for Elam.

Thankfully, his brother answered on the first ring.

"What's up?"

"The dog had a damned tracking device in its collar."

"Hell."

"I'm sending Beth and the kids to you at Hell on Wheels. Get them somewhere safe."

"Will do."

"When you get a chance, call Jace. As soon as he can, have him swing by Keagan's place. I'm going to lock everything up, gather everyone's things, then I'll be ready to head out."

"No need to call. He's here with us. He should be there in fifteen or twenty minutes."

As soon as his brother disconnected, Bodey moved the horses into the barn so that he could remove their gear and rub them down. He wanted to be ready to leave as soon as Jace arrived.

BETH was only a few hundred feet from the gate when she saw the headlights turning off the main road, heading full-speed toward the gate.

Her first thought was that Elam had been able to get to Rocking Horse Ranch in record time. But then, immediately on its heels was the fact that such an idea was ridiculous. He'd only had a few minutes' notice—if that. Even more troubling, was the way that the vehicle was coming in fast. Too fast to be a casual visitor.

As the oncoming truck crashed through the security gate, Beth reacted instinctively, veering off the drive in a large U-turn, then gunning the accelerator. In the meantime, she began furiously honking the horn to warn Bodey.

Thankfully, he must have heard the racket she was making, because he slid open the double doors, allowing her to dodge inside and slam on the brakes.

Behind her, she could hear the doors slamming shut again.

"What is it?" Bodey called out to her as he ran to the truck.

"Someone's coming and they don't look friendly."

Bodey ran around to the other side of the truck and threw open the door.

"Quick, Eric! Get your little sister into the tack room. There aren't any windows, so it's the safest place to be. You'll find some large barrels of grain. Shift them so that you and Dolly can hide behind them. As soon as we know it's safe, we'll come and get you."

Eric nodded, scooping Dolly into his arms. From inside his shirt, Noodle gave a yip and scrambled toward the neckline in an effort to escape—and Beth knew the dog was probably scratching Eric. But other than wincing, he continued to the heavy metal door in the center of the barn.

As soon as the two youngsters were safely inside, Beth turned to Bodey. "What do we do now?"

Bodey leaned inside the rear portion of Elam's truck, flipping up the seat to reveal a cargo area.

"We pray that Elam still has his gear in here."

He offered a soft, "Yes!" when he saw the gun cases and ammo boxes.

Not for the first time since joining Helen at Hell on Wheels, she felt as if she'd been thrust into an alternate universe when Bodey grabbed a dark leather holster and quickly strapped it low on his hips. As he tied the thigh cords, he said, "That smaller box has Elam's pistols. Load them for me. Forget the empty chamber."

Beth quickly did as he asked. She'd already learned that the first chamber was usually kept empty as a safety precaution. To ignore that step meant that Bodey's instincts must be clamoring as loudly as hers.

As she filled each of the cylinders with shiny brass bullets, her stomach bottomed out as if she'd plunged straight down an elevator shaft. For a year now—more than a year—she'd done everything in her power to evade Leroy Vonn and his henchmen. Sometimes, she and her siblings had avoided being caught by the narrowest of margins. But this time, their luck had run out. The confrontation that she had fought so hard to avoid was here. There would be no last minute escape.

She finished loading and carefully handed one of the weapons to Bodey. As he settled it into the holster, she asked, "Can we do this? Can we hold them off?"

Bodey met her gaze with a fierceness that she could scarcely believe—and she was suddenly glad that he was on her side.

"You need to get into the tack room with the kids. Use your phone to call 911."

She shook her head. "I'll call 911, but I'm staying with you."

"Beth—"

"This is my fight, too, Bodey," she said firmly, brooking no argument.

He regarded her intently—and she was sure that he would insist on her retreat. But he nodded—even though it was obviously the last thing he wanted to do.

"Can you shoot a rifle?"

"Yes."

"Load it. Then I want you to head up the ladder to the hayloft."

She opened her mouth to argue, but outside she heard the rumble of a truck engine, then the crunch of gravel as the vehicle came to an abrupt halt.

"I need you to cover me from above. They'll be expecting you to be hidden somewhere. I need you to be our element of surprise."

Beth knew they were running out of time, so she grabbed a box of ammo and the rifle case and headed for the ladder.

It was difficult to scale the nearly vertical treads while holding the case and the box of ammo. But after shoving the box down the front of her T-shirt—much the same way Bodey had been carrying Noodle around—she was able to drag herself up to the loft. Then, in the near darkness, she hurriedly opened the case and began loading the weapon.

Please, please, don't let me shoot Bodey or somehow hurt the kids.

Her pulse roared in her ears as she lay down in the prickly bits of alfalfa that littered the hay loft. She couldn't see Bodey at all, so he must have dodged into one of the stalls.

It seemed like hours—but was probably only a few agonizing seconds—when she heard one of the large doors being rolled back. Her heartbeat became deafening as she waited for her assailant to move into view. When he did, she bit her lip.

John Joseph.

But the man who stood below her bore very little resemblance to the boy she'd once known—or even the person who'd confronted her at Hell on Wheels. Gone was the earnest, homegrown affability, and in its place was a naked, steely-eyed fury. In his hand, he held a very modern, very deadly pistol.

Inwardly, Beth cringed. Yes, she and Bodey were armed. But how were weapons designed to recreate the Old West supposed to match up against something so thoroughly modern?

"There's no use hiding, Mary Grace! Your cowboy isn't here to protect you. We saw him leaving in his truck a couple of hours ago. This time, it's just you and me."

Elam. They must have seen Elam leaving the ranch before Bodey had saddled up the horses. With the Farm leadership in custody, they'd all thought the danger was over.

John Joseph murmured under his breath, gesturing with the pistol, and she realized that he hadn't come alone.

"So is this where you live now? With him? Is this *how* you live?"

John Joseph began creeping up the side of the car, then whipped the gun into the cab as he checked to see if Beth and the kids were crouched down, out of sight. From somewhere below her, Beth could hear stall doors opening and closing.

"You've bought into the whole capitalist agenda, haven't you Mary Grace? Spend, spend, spend until you find yourself so deep in a mire of want and need that you can't get out. That's how they get you, Mary Grace. Bit by bit, the government, with its taxes and regulations, has a stranglehold on everything you do. And what the government doesn't control is under the reins of the greedy, corrupt, capitalist cabal."

Beth watched as John Joseph morphed into something—someone—she hardly recognized. His body grew rigid. His eyes blazed with fanaticism.

When he suddenly looked up, she ducked down as far as she could, but something must have alerted him, because he paused, then murmured to his unseen companion.

"Are you happy, Mary Grace?" John Joseph asked, his voice silky but full of menace. "Has living the great American lie made you a better person? Don't you wish things could be more like they were? Living off the land through the sweat of your own brow surrounded by God's own beauty?"

He lifted his pistol, aiming it right where she lay.

"You were a different person in those surroundings. Kind, loving, giving. And now what have you become? Selfish. Self-involved. Why else would you hurt two defenseless children this way? You ripped them away from the only home they've ever known. You even stooped so far as to bribe the immoral establishment into helping you."

Beth could feel a cool sweat forming at her back, on her lip.

"Does it comfort you at night, knowing what you've become? Or do you quiver in disgust at yourself when you realize what you could have been. The wife of a powerful man."

She shook her head in disbelief. If she'd stayed, she would have been married off to one of Vonn's commanders, a man in his fifties with a heart condition. To call him a powerful man was stretching the truth more than a little.

"But then, you couldn't have known, could you? When you abandoned us—when you betrayed your fellow members—you missed out on a golden opportunity. If you'd stayed, I would have fought for you. You would have been my wife. *Mine.* And in doing so, you would have become the first lady of the Fundamentalist Army."

First lady?

And then she knew. When she'd returned to the Farm to get Eric and Dolly, Leroy Vonn had been conspicuously absent. There had been rumors brewing in the compound that he was ill and that he planned to name a successor.

Was John Joseph now the leader of the group?

Dread coated her tongue with the coppery tang of her own blood and she realized that she'd bitten the inside of her cheek to keep silent. If Leroy Vonn had appointed John Joseph as their leader . . . that meant that the Farm hadn't been stopped by the FBI at all. The Feds had merely slowed them down.

Without even realizing what she was doing, she sighted down the length of her rifle. Her finger curled around the trigger.

She could stop him. She could stop it all. By squeezing a little tighter, she could totally disrupt the governing body of the Farm, and her brother and sister would finally be safe.

And she'd do it. She'd willingly risk spending the rest of her life in prison if her brother and sister could—

The rifle was wrenched from her hands. Whirling, she realized—too late—that John Joseph must have ordered his companion to find his way into the hayloft by some other means than the inner ladder.

When she would have lunged at the stranger, he leveled the rifle and warned, "No way, Missy. Down the ladder."

Damn, damn, damn!

Why hadn't she been more careful? Why hadn't she realized that if John Joseph knew where she was hiding . . . ?

The gunman nudged her with his foot. "Nice an' easy. Down the ladder."

Very slowly, Beth did as she was told.

Too late, she realized that Bodey had told her to call 911 after she'd reached the loft. She nearly cursed aloud at the ramifications of her mistake. Unless Bodey had thought to make the call himself, they were alone in their fight. Unlike the Westerns on TV, there would be no cavalry thundering to help them.

So Beth had to do something to even the odds again.

Gradually, she rolled to her feet, then shuffled toward the edge.

"Easy, now. I wouldn't want you gettin' yourself hurt."

She turned and felt for the top rung with her toe, then eased down, one rung at a time, moving sluggishly enough to annoy the man at the top, but not so slowly that he would know she was stalling.

But, all too soon, her toe touched firm earth.

"Hands up," John Joseph said, from a spot much closer than she'd realized, so close that the tip of his pistol pressed into her skin and she could feel the heat of his body.

"I'll go with you," Beth breathed. With no other weapon left to her, she resorted to bargaining. "Leave them here and I'll go with you—wherever you want to go."

John Joseph laughed and the sound was like ice trailing down her spine.

"You're going to do that anyway."

She closed her eyes, wondering where Bodey was hiding. Had someone already found him? Was he lying somewhere hurt? Bleeding?

"Why?" she whispered. "Why do you want to go to all this trouble to drag someone back into your world who obviously doesn't want to be there?"

"Because I have to save the three of you, don't you see? If you aren't willing to shun the horrors of a diseased state, then it's my duty to do it for you. And I won't let you pollute two innocents—two naturally born members of the Fundamentalist Army—because you want to join the grand cult propaganda being spread by madmen who insist that their way is the only way."

Beth chanced a peek over her shoulder and then shrank back at the rage and zealot fire that burned from his eyes. John Joseph had been well and thoroughly indoctrinated by Leroy Vonn's philosophies. He honestly believed what he was espousing. And he wasn't willing to admit, or even concede, that someone else might have a differing opinion.

She glanced up at the loft again, but John Joseph's pal hadn't yet come down the ladder. She had no way of knowing if Bodey was able to help her anymore. If she was going to do something, she had to do it now.

Drawing on everything she could remember from her training at a self-defense course, her time on the gun range, and yes, her beloved steampunk novels with their take-no-prisoners heroines, she whirled, jabbing John Joseph in the stomach with her elbow. Then, she came down hard on his foot with her heel.

As soon as he loosened his grip, she was dodging out of the barn into the night, knowing that if there was even the slightest chance that Bodey could help, she needed to draw their attackers away long enough that he could gather up the children, get in the truck, and drive to safety.

"Get her!" John Joseph bellowed.

Damning her short legs, Beth ran around the barn, intent on reaching the hill where they'd watched the fireworks. Because of the green lawns around the house and the rolling pastures that branched off from the barn, there weren't many trees and rocks that could provide her enough cover from the moonlight. But if she could get to the top of the hill, she could crouch in the ruins or take cover behind the boulders.

She heard footsteps pounding behind her, closing the gap—and she wasn't sure if it was John Joseph who'd given chase or his companion. A sharp pop caused Beth to flinch and a puff of dirt erupted several yards ahead of her.

Someone was shooting at her!

Beth knew she shouldn't be surprised. John Joseph had made it clear that he wasn't leaving without the children— and she supposed that he didn't much care if she came with them. As long as she wasn't alive to tell tales.

She heard another shot, two.

Beth veered sharply to the left, then to the right, trying not to give her assailant an easy target. If she was doomed to fall, she wasn't going to do it easily.

There was another crack—this time from a larger gun— and Beth felt a stinging in her arm.

Hold on. Hold on!

Bodey was out there somewhere.

This time, she didn't have to fight alone.

BODEY cursed himself for being a fool and allowing Beth to take the vantage point from above. He should have thought things through. But he hadn't realized how the interior light from the barn would cast enough of a glow that John Joseph would be able to see Beth move into position.

Knowing that he couldn't allow any of Keagan's horses to be caught in the crossfire if he needed to use his weapons, Bodey had been leading them to the far end of the barn when the other vehicle had appeared. Willow, picking up on his fear and nervousness, had put up a fight at being drawn into the shadows and it had taken every ounce of horsemanship that Bodey possessed to calm the filly enough to pull her in the stall.

Once there, he couldn't leave again without revealing himself. Even worse, he couldn't get a clear shot. He could only listen in increasing fury and horror as Beth was found, then forced to climb down.

He'd been about to dodge into the open and damn the consequences, when there had been noises and a struggle. To his horror, he'd realized that Beth had decided to fight back.

By the time he'd dodged into the aisle of the barn, John Joseph had already given chase. His companion, hearing Bodey's approach, whirled, lifting the rifle and firing.

The bullet smacked into a support beam over his head but Bodey didn't even flinch. Just as he had a thousand times before on the gun range and in SASS competitions, he whipped his pistol out of his holster. One shot, one knee, and the gunman crumpled to the floor, howling in pain.

Running toward the man, Bodey holstered his pistol and kicked his weapons away. Then, he grasped a halter lead from a nearby hook. Before the assailant could comprehend what Bodey meant to do, Bodey had whipped the thick rope around the man's hands, tying him up much the same way Bodey might do to a heifer during a calf roping competition. Then, so the writhing man couldn't give too much away, Bodey drew back his fist.

"Don't you ever hurt one of mine again," he growled. "If I ever find out you're anywhere near me or my family, I won't be aiming for your knees."

Then Bodey hit him, putting all the power of his fury behind the swing.

Pain shuddered through Bodey's hand from the impact but it was worth it when the gunman's eyes rolled back and he sagged into unconsciousness.

"Eric, Dolly, stay where you are," Bodey called out. "I'm going to help your sister and then I'll be back."

Grabbing Elam's rifle from where it lay in the dust, Bodey ran into the darkness. Following the footprints he could see impressed into the gravel, he loped around the barn, realizing that Beth was heading for the hill.

As soon as he made it into the open, Bodey scanned the darkness. Finally, he made out Beth's slight frame scrambling up an embankment. Downhill and slightly to the right . . .

Shit.

He could see John Joseph's arm outstretched, the tip of his pistol adjusting for the shot.

Bodey whipped the rifle into position and fired.

Crack!

John Joseph cried out, collapsing as if he'd been felled by a giant wind. Bodey quickly chambered another round when the man lifted his head, still grasping the pistol, and prepared to shoot again.

Bodey was already running the few scant yards toward him, using instincts he hadn't known he'd even possessed. He paused only a moment, shot again.

Crack!

John Joseph screamed as the slug went right through his wrist. The gun dropped to the ground, and by that time, Bodey was close enough to kick it out of the way. Then, he chambered another round and stood over John Joseph, eyeing at him down the long barrel of the rifle.

"Go ahead. Move. It will give me all the excuse I need to finish you off," Bodey rasped.

And he would do it. In that instant, he knew that if it took screwing up the rest of his life to see Beth and the kids safe, he'd be more than happy to comply.

Suddenly, his anger at Beth for bargaining with John Joseph sifted away as he understood why she'd done it. In that moment, he would have bargained with John Joseph— bargained with God himself—if he could keep his loved ones safe.

So this was what he'd been looking for all these years.

He'd thought that finding a woman to commit to was a game of happenstance with compatibility and sexual attraction the only considerations. But it wasn't anything like that. Loving someone was giving a part of yourself away. It was surrendering your needs, your wants, your ambitions because that other person in your life was so much more important than yourself. It was a lump in your chest when you thought of them, a hunger to make them smile—because their happiness filled you up and made you whole.

John Jacob lunged, and Bodey didn't even think. Whipping his rifle around, he cold-cocked the man in the temple, then watched in satisfaction as John Jacob crumpled, unconscious, at his feet. Even so, he kept the prone figure in his sights, fearing the man could rouse at any time.

"You all right?" he shouted out to Beth, needing to hear her voice so that he knew he'd reached her in time.

"Yes." The answer was shaky, breathless. It held a note of defiance, too—an echo of her will to escape.

A knot of pride and gratitude formed in Bodey's throat. "Beth?"

He chanced a quick glance at the hill and found her there, slightly bent, her hands on her knees as she fought to get air into her lungs.

"Yeah?"

"This may sound crazy, but I love you. I hope you know that."

There was a long silence, then a hesitant laugh that could have been part of the wind, but he knew it wasn't.

"Actually . . . I've been thinking along those lines myself the last few hours."

The burning in his chest grew so intense that Bodey wouldn't have been surprised if his shirt caught on fire.

"I know you're probably not ready to completely believe it yet—that feeling. But that's okay."

He shot another glance her way and was glad to see that she was already moving toward him. Somewhere out in the distance, he thought he heard the faint wail of sirens and he knew the call he'd made to Elam had resulted in his notifying the authorities.

"I've been thinking . . . since you've said you'll come back to Bliss . . ." He screwed up the last of his courage— more courage than he'd ever thought he'd owned. "If you don't mind, I'll get the plumbing hooked up to the Little House. You and the kids can stay there until you can find something bigger . . . I mean . . . if that's what you want to do. It's peaceful and quiet—and there would be other kids around for Dolly and Eric. You wouldn't have to worry about rent, which would give you a chance to find a job you really like. In the meantime, I can stick to the trailer. It's not like I don't already live there most of the time."

She circled a nest of boulders, moving out of his line of sight for a moment, but he could hear her shoes whispering through the grass.

"Are you sure?" she asked, softly, hesitantly.

"Yeah. Yeah, I'm really sure." He pressed on, his heart pounding more intensely than it had in any competition. Because *this* was vital. Every game, every title, every trophy he'd ever won had been . . . fun. Challenging. *This* was real. Important.

"I've got some land bordering the ranch. There's a little creek that runs through it and some trees. It's not too far from the Big House, but it's far enough to be private. I'm thinking I'll build a house."

No answer—but no demurs, either.

"I'm thinking we need lots of bedrooms, so Eric and Dolly can each have one of their own. A kid needs a little privacy."

Nothing. The footsteps had stopped.

"Then we'll probably want a family room like Keagan has. Maybe even a little bigger so the kids can have a place to watch television, study, or play games. I want them to bring their friends home any time they want. And we'll still be close enough to the ranch that they can go horseback riding and—"

He started when Beth slid her arms around his waist from behind. In one of the sweetest gestures that he'd ever been privy to, she kissed his back before laying her cheek against the indent of his spine.

She was so warm, so vibrant, so *alive,* that he felt completely humbled. Things could have gone horribly wrong in the last few minutes.

"You shouldn't talk like that, Bodey. We've only known each other for—"

"Hell, don't even say it. I know every doubt, every objection that you can say before you open your mouth—because I've gone through the list all on my own." He reached for her arm, pulling her around until he could haul her against his side. He could see flashing lights beyond the house and knew he didn't have much time—plus they had the kids to reassure.

"A couple of years ago, my brother Elam came back from competing in the Wild West Games and proclaimed to one and all that he'd found the woman he intended to marry. Jace and me, well, we tried to talk him out of it. We kept telling him he couldn't possibly know his own mind. But he did. When he married P.D. after waiting more than a year, it wasn't because he had any doubts. It was because he was willing to wait until P.D. was ready. Jace fell hard and fast as well. He might have had a few more weeks on Elam before he made up his mind. But Bronte had just gone through a painful divorce. Again, he was willing to wait."

He looked down at Beth, seeing the glimmer of tears and her own hesitancy. But more than that, he saw a spark of hope.

"Maybe we Taggart men are destined to fall hard and fast, I don't know. But generations of Taggarts have also shown that once we fall in love, we're committed for life. It doesn't matter if you need some time. With all that you and your family have been through, I think you *should* be cautious. You've been running for over a year, living out of a few backpacks, looking over your shoulders. None of you are going to get over that any time soon."

He pulled her close, leaning to kiss the top of her head—loving the way that she was so small and delicate that he could tuck her under his chin.

"I want you to know that I'm going to be right there beside you, so proud of everything you're doing, everything the kids do. In the meantime, I'm going to get a head start on that house so that, if and when the time comes, it'll be ready to be our home."

"*Our* home," she echoed huskily—and when she looked up, he saw a single tear plunging down her cheek. Her words might convey her doubts, but her eyes shone with such love, such joy, that he couldn't mistake its source.

"Yeah. *Our* home."

A half dozen police cruisers and black Suburbans skidded to a stop a few yards away from them. Behind them, came Bodey's own familiar truck. As the doors flew open and his brothers emerged, Bodey held up one hand and set the rifle on the ground with the other so that it was obvious he wasn't a threat. Keeping his arms up in a classic show of surrender, he gestured with a tip of his head.

"That's John Joseph—"

He glanced down at Beth questioningly.

"Connolly."

"John Joseph Connolly. Leroy Vonn appointed him the next leader of the Farm and he came here to abduct Beth Tivoli and her siblings, Eric and Dolly. There's another assailant tied up in the barn."

One of the officers came to relieve Bodey of the rifle and the pistols in his holsters.

For a moment, Bodey was separated from Beth—and his inner barbarian came roaring back to life. But as he was being questioned, he could see a policeman draping a blanket around her shoulders, then ushering her into the front of a squad car.

The front.

She would be all right.

Within minutes, the car was heading for the barn, presumably to gather up the children.

It was the hardest thing that Bodey had ever done to stay where he was rather than rushing to join her. But he knew from her slight wave that she understood his quandary. He would have to be questioned by the police—after all, he'd shot two people. And no matter how justified he might have been in defending his loved ones . . .

He still had some explainin' to do.

But she would wait for him.

However long it took.

EPILOGUE

————•✦•————

BODEY stood nervously on the wide wrap-around porch that surrounded the new house—one that had been dubbed the Out House by his little brother, Barry, because it was located "out behind" the Taggart ancestral homes. Bodey hoped to hell the moniker didn't stick.

Just as he'd promised, Bodey had built the home for Beth. For Beth, and Eric, and Dolly, and him. There were five bedrooms, a huge family room, an ultra-modern kitchen, and a dining area that could hold a farmhouse style table with enough leaves to seat the entire extended family—and then some. Even more importantly, the master suite was on the opposite side of the house, offering a little privacy for Beth and him.

At least, he hoped that was the case. Because after nearly a year, he still couldn't get enough of her. Every day, he craved her smile, her soft laughter, and yes, her passion.

He wriggled a finger under his collar and tugged to ease the tightness.

"Easy, little brother," Elam said behind his shoulder.

"How much longer is this going to take?" Bodey whispered.

"There's no sense even asking. It is what it is and it will be what it will be," Jace murmured.

"Thanks a lot, Yoda."

Thankfully, before his brothers could offer any more sage words of wisdom, the bluegrass band in the corner of the yard began to play a soft, slow ballad. Bodey recognized it as the same song that had been playing the first time he'd danced with Beth.

"Here we go," Elam murmured.

Dolly appeared first, her hair pulled back with a yellow ribbon, her blond ringlets cascading down her back. Her sunflower-colored gown was adorned with layers and layers of ruffles. More than ever, she looked like a living, breathing Goldilocks as she scattered rose petals down the main path that led from the white picket fence to the front door.

Barry was the next person who appeared at the gate. He still had a disgruntled expression on his face at being assigned to be the ring bearer. In his opinion, it was a 'baby' job. Bodey had tried to explain to him that it was an important position in a wedding, but Barry wasn't buying it. He marched down the aisle, double time, and took his place at the bottom of the steps. But when Bodey winked at him, he finally smiled.

Next, came Bronte's girls, also wearing yellow. But where Dolly's dress was an explosion of ruffles, theirs were soft and light and flowy. Somehow, Bronte had managed to weave tiny daisies into their hair, matching the bouquets they held in their hands

Bodey saw Bronte and P.D. join the procession—and he briefly wondered who was taking care of the babies. But a quick glance at the crowd revealed Helen and Syd, each carrying infant boys—so close in age that Bodey knew they were destined to become best friends. Caleb, Elam and P.D.'s little boy, was wide awake and watching the proceedings with big brown eyes, while Dillon, Jace and Bronte's son, slept in a nest of blankets in Syd's arms.

Then, there was no more time to study the crowd of friends—no more time to wonder how the Taggart family